Christmas
Masquerades

By
Request

Christmas Masquerades

AN IMPOSSIBLE DREAM
by
Emma Darcy

CHRISTMAS MASQUERADE
by
Debbie Macomber

STEAMY DECEMBER
by
Ann Charlton

MILLS & BOON®

All the characters in this book have no existence outside the imagination of the author, and have no relation whatsoever to anyone bearing the same name or names. They are not even distantly inspired by any individual known or unknown to the author, and all the incidents are pure invention.

MILLS & BOON and MILLS & BOON with the Rose Device are registered trademarks of the publisher.
Harlequin Mills & Boon Limited,
Eton House, 18-24 Paradise Road, Richmond, Surrey, TW9 1SR

CHRISTMAS MASQUERADES
© by Harlequin Enterprises II B.V., 1998

An Impossible Dream, Christmas Masquerades and *Steamy December* were first published in Great Britain by Mills & Boon Limited. *An Impossible Dream* and *Christmas Masquerade* in 1994 and *Steamy December* in 1995.

An Impossible Dream © Emma Darcy 1994
Christmas Masquerade © Debbie Macomber 1985
Steamy December © Ann Charlton 1995

ISBN 0 263 81135 2

05-9812

Printed and bound in Great Britain by Caledonian Book Manufacturing Ltd, Glasgow

Initially a French/English teacher, **Emma Darcy** changed careers to computer programming before marriage and motherhood settled her into a community life. Creative urges were channelled into oil-painting, pottery, designing and overseeing the construction and decorating of two homes, all in the midst of keeping up with three lively sons and the very social life of her businessman husband, Frank. Very much a people person and always interested in relationships, she finds the world of romance fiction a happy one and the challenge of creating her own cast of characters very addictive. She enjoys travelling and her experiences often find their way into her books. Emma Darcy lives on a country property in New South Wales, Australia.

Emma has been successfully writing for Mills & Boon® since 1983, and has since written more than 60 novels, which have been published worldwide.

AN IMPOSSIBLE DREAM

by

EMMA DARCY

CHAPTER ONE

DISASTERS CAME IN THREES. The whole world knew that was a fact. Danielle Halstead knew it was fact. Therefore there could be no doubting it was a fact.

Dani brooded over this inescapable truth as she went through the motions of getting ready for the day ahead of her. She put on her baggy blue jeans and a comfortable T-shirt dyed in tones of blue and black. The colours not only suited her mood but were practical for the work she had to do. It was the kind of work guaranteed to contribute to her feeling of gloom and doom.

The first disaster had occurred eight days ago. She had hurled away her job. In more ways than one.

It wasn't her fault. She had been confronted by a situation that had simply been impossible to accept. So five years of hard work and dedication had come to an abrupt and sordid end.

Dani had made a lot of sacrifices for the sake of the career she had chosen. She loved being creative with food, and it was no mean feat to have worked her way up to the position of assistant chef in one of Sydney's most reputable restaurants. She had accepted the long night hours, accepted the fact they precluded a normal social life, accepted the loneliness forced upon her by the conditions of her job. But no way in the world could she have accepted what Julio wanted.

She had tried telling him nicely that she wasn't interested. She had tried laughing off his many and varied approaches to her. That forceful and disgusting groping in the pantry had made her burn with furious indignation, and when he had pursued her to the kitchen with more of his vile suggestions, Dani had cooled his lust at point-blank range. Her beautiful, rich, gooey, death-by-chocolate cake had met its death in a glorious splatter. All over Julio. In front of the whole kitchen staff!

That was the end. And since Julio was the boss, the parting of the ways was inevitable and irreconcilable. There was no going back.

The second disaster followed on the heels of the first. Dani's closest neighbour, Mrs. B, had sprained her ankle last weekend. Her livelihood was at risk, since she was in no condition to work. There was only one solution to the problem. Dani didn't have any work to go to. Ergo, Dani could take over Mrs. B's work until her ankle was better.

Which was why she would soon be on her way to clean Cameron McFarlane's house. The prospect did not lighten her step or her spirits. Having cleaned three houses this week as Mrs. B's stand-in, Dani was of the opinion that this work was not high on job satisfaction. She was not about to perpetuate it as an alternative career. The smell of furniture polish and toilet cleaner did not give her the same kick as the smell of a perfectly risen soufflé.

The truth of the matter was she didn't know what to do with the rest of her life. Since that awful scene with Julio, even her ambition to run her own little restaurant had curled up and died. Maybe she would get over the sense of shock and weary disillusionment in time, but right now Dani doubted it.

What she did know was that a third disaster had to be on its way, lurking in the not too distant future. Three in a row. It always happened. Dani comforted her feet by putting on her treasured Reeboks, then heaved a deep sigh and headed for the bathroom to tidy up the rest of her appearance.

The telephone rang.

Dani had no sense of premonition when she backtracked to answer it. She even smiled when she heard her mother's voice.

"I hope I didn't wake you up, dear."

Dani hadn't yet told her parents she was no longer working late hours. She hated the thought of telling them she was out of a job. And the reason. They had never approved of her choice of career in the first place. She forced a bright tone into her voice.

"No, Mum. I was up. What can I do for you?"

"It's about Christmas Day, Dani. You know it's only two weeks away. Nicole rang to say she was bringing her new man with her."

Dani grimaced. Her beautiful brilliant elder sister always had some gorgeous hunk in tow to show off her success at attracting desirable men. She never failed to make Dani feel second rate at the mating game.

"And I was wondering if you were bringing a friend home with you this year."

She had in years gone past, mostly a waiter or waitress working and travelling around Australia, and too far from family to go home for Christmas. Nicole sneeringly called them Dani's lame-duck friends. But because of what had happened with her job, Dani was out of contact with all her friends and acquaintances. Except for her neighbour, Mrs. B.

"I haven't anyone on my list at the moment," she replied. "I'll let you know in good time if I meet someone I want to bring, Mum."

"Thank you, dear. Has Nicole told you her good news?" Pride and pleasure in her voice.

Dani sighed. The perfect daughter had undoubtedly shone again. "No, we haven't been chatting lately. What's the news?"

"She's been promoted. A huge rise in salary. She says she can now afford to put a down payment on the lovely apartment where she lives. Isn't that marvellous?"

"Yes. Marvellous," Dani echoed flatly. The knowledge of what the third disaster was going to be had just thumped into her mind and heart.

Christmas Day.

Two weeks away. There was no question it would arrive dead on time, and it would undoubtedly complete the trinity of disasters.

As her mother chatted on about family affairs, Dani glumly anticipated what would happen when she went home. With her own career down the drain—impossible to keep hiding the fact forever—Nicole, the ultra-perfect daughter who never did anything wrong, would have a field day.

Like a film-clip preview, the predictable scene started playing through Dani's mind.

Daddy looking disapproving. Where was her ambition?

Nicole sweetly saying that Dani not only couldn't keep a job, she couldn't get a man and keep him, either. Of course, it was no trouble for Nicole to have both. Which she would demonstrate, right, left and centre, in prominent contrast to her feckless younger sister.

Mummy rushing in, sympathetically saying it was no good crying over spilt milk, and undoubtedly Dani would eventually do something good.

Daddy and Nicole exchanging knowing little smiles at the complete impossibility of this platitude coming true.

And so on and so on.

Utter disaster.

Dani knew perfectly well that competing with her elder sister was a totally lost cause and not worth thinking about, yet it always rankled that Nicole had been the one born under a lucky star. Not only was she bright and beautiful, but everything seemed to fall out right for her, while for Dani, the world seemed to move in the wrong direction.

She suddenly noticed the time ticking away and hurriedly ended the call from her mother. She would be late for Mrs. B's job at Cameron McFarlane's house if she didn't get a move on. And that was another thing her family wouldn't approve of.

They would never count a middle-aged cleaning woman as someone worthwhile knowing, and certainly not the best kind of friend for Dani to have.

They would be appalled that she had offered to fill in for Mrs. B. That would be called do-gooding of the worst kind. It was not Dani's responsibility. It was not Dani's problem. There was no call on her to volunteer.

For Dani it was somewhat different. She had volunteered before she ever sat down to think if it was her problem. After all, she didn't have anything better to do.

She raced into the bathroom, looked at her reflection in the mirror above the washbasin and screwed her nose up at it. Her hair was a mess. At least she never had to pay a hairdresser to get a permanent wave, Dani thought ruefully. When it came to crinkles and curls, she had an abundance of them. An overabundance. The only way to stop it from looking like a mop of frizz was to grow her hair long and keep it that way, but this morning it was an electric cloud, sticking out everywhere.

As she set about twisting the long thick mass of it into a practical plait, Dani eyed her freckles with her usual distaste. Fine skin might be fine for a country like Norway, but for the hot Australian climate, it was a curse. People said the sprinklings of freckles across her nose and cheekbones were attractive, but Dani couldn't help wishing they weren't there. She wished her skin would go a light gold in the sun. As Nicole's did.

It didn't seem fair that Nicole had inherited all the best genes. *She* had got their mother's beautiful green eyes. The least Dani could have got was her father's sherry-brown colour. But no. Hers were a mixture of the two. Hazel. The common denominator. Like her face. Which was far more round than the perfect oval that set off Nicole's beauty. And, of course, Nicole's hair was a silky honey, not plain medium brown.

Dani knew she wasn't plain, but somehow Nicole always made her feel plain. She had been told plenty of times that she had a cute, friendly face. She had a nice smile, a pert little nose, and her eyes were bright and thickly lashed. But even looking on the good side, Dani had to acknowledge she was never going to add up to *striking*. Like Nicole.

Besides which, if she attracted anyone, it invariably turned out to be the wrong sort of person. She thought of her most recent and galling experience with Julio and shuddered. Her mind instantly switched to Mrs. B. She didn't care what her family said, she liked Mrs. B and she was glad to be able to help her out at this critical time.

Nothing turned out right for Mrs. B, either. Even her name, Brwonkowskivitch, which came from having been briefly married to a Russian emigrant, was difficult to pronounce properly. Her husband had been a con man and a wastrel, and her life was one long string of disasters. Dani felt a stab of deep sympathy for her poor neighbour as she left her flat and raced upstairs to get Cameron McFarlane's house key.

Mrs. B occupied the ground-floor flat, right above Dani's basement bed-sit in the old terrace house, which was handily situated for them in the inner-city suburb of Darlinghurst. It was also cheap, which suited their pockets. Particularly in the resent circumstances.

"Mrs. B?" Dani called out as she knocked on the door.

"Come on in, Dani." Mrs. B's door was unlocked and her voice came from the bedroom. "The key you need is on the end of the sideboard."

"Got it. How's the ankle this morning?"

"A lot better, thank you, Dani. I'm just getting dressed."

"Can I do anything to help?"

"No. You go on. I can manage. Say hello to dear Cameron for me."

Dani grimaced at the indulgent fondness in Mrs. B's voice. Mrs. B always described her job as 'doing for her gentlemen,' and Cameron McFarlane was her most favoured gentleman. He was a famous author, she had boasted, although Dani doubted that. She was a voracious reader, and she was completely unfamiliar with the name Cameron McFarlane. Dani suspected him of being something of a con man since Mrs. B seemed susceptible to charming liars.

"I'll do that, Mrs. B," she called out dryly.

"You'll be able to see all the books he's had published," Mrs. B said proudly. "They're in his study."

His books were about psychology or something like that, Mrs. B had told her, which was probably why Dani didn't recognise his name. "Okay. I'll have a look at them," Dani assured her. "I'll drop the key back to you when I get home and we can have a chat then."

"Have a nice day!"

"You, too. And keep off that ankle."

Dani considered psychology a murky area, fertile ground for cranks and quacks. Books on such a subject had no appeal to her. Her taste in reading ran to historical romances, science fiction and other more entertaining areas of literature.

Nevertheless, she fully intended to check on "dear Cameron's" books. As she headed outside to catch a bus to her destination, she had to concede that if "dear Cameron" lived in Double Bay, psychology must pay well. Double Bay was one of the most expensive areas in Sydney.

It was a beautiful summer morning, sparkling with summer sunshine, but Dani had too much on her mind to appreciate what a fine morning it was. She caught the appropriate bus and brooded about her life as she rode through the city.

Out of a job. No man in tow. Living in what her family considered a dump compared to Nicole's lovely apartment. No doubt about it, Christmas Day would be a disaster for her. Not too many people could be considered a complete failure at twenty-three, Dani thought with grim irony. It was a pity her family couldn't think of complete failure as a spectacular achievement.

The bus eventually came to Double Bay and Dani scrambled out at the stop Mrs. B had designated. She checked the numbers of the houses along the street, not wanting to walk past her destination. They were very up-market houses, only to be expected in this classy suburb. No failures in Double Bay.

She found the address and her eyes widened considerably at how extremely well Cameron

McFarlane's brand of psychology did pay. She walked down a path, which cut through perfect lawns and tropical gardens, and led to a house that could possibly be called one of the architectural wonders of the world.

It had numerous levels and shapes in its structure, and the roof line was quite spectacular with rows of skylights radiating out from a central dome. Dani quite looked forward to exploring the interior. It was certainly the finest home of the four that she had been to this week.

The first had been Mr. Newbold's renovated terrace house at Woollhara. That had been a relatively easy job, and Dani had been quite touched by Mr. Newbold's concern over Mrs. B. He was a widower of about sixty and clearly a lonely man because he had followed Dani around, talking about Mrs. B all the time, obviously missing her company.

Mr. Clifford at Randwick and Mr. Kenway at Elizabeth Bay had both chosen to go out for the day while Dani cleaned their homes. Dani hoped that Mr. McFarlane had gone out for the day, as well. She wasn't in the mood for courteous small talk with a stranger. She could get on much faster if she had the house to herself. Following Mrs. B's instructions, Dani rang the doorbell to announce her arrival, then used the house key to let herself in.

She closed the door behind her and stood stock-still, gaping at the mind-boggling splendour and spaciousness of the foyer. It was circular, like the glass dome set into the roof some twenty feet above it, pouring light onto a pool filled with waterlilies and orchids and other exotic plants. A fountain played softly over the greenery and artfully arranged rocks and what looked like driftwood but was probably specially sculpted pieces to complement everything else.

The floor was patterned with mosaic tiles in terracotta and white. The wall was painted in the palest of terracotta pinks, and had a rich sheen that reflected the light. Four sets of double doors led off from the foyer, counting the entrance doors behind Dani. They were symmetrically spaced—right, left, front, back.

Mrs. B had told Dani to take the left-hand doors to get to the master bedroom suite at the end of the hallway. Her first job in every house was to strip the bed, collect the towels from the bathroom and get the laundry started.

The only sound she could hear was the water from the fountain, so Dani figured she had the place to herself. Otherwise Mr. McFarlane would have come to check her out after she had rung the doorbell. She had been standing here long enough for him to do so. In fact, it was time she got moving.

Her footsteps seemed to echo loudly on the tiled floor as she crossed the foyer to the left-hand doors. It made her feel like tiptoeing, but that was ridiculous. There was no-one to hear her.

The doors opened to a wide hallway, lit by a row of skylights. There were quite a few rooms leading off from the hallway, but Dani didn't bother looking into them. Time for that later. She headed straight for the master bedroom to get started on her work.

She opened the door and came to another dead halt. It was not the sight of the splendour and spaciousness of the room that caused her stillness this time. It was the sight of the naked man on the bed.

First there was the shock of finding she was not alone in the house.

Then there was the shock of the body itself.

It was sprawled out in front of her in the relaxed abandonment of sleep, and it was prime beefcake. No other description could do it justice. It could have leapt to real live flesh and blood from the centrefold of one of *those* magazines.

Dani shook her head in dazed disbelief. She simply couldn't imagine that such a body belonged to Cameron McFarlane. Mrs. B's other gentlemen were all over fifty. This body showed no sign of venerable age. Dani felt a little stab of grateful relief that it was lying front down. As it was, she had a riveting eyeful of male virility. She didn't need any further confirmation on that score.

The man was built like a world-champion swimmer: broad-shouldered, strongly muscled arms and back, slim-hipped, taut cheeky buttocks, long powerful legs. Most impressively athletic.

Dani found her eyes roving back to his bottom where a provocative strip of paler flesh interrupted the smooth tan of the rest of his body. As male bottoms went, it could certainly be classified as cute and sexy. Dani couldn't help thinking she wouldn't mind waking up in the morning to a body like that lying beside her. Of course, he would have to be more than a body for her to want that situation, but purely on an aesthetic level, he was some sight to behold.

Maybe he had a face that looked like it fell off the back of a truck, Dani thought irreverently. It was mostly buried in a pillow from her present viewpoint. His hair was thick and black and straight, cut to collar level at the back. It wasn't closely cropped to his head, so he couldn't really be a world-champion swimmer. The one visible ear was neatly shaped and tucked close to his head. Dani suspected that with so many physical assets, it was unlikely that his face didn't match the rest of him. Some people seemed to get everything.

Well, this wasn't getting the laundry done, Dani told herself. Although she couldn't see how to strip the bed with him sprawled over one sheet and the other screwed up under the lower half of his legs.

Dani considered waking him. That could be a tricky operation. What if he rolled over and stretched out as he swam up from sleep? It could be somewhat embarrassing for both of them. On the other hand, he might sleep on for hours, which would put her behind in her work.

Her eyes dropped to the quilt, which lay rumpled on the floor at the base of the bed. If she covered him with that...very gently...he would never even know she had viewed him naked. Not for sure, anyway. It seemed the best solution. Then she could wake him up without any compunction at all. She had a job to do, and if this *was* Cameron McFarlane—which still seemed most unlikely—he knew perfectly well she had a job to do.

Dani moved forward quietly. As she gathered up the fallen quilt a scrap of black lace and silk fell out. Dani dropped the quilt and picked up the tiny garment. A very sexy pair of female panties. Unless this man was a closet transvestite, there was only one conclusion to be drawn from it. The empty champagne bottle sitting in an ice bucket on one bedside table added to the evidence, and the two champagne glasses on the other bedside table confirmed it.

That certainly settled things in Dani's mind. The laundry had to be done. She even had an extra bit of it. She crumpled the small confection of silk and lace up in her hand and lifted the quilt over the dangerous lower half of lover boy's body. Then she took up a strategic position next to the bedside table.

"It's past nine o'clock," she announced in a crisp, matter-of-fact voice. "And you're messing up my work schedule."

His face burrowed farther into the pillow, indicating that her voice was an unwelcome intrusion.

"Are you Cameron McFarlane?" Dani demanded.

Maybe he was a son or a nephew. She distinctly recalled Mrs. B telling her that all her gentlemen were either widowed or had never been married. This man undoubtedly fell into the confirmed bachelor category, but that didn't prove his identity. On the other hand, what was he doing in the master bedroom if he was only visiting?

The head lifted, albeit reluctantly. Dani suspected he had a hangover from the way he squinted at her out of one eye, but she was right about the face. It more than matched the body. It could even qualify as a matinee idol face.

A wing of black hair flopped attractively over a high wide forehead. His black eyebrows had the kind of punctuated arch that was flirtatiously challenging. The eye that looked blearily at her was blue. A clear, vivid blue. His nose had a strong and rather sharp ridge line. It sat with perfect symmetry above a mouth that might have been wasted on a man, but wasn't on him. A firm, squarish jaw line was darkened by unshaven stubble, but that only added to the he-man virility he emanated. He was handsome all right, and the mature character lines on his face wiped out any plastic glossiness about his good looks. Dani figured he was probably in his early thirties.

"Who are you?" he growled at her.

"How about you answer my question first?" Dani returned reasonably.

"Of course I'm Cameron McFarlane. Who the hell else would I be?"

"How would I know? I've never seen you before in my life," Dani pointed out. "But if you're him, you ought to know who I am. You were notified that I was coming."

He winced, shook his head as though to clear it, then frowned at her. "Not Mrs. B's stand-in?" he muttered incredulously.

"Got it in one," Dani affirmed.

He rolled onto his side, propped himself up on one elbow, pried open his other eye and looked her up and down. It was a good thing she had thought of covering him up with the quilt, Dani decided. He hadn't even checked that he was decently covered. Not only that, he was doing a good job of undressing her, his eyes stripping her of her baggy jeans and T-shirt, and lingering with interest on the pertness of her full breasts.

"You don't look like a cleaning lady," he observed, lifting his gaze to hers again and offering a whimsical little smile.

Dani was not amused. This guy was obviously a dyed-in-the-wool womaniser. "You don't look like a fusty old absent-minded professor of psychology either," Dani retorted.

That surprised him. He cocked one eyebrow in disbelief. "Mrs. B told you that?"

"Not exactly," Dani admitted, her mouth quirking with irony. "I had this image of someone like Freud in my mind. And I had the impression from the indulgent way Mrs. B talks about you that you needed looking after."

His face broke into a slow grin, designed to melt any stony heart at three paces. Dimples appeared in his cheeks. "Oh, I do," he said. "And Mrs. B does it beautifully."

Oh, boy! Dani thought, ignoring the stupid flutter in her stomach. He was a charmer, all right. He undoubtedly had poor Mrs. B curled around his little finger. He probably had every woman of his acquaintance ready to jump hoops for him. Including his obliging companion of last night. Who had left him a souvenir to remember her by.

Dani unloosened the black panties from her hand and dangled them from her finger. "A pity your girlfriend isn't into housework. As it is, I guess I'm expected to do her laundry as well as yours. Which I'll get on with if you'll kindly vacate the bed."

His grin turned into a crooked appeal. "Mrs. B usually wakes me up with a cup of coffee. And then she cooks me a proper breakfast."

Dani constructed a sympathetic look. "Well, you'll appreciate Mrs. B all the better when she's on her feet again, Mr. McFarlane. Meanwhile, you'll just have to hang tough. I'm only here to clean."

She picked up the ice bucket with the dead bottle of champagne, tucked it under her arm, then rounded the bed to collect the two dirty glasses. "I'll take these to the kitchen. When I get back, Mr. McFarlane, I want to strip the bed. I'd appreciate it if you finished with the bathroom as soon as possible, too. That's if you don't want dirty towels left lying around."

She walked briskly to the doorway, constructed a condescending smile, then turned around and bestowed it on him. "If you have a coffee maker, I'll put it on. Now that you mention it, I could do with a cup. Then when you're ready, you can pour yourself as much coffee as you like."

She sailed off down the hallway, leaving him in no doubt that she was not at his beck and call. Cleaning a house was one thing. Being a slave was quite another. Dani would never be a slave to the likes of him.

Cameron McFarlane was the male equivalent of her sister. He was obviously accustomed to everything falling into his lap when and how he wanted it. With his brand of good looks and sex appeal, he barely had to lift a finger for that to happen, and if he was brilliant, as well, life was his ball to play with.

It was positively sickening the way some people had it all. It gave Dani a lot of satisfaction to put "dear Cameron" on the loser's end today. It might only be one little pinprick to his ego, but it did her a power of good to sweep the mat out from under his feet. The bed sheets, in this case. Which was even better. The way he used Mrs. B was shameless.

On the other hand, Dani wished he might find her attractive. Of course, he wouldn't. She was too ordinary for the likes of him. But if he did... Dani's mind blossomed with the beauty of how it would be if she could take Cameron McFarlane home with her on Christmas Day.

She wouldn't be regarded as a feckless failure then. Oh, no! Her father would be most impressed that she had a famous author in tow. Her mother would be dazzled by his looks. And Nicole—Dani almost laughed out loud—Nicole would be green with envy.

An impossible dream, of course. But it was a fine fantasy.

Dani decided to develop it all day, thinking up all the mad ways of making it come true. She needed something to amuse her. Brooding over disasters was too depressing. The proposition of how to turn the third disaster into a triumphant success was much better for her mental health.

It would be even better if she could actually get Cameron McFarlane to do it.

One day out of his life. That was all she wanted. One beautiful, scintillating day that would make up for all the put-downs and disapproval she invariably suffered from some members of her family. In fact, if she didn't have her grandmother to stick up for her, as Grandma always did, Dani would be tempted not to go home at all this Christmas.

But with Cameron McFarlane in tow...

The question was... how to get his cooperation?

CHAPTER TWO

THE WAY TO A MAN'S HEART was through his stomach. Or so her grandmother said. It had been one of the reasons Dani had become a chef.

Experience showed getting to a man through his stomach was not a well-proven fact. Certainly not as well-proven as disasters in threes. Dani had never told her grandmother this. However, she was now desperate, and since it was an old saying, she was prepared to give it the benefit of the doubt just one more time.

If she had one superlative talent, if there was one sure way for her to make a unique impression on anyone, cooking was it. Not even Nicole could do with food what Dani could do with food.

Therefore, while it was somewhat galling to back-track on cooking Cameron McFarlane a proper breakfast, the thought of maybe getting him to come home with her on Christmas Day made it a prime tactical manoeuvre.

Apart from which, she could then get him talking while he ate it. Communication had to be established if she was to probe for possibilities to pounce on. And develop. She probably didn't have a chance in hell of capturing his interest. But what the heck! She had nothing better to do, and it was much more interesting than doing laundry.

Dani found the utility room, tossed the black panties into the laundry tub, then opened the next door, which happily led into the kitchen. It was a beautifully equipped kitchen, designed for efficiency of movement and with great preparation space. Like the rest of the house—what she had seen of it so far—no amount of money had been spared in providing the best. Dani beamed her approval.

Having dumped the ice bucket and glasses in the sink, she examined the contents of the refrigerator. She spotted half a leg of ham, some free-range eggs and a collection of cheeses. The fruit and vegetable holders yielded up more goodies—button mushrooms, tomatoes, shallotts, oranges, mangoes. No doubt about it, she could deliver. Piece of cake!

Armed with this knowledge, Dani returned to the master bedroom. Cameron McFarlane had obligingly vacated the bed. She stripped off the sheets and pillow slips, bundled them under her arm, then headed for what had to be the door to the ensuite bathroom. She pressed her ear to it and picked up the sound of a running shower. She knocked on the door, then opened it a couple of inches so he could hear her voice.

"Hey, you in there," she called out. Best to get things on an informal basis as fast as she could, Dani decided. "Do you feel up to eating a proper breakfast?"

Silence . . . except for the running shower.

Dani pushed the door open a little farther and raised her voice. "Cameron? Can you hear me?"

"I heard you." Derisive.

"You didn't answer." Accusing from her.

"I'm contemplating what caused the sudden change of heart." A mocking drawl.

"Christmas spirit," she replied. It was more or less the truth. It certainly had something to do with Christmas, anyway.

"It came upon you with a flash of light, did it?"

"You want to stand there under the shower, psychoanalysing the spirit of Christmas, or do you want breakfast? This offer is one time only. It is not open-ended."

Pause for thought. "Can you cook?"

Got him, Dani thought. "This is your lucky day. You're talking to one of the world's leading experts."

There was a gurgling sound that could have been a scornful laugh. "Okay. You can try," he answered, and there seemed to be a thread of indulgence or smug amusement in his tone.

"Keep thinking like that, Cameron, and we are definitely *not* going to get on like a house on fire."

"I promise to eat it."

The ultimate insult! So much for trying to be attractive, Dani thought. She considered serving him up two charred pieces of toast and eggs that had been cooked to the consistency of rubber. Serve him right. Pride wouldn't allow it.

"I haven't got all day, so hurry up out of that shower. I don't like to be kept waiting," she warned. The picture of charred toast loomed invitingly. "If you do keep me waiting, it will be all the worse for you."

"I'll be there when the whips are cracking," he said, and there was no doubt about it this time. Laughter in his voice.

Dani frowned, suddenly wondering if he was into whips and kinky things like that. She had heard of such deviants. If he was, she would simply have to cross him off her list of people she could take home on Christmas Day. Which was a shame, because he was the only eligible male on it.

She shut the bathroom door loudly to punctuate her departure, then whizzed to the other end of the house. Having dumped the bed linen into the washing machine, she poured in some detergent and turned the appropriate switches. With a bit of trial and error she heard water start to run into the machine and decided she had got the switches right.

Her activity in the kitchen carried far more confidence. She put the coffee maker on, cut up some oranges and a mango and put the fruit pulp through the blender, then prepared all she needed to cook the perfect nutritional breakfast. Having completed that task, she set a place for him in the breakfast alcove adjoining the kitchen, then paused to admire the view from the window there.

A swimming pool glittered beyond a huge paved terrace. A barbecue arrangement had been built on the kitchen side. Luxurious outdoor furniture was spread out for the ultimate in convenience and comfort. Beyond the pool, the ground fell away in landscaped terraces to the harbour front.

Cameron McFarlane had a prime position, Dani thought. Quite clearly he wanted the best and went after it. Which was somewhat dampening. Dani quickly shrugged it off. Nothing ventured, nothing gained. Besides, she might not be the sexiest or most glamorous girl of his acquaintance, but she was willing to bet she was the best cook.

She went to the stove and put the pans on ready to heat. When she heard him coming she poured the fresh juice from the blender into a long glass. As he entered the kitchen, she turned to him with her best smile.

"Try this," she invited, offering him the fruit drink.

Her heart gave a little jiggle as he walked towards her. On his feet, he was certainly an imposing figure of a man—over six feet tall, Dani assessed—and the physique she had surveyed in the raw was just as impressive clothed in blue shorts and a white knit sports shirt. His cleanly shaven face looked even more handsome, and there was a nerve-steeling glint of devilment in the blue eyes. Dani had no trouble reading the intention. He was disposed to have a bit of fun with her.

"I'm sorry," he said condescendingly. "I've forgotten your name."

What a put-down! Dani instantly crossed him off her list. Too cocksure. Too arrogant by far. And no matter how stunningly gorgeous he was in the flesh, the last thing she needed at her side on Christmas day was a guy who would put her down in front of her family.

"Danielle Halstead," she answered curtly.

"Ah!" he said, as though remembering. "And people call you Dani."

"That's true."

"I didn't initially connect you to Mrs. B because I thought she was sending a male cleaner in her place." He switched on a dazzling smile. "I'm glad I was wrong."

Dani sternly told her heart to stop misbehaving so stupidly. Of course he was glad he was wrong! He was getting his breakfast cooked, wasn't he?

"Well, Dani, let's see what one of the world's leading experts can do with breakfast," he said right on cue, confirming her opinion of him.

She had been absolutely stupid to even think of backtracking on breakfast, Dani thought resentfully. The only pleasure left in it was to make him eat his condescension.

"Breakfast will be ready in ten minutes," she said dismissively, but he didn't take the hint to move away and sit down. He propped himself against the cupboards in a relaxed pose, clearly intending to enjoy watching her efforts. "How do you like your coffee?" Dani bit out.

"Black and two sugars."

She poured him a cup and shoved it along the counter towards him. "Is the fruit juice to your taste?"

"Delicious." A flicker of curiosity. "Where did Mrs. B find you?"

"I'm her neighbour."

"As in the good Samaritan?"

The light tinge of mockery caught Dani on the raw. It was the kind of thing Nicole would say, and precisely how she would say it. The idea of taking

Cameron McFarlane home for Christmas was clearly
a disastrous one. Nicole and he would hit it off like
soul mates.

"I suppose you think I'm stupid for volunteering to
help a woman who depends on her cleaning jobs to
make a living?" Dani snapped.

His eyes sharpened, noting the flush on her cheeks
and the bright belligerence in her eyes. "No, I don't,"
he said quietly.

"And I suppose you think I'm stupid for volunteering to cook your breakfast?" Dani steamed on.

He held up a hand in a trucelike gesture. "Hey, wait
a bit! You're getting excited . . ."

"Don't take me for granted, Mr. McFarlane."

"Cameron?" he tried, eyebrows slanting appealingly.

"Don't take me for granted, Cameron. I'm not one
of your women." She managed a sneer. "I was being
nice to you. That's all."

Both hands up in appeasement. "Okay, okay. I got
off on the wrong foot—"

"You certainly did."

"And I'm going to start again."

"Fine!"

"Everything forgiven?"

It confused Dani for a moment. He looked genuinely contrite. He sounded genuinely contrite. And
that didn't seem to accord with the character she had
given him. She swung away and took herself over to
the stove to start cooking his breakfast.

"Mrs. B hasn't got any family, you know," she said
by way of bridging the awkward little silence.

"I know."

She snapped on the gas-ring switches to heat up the pans, then beat the eggs with unnecessary but satisfying vigour. "You mean a lot to her. For some reason, unknown to me, she likes you."

"Maybe I've got some good points," he suggested whimsically.

She beetled him a sceptical look. "Maybe Mrs. B is a lonely old woman who likes to mother you."

"There's nothing wrong with that," he pointed out peaceably.

"No. There isn't anything wrong with that," Dani agreed grudgingly. Except he obviously took advantage of it.

"Well?" Another appeal for her goodwill.

"You know what would really give Mrs. B pleasure?" Dani fired at him.

"What?"

"If you sent her some flowers and a get-well message."

"I hadn't thought of that."

She shot him a look of appeal. "It wouldn't hurt you, would it? To make her feel...well, missed...and cared about? I know she's only your cleaning lady, but you did say she looks after you beautifully."

"You're right," he agreed good-naturedly. "What's her address?"

Dani told him and he moved straight to the wall telephone. She turned her attention to the stove and began cooking. The order of two dozen red roses brought a smile to her lips. Mrs. B would think it was a slice of heaven. A cynical little voice whispered that

Cameron McFarlane was probably well used to sending red roses, and it wouldn't really mean a thing to him. But at least he hadn't baulked at doing it, one point in his favour.

He dictated his message for the card. "Missing my favourite lady. Cameron."

What a womaniser! Quite cynical. All the same, Dani had to admit Mrs. B would love being called his favourite lady. Dani heaved a deep sigh of satisfaction. It was nice to have nice things happen to you. For someone like Mrs. B, nice things happening weren't exactly thick on the ground.

Dani popped two slices of bread into the toaster, pressed the button on the microwave to heat up the plate ready for serving, turned the omelette, checked that the tomatoes and mushrooms were nicely simmering, added a sprinkling of shallots and felt supremely content with the delicious smells drifting up to her nose.

"Am I redeemed?"

The note of hopeful appeal in his voice made her mouth twitch, despite her inner disapproval of him. She flashed him a derisive look. "That depends on your motive. Which, I suspect, would not bear too close an examination."

"I take it that breakfast is my reward," he said dryly.

The microwave pinged. The toast popped. She swiftly spread butter over the toast, removed the warm plate from the oven, arranged his breakfast on it with deft artistry, flicked off the gas switches, then turned to face him with her offering.

"It's not burnt. Sometimes it pays to be generous," she tossed at him as she carried the plate to the alcove.

He followed, sniffing appreciatively. "Smells great. Looks great..."

"I happen to be—"

"Yes, I know." He grinned at her as he sat down. "One of the world's leading experts. I shall not doubt your word again. New start. Right?"

Dani allowed herself to feel somewhat mollified even though his charm was the ultimate in slick. "Right," she agreed, wondering if she could risk putting him back on the list.

He was open to suggestion. He was good at pretending an interest. He had dropped that off-putting arrogance. The question was... how to make it worth his while to do what she wanted of him? After all, he probably had his own family to go to on Christmas Day. On the other hand, Cameron McFarlane did not impress her as a committed family person.

"Why do I get the feeling that you're measuring me up for another strike?" he inquired.

Those twinkling blue eyes really were dynamite, Dani thought. "Eat," she commanded, and left him to do so while she cleaned up in the kitchen and thought some more.

If she could get him to turn in the right kind of performance, he would certainly do the trick of side-tracking her family from asking all the burning questions Dani didn't want to answer. But first she had to capture his interest, and not just play interest. He had read her correctly. She did need to strike him, somehow...

"This is a superb omelette," he said.

Back to cooking, Dani thought. Perhaps her grandmother *was* right. If she made him a very special lunch to top off the breakfast, and started being really nice to him...

"I'm glad you're enjoying it," she said, beaming him a bright smile.

"Why don't you have a coffee break and come and join me at the table?" he invited. His eyes merrily teased her as he added, "In the spirit of Christmas, peace and goodwill."

The perfect opening. "Thank you," Dani said with real gratitude. "I'm about ready for a cup. Want a refill on yours?" she added, demonstrating her goodwill.

"Please."

She provided them both with coffee and then sat down opposite him. He was making short work of his breakfast, eating with relish. So he ought, Dani thought smugly. He wouldn't get a perfectly cooked breakfast like that every day.

"Do you have a family you go to for Christmas?" she asked.

The pleasure on his face seemed to click out, leaving it oddly expressionless. His eyes lost their sparkle. "No family," he said with forced lightness.

"I'm sorry," Dani said automatically, sensing an aloneness that she had not associated with him before. Although she sometimes wished to be free of ties of obligation, she would never wish to be completely cut off, on her own.

His lips stretched into a sardonic little smile. "No need to be. I do quite well by myself. What about you? A large family?"

Dani sighed. "Not so much large as heavy."

He looked quizzical. "A *heavy* family?"

"There are always expectations to live up to," Dani answered dryly.

His face broke into a grin, sunshine emerging from a cloud. "Like becoming one of the world's experts at cooking?"

"Something like that." It was far too soon to outline her problems. She had to check out the possibilities first. "So what do you do with yourself on Christmas Day?" she asked.

He shrugged. "There are always invitations I can take up if I want to."

Naturally, Dani thought. A man like him would be welcomed by a lot of people, particularly women. "Anything special this year?" she probed.

He shook his head. "I'll probably spend a quiet day here. I'll be flying out to the United States early on Boxing Day."

At least she had the all-clear. He was free to accompany her home, if she could get him to cooperate. That was a big if. Dani tried to rally her confidence. It was a pity she wasn't any good at flirting. Nicole was so expert at it that Dani had automatically declined to bother with such an art.

Cameron McFarlane cleaned his plate with a piece of toast, then sat back with an air of complete satisfaction. He gave her a twinkling look of approval that had her toes curling. "How did you learn to cook like that?"

"With a great deal of application," Dani answered with a self-derisive laugh. Stick to cooking, my girl, she told herself. It was her best bet for softening him up to see things her way.

The telephone rang and Cameron pushed his chair back to get to his feet. Dani started to rise also, figuring she had better get to the cleaning if she was going to take time off to concoct a seductive lunch.

"Stay. Finish your coffee," he urged.

"It's finished. And I've got work to do."

He grimaced at her argument as he moved to answer the telephone. Dani picked up his breakfast things and took them to the sink. She heard his end of the brief conversation while she stacked the dishwasher. He didn't sound too happy with what was being said by the other party on the line. In fact, when he hung up the telephone, he gave vent to some colourful curses.

"Something wrong?" Dani asked sympathetically.

He rolled his eyes. "I can't believe it! The man burst into tears on me. A grown man..."

"There must have been a reason."

Frustration edged his voice. "No reason at all. I hired these people to cater a party tomorrow night. They're supposed to be the best. Gourmet food. Reliable quality. Perfect service..."

"Peregrine and Sylvester."

"Yes." He looked startled at her knowledge.

"And that was Peregrine to say he couldn't possibly cope." It was a statement from her, not a question.

Cameron nodded.

"And when you remonstrated, he broke into hysterical sobs." Another statement.

"How on earth could you know that?"

"Elementary. Peregrine and Sylvester specialise in high-tone parties."

Cameron looked bewildered. "So?"

He obviously needed more explanation. Dani patiently gave it to him. "It's a wonder Peregrine thought to call and cancel at all. About ten days ago he attempted suicide in a very half-hearted way. Quarter-hearted is probably more accurate."

"Whatever for?"

"Because Sylvester was lured away by another lover. It was only a temperamental suicide, of course, to blackmail Sylvester into coming back, but I'm afraid it didn't work. The faithless Sylvester has flown off to Venice. The word in the trade is that he's been promised a luxury train trip on the Orient Express as well as fun and games amongst the gondoliers."

"My God! How did you find all this out?"

"Gossip. Everyone gossips like mad in the trade." She gave him a wise look to punctuate the point in case he was slow to catch on.

He winced.

Dani decided some defence of her profession was in order. "Peregrine and Sylvester are usually very professional in their work, but they do have their little emotional traumas now and then. Sylvester will eventually come back. I'm told he always does. Then things will go straight back to normal."

"What about my party?" Cameron complained.

"You could postpone it for about six months," Dani offered helpfully. "By then . . ."

"What connection do you have to the catering business, Dani?" Cameron asked curiously.

"I've been working as a chef for years. For the past twelve months I've been assistant chef at Julio's Restaurant," she added with considerable pride. The fact that she was no longer there wasn't relevant.

His face cleared of all puzzlement. It was as though a light had been switched on behind his eyes. They turned to an incandescent blue. "A chef. A trained chef." His mouth widened into a distinctly wolfish grin. "What are you doing tomorrow night, Dani?"

A thousand-watt light globe suddenly clicked on in Dani's mind. The gold specks in her hazel eyes gleamed very brightly. "Expensive," she said. "Very expensive."

It did not deter him one bit. He leapt at the bait with teeth still bared. "How much would it cost me to lure you into catering my party?" Bribery and corruption obviously no object.

"Well, Cameron," she said with a lilt. "I can see you'd be socially embarrassed if you couldn't feed your guests the way you want to. And since I have a very fine understanding of social embarrassment, maybe . . . just maybe . . . we can work something out. Come to an understanding, so to speak."

He looked at her warily. "You would consider doing it? You can get out of your job at Julio's?"

She wasn't about to admit she was already out. When it came to bargaining, Dani was no dumb chick. "I can, with some considerable effort, make myself free tomorrow night," she said slowly. Then in a dubious tone, "How big is the party?"

"Small," he encouraged. "Only about twenty people."

"Piece of cake." She wanted him encouraged, too. "You'll do it for me, then?"

"Maybe. I could do something really special."

"Wonderful."

"No quibbles about the cost of gourmet delicacies?"

"Spend whatever you need to."

"And then there's my time and trouble and expertise..."

"How much do you want?"

"Nothing. Nothing at all. It's not a question of money for me..."

"What do you want, then?" Frustration.

Dani smiled. She couldn't stop the smile from widening into a grin of calculating triumph. "I'll swap you..."

"Yes?"

"This party, if I can have..."

"Yes, yes?" he pumped eagerly.

"*You*—body and soul—on Christmas Day!"

CHAPTER THREE

DON'T COUNT YOUR CHICKENS before they hatch. That was always Grandma's advice. Yet Dani couldn't help feeling elated. As she made her way home, she severely cautioned herself that there was many a slip 'twixt the cup and the lip. But she was driving one of Cameron McFarlane's cars!

Despite all her commonsense attempts, it was proving impossible to bring herself down to earth. Bursts of glee kept bubbling through her. She had actually done it! Pulled off the impossible dream!

While Christmas Day had not yet come and gone, Cameron McFarlane had given his word that he would play his part. Dani had no doubt he could do it. Glorious scenes of the impact he would undoubtedly make on her family zipped in and out of her imagination. The scenes with Nicole were especially satisfying.

Success was very sweet, Dani thought exultantly. She hadn't precisely got to Cameron's heart by way of his stomach, but what she had achieved through her cooking was more than she had expected, so life was definitely looking up. Luck—in the form of Peregrine and Sylvester's dereliction of duty—had been on her side. She had every right to feel happy and high-spirited.

Dani laughed as she remembered Cameron's initial reaction to her proposition—totally stunned surprise. Then as she had explained more, his expression gradually changed to whimsical amusement. He declared it would be his pleasure to be at her side on Christmas Day, and fulfilling his role would be a piece of cake. Which was very sporting of him, considering the way she had gone about it.

He had also been rather sporting earlier when he had sent the flowers to Mrs. B. And she had really enjoyed planning the party with him. She couldn't have asked for a more cooperative partner. He had agreed to the shopping list she had made out, and lent her the car so she could get about more freely. Generous as well as sporting, Dani thought warmly. On the other hand, it must have been perfectly plain to him that there was a lot for her to do if she was to deliver what he wanted.

It was in his own interest, she reminded herself. Yet he could have left all the party work to her once the bargain had been struck between them. Instead of which, he had readily accepted the argument that there was only one of her, not two like Peregrine and Sylvester. He had followed her around the house while she cleaned, Dani delegating little jobs for him to do while he asked what she intended to serve and discussed how best it could be organised.

There had been other, more personal questions, as well. Dani had sparred with him over those, not prepared to give too much of herself away. What they had was a business agreement. Pure and simple. As it was, she found Cameron McFarlane too attractive for her own good. There was no sense in letting herself be charmed into weaving fantasies about him that couldn't come true.

Although she had got him for Christmas Day!

Dani was able to park right outside the terrace house where she lived. Not many people owned cars in this street, and certainly not a luxury model like a BMW. She hoped it would be safe overnight. Darlinghurst was not the most salubrious of suburbs, but Dani's immediate neighbourhood was relatively quiet and respectable.

She quickly carried this afternoon's purchases down to her bed-sit, then raced up the stairs to see Mrs. B.

"It's Dani," she called out from the communal hallway.

"I'm in the sitting room, Dani," came the reply.

The front room of the ground floor was Mrs. B's bedroom. It was sealed off from the hallway because of the staircase that continued up to the top-floor flat. This was occupied by a couple whose marital conflicts could be heard on all levels, and a fair way up the street, leaving Dani and Mrs. B to wonder how and why they could bear living together.

The ground-floor hallway ran straight through the house to the laundry they all shared, but the door halfway along it opened into Mrs. B's sitting room, and it was slightly ajar so that Mrs. B could listen to any comings or goings. Even the fighting couple upstairs were company for her... of a sort.

Dani heard *Wheel of Fortune* click off as she reached the door. "You don't have to stop watching TV, Mrs. B."

Since it served for most living purposes, the room was cluttered with furniture. Mrs. B sat in her favourite armchair, resting her injured ankle on a footstool. The remote control for the television set was poised in her hand, but it was instantly clear that she had no further interest in watching the programme. Her brown eyes glowed with pleasure, giving her rather homely face a lively attraction.

"Oh, Dani! You'll never guess. I've had the most wonderful day," she enthused.

Dani spotted the red roses on the dining table out of the corner of her eye, but she didn't let on that she'd seen them. "Has the swelling in your ankle gone down?" she asked brightly.

"Almost." Mrs. B waved a dismissive hand. "I had a visitor. Henry Newbold. You know, from the Woollhara house I clean on Mondays."

Dani didn't have to act her surprise. She had been expecting to hear something else. But she easily recollected the widower who had been so concerned about Mrs. B. "That was nice of him," she said.

"Yes. And he brought me a box of chocolates and stayed a while to chat." Mrs. B was quite pink-cheeked about it. "He asked if he could call me Hilda."

Dani raised her eyebrows. A romance in the offing? She smiled as she mentally paired them together, Mr. Newbold's stiffly upright military bearing and dignified white mane of hair, Mrs. B's somewhat roly-poly build and the dyed red-grey hair permanently waved with a vengeance. However oddly matched they seemed, opposites did attract, Dani reminded herself.

Even if it was only an easing of mutual loneliness, it was something.

"He did seem to miss you a lot on Monday," Dani encouraged.

"Yes. He told me. And he seemed quite put out when the roses arrived."

"Ah!" said Dani, turning her head to acknowledge the splendid arrangement of perfect blooms. Maybe it hadn't been such a good idea after all.

"Quite put out," Mrs. B repeated with satisfaction. "Dear Cameron sent them."

"He told me he was going to," Dani affirmed, keeping her role in the affair undercover.

"I had to explain to Henry that Cameron was one of my gentlemen. Quite a young man, and like a son to me. Henry said he understood that anyone would like to have me as a mother." Her ample bosom rose and fell in deep pleasure.

Dani smothered a sigh of relief. The gesture had obviously worked out even better than she had anticipated. "Well, Cameron certainly speaks very fondly of you," she said, happy that Mrs. B felt so happy.

"A dear boy. A very dear boy, thinking of me like that."

Dani didn't think that Cameron McFarlane could properly be called a boy, but she held her tongue. "Here's your share of today's wages," she said, stepping over to the sideboard and tucking the notes into the handbag that sat there.

"I don't like taking that money from you, Dani," Mrs. B protested. "You're doing all the work."

"Half and half. We agreed, Mrs. B. I wouldn't have any work at all but for you." She grinned. "And because of you, I've got a job for tomorrow night." She explained about Cameron's party and the caterers cancelling at such impossibly short notice, but she kept the bargain they'd struck to herself. "So it's good news all around," she finished with a smile.

"That's wonderful, dear! I'm sure you'll manage very well."

"I need to get a few things done tonight, Mrs. B, so I won't stay. Are you all right for everything? Anything I can get you?"

"Don't worry about me, Dani. I can manage quite well now."

She looked as though ten years had been taken off her age. It was amazing how a few little lifts in life could make so much difference. Dani was well aware of the bounce in her own step as she went downstairs.

Her mind hummed with plans while she took a refreshing shower. First she would make her death-by-chocolate cake. While that was in the oven, she would whip up the avocado dip and start on the crêpes. It was so good to feel a sense of purpose. She wanted to show Cameron McFarlane that he was getting an excellent bargain. Really impress him.

The thought came to her that she didn't have to wear her whites on this job. It was quite different to being a chef in a restaurant. She could dress up. After all, she would be mingling among the party guests as she served them, and it was better if she didn't stand out like a sore thumb.

She could wear her little black dress. It was discreet. It was also the most feminine thing she owned. Dani baulked at calling it sexy. She was *not* Nicole. She was *not* trying to compete for Cameron McFarlane's interest. *His* kind of woman would undoubtedly be a knockout, and Dani did not delude herself into thinking she could belong in that category. Not even with all flags flying. However, she could . . . well, try.

She wanted to look her best. That was reasonable. And she didn't want to look too much out of place. It was an opportunity to show Cameron he wouldn't be accompanying a complete frump on Christmas Day.

Dani towelled herself dry, slipped on some fresh clothes, then headed for the kitchen where she had dumped all the shopping bags. She was in the middle of lining up the ingredients for the cake when the telephone rang. A glance at the oven clock showed 6:25. Frowning over who might be calling her at this hour, she hurried to answer the summons.

"Well, I finally got you." Nicole's voice.

Dani sighed. Probably ringing up to gloat. It was never for a nice sisterly chat. "Mum told me about your promotion. Congratulations, Nicole," she slid in before the gloating got into full stride.

"Oh!" Disappointment. "Well, I've been trying to reach you all day. When I couldn't get you at home, I rang Julio's. You could have warned me you'd lost your job." Accusing.

The fat was in the fire! Dani gritted her teeth. "I didn't *lose* my job, Nicole. I walked out."

"What on earth for? You won't get a better position than you had at Julio's."

"It wasn't healthy for my social life."

A short disbelieving silence. "And that's more important to you than a career?" Absolute scorn.

"I'm evaluating my priorities," Dani said loftily.

A snort. "How's your bank balance, Dani?"

"How's yours?"

"*My* bank balance is not in question since I have the good sense to know how to forge ahead in my career. I'm merely asking about your finances because Christmas is coming up. You obviously need guidance on buying presents. I don't know what you thought you were doing last year—"

"They were fun gifts, Nicole. Haven't you ever heard of fun?" Dani interposed.

"Useless rubbish." Contemptuous dismissal. "As it happens, I saw a marvellous gift you can buy Mum..."

Dani seethed while Nicole described the marvellous gift. She had been suffering this kind of put-down all her life from Nicole, as though she couldn't be trusted to choose anything good, as though she had no taste at all in anything. Except food. Which didn't count with Nicole because she was always dieting.

Besides, the gifts she had brought last year had given everyone a laugh. Everyone except Nicole. No sense of humour at all. At least, not where Dani was concerned. She hadn't even raised a smile at her gift. Just rolled her eyes and turned up her nose as though it was a bad smell. Dani had bought her expensive

Lancôme soap this year, so she could wash the bad smells away. Nicole wouldn't turn up her nose at that.

"If you don't have enough money, I could go out of my way and lend you some. For a short time. Until you regain your senses," Nicole finished with typical condescension.

"Thank you for the thought, Nicole," Dani said with tightly held restraint, "but I've already bought Mum's Christmas present. And everyone else's."

A frustrated sigh. "I suppose you were out looking for another job today."

"No. I was with the latest man in my life."

"What?"

"You heard me, Nicole. Man, as in m-a-n."

"Another lame-duck boyfriend?" It was an out-and-out sneer.

Dani suffered a sudden rush of blood to the head. She was sick to death of this sniping from her oh, so superior sister. For once in her life she had a big gun up her sleeve, and the temptation to roll it out and fire it was overwhelming. It wasn't every day she could play one-upmanship with her elder sister. Christmas Day would be the big pay-off, but this was certainly a timely little bonus.

"Oh, I wouldn't call Cameron McFarlane a boy, Nicole. Not even a friend. He's a man."

"Who? What name did you say?"

"Cameron. Cameron McFarlane. He's a famous author. While I haven't asked his exact age, he certainly doesn't look like a boy. He doesn't act like a boy. He doesn't feel like a boy. I'd say he was definitely all man.'' So cop that, Nicole, Dani added to herself.

"You don't mean you've let yourself get involved with *him?*" Nicole answered her.

"Oh? You know Cameron, do you?"

"Of course I do. God almighty! Why do you always have to be a silly naïve little fool?"

Dani came off her high with a thump. Anger stirred. "I hope you have a good reason for saying that, Nicole."

"You want to join the queue? Be a chapter in his next book? Why, do you suppose, he's interested in someone like you?"

"He happens to like me," Dani grated.

"Sure!" Nicole scoffed. "An ignorant little virgin. As foolish as they come."

"I'm not!" Dani cut in hotly.

"He'll string you along and seduce you..."

"What's it to you, Nicole? You've been gallivanting through men's bedrooms for years. You're living openly with a man right now. You're not prepared to marry him. So why hassle me and my choices? Maybe I want to be seduced."

Silence. Then, grimly, "He'll use you for his own purpose, and that will be the end of it. He's a notorious womaniser. I thought you'd have a bit more pride than that, Dani."

"And what makes you such an authority on Cameron McFarlane?" Dani challenged fiercely.

"My PR firm handles his publicity in Australia. His latest book, *The Psychology of Sex,* is currently top of the best-seller list. Been there for ten weeks. He's just finished a term of guest lectureship at Sydney University. His next book is to be called *The Psychology of Sexual Experience in the Modern Woman*."

Hell! Dani thought. What had she got herself into? No wonder his brand of psychology paid well. Nothing like sex to sell a lot of books. And no doubt he was a first-hand authority on the subject. But that really had nothing to do with her and the bargain she had made with him. Nevertheless, she couldn't let Nicole know that.

"Which all makes him a fascinating man," she said as blithely as she could.

"Dani, I know him. You are mincemeat to him. Believe me. Get out before you're badly hurt."

"How well do you know him?" Dani demanded, refusing to budge. Nicole was obviously green with jealousy that a man like Cameron McFarlane was paying her ineffectual little sister any attention at all.

"Intimately."

A chill spread through Dani's veins. The glorious vista of triumph on Christmas Day wavered before her eyes, threatening to disintegrate. "Are you telling me that you've had sex with Cameron McFarlane, Nicole?" she demanded flatly.

"Don't be so crude, Dani."

"I'm not crude, Nicole. I'm honest. Isn't that why I'm such a cross for you to bear? Because I'm not smart and polished and sophisticated like you?" she went on, hating—absolutely hating—the idea that Cameron had bedded her sister. Unfortunately it was all too believable.

"I have tried to help you—"

"I don't want your help! I want the unadulterated truth. Have you, or have you not, been where you told me not to go?"

There was a long pregnant pause. An exasperated sigh. "You make such stupid choices, Dani—"

"Yes or no?"

"I'm only trying to protect you—"

"Yes or no?"

"He's a high-flyer—"

"Yes or no?"

"Yes!"

"Thank you."

Dani crashed the telephone receiver down in a mountainous rage against the stinking rotten fate that had led her to Cameron McFarlane and the hope that she could be a winner for once. She should have known it was too good to be true. When had she ever been a winner against Nicole? Never!

She hugged her chest to hold the pain of it in and tramped up and down the small room to work off the volatile energy charging through her. This was what came of counting chickens before they hatched. A rotten egg right in the midst of her nest of beautiful dreams.

Damn Cameron McFarlane and his careless womanising! He was no better than a rooster in a henhouse. And Nicole, of course, would have been right up his alley. Two of a kind. Sharing the highest perch above all other lesser mortals.

What a fool she had been to think that anything with a man like him could work out right for her! Dear God! Those black silk and lace panties could have been Nicole's. The thought of his naked body in intimacy with her sister's . . .

It was sickening.

Even worse was the thought of how it would have been if she'd taken him home with her on Christmas Day with Nicole knowing . . .

Sick, sick, sick.

At least she had been spared that dreadful humiliation. But now Nicole could preach about her unwise involvement with Cameron, and the loss of her job, and Christmas Day was going to be hell! So much for averting the third disaster! She had compounded it a hundredfold!

On top of everything else, she still had to do Cameron McFarlane's party with no reward for all her labour. Just because she had to reject his side of the agreement, it was no excuse to ignore her side. She had already spent a sizeable chunk of his money, and there was his car parked outside, and he was depending on her to keep her word. She had no choice but to deliver on tomorrow night's party. Her sense of integrity, her sense of professionalism, would not allow her to do anything else.

But she wouldn't bother with her little black dress. If Cameron McFarlane didn't approve of her chef's whites, too bad! Expertise was expertise, and he could jolly well be grateful for what he got. All she was going to get was a big fat zero.

Dani trudged out to the kitchen. There was work to be done and she might as well get on with it, but there was no joy in it. No joy at all. She was face to face with the undeniable, unpalatable, unchangeable truth. There was simply no escaping the fact that disasters came in threes.

CHAPTER FOUR

"The best laid schemes o' mice an' men gang aft a-gley."

A good word, *gang,* Dani thought glumly. Everything always seemed to gang up against her. It was a wonder Cameron McFarlane's BMW was still in the street this morning. No-one had crashed into it, either. That was probably because it was part of *his* scheme. Only *her* schemes got shot to ribbons. And it wasn't going to be much fun telling him that she had changed her mind about Christmas Day.

She brought the car to a halt in Cameron McFarlane's driveway and sat staring blankly at the closed garage doors, mentally gearing herself to face the inevitable. Cameron would want to know why she had changed her mind. Pride insisted that she not tell him it was because he had bedded her sister.

No doubt he would be only too ready to accept any reason. After all, she had pressured him into it. What possible pleasure could there be for him in spending Christmas Day at her side? Much as it pained Dani to acknowledge it, Nicole could very well be right. She probably was a silly naïve little fool.

The garage door in front of her tilted open. Then the man himself was there, smiling at her, looking bare and bronzed and stunningly physical. He was wearing luminous red swimming shorts. That was all. And the shorts were briefer than brief. However spectacular the red was, it did not compare with the rest of the spectacle on show.

Dani's heart contracted. *Man* was right. But he was also a man who had intimately shared all that compelling maleness with her sister. Which put him absolutely off-limits as far as Dani was concerned.

He waved her forwards. Dani started the car and drove into the garage, telling herself she was here to do a job and that was all she was here for. She had to wipe her mind of everything else concerning Cameron McFarlane.

He opened her door as she switched off the engine. "More convenient for unloading in here." His voice was warmly welcoming. His smile was heart-stopping at close quarters. The twinkling blue eyes aided and abetted its striking power. "I had a feeling you'd be meticulously punctual. It's right on the dot of one o'clock."

"I keep my word." It came out sharply. Dani was more on edge than she wanted to be. She fiercely wished she didn't find him so attractive. It wasn't fair.

"So do I," he assured her, as though picking up the doubt in her mind.

Dani heaved a rueful sigh. It would have been easier for her if he'd turned out to be an absolute rotter, but she had the suspicion that somehow she intrigued him, and he would have played his part to the hilt on Christmas Day. In a way she was glad about that. It showed that her judgement wasn't always wrong. But it didn't help the situation.

She swung her legs out of the car and stood up, lifting her gaze to his reluctantly. She caught him in the act of giving her the once-over. Couldn't help himself, Dani decided cynically. An automatic reaction to the proximity of a woman. Not that he would get much satisfaction out of her. She was not dressed to show off her femininity. She was dressed for work.

The white Reeboks on her feet were the most practical shoes for her profession, expensive but well worth the money in terms of comfort since she was on her feet all the time. Her sage-green shorts—it was a very hot day—were baggy and almost knee-length. Her lemon and white top was loose enough to let the air circulate between the fabric and her skin. Her face was undoubtedly shiny from the heat since she hadn't bothered with make-up, and she had woven her thick, unruly hair into a plait from the top of her head to the nape of her neck.

It surprised her when his gaze flicked up to hers and she saw a gleam of approval—pleasure?—dancing in the blue eyes. And the smile had grown broader. It cracked her defences wide open. For some perverse reason he liked her precisely the way she was. She could feel it. But it was no good feeling it. She steeled herself against the fluttery vulnerability he evoked in her and handed him the car keys.

"There's some stuff in the trunk to be carried in, if you wouldn't mind," she said flatly.

The smile didn't falter, but one eyebrow was slightly raised. Probably psychoanalysing me, Dani thought.

Which wouldn't get him very far with her. She had a built-in resistance platform—namely Nicole—that he would never get past, no matter how clever and like-able he was.

"You sound tired, Dani. Is this going to be too much for you?"

Pride in her own abilities came to the fore and made up her mind as to her course of action. She wanted no distraction from producing her best. "Piece of cake," she said, "but business before pleasure."

He could take that any way he liked because Dani knew what she meant. She would do the job first. Then she would tell him she didn't need him any more. Not for Christmas Day or anything else. No need to go into details. Then he could get about his business, and she could get about hers. Which, at this point in time, was non-existent except for Mrs. B's cleaning. The sprained ankle would certainly be better by next Friday, so Dani wouldn't have to see Cameron McFarlane again after tonight.

There was a moment of consideration from him. "Right," he agreed. "Tell me what you want me to do."

Which was generous of him. And immediately changed the nature of the relationship between them. There was none of the casual bantering he had gone on with yesterday. She was the professional, and without knowing it, Dani exuded a self-confidence, a knowl-edge of her powers, a high degree of practical effi-ciency in her every word and action. She was in charge, and he subtly acknowledged it, doing her bid-ding without any argument, standing back and watching her in an admiring way if there was nothing he could do to help her.

It was a companionable afternoon. If only Nicole hadn't spoilt everything with her revelation, it would have been a very pleasurable afternoon. As it was, Dani had to continually put clamps on her responses to Cameron's almost-naked nearness and his obliging good nature.

She was also conscious of some private assessment of her going on in his mind. Perhaps she was only imagining it. Perhaps it was because she now knew what he wrote about—what he was famous for—that she kept thinking he was viewing her as an interesting subject. Whatever... She was disturbingly aware of his presence and found it increasingly difficult to keep her guard up against the compelling charisma of the man.

It was a relief when all the preparation was done and she could get away from him for a while. Cameron had offered her one of the guest bedroom suites to shower and change and generally refresh herself before the party.

Dani had little to do in regard to her appearance. Her hair was fixed in the neat plait. She had quite deliberately brought no make-up with her to punctuate the point that she was rejecting every intention of trying to look attractive for Cameron McFarlane. However, she did linger in the shower, needing to wash away the tension that somehow had her feeling all her nerves were as taut as piano wires, ready to twang at any provocation.

She pulled on her white trousers and was doing up the side buttons of the white tunic when a dreadful thought struck her. What if Nicole was invited to this party? Dani closed her eyes and shuddered. She should have brought the little black dress to wear. She should have . . .

No! Cold hard reason asserted that whatever had gone on between Cameron and Nicole was over. Past history. And the way Nicole had spoken about him meant that Cameron had dumped her, not the other way around. Therefore, Nicole's pride wouldn't allow her to be here even if she had been invited. Dani breathed freely again. The humiliation of being seen by her sister as Cameron's cook instead of his girlfriend was not about to be heaped on her head.

Six more hours should see the mess through, Dani consoled herself. She squared her shoulders and set off to do a last-minute check of everything. The guests were supposed to start arriving at eight o'clock. She had twenty minutes' grace to ensure that nothing had been forgotten.

The set of double doors opposite the entrance to the foyer opened to a living room, which to Dani was the acme of casual elegance. The tiled floor, which continued from the fabulous fountain foyer, was broken by squares of geometrically patterned carpet. Around these were grouped leather lounges and armchairs, serviced by low granite tables. Brass sculptures were mixed with indoor ferns and palms. A magnificently provisioned bar ran along one wall, with a brass foot rail and leather and brass bar stools. The wall facing the outside patio and swimming pool was all glass, with sliding doors that readily expanded the huge entertainment area. For the kind of informal party planned for tonight, it was absolutely ideal.

Cameron was behind the bar, filling ice buckets and planting bottles of champagne in them. "Have a drink with me before the madhouse begins," he invited. "You've more than earned a few minutes' relaxation, Dani."

She hesitated, reluctant to ease the barrier she had drawn between them. Yet it seemed churlish to refuse. "All right."

She was conscious of his eyes flicking over her chef's uniform as she walked to the bar. She half-expected a comment on it, but none came. She had the impression he was totting another configuration up in his brain, and he didn't particularly like the answer it was pointing to. She slid onto a bar stool, trying not to notice how well his white trousers fitted him, nor how the navy blue shirt seemed to deepen the colour of his eyes.

Before Dani realised what he was doing, there was a loud pop, and he was pouring champagne into two glasses. "I didn't mean you to open a bottle just for me. A soft drink..." His smile choked off the rest of her protest.

"I thought it was time for us to drink a toast."

"A toast to what?"

"Our partnership." He handed her a glass and clinked it with his.

"Short and sweet," she muttered, then sipped cautiously at the wine. It was very nice but she couldn't afford to let anything go to her head.

"Will they be missing you at Julio's tonight?" Cameron asked.

"No."

"Have any difficulty getting the time off?"

"No."

"They can do without you?"

Dani shrugged. "They have to. I don't work there any more."

He frowned. "I thought you said . . ."

"I did work there until a week ago." She gave him an ironic little smile. "It was easy to make myself free for you. I've now joined the army of the unemployed."

"Why?" Curious rather than critical.

Her smile became more crooked. "We had a difference of opinion about something."

She took another sip of wine. Throughout her time at Julio's she had tasted the odd glass of good wine from the unfinished bottles left behind by customers. This champagne was very good. Creamy was the way the experts described it.

"You're a woman of very strong opinions," Cameron remarked, more of a question than a statement, his eyes teasing and probing at the same time.

"No, I'm not. I have a very open mind." So much for his psychoanalysis, Dani thought. Her eyes flashed a warning. "What I do have is a strong sense of where I'm going and what's right and wrong for me."

His mouth quirked. "I stand corrected . . . again."

"I'd give it up if I were you."

"And if I don't?"

"You might learn something you don't want to learn."

He laughed. "You can put me into a neatly labelled pigeonhole, but I can't do that to you?"

"That's about the size of it," Dani returned loftily.

His grin held an appreciative warmth that tingled right down to Dani's toes. "I must admit you are proving to be a challenge. Rather unique... amongst the women of my acquaintance."

"Of which there are undoubtedly many," Dani snapped, trying desperately to reline her defences and squash her vulnerability to his undermining charm.

She had to get his mind off her. She didn't need to have him burrowing under her skin. Dani frantically searched for a way to divert his attention away from herself. Then a flash of inspiration hit.

"In fact," she said brightly, "I've been wondering what's wrong with you. Now I know."

One eyebrow rose. "Does something have to be wrong?"

"Oh, yes. Quite definitely yes."

"Why?"

"Because you're not married. That's unnatural. You haven't got a lack of choice," Dani pointed out reasonably. "And you're thirty-something years of age without having achieved a permanent relationship with a woman you can live with. Which leaves two alternatives as I see it."

"Which are?" He looked amused.

"You're either inordinately fussy, and horribly self-centred. Or..."

"Or?"

"You're not really interested in women at all."

"What?" That wiped the amusement off his face.

"It's a theory," Dani went on matter-of-factly. "What's a man trying to prove when he keeps fluttering from woman to woman? Doesn't that suggest that something is wrong with him? That maybe he's not sure of his sexuality?" There, take that, she thought. A little bit of psychoanalysis from Dani Halstead.

"Maybe he simply hasn't found what he's looking for," Cameron muttered.

"Maybe the fault lies within himself," Dani countered, then shrugged with a sublime air of indifference. "But whatever the cause, it's none of my business."

The door chimes sounded.

Dani grinned at him. "Action stations!" She slid off the stool to head for the kitchen. "Have a good party, Cameron," she tossed over her shoulder. "Maybe you'll find what you're looking for tonight."

He muttered something she didn't catch. Dani was laughing to herself. She had set him back on his heels, good and proper. Taught him a lesson. She figured Cameron McFarlane could do with quite a few lessons. He was far too smug about his own powers. She propped herself against the kitchen cupboards, sipping happily at the glass of champagne until it was time to start the first round of hors d'oeuvres. An hour later the party was really humming. People were floating on champagne as though there was no tomorrow. "Are you celebrating something?" Dani asked Cameron when he carried an empty tray out to the kitchen.

"Ten weeks on the *New York Times* best-seller list," he affirmed. "Got any more of those little crêpe things with the lobster and mango fillings? Or the spinach and cheese?" he added hopefully. "They went like hot cakes."

"About ready to come out of the oven. I'll bring them in." She flashed him an accusing look. "You said about twenty guests. I did a head count of twenty-eight."

An apologetic grimace. "People bring people. I'm afraid two more have just arrived. Is it a problem?"

"I'll manage."

He curled an arm around her shoulders, dropped a kiss on her forehead, then gave her a dazzling smile. "I'll take you out to dinner tomorrow night to compensate."

He left her feeling pole-axed. "Damned womaniser," she muttered to herself. It was a thought that was repeated continually throughout the evening. Women hung on him, if not physically, on his every word. Despite the number of guests, he was the central focus of the party, and that never wavered.

When Dani moved out to the barbecue to start cooking the shelled king prawns in the garlic butter, somehow Cameron was at her side, and the party seemed to naturally gravitate out to the patio area and around what she was doing. He was like the Pied Piper, Dani thought, except these were women following Cameron McFarlane, not plague rats following a musician.

But it worked well because the guests were there to help themselves as soon as she had concocted the first culinary delight from the barbecue. The moment the prawns were ready, Dani poured some warmed olive oil through the pre-cooked *cannellini* to keep them separated, spooned through the caviare, then added the sizzling prawns.

The combination of white beans, black caviar, and red prawns, not only looked great but tasted great as well. Dani transferred the steaming dish to the buffet table where a range of salads stood ready, and Cameron's guests were not backward in coming forward to pounce on the new offering by the chef. Dani allowed herself a smug little smile as she returned to the barbecue to start on the Hawaiian lamb kebabs.

"Delicious. Best prawns I've ever eaten."

She glanced up from her cooking to find herself face to face with a gorgeous blonde with a gaping cleavage. It made Dani glad she hadn't worn her little black dress because it would have made a very poor comparison to the stunningly sexy black dress this woman wore. Dani suspected she was the owner of the black silk lace panties she had found in Cameron's bedroom the day before. It was the same blonde who had been draping herself on Cameron whenever he stood still long enough for her to do so.

Dani forced a smile. "I'm glad you enjoyed them."

"Where did Cameron find you?"

"In his bedroom," Dani answered matter-of-factly. No way was she going to admit to this woman that she'd been cleaning Cameron's house yesterday. And doing her intimate laundry.

The blonde seemed stunned. Dani pointedly returned her attention to the kebabs, which she began to turn over. Let Cameron explain, she thought savagely. If he wanted to. The blonde was his business, not hers.

"When did you meet?"

"Yesterday morning. About nine o'clock."

"That figures."

The edge of bitter irony caused Dani to glance up from her cooking again. The blonde gave her a woman-to-woman little smile.

"He didn't want me to stay the whole night with him." She looked Dani up and down. "So what have you got that I don't have?"

Dani decided to backtrack fast. She didn't want to give the wrong impression and get into an altercation over Cameron McFarlane and his love-life. "I didn't jump into bed with him, if that's what you're thinking," she said bluntly. "Certain circumstances arose and he needed a chef. Which is what I am. Apart from that, I haven't got anything, really. I just go my own way..."

The woman stared at her in disbelief. "You must have something. He's been keeping an eye on you all evening, so I know he's attracted to you."

Dani didn't believe that for a moment, but even if she wanted to believe it, the image of him and Nicole... Dani shuddered. "Too bad!" she said, doing her best to sound casually indifferent. But inside she was feeling confused and disturbed. She kept on turning the kebabs as though that was the only thing that interested her. She wished the blonde would go away.

She didn't. "You are unbelievable," she accused. "Every woman here wants an invitation into his bed."

It exasperated Dani. "Look," she said confidingly, "if you want him, it's all right with me. I don't mind. Really I don't."

"Hell!" said the blonde. She looked dazed and confused beyond belief.

"Anybody here can have him, for all I care." Dani was getting into her stride. "Consider him up for grabs. It means absolutely nothing to me."

"*You* don't mind?" Her jaw was agape.

This was dragging on, and Dani needed to concentrate on her cooking. "What do I have to say? You've got my permission, if that's what you want. Anyone here who wants to bed Cameron McFarlane has got my permission. Now if you don't mind..."

The blonde walked away as though her world had suddenly collapsed.

Dani could only half concentrate on the kebabs, but she had become so automatically good at what she did that even half her mind could produce better results than most people attained with their full minds.

Damn people with silky blonde hair and big cleavages, she thought. But she had learned years ago not to compete. She had to use the equipment she was born with to full advantage and let the others with more favoured genetics look after themselves.

The thought that Cameron McFarlane could find her attractive—more attractive than the well-endowed blonde—was too much to credit. If he was keeping an eye on her, it was probably because he was piqued at her resistance to his charm. Which was because of Nicole. Otherwise she would have been mincemeat for him, as Nicole had charmingly suggested.

Perhaps she was an amusing curiosity to him, a subject for a chapter in his next book, another of her sister's sweetly acid suggestions. Or maybe he was merely checking that she was handling his party with the expertise she had promised. He couldn't be truly attracted. The blonde simply wasn't getting the attention *she* wanted from him, and looking for reasons to explain her own failure.

Dani switched off the grill, arranged the kebabs on their serving plates, carried them to the buffet table, then left the guests to their appetites. While they were occupied on the patio she did a fast clean-up in the living room; glasses into the bar dishwasher, trays to the kitchen. All that was left of her hors d'oeuvres were a few curls of celery and carrot sticks which she had placed around and between the rolls of smoked salmon. There wasn't even a scraping left of the avocado dip.

Dani had set out a fine array of cheeses and crackers on trays and was working on the fruit platters when Cameron breezed into the kitchen, beaming benevolence and his strong male charisma. "Need a hand with anything, Dani?"

"No, thank you," she snapped.

It halted him in his stride. "Something wrong?"

"What could be wrong? Your guests are golloping up everything I put in front of them. There are now forty of them instead of twenty. So far I've coped. Under severe difficulties. Any more questions?''

"The food has been superb, Dani. Wonderful. Compliments all around.'' He was still looking at her quizzically. "Are you angry about the extra guests?''

"I'm not angry about anything. I'm simply doing my job.'' She shot him a meaning look. "Yours is to entertain your guests. So go on back to it.''

He frowned. "Did Simone say something to you?''

"Who's Simone?''

"When you were cooking the kebabs.''

"She said the prawns were great. I gave her permission to bed you any time she liked.'' She nodded towards the cheese and crackers. "You can carry one of those trays to the guests if you want to do something useful.''

"You gave her permission?''

He looked dumbfounded.

It gave Dani a sweet sense of satisfaction. "Simone—if that's her name—seemed a bit disturbed. She had the weird idea that you fancied me.'' Dani rolled her eyes and turned to the fruit platter. "When you give her back her silk lace panties from Thursday night, you might reassure her that I'm not on your list of conquests.''

Cameron picked up a tray, then paused. Dani could feel his eyes boring into her, but she didn't look up from the Kiwi fruit she was peeling.

"I think this is getting out of hand,'' he said, his tone clearly one of vexation.

She shook her head. "It doesn't bother me, Cameron.''

"I think I've got some explaining to do..."

"The guests," Dani said pointedly. "And they don't bother me, either. The more people who like what I do, the more satisfaction I get from it."

It was true. Usually. Somehow pleasure in her work was escaping her tonight. She wished Cameron would go and leave her alone. Instead he stepped towards her, put a hand on her shoulder and gave it a gentle squeeze, commanding her attention.

"I like what you do, Dani," he said softly, his blue eyes serious for once, and dark with some deep purpose. "Very much," he added in a low throb. Then he favoured her with his heart-stopping smile and left her to her work.

In a most uncharacteristic burst of frustration, Dani stabbed her peeling knife into a piece of pineapple. Surprised at her own strength of feeling, she lifted the piece of fruit to her mouth and chewed it. Cameron McFarlane was not for her, and that was that. He could switch on all his charm until the cows came home. He was unalterably off her list.

She finished her arrangement of tropical fruits inside the pineapple shells, piled fresh berries around them, interspersed these with chocolate-coated orange peel, then admired her handiwork—artistic and mouth-watering. It was a pity she was feeling so sour with life in general. Without a doubt, her catering was first class.

Dani spent the next hour discreetly cleaning up after the hot courses, filling the dishwasher, emptying it, washing the large trays and serving plates. Music was blaring, people were dancing, and the cheese and fruit were being picked at with relish. From the way things were going, she couldn't anticipate an early end to the party. It was very much in full swing.

At midnight she rolled out the trolley with the coffee things and her death-by-chocolate cake. Most of the guests partook of both, but as a hint for them to go home, it was a dismal failure. They were still partying on an hour later, and the chocolate cake was all gone.

Dani did another clean-up, then sat in the kitchen drinking coffee. Her job was done. She felt tired and drained and exhausted, totally spent physically, mentally and emotionally. By rights she could go home now. Somehow she didn't want to.

It was nonsense to think she had to speak to Cameron before she went. She didn't have to. But she did want to know if he would accept her decision to release him from his part of the bargain. Would he accept it with relief? Would he argue? Apart from which, there was a dreadful fascination in finding out if Simone was going to lose another pair of knickers tonight. Or would it be someone else?

She was brooding over these highly questionable questions when Cameron swept into the kitchen again. "Business done," he declared. "Time for pleasure. Come and join the party, Dani."

She viewed him with jaundiced eyes. "No, thank you. I'll just wait here and clean up after they're all gone." For some stupid reason she cringed inwardly as she added, "Unless I'd be in the way of, uh, other arrangements."

He grimaced. "Somewhere along the way," he said slowly and seriously, "you have got the wrong idea."

He took her hand, the one that was not curled around the coffee mug. His eyes seemed to say that the only other arrangement he had in mind was with her. Which sent Dani's pulse into a skittish canter. His fingers stroked over hers, pressing their persuasion.

"I wouldn't allow anything to stand in the way of our agreement, Dani. I want you to come and enjoy yourself with me. When everyone's gone, I'll help you clean up, if you insist we have to do it."

Stop it now, Dani's mind screamed. *Right now!* It was the perfect opportunity. Then she could go home with a clear conscience.

Instead she allowed him to draw her off the kitchen stool. Once on her feet she dredged up the energy and willpower to do what had to be done. She began by deliberately extracting her hand from his. He frowned at her pointed disengagement from him.

"There's something I have to tell you, Cameron." She forced the words out determinedly.

"What?"

"The agreement is off. I've decided I don't want you with me on Christmas Day," she rushed on. "You were in a fix over this party, and I wouldn't let you down after giving my word, so I did the job you wanted. But I don't want anything in return from you."

"Why not?" he demanded.

"You're not what I want," she stated flatly. "I've crossed you off my list."

He looked incredulous. "You think I can't do what you want?" The challenge in his voice carried a confidence that aroused Dani's resentment of what she perceived as his careless acquisition of any woman he fancied.

"You think you're God's gift to women," she accused hotly. "Well, let me tell you that my grandmother and my mother and my father will spot you for a fraud in no time flat!"

"The hell they will!" he retorted with strength. "One thing I'm not, and never have been, is a fraud. I wouldn't have got to where I am if I were a fraud. I wouldn't have agreed to our bargain in the first place if I hadn't wanted to be with you."

"And why, might I ask, do you want that?" Dani scoffed.

His anger melted into something more disturbing. "Because you're the most provocative package I've ever been presented with."

Dani was outraged. "I am *not* provocative. I've *never* been provocative. I don't believe in being provocative."

"No?" He raised an eyebrow, but the sternness of his mouth...was it a trace of anger? "Then why have I thought of nothing but you since you woke me up yesterday morning?"

Dani didn't have an answer to that. "I'm *not* a package."

"Yes, you are, Dani. A package full of surprises. A package I want to open. And find out all there is to know of what is inside." He moved forward and slid one hand around her waist. "The wrapping is interesting. I want to know what it's hiding."

He was pulling her closer. Dani lifted her hands to his chest to push away. "This isn't a good idea, Cameron," she warned in quick, urgent words.

"It feels good." His other hand completed the encirclement of her waist. His eyes burned into hers, denying there was any ground for her to protest. "I've been wanting to taste that saucy mouth. It begs for exploration."

"No, it's not begging," she choked out. Her throat had gone all tight. It felt paralysed. Her whole body felt paralysed. There was suddenly something very mesmerising about the way his mouth was coming towards hers. She was like a mouse waiting for the predator to strike. She made an enormous effort to concentrate on what had to be done. "I don't think..."

"This is not the time for thinking."

Then his lips were brushing over hers, a soft tingling contact that was both sensual and seductive. Dani struggled with herself. Of course, she couldn't take him home with her on Christmas Day. That was definitely out. And she certainly couldn't have him as a lover. That was just as definitely out. But a kiss... well, there was no harm in that, was there? And she was entitled to it, wasn't she? Just to see what it was like with him?

CHAPTER FIVE

THE QUESTION became academic as Dani lost her train of thought. His mouth was warm and soft and mobile. It didn't feel too badly at all. In fact, it felt very good. And she was far too tired to fight Cameron off.

She had no remorse at leaning more of her weight against him. He appeared to take the slump of fatigue as encouragement, his mouth weaving a symphony of sensation over her lips. He gave her such comforting support that she let herself sag into his secure embrace, pressing her breasts against his chest as his mouth began to work more vigorously over hers. She liked the texture of his lips. Quite instinctively she moved her tongue slowly but fleetingly over their graduating softness.

Cameron McFarlane apparently took this as further encouragement. He started exploring her mouth with his tongue, long sensual rolling movements that were intensely exciting and left her feeling like quivering jelly. She was boneless, weightless, soaring like an eagle, but there were things she wanted to try, things she'd never thought of before, things she had never imagined doing . . . like finding out if it was just as exciting to explore his mouth in the same way.

And her hands itched to do things, too. They played over his neck. She sensed it had something to do with nerves. She didn't know how she knew, but it felt right, and Cameron McFarlane seemed to be responding just right. For some reason he was uttering short little moans, but he was aroused by her touch, no doubt about that. And she felt feline and graceful.

Yes, for the first time in her life she felt graceful, as if her body had been made to belong right where it was, and Cameron led her into an intensely exciting rhythm that united their mouths and stomachs and hips. She liked where she was, she liked what she was doing, she liked what *he* was doing to her. It felt as if her world had gone into overdrive and she was spinning into a new dimension.

She had tried kissing before, but it had not been the same, never like this. The boys had been so gauche, so awkward or so greedy to take. Whether it was their lack of giving, or the fact that she had not been so involved emotionally to be all-giving, the result was the same. Dani never had any trouble repulsing physical advances that didn't please her.

Nicole was half right. She was a virgin. But she was definitely *not* foolish about it. It had never felt right before, and why should she give sufferance to something that didn't feel right? It was not that she lacked curiosity or confidence in herself. She simply refused to give a man pleasure that he could not return. That was one of the lessons she had learnt from the women's movement over the past twenty years—a woman had rights. And Dani believed in exercising them.

One of Cameron's hands trailed up and down the curve of her spine, caressing a shivery line of pleasure. Then it found another line, moving under her upstretched arm and stroking the soft swelling edge of her breast. Dani had an irresistible urge to touch him, too. Ever since she had first seen him she had secretly wondered how it might be.

Experimentally she ran her hands down Cameron McFarlane's back. She felt his muscles contract... ripple. This man was sensitive. Temptation urged her on. She eased her body back a little so that she could bring a hand up to the open neckline of his sports shirt. The buttons seemed to fall open for her. She felt his skin goose-prickle under her touch. Her mental and emotional fatigue washed away in a drugging sense of her own pleasure. It was marvellous that he responded like this. He really responded to what a man should respond to.

A numb amazement spread through her mind. No wonder women chased him in droves. He seemed to be instinctively tuned to their needs. A man in a million. But how could she possibly keep him when he had such attributes? He probably *was* God's gift to women. And she couldn't have him, anyhow.

Regret ran through her like a river of lead. She had to stop this. Yet she couldn't cut this kiss off abruptly. Not the kiss of a lifetime. As sad as it was, though, she had to end it.

Intuitively he knew what she was doing and he didn't resist. The pressure of his mouth lightened until their lips were barely grazing. They moved apart, came back to taste the sweet temptation of each other time and time again, intoxicating little frissons of magical electricity, sipping at the entrancing pleasure.

Then Dani lowered her head for the last time and leant it against the warm haven between his shoulder and chest.

His voice was husky as his lips feathered past her ear. "Let's go to bed," he whispered.

There was no question about what she wanted to do. Her stomach, her breasts, her nerves were screaming out for more of the same kind of enthralling experience. It was only with considerable difficulty that Dani forced into her unwilling mind the image of Nicole with him. But she did it. This was the time for sanity. She had to put a stop to what was going on between them and what he was suggesting. Decisively. No matter how hard it was. She remembered a line from *My Fair Lady* and it tripped off her tongue.

"Not bloody likely."

That should do the trick, she thought. And to help it have its decisive effect she mustered up what strength she could and took a step backwards, away from his wandering hands and arms.

Cameron McFarlane looked dazed, drugged, bewildered. "What did you say?"

"Not bloody likely," Dani repeated for him.

Still he couldn't seem to comprehend that she was rejecting the idea of going to bed with him. "What?" he asked incredulously.

If ever there was a time for firmness, this was it, even though she was shaking inside. "The answer is no," Dani said emphatically.

He shook his head as though to clear it. "I was getting a different message a few moments ago."

"I was checking you out."

"You were checking me out?" His voice was strangled with disbelief.

"To see how good you were at kissing."

"And?"

"You were surprisingly good."

"So?"

"That's all. I don't want anything more from you. I don't want to see you again."

"Why?"

"There are reasons..."

"What reasons?"

Dani found it very difficult to say. The question conjured up images that turned her stomach.

"Forget it," she said. "Go find Simone."

"I can't forget it. I don't want Simone."

He sounded very passionate about it. Dani thought the only thing to do was give him some down-to-earth practical advice. "Then sleep by yourself, Cameron. Do you good for a change."

"Tell me what's wrong!"

Quite clearly he wasn't in the mood for taking advice. He seemed angry. Very angry. Dani sighed. Nothing she touched ever turned to gold. At the present moment, everything she touched turned into a disaster. There may as well be another one, she thought, feeling more miserable than she had about everything else. But the truth was the truth. She gave it to him, right between the eyes.

"You slept with my sister." And you can't put spilled milk back in the bottle, Dani thought as she fiercely added, "As far as I'm concerned, that ruins anything there could be between you and me."

A primitive pride blazed from her eyes as she watched Cameron McFarlane pass beyond the initial shock of having to face up to the consequences of his actions. She saw the resentment of being made to pay for something he didn't care about, the burning frustration of not getting his own way, and finally the determination to pursue what he wanted despite everything she had said.

He didn't like rejection, she thought. He had been aroused. Maybe he'd never been rejected before by a woman when he was aroused. He certainly didn't like it. It wasn't necessary to be a professional psychoanalyst to feel that. Yet he didn't have to suffer the physical frustration she was feeling. He could walk straight back to his party and find solace with his pick of any number of women. Including Simone.

Although that kiss had been an incredible revelation to Dani, it couldn't have been so amazingly special to him. For a man of his experience, there'd probably be nothing new left to feel. He'd done it all before, countless times. With her sister, as well. No matter what he said or did, Dani was not about to forget that. She had gone as far as she could let herself go with him. This little episode in her life had to be finished with now.

"I'm going to ring for a taxi," she stated firmly.

"No, you're not!" Ruthless determination tightened his jaw. "Not until we've got this situation sorted out."

"There's nothing to sort out," Dani corrected him. "What's done is done."

"I can see that," he agreed with her. "And it was done between the time you left me yesterday and your arrival here today. Which accounts for the change in your attitude towards me, your intense concentration on your work this afternoon and the flak you've been giving me tonight. Right?"

"Right!" she snapped, finding his analysis distasteful in the circumstances.

"Right!" he snapped back at her. "Now who the hell is your sister? To my certain knowledge I have never slept with a woman by the name of Halstead." His eyes blazed over her. "Although I most certainly want to."

Dani instantly felt a deep and bitter resentment on her sister's behalf that he couldn't remember her name. It was totally damning. No doubt about it, he was nothing more than a rooster in a henhouse. Nicole was right. He only used women for his own purposes, and that was the end of it. He didn't care enough to remember them afterwards.

"My sister's name is Nicole. Nicole Halstead. I dare say you didn't get as far as her surname," she answered coldly.

"I know *everything* about every woman with whom I've shared any intimacy," he retorted with grim authority. "I do not know a Nicole Halstead."

"You do so!" Dani told him in towering disgust at his lies.

"I tell you I don't know," he insisted in angry challenge. "If you're so sure of your facts, tell me when and where."

"Nicole works for the PR company that promotes your books in Australia," Dani recited accusingly. "Does that jog your insultingly blank memory?"

It still took him a few moments to make a connection. Then he said with a look of total perplexity, "*That* Nicole?"

He sounded incredulous, which put Dani slightly off her stride. "She happens to be my sister," she reminded him fiercely.

It was a warning. No matter how mean and bitchy Nicole might be, Dani had a very strong sense of family loyalty, and she was not about to allow Cameron McFarlane to put her sister down any more than he had already done by supposedly not remembering her.

There was not one wavering flicker in the blue eyes that glittered at her with triumphant satisfaction. "She was introduced to me as Nicky. I didn't learn her last name. If it was ever given. And I have not slept with your sister," he declared with ringing conviction. "Never. Not once."

Dani's eyes narrowed. "How do you know you haven't? You obviously can't remember."

"My memory is faultless on people I have met. Your sister is a slight—*very* slight—business acquaintance. She has never been, and never will be, anything more than that in my life," he said emphatically. "To put it succinctly, she is not on my list."

"Your *list!*" Dani snorted in contempt.

His eyes derided her contempt. "You have a list. I have a list. And I don't care to be crossed off *your* list because of some mistaken notion that your sister is on *my* list."

This put Dani in a fix. She didn't want to tell him that hers was an imaginary list. Besides, they were getting off the point. "How come Nicole says you did sleep with her?"

"How would I know why Nicole says I did?"

"You're accusing my sister of being a liar."

"I think she's very much mistaken. Or..."

"Or what?"

One eyebrow rose. "Or your sister has a very vivid imagination."

To Dani's certain knowledge, Nicole had no imagination at all. And she didn't make mistakes. Her sister was utterly dedicated to facts and figures, which she threw at Dani at every opportunity. So one or the other of them was lying. The trick was, which one?

She eyed Cameron McFarlane suspiciously. He looked very confident of being in control again. But he was supposed to be a master of psychology. Having been thrown off stride himself, it would be an effective counterstrike to throw her off stride.

"I'll think about it," she said.

"Dani, if I went out on the patio and swore black, blue and brindle that you hopped into bed with me yesterday morning, don't you think most people would believe it?"

"Probably," Dani acknowledged reluctantly.

"That's the position I'm in," he said persuasively. "How can I prove I didn't do something?"

He had a point. But he could still be lying. Yet if it was Nicole who was lying... Why, why, why would she do that?

"I don't like you very much," she said, half to herself. Although it wasn't true. If Nicole had told a great big lie, she could get to like Cameron McFarlane a great deal. Too much, really. Which would lead to another inevitable disaster.

His hands were on her shoulders, softly kneading them. "You did like me yesterday, Dani. After we made our bargain, you were beginning to like me quite a lot." He raised a challenging eyebrow, and the blue eyes bored into hers. "Are you going to let a lie spoil what we could have together?"

Dani's stomach churned with uncertainty. She wished she could give in to the temptation of his touch, to let him be close to her again. The memory of how it had felt with him clouded her thinking. She struggled to regain good, sound reasoning. If Nicole had lied... But then, there was Simone, as well. How could she know what was true or not?

"You like blondes," she stated accusingly.

"I don't like blondes!" Cameron rasped in exasperation. "I don't care what colour a woman's hair is. It can be black, red, green, purple...." He paused to catch his breath.

"They're all the same to you as long as they perform in bed," Dani finished for him.

The pupils of his eyes seemed to contract. "You've got the wrong idea about me, Dani," he bit out.

"In what way?" she asked sceptically.

"I like women. As people. I like you as a person."

"And Simone?"

"Is a very nice person. But I'm not in love with her."

Dani stared at him.

He shrugged. "Simone is doing her doctorate. We have had a mutually satisfying relationship. There is no commitment to each other on either side." He paused, his eyes boring into hers. "Something wrong with that?"

Dani was fairly sure Simone would have liked a commitment, but Dani was not here to fight Simone's battles. She shrugged. "That's your business. It has nothing to do with me."

He sighed. Heavily. Then very softly he said, "I want *you*, Dani." And the desire warming his eyes made mincemeat of Dani's stomach.

Fortunately her brain was still in reasonable working order. Right now he wanted her. Dani couldn't disbelieve that. But only a couple of nights ago he had wanted Simone. And before that, her sister? How many other women had contributed to his list? Dani really didn't care to be part of a list.

"Why should my sister lie to me?" she demanded.

He shook his head. "God knows! You'll have to ask her. Maybe she's jealous of you. I don't know."

This wasn't getting her anywhere. "I'll think about it," she said again.

Desire slid swiftly into speculation. "I don't know for certain what's on your sister's mind. I do know for certain I'm telling the truth," Cameron stated decisively. "I did not sleep with your sister. I was not even tempted to sleep with your sister. Perhaps she resented that. She let me know, in the subtle way that women have, that she was available if needed. I did not react to it because I do not take up with any woman on the basis of her giving me the green light. Believe it or not, I do have a strong sense of discrimination as to what I want, when I want it and with whom."

Dani considered all of this for several moments. Maybe he wasn't quite the womaniser Nicole had painted him. He wasn't exactly celibate, either. However, it was hardly reasonable to expect a man of his years not to have had a few relationships in the past. If Cameron McFarlane was telling the truth, if he really had rejected Nicole's come-on and preferred her, Dani Halstead... A glorious light switched on in Dani's brain, and Cameron McFarlane went up in her estimation like a supersonic elevator.

One question came uppermost to mind. "Why me, then?"

He smiled. It was a winning smile. A smile that radiated happiness and well-being. A smile that Dani decided she'd better be suspicious of, because it was doing a lot of damage to her inside, and that could be very dangerous if he was an out-and-out liar.

"You're enchanting. Natural, uninhibited, and with a deliciously tart dash of spice. After that kiss we shared, I have a strong feeling that we fit together."

"Well, I'm not too sure I find you enchanting, Cameron," she quickly derided. "Or that we fit together all that well." The suspicion remained, however, that he could be right. And if he really, *really* preferred her to Nicole... "I'm going to check back with Nicole and hear her side of this before I'll consider being enchanted by you." She paused and raised her eyebrows. "Can you live with that?"

The smile turned into a grimace. Frustration tightened his face. He finally relaxed into a resigned sigh, his eyes mocking the resolution in hers. "I guess this means you won't be staying the night."

"As I said before, I'm going to ring for a taxi."

"I'll take you home."

"No, you won't. You've got guests to tend to."

"Damn the guests! They can look after themselves."

"That's very selfish. You invited them."

"Only half of them."

"That's not the point. You're the host. Besides, I don't want you taking me home. I don't know yet if I want to be with you or not. And until I make up my mind about that..."

"Dani, I've told you the truth," he appealed with an edge of strong feeling.

"If it's the truth, it will still be the truth tomorrow, and the next day, and the next day," she argued. "Think of it this way, Cameron. You may not want me by then, anyway. And that will settle things for both of us."

"You like having things your own way, Dani Halstead," he grated between his teeth.

"A woman has to do what a woman has to do," Dani tossed off.

His chagrin crumbled into a ripple of soft laughter. "Why fight it?" he said, lifting his hands from her shoulders and shaking his head. "Take your taxi, if you must. Tomorrow is another day." His eyes flared with the promise that they would meet again... and with a different outcome.

Whether that was male pride or serious intent, Dani couldn't be absolutely sure. She knew that she very definitely needed a breathing space to work things out in her own way.

He insisted on giving her money for the taxi fare, which Dani readily accepted since she had done a great deal of work for him and it wasn't by any means sure that she would get any compensation for it. That remained a very grey area for the present.

There were still some fifteen or so guests lingering at the party—Simone amongst them—when the taxi arrived. Cameron made a point of escorting Dani to the waiting cab. "Thanks for all the work you put in, Dani," he said as he saw her settled onto the back seat. He made no reference to tomorrow.

She looked at him, a flash of cynicism in her eyes. "It was an interesting experience, Cameron," she said, but her heart was heavy.

Cameron touched his fingers to his lips and threw her a kiss as he shut the door. It was a charming gesture. He was very good at charm. Very good at everything.

She didn't look back as the taxi moved forward. The equation was very clear to Dani. If Cameron

McFarlane truly wanted her, he would come after her. On the other hand, if he had been lying through his teeth in order to win some brief satisfaction tonight, he knew the game was up and there was no point in pursuing her even if he wanted to. Either way, nothing could be settled until tomorrow, so there wasn't much point in thinking about it.

For some reason Dani had a blinding headache by the time she arrived home. She was not prone to headaches. It must be because of having all her emotions scrambled around, Dani decided.

She took a quick shower, pulled on her nightie, then undid the tightly woven plait and fluffed her hair out, hoping that might ease the problem. As an extra measure, she took two aspirin tablets before falling into bed.

She tried to go to sleep, but she couldn't help thinking about that kiss and remembering how it had felt. She wished she could know all that might have followed on from it. She figured that would be very worthwhile knowing. At least once in a lifetime.

She was only twenty-three years old, she consoled herself, and Cameron McFarlane couldn't be the only man in the world who knew how to respond to a woman. If she couldn't have him, that was that. Nevertheless—although it wasn't a nice thing to contemplate—she wouldn't mind too much if she found out Nicole had misled her.

And if it was true Cameron McFarlane wasn't the rooster in the henhouse she thought he was, well, she wouldn't mind that, either.

Of course, neither factor would have any meaning at all if he didn't come after her. Dani was through with counting chickens before they hatched. No doubt about it. As Grandma said, a bird in the hand was always worth two in the bush.

Somehow this piece of wisdom did nothing to ease the dull throbbing pain in her head and heart.

CHAPTER SIX

DANI WAS DREAMING about chasing birds through a confusing wilderness of bushes when a banging on her front door woke her up. It was a relief to get out of that dream. For some reason she had birds on the brain.

She squinted at her bedside clock, which showed it was almost ten. But it was Sunday morning, and she wasn't expecting any visitors. If it was Mrs. B she would have come to the stairwell door not the outside one. So it couldn't be her or one of the upstairs couple. Unless perhaps one of them had accidentally locked himself or herself out of the house. That had happened before, particularly after a raging argument.

Dani dragged herself out of bed. At least her headache had dissipated overnight. The morning could be faced without wincing. She drew on her cotton robe, pushed her hair away from her face, then went to the door to answer the summons, which persisted.

Dani could hardly believe her eyes when she found Cameron McFarlane on the basement landing. His handsome face instantly beamed with pleasure at seeing her. Because of her untidy state Dani was half-hidden behind the door, but that was no protection.

His smile was bright enough to dizzy her, and the rest of him—in blue jeans and a white cotton pullover—emanated vibrant vitality.

"What are you doing here?" she asked dazedly.

"It's tomorrow," he replied. "The sun is shining. It's a beautiful day. I've come to take you out with me."

She stared at him, struggling with the temptation he held out. He *had* come after her. Which meant he really did want her, didn't it?

But she still didn't know if he'd been lying about Nicole or not.

"You woke me up," she said, stating the obvious while she tried to get her thoughts in order. "I'm not dressed," she added, self-consciously aware that her body was singing its own treacherous song of excited pleasure at having Cameron here with her in the light of another day.

His eyebrows slanted appealingly. "I did allow you eight hours' sleep. Which is more than I got, tossing and turning and thinking of you. Throw some clothes on, Dani, and let's take off."

Dani paused for serious consideration. Her hand automatically went to her hair.

"Don't worry about your hair," he urged. "It's beautiful the way it is."

Beautiful? It must be a mess, Dani thought. And Cameron was bombarding her with charm. She frowned at him. "I haven't rung Nicole yet."

"Then do it right now." Something feral glittered into the blue eyes. "In fact, I'd like to speak to her myself."

No, Dani thought. This is between Nicole and me. Private family business. And a serious matter, as well. At least to Dani, it was. If Nicole had vilified Cameron McFarlane's character out of malice and spite, that was very disturbing. After all, they were sisters.

"I want to speak to Nicole alone, Cameron," she said decisively.

He hesitated, obviously reluctant to let that happen. His eyes burned into hers, reminding her of how they had felt together, reminding her of all he was offering her. Dani felt extremely conscious of not being properly dressed. Her body, under the free-flowing nightie and robe, was remembering all the sensations of last night's embrace, and the desire to explore that experience further was little short of overwhelming. Perhaps Cameron sensed it and was satisfied with his effect on her. He relaxed into another charming smile.

"Go to it, then. I'll drop in on Mrs. B and have a little chat with her. I expect you to be ready to go when I come back."

Dani hastily closed the door and leaned against it, taking several deep breaths to calm her racing pulse and pump some strength into her legs. Cameron McFarlane certainly was dynamite when he chose to exert the power of his attraction. She shouldn't have let him kiss her, Dani thought. It had closed the distance between them with devastating force. Distance that she had to keep if Nicole had not been lying.

Dani pushed herself away from the door and headed for the telephone. She dialled her sister's number, feverishly hoping Nicole had not gone out this morning, because she didn't know what she would do if the burning question couldn't be resolved. That Cameron had wanted to speak to Nicole suggested he was innocent. Or did it? Perhaps he had the power and influence to threaten Nicole's career. Dani suspected that Cameron McFarlane could be very ruthless when it came to getting his own way.

Did he really find her so attractive?

Or was it a case of not being finished with her until *he* decided he was finished?

Answer me, Nicole, Dani thought with growing impatience as she waited for the telephone receiver to be picked up at the other end of the line. It felt like an interminable length of time before it was. Yet when Nicole's voice did answer the call, Dani was immediately plunged into a ferment of uncertainty. How was she to ask if her sister had lied about Cameron? It was so shaming and offensive, whatever the outcome.

"Who's calling, please?" Aggrieved.

"It's Dani," she blurted. "I...I need to know if you said those things about Cameron because... because you wanted to protect me from being hurt."

Silence.

"Nicole? Please? I really need to know," Dani appealed desperately.

More silence. Then, tersely, "If you're intent on making a fool of youself over Cameron McFarlane, Dani, go right ahead. The decision is yours."

Dani sighed. The metaphorical washing of hands. Which wouldn't do in this case. "Look, Nicole," she tried again. "Maybe I'm not the kind of sister you'd like to have. We don't seem to have much in common. But this is important to me. You see—" there was no way around it, she had to say it straight out "—you see . . . Cameron swears he didn't sleep with you."

"You asked him?" Shock, swiftly escalating to outrage. "How dare you talk to him about me! How dare you . . ." Nicole choked on her fury.

Dani winced. Why hadn't she thought of the bitter wound to Nicole's pride? If Cameron McFarlane was telling the truth . . . "I'm sorry," she rushed out. "I didn't ask him, Nicole. He kind of pressured me into giving him the reason I was refusing to . . . to see him any more. And he swore that he hadn't had that kind of interest in you."

"And you believe him." Blistering resentment.

"Nicole . . ." Desperate appeal. "I didn't know what to believe. I thought maybe . . ."

"Believe what you like, Dani."

It was now Nicole's turn to crash the telephone receiver down and put an emphatic end to pursuing the painful point any further.

Dani felt both frustrated and deeply disturbed as she slowly returned the receiver to its cradle. Nothing would ever be the same again. She had given Nicole the ultimate insult. If Cameron McFarlane had rejected Nicole, and really wanted her, Dani, then Nicole would certainly consider that the greatest insult she had received in her life.

Why did it have to be like this? Why couldn't she and Nicole be friends? Nicole treated her almost as if she was a competitor, yet Dani had gone out of her way *not* to compete with Nicole. Tears burned her eyes as she removed her hand from the telephone. She felt chewed up inside. A mess.

She probably shouldn't have doubted her sister's word. She should never have revealed what Nicole had said to Cameron McFarlane, shaming her sister just because he got under her skin. Dani didn't have to see him again, but Nicole undoubtedly would in the course of her work at the PR company. Why hadn't she thought of that?

Nicole would never forgive her. Never in a million years. Nicole might not have liked Dani much before, but now she would hate her. The burning tears welled up and overflowed. Dani slumped on her bed in defeat. Another disaster. Nothing turned out right for her. Not ever.

But there was no point in sitting here moaning and groaning about the situation. She had to make up her mind what to do about Cameron. He would be coming back for her soon. Dani got herself moving while she thought about Cameron McFarlane's persistence.

She had a quick wash then hurried through her dressing, automatically choosing her favourite skirt and matching blouse. It was not an expensive outfit, only polished cotton, but the tiny floral print in oranges and greens and browns suited her colouring, and Dani was not completely without vanity. Whatever she decided to do about Cameron McFarlane, some core of feminine pride inside her wanted him to see her looking nice for once. She quickly fastened the stylish belt in tan leather around her small waist and slid the matching sandals onto her feet.

When the expected knock came on her door, Dani was sliding a couple of combs above her ears, bringing some order to the mass of waves and curls that tumbled to her shoulder-blades. Her bathroom mirror reflected a pale face, and the freckles across her nose and cheekbones seemed to stand out more than usual. Could a man like Cameron McFarlane really want *her?* Dani asked herself. Had Nicole lied out of spite and jealousy?

Damn Nicole! Dani thought fiercely. She'd been interfering in *her* life, *all* her life, making her feel second-rate and not worthy of notice. For whatever reason he had, Cameron McFarlane was certainly taking notice of her. And if Dani wiped everything else out, the plain unvarnished truth was she *wanted* to be with Cameron McFarlane. She *wanted* to explore the amazing and exciting sense of rightness with him.

Having made her decision, Dani applied a soft coral lipstick to put some colour on her face, then went to confront the man whose desire for her was about to be measured.

She opened the door and was once more swamped by the impact of his compelling physical presence. His blue eyes glittered with pleasure as they took in her appearance, and the smile he gave her was a force-ten heart stopper.

"Great! You're ready."

Dani took a quick breath to ease the constriction in her chest. "More or less," she said evasively.

"Nicole came clean."

He said that with such confidence it was difficult not to assume he was innocent. But being a master psychologist, he might have worked out that Nicole had a career to protect. It was not conclusive.

"More or less," Dani replied, even more evasively.

"So now you know you can trust me."

"That might be overstating the case a trifle."

"Learn to trust your instincts, Dani." The advice had a liberal coating of self-satisfaction.

Trusting her instincts was one thing that Dani was *not* going to do. That could be far too dangerous with this man. She took a deep breath and asked, "What have you got in mind for today, Cameron? You didn't say earlier."

"How about a swim? It's hot now, and it can only get hotter. Unless there's something specific you'd like to do, we can laze around the pool today, then go out for dinner this evening." He grinned. "Consider me your slave for the day. Tell me what you want and I'll give it to you."

"That sounds fair," Dani said, unable to stop herself from responding to his flirtatious grin. "I'll collect the things I need."

A few moments later Dani joined him on the basement landing with her beach bag. Her heart was pumping so excitedly that she was already locking the door behind her before she remembered Mrs. B and her bad ankle. She shot Cameron a look of appeal.

"Would you mind waiting a bit longer? I should check on Mrs. B to see if she needs anything."

"No need. She's mobile again. One could almost say spritely." His eyes danced with amusement. "Besides which, she has company. A gentleman by the name of Henry Newbold. He's taking Mrs. B out to lunch."

"Oh! How lovely for her!"

Dani was so pleased for her friend that she barely noticed Cameron relieving her of her beach bag, but she certainly noticed his arm sliding around her waist as they went up the basement steps together. Her whole body was vibrantly alive to the warmth of his hand on her hip, and the brush of his body against hers was oddly mesmerising. Dani did not recollect her wits until she was seated in the front passenger seat of Cameron's car.

Why did it feel so different with him? Dani wondered, perplexed and disturbed by the intensity of the response his touch drew from her. She could be in big trouble before this day was out if she didn't put some firm control on proceedings. If Cameron thought last night's kiss represented a go-ahead signal, she had to scotch that idea immediately. Otherwise lazing around his pool might lead to all kinds of complications, including his bed.

It was all very well feeling strongly attracted to him, but she didn't want to end up being used for a chapter in his new book. For the life of her, she couldn't understand why he should choose to want *her* above Nicole. Or Simone, for that matter. It made no sense to her.

Cameron took his seat beside her. The closing of his door seemed to lend an intimate atmosphere to their togetherness. Dani frowned at him as he flashed her a smile that expressed far too much satisfaction for her comfort.

"I'm still not sure I like you," she blurted out, feeling a need to prick his confidence.

"Today's the perfect opportunity for you to find out that you do," he replied, not the least bit pricked.

"I'm coming because you owe me a day," Dani declared, spelling out the terms for his conduct.

That seemed to galvanise his attention. The blue eyes speared into hers. "Am I to understand Christmas Day is still off, Dani?"

She grimaced. "Well, it won't work any more, Cameron. It would cause trouble within the family, and I don't want to do that."

"I see," he said grimly. "So Nicole didn't back off."

"In a way she did," Dani assured him quickly. "But she knows you, Cameron, and that spoils the effect I wanted. Whether it's true or not, you have a reputation of being a womaniser, so it won't do me any good to turn up with you."

He frowned. "What effect did you want?"

"To turn the spotlight of interest onto you instead of me. You happen to be the archetype of all the qualities my family admires." She shrugged. "Hopelessly superficial, of course, but that's the way they judge."

"Superficial..." The word clearly stuck in his throat.

"You know... handsome face, good physique, highly successful in your chosen career, rolling in money, smart dresser, charming manner..."

"Those qualities mean nothing to you?" he asked, a quirky little smile on his lips.

"Oh, I wouldn't knock them. I was quite prepared to use them," Dani acknowledged. "But compared to other things, I don't think they're terribly important."

"Like what?"

"Having a good heart, kindness, honesty, loyalty, fidelity... things like that."

He flashed her a challenging look. "It will be interesting to see how honest *you* are, Dani."

Which gave her food for thought as he started the car and drove them toward a day of highly questionable togetherness. She wanted him. There was no denying that. But people could want a lot of things that were not good for them.

"What was the difference of opinion that caused you to leave your job at Julio's?" Cameron enquired, surprising her out of her worrisome reverie.

It was a safe subject, Dani decided. She explained what had happened with Julio and how disillusioned she felt with the whole business.

Cameron made sympathetic comments that sounded sincere. Then he slanted her an enquiring look. "So what are you going to do now?"

Dani shrugged. "I haven't made up my mind yet."

He smiled as though he was pleased she had no immediate plan. "I'm sure something will turn up," he said.

Not for her, Dani thought. *He* might be lucky, but she wasn't. She needed to prove herself on every job she obtained, and none of them had come easy.

When they came to a halt at Cameron's house, Dani felt ridiculously nervous about getting out of the car.

It had been a bad idea to come here, she thought. She should have insisted on a public beach. Or somewhere public.

Cameron, however, made no attempt to touch her when she alighted. He led the way into the house, keeping to a relaxed charming manner as he invited her to use the guest suite she had used last night for changing her clothes.

There were a few moments of high tension when she went out to the patio in her bathing suit and saw him in his. Dani had more than enough curves in the right places and her yellow maillot displayed all of them. Cameron showed a fascinated interest in mentally mapping every one. At the same time, Dani couldn't help staring at him in the light of what she had felt in last night's embrace.

It was Cameron who broke the dangerous enthralment, moving not towards her but away, inviting her to share the pool with him. The cold water was a good dampener for more than the summer day's heat. They swam and floated and swam some more. Cameron gradually put her at ease with a mixture of good humour and charm, laughing at things she said and never letting their conversation flag long enough for any discomfiting silences to develop. He seemed interested in her ideas and experiences, and he readily reciprocated with stories of his own.

He did not act or talk like a womaniser, Dani thought with relief. She slowly came to the realisation that the only evidence she had of his womanising was his relationship with Simone, which had been a mutual affair.

She remembered his insistence that he did not bed women indiscriminately. On the other hand, how had he gathered the material for his book *The Psychology of Sex?* That seemed to suggest a lot of first-hand experience. Dani decided she had better get hold of his book and read it for herself.

He undermined other preconceptions she had by cheerfully making them salad sandwiches for lunch and proving himself perfectly capable in the kitchen. He drank a soft drink with her, not criticising her choice or attempting to persuade her into trying anything alcoholic. Dani could not have asked for a more considerate host, nor a more pleasant and stimulating companion. She could not help liking him. Very much.

They were relaxing on the sun loungers after lunch and Dani was feeling a lovely warm contentment when Cameron indirectly reopened the question about Nicole. "Family is important to you, isn't it, Dani," he remarked, rather than asked. His eyes shot her a look of warm approval that Dani found a bit confusing, since one of her family had supposely maligned him.

"Yes, it is," she replied staunchly, then tried to get the subject on an impersonal level. "I think everyone has a need to feel part of something. Roots of one kind or another. I guess you must miss that, not having a family yourself."

A sardonic smile curled his mouth and his eyes went hard. "Some things are better missed."

"What happened, Cameron?" she asked impulsively. "How did you come to be so alone?"

He shrugged dismissively. "Ancient history, Dani. Tell me about your family." He flashed her a curious look. "Do you love them?"

"Yes." She gave him an ironic smile. "Although sometimes I don't like them too well. Except for Grandma. Grandma is special. When I grow old I want to be just like my grandmother."

Warmth crept into his eyes and seemed to caress her. "Why?"

Dani took a deep breath and tried to ignore the tingly feeling running riot through her body. "Because she's so wise and loving and doesn't try to interfere. She believes in letting people live their own lives, but if you ask her for guidance, she helps without being bossy. I've had some of the best times of my life with Grandma."

"Where does she live?"

"On a little five-acre farm outside Camden. It used to be a much bigger farm, but most of it was sold off to land developers after Grandpa died. Grandma held on to enough so she can still keep her dogs and goats and chickens and have her fruit trees and vegetable garden. Mum and Dad are always on at her to sell up and settle in a retirement village close to them—" she flashed him a triumphant grin "—but no-one's going to get Grandma to do anything she doesn't want to do."

Cameron grinned. "A very strong character?"

"Very independent. Dad says she's old, stubborn and just plain ornery, but there's nothing feeble-minded about Grandma."

In fact, her pithy comments on life often discomfited her family, particularly Nicole, who thought she knew better than anyone. But Dani didn't want to mention Nicole to Cameron.

"Is she your father's mother?"

"No. My mother's. Dad's parents are dead. We never saw much of them. Usually we went to Grandma's for school holidays."

"What did you do there?"

Dani regaled him with stories from her childhood. Cameron listened with such fascinated interest that Dani had the strong impression his childhood had been very different from hers. She wanted to ask him about it, but he skilfully blocked every attempt she made, turning the conversation back to her life. Not that she minded telling him, but she was conscious of him learning a great deal about her and telling very little about himself.

All the same, it was a most enjoyable afternoon. It was only as she was changing to go out to dinner with him that she realised Cameron could have been playing some masterly game of psychology, beaming interest and approval at her to persuade her into revealing so much. On the other hand, why would he want to know if he wasn't really interested?

Cameron took her to a little French restaurant in Paddington and he told her stories of the strange meals he'd had in foreign places. He had her laughing and enjoying herself so much she didn't stop to think his experience was so much wider than hers that she couldn't possibly be a match for him. His eyes kept telling her he was enjoying her response to him, and Dani felt giddy with pleasure.

The meal they had was fine and beautifully presented, and as it turned out, Dani was well acquainted with the chef, having worked with him before she moved on and up to Julio's. She sent him her compliments via their waiter.

In his typically flamboyant style, Henri appeared in the dining room a few minutes later, calling out her name as though she were a long-lost relative. Dani laughingly rose from her chair to be greeted by smacking kisses on both cheeks. Then, of course, she had to introduce Cameron, who looked on with tolerant amusement while Henri poured forth a torrent of words.

"I have heard everything! Julio, upsetting you like that. Deplorable, *chérie*. Terrible. He should be guillotined for disturbing an artist such as yourself. You were right to leave. It is Julio's loss. Who else can make so well the apple pie with the crushed almond pastry? Who else . . ."

"Your pear and ginger pudding is not to be scoffed at, Henri," Dani replied, cheered by his championship.

He made a smacking sound with his lips, tried to look modest and failed hopelessly. "Ah, my Dani! What times we had together! A kitchen with both of us. Let it be so again. If you have not yet secured another position, join me here. I realise it would be a step down for you, *ma chérie,* but our reputation is growing. Who knows where the future may take us? Together we would be strong . . ." Henri looked towards the ceiling with the air of a man who was vouchsafed a vision that would change the world.

The offer took Dani by surprise. She hesitated, but above all else she needed a job. "That's so kind of you, Henri. But impulsive. Don't you think..."

"No!" said Cameron.

"The marvellous things we would create!" enthused Henri, kissing her again.

Dani was doubly distracted.

"Don't do it," said Cameron. "Don't even think about it."

"Why not?" asked Dani.

"Is there some reason?" Henri enquired, forced to take notice of Cameron.

"I've found a job for Dani."

The flat declaration startled both of them.

"You have?" Dani queried disbelievingly.

"The perfect job for you," Cameron asserted.

Dani turned to Henri in some confusion of mind. "Henri, I have to think about this."

"Of course! Think all you like. But you and I, *chérie*. That is worth thinking of. The masterpieces we would create..." He wandered off with the air of a man besotted by his own creations.

Dani sank back onto her chair and looked searchingly at Cameron. He appeared very serious. Had someone in the trade been at the party last night? Or someone who knew someone? Was that why he had been sure something would turn up for her? But why hadn't he told her about it earlier?

"What job have you found for me?"

"One where you can do as you please."

"That sounds good."

"You will have complete control."

Dani's eyebrows shot up. That was unusual. Dani had found a great deal of ego and megalomania in all the kitchens she had worked. Even Henri was temperamental. "You mean I'll be in absolute charge of everything?" she asked incredulously.

"Absolute authority. Total freedom of choice."

"That sounds great." Dani leaned forward eagerly, her eyes sparkling with excitement. "When do I start?"

"Tomorrow."

"Where?"

"At my place. As my personal chef."

Dani's excitement fizzled out. She came back to earth with a thump, all her suspicions about him charging through her mind. Cameron had led her right down the garden path, flattering her, entrancing her, breaking down barriers with consummate skill, but she wasn't so naïve that she couldn't see *come in, sucker* written all over this offer. He had wanted her to go to bed with him last night, and this was clearly the next step to achieving that end.

"You can't afford me," she said disdainfully.

His eyes glittered a derisive challenge. "Yes, I can."

"Maybe you can, but I don't want it."

"Why not?"

"It's a live-in position."

"Yes."

"And something else is going to be involved besides cooking."

"Does that frighten you?"

"Any sensible person would be wary of a job like that, where tenure doesn't depend on the quality of the cooking," she mocked. "Besides which, you're flying off to the U.S. on Boxing Day, so it's hardly worth my while to tie myself up with you, is it?"

"Perhaps I won't go. Perhaps I'll want to take my personal chef with me. Consider it a trial run, Dani. A checking-out process, if you like. You'll be well paid for the work, so you won't be out of pocket."

Dani favoured him with a look of arch scepticism. "You may have had a lot of trial runs in your life, Cameron, but let me tell you, they're not my style."

"I said you had complete freedom of choice, Dani. I give you my word that nothing will happen that you don't want to happen."

"How good is your word?" she scoffed.

"As good as yours, Dani Halstead. Every bit as good as yours. And possibly—" the blue eyes bored into hers "—a lot better."

The challenge to her honesty was like a punch to the heart. Dani stared at him, fiercely justifying her stance with him to herself. Yes, he was attractive. More attractive than any other man she had met. Probably more attractive than any man she would ever meet. She had spent a wonderful day with him and she did like him. Enormously.

She wanted to have more time with him, time to know him better, time to feel her way with him and find out if they had a future. He was handing her that opportunity. But what motive did he have? He couldn't be considering anything lasting between them, could he? Why would he? She was no match for him.

He leaned forward, reached across the table and took one of her hands in his. His fingers stroked across her wrist, softly, seductively, persuasively. "Give it a chance, Dani. That's all I'm asking."

In his eyes was the promise of the rightness she had felt with him last night, the promise of all the possibilities in the world between them. But was it a deception? An illusion? A mirage conjured up by her own secret desires?

Dani's body rebelled against the caution in her mind. Her heart pumped a wild *yes*. Her stomach melted with compliance. Her legs denied any strength to walk away. Her lungs refused to breathe properly until she was prepared to consider surrender.

"I'll think about it," she managed huskily.

"Tomorrow," he pressed.

"All right. I'll give you an answer tomorrow. After I've done Mrs. B's cleaning."

"What time will you be home?"

"Five o'clock."

"I'll be there."

He released her hand and sat back, emanating a supreme confidence that he would win his way with her. Dani didn't know if she cared any more if he did. There was a time in life when it was necessary to throw caution to the wind. Perhaps this was the time for her.

And who knew? Maybe the way to a man's heart was through his stomach!

CHAPTER SEVEN

THE NEXT MORNING Dani found out that Mrs. B didn't need her as a stand-in cleaner any more. She had contacted a professional cleaning service, which assured her they could take over her run permanently, and she was about to recommend it to her gentlemen. Mrs. B had decided she was never going to do cleaning again. Except for Henry, of course. Mrs. B was moving out to a new life. No more loneliness for her. From now on it was going to be Hilda and Henry together in his Woollhara home.

Which left Dani with a great hole in her life. Her one close friend was deserting her for a man. Not that she minded about Mrs. B settling in with Henry Newbold. She was happy for her. But with no-one near by to talk to, it did mean a lot of lonely days and nights stretching ahead of her.

As it was, she was unexpectedly free for the day, with a heavy decision hanging on her mind. It wasn't that she didn't know what she wanted to do. That was not in question. She simply didn't understand what Cameron McFarlane saw in her, apart from her first-class cooking. Dani didn't like walking into a situation she didn't understand. It made her feel out of control.

Despite all the disappointments and disasters Dani had weathered over the years, she never felt she couldn't control her life. Occasionally she made judgements and decisions that didn't work out properly, but that was to be expected. Everybody did that. It happened more frequently to her because luck was definitely against her.

Nevertheless, she always picked herself up and moved on, she hoped steering a wiser course into the future. The problem with Cameron McFarlane was that she had more than a sneaking suspicion that to become his personal live-in chef had a few consequences. However much she wanted to be with him, it appeared to be the height of folly rather than a rational, sensible decision with a happy ending.

Yet Mrs. B's good opinion of Cameron kept playing around in her mind, teasing her into a different perception of his character. Mrs. B had been delighted she and Cameron had got on so well that he had wanted to spend all yesterday with her.

"Such a kind man. I really shall miss doing for him. All the treats he's given me . . ." She smiled with fond remembrance. "But it will be nicer sharing with Henry."

"What treats, Mrs. B?" Dani questioned.

"Oh, there was always food he didn't want because he'd be away. And complimentary tickets to the movies. Every time I mentioned a movie I'd like to see, somehow someone gave him a ticket to it that he didn't have time to use and he'd give it to me." Her brown eyes twinkled brightly in delighted anticipation of a happy outcome to another romance. "He's a good man, Dani. The kind who'd really look after you. You do like him, don't you?"

Dani's agreement had made Mrs. B look extremely satisfied, as though everything was neatly settled in her mind. Not so in Dani's. Yet she was forced to continue revising her judgement of Cameron McFarlane. He hadn't been conning Mrs. B with his charm. He had given at least as much as Mrs. B had given him. Possibly more. She remembered his readiness to oblige in sending Mrs. B flowers and felt ashamed of her cynicism.

Maybe he did have a good heart. She couldn't doubt he was generous. Maybe he had no bad motives at all. Was it possible he was totally sincere in all he'd said to her?

Since the wisest person she knew was her grandmother, Dani figured that her free day could be fruitfully employed talking a few things over with her. She could not, of course, spell out the details, but a general overview of things could very well clear up a few murky areas in her brain. Dani wanted to have all her wits about her, her facts absolutely straight and a sensible decision under her belt when Cameron McFarlane came for her this afternoon.

A telephone call ensured that a visit was more than welcome, and Dani set off, her spirits automatically lifting as she took the train that her grandmother would meet at Camden, on the south-western outskirts of the city. Dani loved going to Grandma's place.

Nicole had hated their holidays there, always complaining there was nothing to do. But that was mainly because Nicole recoiled from getting her hands and clothes dirty. Nicole had never known how to have fun and probably never would. Which was a pity. It was one of the few times that Dani didn't envy Nicole—in fact, felt a stab of sympathy for her.

Dani wanted to talk to Grandma about Nicole. It was not something she had done before, because most of the time she wanted to forget Nicole. Dani had made up her mind that she believed Cameron's assertion about not having any intimate association with her sister, but she wanted a clearer understanding of Nicole's motives for saying what she had said.

She hoped Grandma had some useful insights because Dani wanted to smooth things over between herself and her sister. After all, Christmas was Christmas, they were family, and that particular day was hurtling towards her like an express train.

Time seemed to slip by very quickly and suddenly the train was pulling in at Camden. Dani hurried off and raced out of the station to where she knew her grandmother would be waiting. She grinned at the spritely white-haired lady who waved to her from beside the blue pick-up truck she had been driving for the last twenty years.

Her grandmother's wild mop of curls was cropped short for practicality, and she wore her "town clothes," which were always pink. On this occasion they were candy-striped cotton trousers and a matching overblouse.

They hugged and kissed, and Dani was quite sure if she hadn't seen Grandma for ten years instead of two weeks, the warmth and affection of the greeting would be the same. Grandma was unflappable.

They piled into the truck for the twenty-minute trip out to the farm. No comment was made about Dani's visit on a Monday, since Monday was her usual day off work anyhow, and Dani prompted her grandmother into telling all her news.

One of the dogs had a new litter of pups, and the rooster in the henhouse had given the alarm that a fox was about. He was a feisty bird, well worth his keep. He knew how to protect his hens. There was certainly a place for such roosters, Dani thought, and wondered if Cameron McFarlane would ever care enough about her to be protective.

When they reached the farm, Grandma and Dani did the rounds of the animals, then with all due greetings made, they settled at the table in the huge country kitchen, which was Grandma's domain. Over a cup of tea and Grandma's pumpkin scones, the old lady regarded her grand-daughter with shrewd probing brown eyes.

"So what's wrong, Dani?" she asked quietly. "Why have you come to visit me today?"

Dani heaved a rueful sigh. Nothing got past Grandma. She could spot a lie coming a mile off, and if any mischief had been done behind her back, somehow she always knew about that, too. She explained it away by saying the birds told her, but Dani figured she had some sixth sense.

"I'm trying to work something out, Grandma," she started hesitantly.

"Fine," her grandmother encouraged. She moved down to the far end of the table, where her tapestry frame was set out on a special cloth. She threaded a needle with one of the coloured wools, gave Dani her listening smile and started stitching away.

This is it, Dani thought. The big one. It wasn't a time for half-measures. She had to go in boots and all. "It's about a man, Grandma."

"Fine," said Grandma non-committally.

Dani took a deep breath. "Nicole told me something about him—" impossible to specify what "—but I don't think it was true."

Grandma looked up. "Why don't you think it's true, Dani?" she asked quietly.

Dani paused for reflection. Why didn't she believe Nicole? It certainly suited her purpose not to believe her. But it went deeper than that.

"It doesn't *feel* right, Grandma."

It was as simple as that, really. All the vibrations she was getting from Nicole and Cameron McFarlane . . . they didn't fit together. Someone was lying, and all her instincts said it was Nicole.

"Then perhaps Nicole is lying," Grandma said quietly. Her stitching never altered a beat. Calm, unflappable, imperturbable.

"But why, Grandma? Why should Nicole tell such a dreadful lie?"

Grandma looked up at her. "There could be a lot of reasons, Dani."

"Such as?"

"Perhaps Nicole is jealous of you. Perhaps she envies what you could have."

"Ha!" said Dani with derisive scorn. "Nicole, jealous of me? Fat chance, Grandma! Nicole is the one who has everything. She's—"

"Has she, Dani? Has she got everything?"

She didn't have Cameron McFarlane, Dani thought, and Cameron had also suggested Nicole might be jealous of her. That had to be the answer, Dani decided. Nicole had wanted Cameron and she hated the thought that he preferred her younger sister. Although Heaven alone knew why he did!

"Nicole is beautiful, Grandma. She's brainy—"

"Do you think that's so important, Dani?"

That stopped Dani in her tracks. Only yesterday she had made the same point to Cameron McFarlane, listing his on-show attributes and telling him they weren't the most important things, that they weren't enough for her when it came right down to the nitty-gritty. But would men think the same way about Nicole? The evidence was overwhelmingly against it.

"Well, they're assets most people would like to have, Grandma," she defended.

Her grandmother made no reply. For long minutes Dani watched her carry on with her stitching, her hands moving rhythmically and methodically in their repetitive task. Dani loved Grandma's hands. They were old and gnarled and weather-beaten from farm work, oversized for a woman, but they were the tenderest, most comforting hands in the world.

They had consoled and soothed her when she was hurt, bathed her forehead when she had a childhood fever, gently delivered all kinds of animals. They were capable, loving hands. Dani hoped that when she grew old, she would have loving hands like that for her grandchildren.

Suddenly the shrewd brown eyes snapped up and looked quizzically at her. "Do you really, Dani? Do you really want that?"

Which left Dani bewildered. "Want what, Grandma?"

"To be like Nicole."

The thought flabbergasted Dani. She had sometimes wondered what it would be like, but to be actually like Nicole . . .

"Certainly not, Grandma. No way! I'd much rather be me."

Grandma gave a self-satisfied little smile as she went back to her stitching.

"There is one other thing, Grandma . . ."

"I'm all ears," Grandma encouraged.

"It's a man."

"The same man?"

"Yes."

"Well?"

Dani blurted it out. "I don't understand why he's attracted to me."

Grandma looked up. "Don't you think you're attractive, Dani?"

"Well, yes, but I'm not Nicole." Or Simone, either, she thought.

"Beauty," said Grandma portentously, "is in the eye of the beholder."

Dani was disappointed. She had expected more from Grandma than that. Dani didn't see how she could base her life on such a dubious proposition. It simply didn't have the same ring of truth about it as "disasters come in threes" or "the early bird catches the worm." She suspected it was in the same vein as "the way to a man's heart is through his stomach," which had yet to be verified in Dani's experience.

"Well, Grandma, would you like me to make us some lunch?"

She started to rise, but Grandma said, "Sit down, Dani. I think I have to tell you a story." She gave Dani her sweet imperturbable smile that seemed to embrace a great experience and knowledge of the world.

Dani sat. There was more to come. Maybe she would still get some light thrown onto her problem, some wise advice that would illuminate the path and the darkness ahead.

Grandma sat back complacently, taking her time. Grandma was never hurried in anything she did. "It's a fairy story," she began, and resumed her stitching. "But for all it's a fairy story, it's true enough." She glanced up momentarily. "See what you can make of it, if anything at all."

Dani waited.

"Once upon a time, a long time ago, there was a young girl. She was pretty enough, and attractive enough, but she had one glaring fault."

Dani had a prickling sensation that she knew what was coming. She didn't like it. Not one bit.

"The fault in the girl was grotesque. She was always conscious of it and tried to hide it." Grandma took one long pull of the tapestry wool so her arm was extended to its fullest extent. "You see, Dani, this girl had very huge, ugly hands. She tried her best to keep them out of sight. She put them behind her back. She sat on them. Mealtimes were a terrible torture because they exposed her hands to everyone's critical view.''

''I wouldn't think like that, Grandma,'' Dani interjected defensively.

''Of course not, my dear. Anyway, this little girl grew up and one day she fell in love with a man.'' Grandma smiled an inner solitary smile. ''Very much in love,'' she said firmly. ''One day this man asked her to marry him. And do you know what this silly girl did?''

Dani shook her head. Her throat had gone dry. She had no idea what was coming next.

''Well, this silly girl,'' Grandma continued, ''said to the man, 'How can you love me when I've got such ugly hands?' She then held her hands up in front of his face to prove her point. Oh, she was such a silly girl then.''

''What happened?'' Dani croaked.

''Fortunately for the girl, the man she loved was a very sensible man. He didn't tell a lie and say to her that she had the prettiest hands in the world. No, what he did was quite different. He looked her firmly in the eyes and said, 'If you love me, you'll forget you ever said that to me, as I'm going to forget you ever said it. Otherwise every time I see your hands I'll think how ugly they are. I love *you*. Not your hands. Between us, I never want your hands to be mentioned again, not in all our married life. If you don't keep to that, they'll become a stupid issue, and someday dreadful wound-

ing words will be spoken that will never be forgiven.'
And the girl, at last, got some sense and promised him
she would never mention her hands again or let them
get in the way.''

Grandma stuck her needle into the side of her tapestry with the air of having finished all she wanted to
say. She sat and gazed contentedly through the kitchen
window, looking out over the long back yard with her
animals and vegetable garden. Her domain.

Dani felt she had got the point. It didn't do any
good to let shortcomings get in the way of something
that could mean an awful lot to you. In fact, Dani
made an instant resolution never to think about her
freckles again. She wasn't going to throw Nicole in
Cameron's face again, either.

Dani cleared her throat and spoke her heart. "I love
your hands, Grandma."

"So do I, my dear," she answered softly.

"Hands were never mentioned again, Grandma?"
Dani hated asking, but she needed to know.

"Only once," Grandma said. "Only once." A smile
lit her face, a smile of serene inner satisfaction and
contentment, a radiance of benign appeal.

"What happened?"

"Oh, a very rude man once made an unseemly remark..."

"And?"

"Your grandfather had a lot of Irish in him, Dani.
He really believed in the things he believed in. He hit
the man once—what a blow it was!—straight between the teeth. The man went down like a lead bal-

loon. Blood everywhere. He didn't bother getting to his feet.''

Dani looked at her grandmother in shock. Here was a woman who wouldn't hurt a fly, who went out of her way to give compassion and support to those who suffered, but her face was suffused with supreme pleasure in the painful blow that had been struck on her behalf. It was clear that she had drifted off into another world, a world of dreams where love blossomed and grew in richness and strength, and there had been happiness and laughter and tears. Another world, which was still very real and vivid to her.

Dani didn't interrupt her reverie. She understood precisely what Grandma was saying.

What are defects to you might not be defects to others...unless you let them get in the way. If you were confident in yourself, no-one noticed. If you weren't confident, then it would automatically get in the way.

When it came to real love, superficial things like that simply didn't matter. The word *love* gave Dani a pleasant little tingle along her spine. Was she in love with Cameron McFarlane? Could anyone fall in love that quickly?

A strong sense of decision swept through her. She was going to see this feeling through, whatever the truth and the consequences. She had to take the chance that everything might turn out right.

Time slipped by. Dani made lunch for her grandmother who seemed content to sit dreaming of other times. But Dani had to get herself organised. She had another appointment today. Her mind was made up, and she was ready to act on her decisions.

She rose from her chair, knelt beside her grandmother and placed her head upon the loving hands so carefully folded together on her lap. "I love you, Grandma."

One hand slid away and lifted to caress Dani's tangled brown curls. "I love you, too, Dani."

A most satisfying visit, Dani thought, as they made the trip to Camden station. She felt there had been a new and significant development in her relationship with Grandma. More adult... more something... she didn't know what.

But she certainly understood Grandma much better now. She wondered what she would do if Grandma died. She realised it was inevitable, and what would happen was that she would have her own children, and they would have their children, and if everything worked out right, one day she would become just like Grandma and be wise and able to help people.

Dani gave her grandmother an extra big hug at the railway station, but it was Grandma's words that arrested her. "I'll look forward to meeting your man on Christmas Day, Dani," she said simply, but there was a knowing twinkle in her eyes.

On the train journey into the city, Dani pondered those words and their significance. Damn Nicole! she thought. Dani had to live her own life. She had found her wings and she was going to fly and soar into the unknown, into a new life. And when Christmas Day came, if Cameron wanted to be with her at her family home, she would be proud to take him to meet Grandma.

Dani could hardly wait for five o'clock.

And Cameron McFarlane.

CHAPTER EIGHT

CONSCIOUS OF TIME ticking away, Dani whizzed around her flat, packing all the things she needed to take with her. She carried a box of perishable food to the top flat and left it outside the quarrelling couple's door. When she was satisfied that she had everything organised, she set to work on her appearance.

She washed and blow-dried her troublesome hair. If Cameron thought her hair beautiful, she wasn't going to hide it in a plait. It ended up rather like a wild halo of crinkles and curls around her face, but at least it was a shiny brown. And if she took away the freckles across her nose and cheekbones, there wasn't much wrong with her face.

Cameron had said she had a saucy mouth that begged to be kissed. Her nose wasn't perfect but she didn't mind the little tilt at the end. As for her eyes, well, hazel could be more interesting than plain green or brown, and she did have thick curly lashes. From now on she was going to think positive.

For good measure, she put on the clothes she had bought for Christmas Day. The well-tailored white trousers and the boldly striped red and white jersey top were really quite striking on her, Dani thought. One thing she did have was a well-proportioned figure.

Cameron thought so, too, or he wouldn't have stared at her in her yellow maillot.

Dani worked herself up into feeling absolutely great about herself by the time Cameron called for her at precisely five o'clock. Then, despite all her marvellous resolutions, she took one look at him and her new-found confidence cracked. He wore a light grey business suit that not only emphasised the striking features of the man, but impressed on her that he could take his place in any circle he chose and be the centre of it. He emanated a self-assurance that no-one could take away from him, while Dani felt herself deflating like a pricked balloon.

Nevertheless, he was here for her, and at least she was a damned good cook, Dani argued fiercely to herself. She would make him appreciate that, if nothing else. Her eyes challenged his with tigerish pride.

"We haven't talked wages yet," she said, stubbornly determined on making him respect her professionally and not take anything for granted.

Cameron named a daily rate that was more than Dani had earned in her life. And for considerably less work. She swallowed three times to counteract the tremulous upheaval it caused inside her. So much money could only mean that Cameron was very intent on having her. She desperately hoped he didn't think he was buying more than her expertise in the kitchen. Her love, her body, her feelings were not for sale. Or maybe he thought . . .

"If that's meant to cover house cleaning as well, you can forget it, Cameron," she asserted. "Mrs. B has undoubtedly informed you that she won't be cleaning your house any more. And neither will I. House cleaning is not my vocation in life. I was only helping out a friend.''

Another thought struck her before he could reply. ''I should also tell you that I don't believe in double standards when it comes to housework. Or in any other area. As far as living in the same house is concerned, you pick up after you, and I'll pick up after me.''

''I've already contracted the cleaning service Mrs. B recommended to do that work, Dani,'' he assured her, amusement dancing in his eyes.. ''Your job is to be my personal chef. Nothing more, nothing less.''

''That's all right, then. I don't want you to have any false expectations.''

''How could I with you?''

Dani didn't like the sound of that. Maybe he had lost interest in wanting her. She frowned at the way his mouth was quirking. ''What's that supposed to mean?'' she demanded.

The quirking stretched into a wide grin. ''Dani, you lay everything straight on the line. Which I like, I might add. It's a most refreshing change from the usual artifice that most young women employ.''

Dani's heart gave a pleasurable little skip. He liked her for being the way she was. Maybe Grandma was right after all, and Cameron found nothing wrong with her. She gave him a brilliant smile. Her bright hazel eyes sparkled loving approval at him.

It seemed to cause his grin to falter. A strange look flitted over his face, as though he had suddenly been struck by some new thought. He was staring at her, but his eyes had the glazed expression of being inwardly focused. It played havoc with Dani's stomach. Then, whatever it was, he snapped out of it and leaned down to pick up the packed suitcase that stood by the door.

"Let's go," he said.

Dani had a strong premonition of the hand of fate as she locked up her flat and followed Cameron to his car. They were going off together, going to be together day in and day out. Maybe she would never come back to live in the old terrace house. Just like Mrs. B.

"I haven't bought any food for dinner tonight," she said as Cameron drove them towards his home.

"I did." He flashed her a smile. "You can take over the buying tomorrow. Then you can keep surprising me."

She laughed out of sheer nervous excitement. "Have you any definite dislikes that I shouldn't cook, Cameron?"

"Tripe. I hate tripe. And liver. Nothing with liver. I'm a very plain eater." His eyes sparkled at her. "I'm looking forward to being educated to higher and better things by one of the world's leading experts."

"I'll balance plain with fancy. That way you're guaranteed something you can enjoy as well as something you can try."

"Precisely my formula for life."

Dani didn't know if she approved of that or not. She had a keen admiration for the mind of Cameron McFarlane, but his heart was still very much a mystery to her. She hoped that in time it would be revealed to her.

When they arrived at the house in Double Bay, Cameron carried her suitcase to the guest bedroom suite she had used before. "Take your time unpacking," he invited. "There's no hurry to get to the kitchen. I'm happy to eat when you're ready."

She favoured him with another brilliant smile for being so nice and obliging. Cameron's gaze fastened on her mouth for several heart-kicking seconds, then swept to her feet before slowly lifting to her eyes again. "I have a house rule, too," he said.

"Oh?" Dani choked out.

"No chef's uniform." He smiled. "I like what you're wearing much better."

Dani could feel her whole body flushing with pleasure. "What about when you have guests?" she asked.

"Then you will be the hostess as well as the chef."

Dani was filled with delight that he wanted her at his side amongst his smart friends and associates. There was only one problem. "I may not have appropriate clothes for that, Cameron."

"Then it will be my pleasure to find and purchase the appropriate clothes for you to wear."

Dani took a deep breath. This was tricky ground. She wasn't sure she should find it acceptable, but the thought of having clothes that Cameron wanted to see her in was very seductive. Something very female inside her insisted any protest was stupid.

Cameron's gaze wandered down to the rise and fall of her breasts, lingered a moment, then flicked up again. "Definitely a pleasure," he said with another smile. "You have a perfect body, Dani."

Beautiful hair, perfect body, and he liked her being straight with him. Dani's cup of happiness was flowing over like a fountain.

It was only after he left her to her unpacking that she cautioned herself about his intentions towards her. Getting her into bed with him was one of them. Cameron had made no bones about that. But he had more or less promised not to pounce. Freedom of choice, he had said. But if she didn't choose when he wanted her to, what then?

Dani did her best to shrug off the question. She was here with him now. No point in crossing bridges until she came to them. Maybe she could alter the courses of those bridges anyway. She was not without some power, since he wanted her. She also had the will to fight for what she wanted.

When Cameron joined her in the kitchen, Dani had already planned the menu for dinner. He had changed into casual clothes, and Dani was somewhat distracted from her preparations for a while. His jeans made her very aware of his extremely virile masculinity, and he hadn't bothered doing up all the buttons on his white sports shirt, which left a deep V of smoothly tanned chest. Dani wondered if it was deliberate enticement for her to touch him there as she had the other night.

Yet he talked to her in a perfectly natural manner, and Dani's inner tension gradually eased away in the pleasure of his company. She braised lobster medallions in white wine and served them with a salad. She cooked steaks on the barbecue, having already popped a cheese and potato dish into the oven. She accompanied this with snow peas and honeyed carrot sticks. Finally she produced perfectly baked pears with a fresh strawberry sauce and ice-cream.

Cameron was full of appreciation. Dani glowed more approval at him. When she brought up the subject of food expenses, he said she could break the bank for all he cared, so long as she kept giving him meals as marvellous as that. She had an absolute free hand to buy whatever she liked. He would meet all bills with pleasure.

Dani was beginning to think there might be a lot of truth in the saying, "the way to a man's heart is through his stomach." If his stomach was properly satisfied, it probably softened up his heart for easier entry. Anyhow, it seemed like a good idea to test this theory and see if Cameron would open up to her.

Having cleaned up the kitchen, Dani took their after-dinner coffee into the living room where Cameron was lazily stretched out on one of his leather armchairs looking supremely content. She was conscious of his eyes glittering over her in an excitingly possessive way as she sat on the chair beside his. Dani had to compose her mind before introducing the subject she wanted to talk about.

"I've told you practically all about myself, Cameron," she pointed out. "I'd like to know more about you."

He gave her an indulgent smile. "What do you want to know, Dani?"

"About your childhood."

The smile turned into a grimace. "I prefer to forget that."

"Why?" She wasn't going to let him evade her questions tonight.

He flashed her a sardonic look. "I'm not confused about my sexuality, Dani."

She flushed at the reminder of her provocative suggestion.

He grinned at her embarrassment. "Nor do I believe I'm overly self-centred or fussy. I simply know what I want and don't want. And I don't want you psychoanalysing my childhood and coming up with the wrong answers."

"Then tell me the right answers," she argued reasonably.

"The right answers are that I learnt the right lessons, and I don't intend to make the mistakes first-hand experience taught me were destructive," he answered dryly.

"Like what?" she persisted. "What harm can it do to tell me about it if your family are all gone?"

"They're not all gone. I simply disowned them," he stated matter-of-factly.

Dani stared at him in shock. "You disowned them?"

"It was better for them. Better for me." His eyes softly mocked as he added, "Life is not always the straight line you want it to be, Dani."

"How is it *better?*" she demanded.

"My father has a family. My mother has a family. Both are separate from the other. My parents are much happier not to be reminded that they were once married to each other.''

The child of a divorce, and a bitter one, Dani guessed. "But what about you? Don't they care for you?"

"I embarrass them."

"Why?"

"Because I know too much about them. I know what they want to forget."

"Like what?"

He gave her a twisted little smile. "Dani, people don't like to be faced with their uglier side. My parents were not into parenting when they were married to each other. Their marriage was a battle ground. Robbie and I were merely weapons they hurled at each other. When they divorced, Mother got custody and quickly shoved us into boarding school so she could get on with her love-life, and my father got loaded with exorbitant fees. Mother was a winner. She liked to win everything. Sending Robbie and me to boarding school was a complete win for her."

No loving at all, Dani thought sadly. She was no longer surprised that he shied clear of marriage if that was his childhood experience of it. But what of his brother or sister? "Robbie?" she asked.

He winced. "My younger brother."

"Where is he now?"

Cameron's face took on a shuttered look. "He drowned when I was fifteen. It happened the day after his thirteenth birthday."

His jaw tightened. A muscle in his cheek contracted. His hands, which had lain relaxed on the armrests of the leather chair, curled into knuckle-white fists as though he wanted to hit out at the fate that had taken his brother from him.

Dani hesitated to intrude on a grief that still had the power to pulse through him with such angry violence, yet she felt it might do him good to talk about it instead of keeping it bottled up inside him. "How did it happen?" she asked softly.

He flashed her a look that was both haunted and resentful before he tempered it to flat derision. "We were spending our obligatory time with Father during school vacation. We went fishing. A storm came up suddenly. The boat was capsized by a wave. It was late evening. We hung on to the boat. No-one came looking for us. Night fell. Robbie got tired. A large wave crashed into us and he slipped off. Off into the darkness. I couldn't find him. I searched for hours. He never came back."

Flat, toneless, as if somehow he had failed. No appreciation of the strength and courage he'd shown.

"What happened to you?" Dani asked, wanting to draw him out of the past and back to her.

His mouth twisted as though he hated his own survival. "The next morning I was found by a fisherman."

She wanted to say, "I'm sorry, Cameron. I'm sure you tried the best you could," but that wasn't the best way to show caring and compassion. Touching was better than words. Grandma had shown her that. So she reached out and gently covered his closed fist with her hand, her fingers softly stroking until his hand relaxed under hers.

His eyes regarded her quizzically for several long moments before he spoke. "I'm glad you didn't say anything. No false sympathy."

"There are no words for what you've endured, Cameron," she said quietly.

His fingers slowly and deliberately linked with hers, giving a tactile acceptance to an empathy he had neither invited nor expected, but which was there...the beginning of true closeness between them, a lowering of barriers.

"You know what I hated most?" he said, his mind still dwelling on the past.

She shook her head.

"My parents attending Robbie's funeral. Supposedly mourning their son." His voice carried a dark mockery as he added, "They fought over him...even there."

Like the couple in the upstairs flat, Dani thought. "I understand," she whispered. "In a way I've heard it all before. I don't want it to happen to me."

"Nor me."

They sat together holding hands, enjoying togetherness in their mutual thoughts. Dani wondered if Cameron had too deep-rooted a prejudice against marriage to ever consider it. Yet staying alone and single and having the occasional affair wasn't the way to handle life and get the best out of it. Life was about loving. Loving was about life. Dani was sure of it.

"I've never told anyone about that before," he mused, more to himself than to her.

Dani wondered if it was some revelation to him that he had opened up to her. She couldn't help feeling uniquely privileged. It had to mean he trusted her with his confidence. Perhaps it meant even more than that, she thought hopefully.

"You don't see your parents any more?" she asked.

He shook his head. "That stopped after I started publishing. Psychology sweeps the human soul bare. My parents tend to take my books personally. I must admit my experience with them did give me the desire to know why people are the way they are. Why they do what they do. How people make their own worlds. A search for reasons. A search for solutions."

"What solutions have you found?"

Any brooding darkness in his soul was banished as he smiled at her. His blue eyes danced teasingly as he repeated the very words she had spoken to him yesterday. "That having a good heart, kindness, honesty, loyalty, fidelity...things like that...will get you through most problems."

Then he lifted their linked hands to his mouth and brushed his lips over her knuckles. Dani's heart jolted.

"Even better if you mix all that with some loving," he murmured, his eyes warming to more than teasing.

"I think it's time I said goodnight, Cameron," Dani managed to force out.

He kissed her hand again, his eyes steady on hers, watching, wanting. "Are you sure about that, Dani?" he asked softly.

"Yes." Her throat felt so constricted it was barely a whisper. She swallowed hard then added, "Thank you for talking to me."

He sighed and gave her a whimsical little smile as he released her hand. "My pleasure. I hope you sleep well."

"And you," she said, willing strength into her shaky legs as she stood up.

She was extremely conscious of him watching her as she left the living room. Her skin tingled all over, and the back of her neck positively prickled. *It is too soon,* Dani kept reciting to herself. *Far too soon.* But she didn't let herself think about what it was too soon for until she was safely in bed with the lights out.

What would it mean to Cameron?

Dani knew what it would mean to her.

And if it was the beginning of the end, she would shrivel up inside for evermore.

CHAPTER NINE

THE NEXT MORNING Dani made up menus for the rest of the week and wrote a shopping list to cover everything. Cameron insisted on accompanying her to the markets, saying it would be a new experience for him. Dani was only too happy to spend the whole day with him.

It was fun shopping together. Cameron waggled his eyebrows over some of her choices, but she challenged him to wait and taste. He seemed blithely unconcerned about the cost of anything, even adding a few very extravagant items to her shopping list. Like black cherries, which were obscenely expensive.

"I like cherries," he said, popping one into his mouth and eating it with a blissful look on his face. His eyes twinkled with teasing devilment. "Of course there is one thing I'd like better..."

Dani declined to ask. He had already informed her that oysters were well known for their aphrodisiac properties, were very healthy, and they should both eat plenty of them. With an air of complete innocence, he stocked up on French champagne, extolling its qualities and the delightful way it bubbled through one's head. Dani couldn't help laughing at his good-humoured suggestiveness, and the way his eyes made love to her, had her heart in a constant state of barely repressible exhilaration.

But while Cameron was certainly an expert and exciting player at love, Dani still wasn't sure that *his* heart was involved. In her need to know and understand him, she decided she should waste no time in reading up on how he thought in the books he had written. She waited until dinner was over that night, then asked Cameron if she could borrow one of his books from the study.

"Not one of mine, Dani."

"But I wanted..."

The blue eyes were suddenly very hard and serious. "No. Any other book. I don't want you reading mine."

Dani felt bewildered. "Why not?"

"Because those books weren't written for you."

Still she didn't understand his objection. "I know that, Cameron, but I might learn something about you from them."

"No. There's nothing for you to learn from them, Dani. You're far better off the way you are."

"What do you mean... the way I am?"

His mouth curled into an ironic little smile. "Not screwed up. You've got a straight line in your head, Dani. It's a *good* straight line. Believe me. I know. And I wouldn't want anything to mess up that straight line."

She challenged him. "Do you think I'm a simpleton, Cameron? That I can't read things and sort out what's right or wrong for me?"

"No. But when I make love to you, I don't want you thinking you should be doing anything that doesn't come naturally to you." His eyes took on a gleam of sheer animal wickedness. "You can learn far more about me that way. Much more enthralling than taking one of my books to bed with you."

Was it all sex with him? Dani worried. Nothing else? "I think I'll stick to a book tonight," she said, and took herself off to the study, out of Cameron's firing range.

THE NEXT MORNING he announced he had invited a number of people for dinner on Thursday night so they had to spend today shopping for an appropriate hostess outfit for her. He did not want her to feel pressured for time tomorrow.

"How many people?" Dani demanded. "You should have told me yesterday when we were buying food."

"Only eight including us. And it doesn't have to be anything special, Dani. I want you at the table with me, not in the kitchen. So, if you can prepare everything beforehand . . ."

"Last time you told me twenty and it ended up forty," Dani reminded him pointedly.

"That was a party. Who can control a party?" he contended. "This is a sit-down dinner. No gatecrashers, I promise."

"Are you absolutely sure of that, Cameron?" she asked suspiciously.

"I give you my word." His eyes twinkled at her. "Which I have amply proved to you so far."

Dani had to concede he had been as good as his word, even against his inclinations. She smiled. "Okay."

"Right! So we go shopping for clothes. There are some fine boutiques at the Double Bay centre."

"They'd be dreadfully expensive, Cameron," Dani quickly warned. The Double Bay centre was well-known for its luxury boutiques, catering to the tastes of the wealthy who lived in the area.

"Dani, I am not concerned about money. We get what I think is appropriate," he declared with decisive finality.

Dani found out that what Cameron thought appropriate was absolutely out of this world. It was made of silk chiffon, printed in a glorious array of colours, a rich vibrant green, royal blue and purple, but predominantly bright yellow and orange. The flowers on the bodice were beaded to emphasise the colours and make them sparkle brilliantly. A wide band of black, elasticised to cling to the curve of her waist and hips, separated the bodice from the skirt. The latter consisted of three layers of chiffon, falling to different lengths in a cascade of handkerchief points. It was a skirt that made Dani want to twirl around and dance. She couldn't resist a couple of twirls when she paraded the dress for Cameron's approval. It was the most beautiful, the most feminine, the most stunning dress Dani had ever seen, let alone worn.

"Perfect!" Cameron declared, his eyes laughing at her as though he knew exactly how she felt.

There was only one drawback. She couldn't wear a bra with it. The back of the bodice plunged in a deep cowl that dipped right to the waistline. Who cares? she thought. The dress was working some magic on her. She felt beautiful in it. Beautiful and sexy and deliciously wicked. And it felt good to feel that way. Particularly with Cameron looking at her as though she was all he could ever want in a woman.

He insisted on buying a black beaded evening bag that went with the dress, and then, of course, they had to get the right shoes. Nothing but a Christian Dior pair in black and gold would do.

"This has to be costing you a fortune, Cameron," Dani whispered guiltily.

"I'll write another best-seller," he insisted.

Dani simply couldn't argue. She had never believed she could ever look striking, but she could. She really could in the dress Cameron had bought her. And a million stars were popping off in her head. What was money compared to that feeling? Even if it was only a once-in-a-lifetime feeling, it was worth it. And she loved Cameron for giving it to her.

Of course she loved him for other reasons, too. All of them were bubbling inside her as they took their marvellous purchases home.

"Happy?" Cameron asked.

She laughed. "I suppose it's mad to be happy about a dress..."

"No. It's good to be happy, Dani. And it makes me feel good to see your eyes sparkling like a Christmas tree." He slanted a wry little smile at her. "I'm tempted to take advantage of it, but I won't. This isn't an attempt to put pressure on you."

"You couldn't, even if you wanted to, Cameron,"
Dani said with utter certainty.

He laughed softly to himself, then shot her a twinkling look of approval. "I prefer you to choose."

That was fine by Dani. She hoped that when it came
time to choose, Cameron would have more on his
mind than immediate gratification.

For the rest of the day, Dani felt there was a new
closeness between them . . . a warmer understanding,
an intimacy of feeling, a deep happiness in being together. When she went to bed that night she wished she
was not alone. She craved the sense of togetherness
they had been sharing. She missed it.

Dani was up bright and early the next morning, excited about being with Cameron again, excited about
tonight's dinner party, when she would wear the dress
for him. She was brimming with the joy of life as she
bustled around, getting Cameron's breakfast ready.
When he came into the kitchen he looked happy, too.
He smiled as much as she did, and every time their
eyes met it was with warm pleasure. Dani felt like
dancing or shouting from sheer happiness.

Later on in the morning they had a swim together
and Dani was towelling herself dry when she heard the
telephone ringing in the kitchen. She called out to
Cameron who was still swimming his daily fifty laps,
and he called back for her to answer it until he could
get there. Dani had no concern about doing so. It was
a perfectly reasonable request.

"Cameron McFarlane's residence," she announced into the receiver.

Silence.

"Who's calling, please?" Dani inquired pleasantly.

"You're the chef who was there last Saturday night, aren't you?" came an accusing female voice.

Dani instantly bridled. What woman from the party was calling Cameron? And why? "Yes, I am. Cameron is in the pool. He'll be here in a minute," she explained coolly. "If you would please hold on..."

"Well, I'm glad to know you're human," came the acid comment.

"What makes you think that?" Dani demanded, highly suspicious of the remark.

"I spoke to you, remember? Simone. Simone Lessing."

"Oh, yes!" Dani affected surprise over her inner dismay. She didn't care for the idea of Simone ringing Cameron. Not one bit!

"So you decided it might not be so bad to keep on bedding Cameron, after all," Simone taunted.

Dani dragged in a deep breath. "Simone, Cameron told me you were a very smart lady. Really clever. Doing your doctorate at the university. Among other things. He also thinks you're a very nice person. I'm sure you must be or he wouldn't have spent so much time with you."

Dani paused for the other woman to take stock of her niceness. Then she delivered the punch line. "What I can't understand is how you could think of him as nothing but a stud. Cameron is much more than a great male body, and if you—"

"Thank you, Dani," said his quiet voice behind her.

She swung around to meet eyes that seared hers with questions. All of them uncomfortable. But she had to defend him, didn't she? Simone deserved the feminine equivalent of a knuckle sandwich for thinking about him the way she did.

Cameron took the receiver out of her hand, his eyes still burning into her as he spoke into it. "I apologise for keeping you waiting, Simone. What can I do for you?"

Sheer black jealousy swept through Dani. She turned her back on Cameron and his conversation with his all too recent lover and marched over to the kitchen sink. She turned on the cold water and started washing the grapes she had left there. She heard Cameron say yes, no, thank you, then the click of the receiver being hung up.

"What was that all about, Dani?" he asked quietly.

Grapes were dropping off the bunch everywhere, but Dani didn't notice. She kept on washing as she bit her reply out through fiercely clenched teeth.

"I thought you didn't like being regarded as a womaniser."

"I don't."

"So how come you were dumb enough to go to bed with a woman who thinks that?"

A pause for consideration. "A mistake on my part. We seemed to have a lot in common to begin with. Was she being nasty to you?"

"Is *she* one of your guests tonight?"

"No."

"If you ever bring her here again, don't expect me to cook for her. She might be nice to you on the outside, but inside she's a bitch."

"Simone will never be invited here again. I'm sorry she upset you, Dani."

"So you should be," she muttered. "No taste. No depth. You should have known better."

"Perhaps I couldn't find anyone better until you came into my life."

"Convenient. That's what it was with Simone."

"I guess you could say that."

"Well, if you think I'm another convenience . . ."

"No. I definitely don't think that. I doubt that anyone could think of you as a convenience, Dani. More like a force of nature."

She heard the smile in his voice and didn't know whether to be angry or mollified. "Well, so long as you've got things straight now . . ."

"Very straight." He came up behind her and dropped a soft kiss on her bare shoulder. "Thank you for standing up for me. I'm glad you think I've got a great body. And you'd better stop mangling those grapes if we're to have them tonight."

"Oh!" said Dani, her concentration shot to pieces by the touch of his warm lips on her skin. She jerked her hand up and turned off the tap. "If we're going to get any dinner tonight you'd better stop distracting me, Cameron McFarlane."

He sighed. "Another cold swim. Just when I thought you were warming to me. Well, I guess I'd better go do penance for my former sins so you'll forgive me enough to make me some lunch."

He left Dani smiling to herself. She couldn't help it. She wondered if he could charm birds out of trees. Then she wondered why he thought she was a force of nature. She finally decided Simone didn't matter. What had happened in Cameron's past was no concern of hers. What happened in the future was something else entirely.

Dani wasn't sure where she was going with Cameron. For better or for worse she loved him, which meant she probably would end up in bed with him. But how much that would mean to Cameron she didn't really know. Did he ever think of getting married? Having children and creating a family? Was that in his formula for life?

Dani was none the wiser when she left the kitchen to get changed for dinner. Everything was prepared as Cameron had dictated, leaving the minimum of work for her to do once the guests arrived. It was only a matter of popping a few things in the oven at the appropriate time and serving the courses she had planned. Cameron would handle all the drinks and wines.

She had spent some time during the afternoon washing and blow-drying her hair, happily aware that her wild cloud of crinkles and curls looked absolutely right for her dress. She bundled her hair up in a cap, had a quick shower, then took great care with her make-up. Oddly enough, even her freckles seemed right for the dress, as well. She didn't worry about trying to cover them up. She used green eye shadow and a vibrant orange lipstick and touched up her thick lashes with mascara.

The silk chiffon had a lovely sensuous feel as it slid over her bare breasts. Black shoestring ties at the back of the neck fastened the bodice of the dress in place. Dani did them up then fluffed out her hair and did a few twirls around the bedroom, feeling like a beautiful barefoot gypsy as the wonderful skirt floated out around her. It was a pity she had to put shoes on at all, Dani thought, but she could hardly be a barefoot hostess.

She heard music playing the moment she stepped into the hallway. Cameron had put on a calypso disc, and the beat was infectious. Her feet itched to dance. She found Cameron in the living room and came to a heart-pumping halt as he stared at her and she stared at him. He wore all black. A black open-necked silk shirt with softly flowing sleeves. Severely tailored black trousers. He looked like a gypsy, too, dark and dangerous and magnificent, his vivid eyes flashing blue fire.

He suddenly grinned. "Shall we dance?"

Dani laughed and twirled towards him. "Yes. Let's dance."

He caught her in his arms and led her into a wild tango. It was certainly playing with fire, but Dani didn't care. It was madly exciting and marvellous, and the desire glittering in Cameron's eyes ran like a fever through her blood. When he swept her hard against him, she revelled in the power of his body, the tensile strength that seemed to envelop her. When he swung her away from him, her body zinged with anticipation for the next time he would catch her, bending her over his arm, leading her wherever he willed.

The doorbell rang.

Which was probably just as well, Dani told herself, or things might have got completely out of hand. However, it was difficult to stifle a pang of regret that they had been interrupted, and she couldn't bring herself to protest Cameron's arm around her waist as he swept her with him to greet his guests in the foyer.

Two couples arrived together. The men were in their thirties, the women in their late twenties, Dani judged. Cameron introduced her to them and Dani tried her best to remember their names, reciting them over to herself, Ken and Barbara, Colin and Jill. All four of them seemed to have trouble tearing their eyes away from her, which was amazing since Cameron was standing beside her.

I really am *striking*, Dani thought exultantly, and shot a loving look at Cameron for making it possible. He hugged her closer to him as they ushered the guests into the living room, and Dani couldn't resist giving him a hug in return.

For the next ten minutes, Dani revelled in her role as hostess. Cameron poured champagne while she made small talk. Both the women admired her dress and asked where she had bought it. The men were content to simply admire her. No-one was yet interested in the tray of hors d'oeuvres, which was set on the low table between the leather lounges.

When the doorbell rang again, Cameron went to answer it. She was feeling wonderfully confident and happy, chatting away to Barbara and Jill, when Cameron ushered in his last two guests. She looked up in bright expectation of meeting another nice couple, and her smile froze on her face when she saw who was with Cameron.

Nicole!

And her current live-in.

Dani was numbly aware that Nicole's smile had frozen on her face at the sight of her, as well. Total shock between them.

CHAPTER TEN

DANI WRENCHED her eyes away from Nicole and looked at Cameron. His eyes were serious, looking at her with sombre purpose. Dani's heart performed an agitated little jig. He had something in mind, all right. But what?

Cameron smoothly carried out the introductions, and Dani could not help but admire the way Nicole recovered herself enough to acknowledge them. It helped speed Dani's recovery. She managed a fair semblance of composure when Cameron blithely informed everyone that Nicole was Dani's sister.

This raised the usual comments that they did not look at all alike, but for the first time in her life, Dani realised she was not coming off second-best in this comparison. Nicole was wearing a classic little black dress, extremely elegant and undoubtedly expensive, but tonight she was a pale moon to Dani's blazing sun. Nicole's eyes were very green as they took in Dani's dress and scanned her appearance.

Cameron guided Nicole and her present lover onto the lounge directly opposite Dani. He supplied them with glasses of champagne, then with the air of a conjurer who has performed his best trick of the evening, he settled on the armchair beside Dani and gave her a triumphant grin.

It slowly dawned on Dani that he'd had this confrontation in mind when he'd bought the dress for her. He had meant her to outshine Nicole. Perhaps he wanted to drive home to her that *she* was his choice. Not Nicole. Or any other woman.

Perhaps he had been so patient about getting her into bed because he wanted to get Nicole's lie out of the way first. Perhaps he was going to force the truth tonight. Yet a dinner party with other people present was hardly the place or time. Particularly with Nicole's lover here, as well. It would be in dreadful taste. Dani shook her head. The fact that Cameron had invited the two of them together was proof enough he hadn't slept with her sister.

Perhaps he thought this was a good peace-making gesture. One look at the barely veiled hostility in Nicole's eyes told Dani it wasn't going to work. The fat was in the fire. Nicole could hardly wait to pounce on her with bared claws.

Dani suddenly had a deeper appreciation of Cameron's insistence that she organise things so she didn't have to spend much time in the kitchen. She stayed with the guests while all the hors d'oeuvres were eaten, giving Nicole no opportunity at all to strike at her. When they went into the dining room, there was the business of being seated. Then Cameron was asking everyone's preference on wines while Dani made a discreet exit to the kitchen to bring in the first course.

Nicole was seated at the other end of the table from Dani so the congenial atmosphere was maintained while the cold cucumber soup was eaten. Cameron praised its delicate taste and kept smiling at Dani in a possessive kind of way. Stirring the pot, Dani thought, and could have kicked him, except she was placed between two of the male guests and not within striking range of Cameron.

The moment she rose to gather up the soup plates, Nicole was also on her feet, projecting sweet sisterly consideration. "I'll help you, Dani," she said.

Short of tearing plates out of her hands and making a disgraceful scene, there was nothing Dani could reasonably do to stop her. She shot a fulminating look at Cameron, who beamed a benevolent smile back at her.

The moment the kitchen door was closed behind them, Nicole opened fire. "What on earth are you thinking of, letting Cameron McFarlane parade you around like a whore?"

"Do you think of yourself as your lover's whore?" Dani retorted fiercely.

"I have a job and can afford this dress. I keep myself," Nicole snapped.

"I keep myself, too, Nicole. These clothes come with the job of being Cameron's personal chef."

"His what?"

"His personal chef. He offered me the job and I took it. I cook all his meals for him and he pays me a . . . a very large salary."

"Don't tell me you're not sharing his bed, too." Contemptuous scorn.

"I have my own bedroom. In which I sleep alone." She glared her contempt at Nicole. "People in glass houses shouldn't throw stones. And while I'm on the subject, you can tell me why you lied to me about sharing Cameron's bed yourself.''

Nicole affected a lofty look. ''It was for your own good.''

''I don't need you to make those decisions for me, Nicole.''

''Yes, you do. You never take a damned bit of notice of anything except what *you* want to do.''

The furious resentment in Nicole's voice rang bells in Dani's mind. ''You're jealous of me, aren't you, Nicole?''

Nicole's mouth tightened and her green eyes blazed with pride. ''Why should *I* be jealous of *you?*''

''I don't know,'' Dani answered truthfully. ''But you are. So why don't you spit it out, Nicole? What is it about me that gets under your skin?''

A number of expressions warred across Nicole's face, finally firming into angry decision. ''All right. I'll tell you. You do things. You don't care what anyone thinks about them. You go your own way regardless of...of anything at all. Breaking all the rules. And because you're the baby of the family, you're allowed to get away with it.''

Dani stared at her sister in bewilderment. ''What rules have I broken?''

''All of them! All the rules I had to live by. You wriggled out of them. You could get your clothes dirty. You weren't sent to bed early when you were a little kid. You were allowed to stay up until my bedtime. You could get rotten grades at school. Nothing was *expected* of you. I took the brunt of all the expectations in our family. While *you* were spoilt rotten and went your own sweet merry way.''

Dani frowned as understanding started weaving through her mind. ''But you get all the approval, Nicole,'' she reminded her sister.

''I paid for it!''

''Yes. I guess you did,'' Dani said slowly, sympathetically. ''I'm sorry, Nicole. I didn't realise...''

''No. You never have thought about me. All the times I had the responsibility of minding you, and if you did something wrong, I got the blame for not looking after you properly. But *you* never took any damned notice of *me*.''

Dani shook her head. ''But you were always so prim and proper. You never wanted to have fun.''

''That's all you've ever thought about. Having fun!''

''Is there something wrong with that?''

Nicole glared at her. ''Of course there's something wrong with it! Why should you have fun?''

''I can tell you it hasn't been much fun for me having you always held up as the perfect model daughter,'' Dani retaliated. ''The bright one. The beautiful one. The one who never did anything wrong. How do you think that made me feel? Dim scatty Dani with the frizzy hair and freckles.''

Nicole frowned.

''I couldn't compete with you, Nicole. Just thinking about you made me feel crushed all the time because you were always better than me at everything. Don't you see?'' Dani appealed. ''I had to go my own way to survive as the person I am. If I tried to be like you, I was always going to be a loser, Nicole. Look at you..."

A funny little smile quirked at the corner of Nicole's mouth. "Look at you—" her eyes ran over the turbulent cloud of crinkles and curls "—even your frizzy hair looks beautiful tonight."

"But yours looks beautiful all the time, Nicole."

Her sister heaved a rueful sigh. "I guess we both have our resentments."

"We've never really talked about them. But believe me, I've been terribly jealous of you at times," Dani confessed.

"Really?" Nicole looked unsure.

This seemed almost incredible to Dani. "Dad's so proud of you. I'm the also-ran who might possibly do something good some day. But that's open to grave doubt," she added with heavy irony. "You're the shining star in our family. I think you always will be, Nicole. Whatever price you paid for being the first... you are the first."

Nicole grimaced. "Grandma always takes your side."

"Can't I have someone taking my side?"

"Why should she, when you never do anything right?"

"Maybe she likes to see me acting independently. Doing what I want instead of what everyone else wants."

"A chip off the old block," Nicole half jeered. "I can see you ending up as ornery as Grandma, Dani."

"I hope I do. I think Grandma is a great person."

Nicole looked disgruntled, as though she wanted more argument but couldn't bring anything suitable to mind. "You'll end up in Cameron McFarlane's bed, too," she finally said. "If you're not already there. He's not doing all this for nothing."

Dani was only too well aware of that. "If I do, it will be because I love him, Nicole."

The kitchen door opened and Cameron breezed in. "Anything interesting going on out here?"

"Oh, my God! The dinner!" Dani whirled to rescue the dishes she had put in the oven before the soup course.

"I'll leave you to it since you're the expert," Nicole said with a touch of the old spite.

Ingrained attitudes died hard, Dani thought, pulling on her oven gloves. Nevertheless, the spite had less acid than usual, and now all their grievances had been aired, perhaps they could be a little more sisterly to each other in future.

Nicole and Cameron exchanged false smiles as he opened the door for her exit. "Everything all right, Dani?" he asked with a look of concern.

"Fine!"

"Need a helping hand?"

"I think you've *helped* quite enough tonight," she said pointedly. "Go on back to your guests, Cameron. I'll get this served up in a minute."

"They can wait another minute," he said, his eyes twinkling with mischievous purpose as he moved towards her and swept her into his arms.

"What do you think you're doing?" Dani demanded, waving her heavily gloved hands in protest.

"It's been a long time since last Saturday night," he said, and claimed her mouth with his, effectively silencing any further protest.

Dani's mind was torn in two. This wasn't the right time. Yet he was kissing her so beautifully, so temptingly, that everything within her cried out to respond. But her hands were trapped in the stupid padded gloves, and she didn't like the helpless feeling that gave her. Cameron was in control of everything, while she... With an inward sigh Dani gave in to what he was doing to her. He was so good at it, and it *had* been a long time since Saturday night.

She completely lost track of time, place and circumstances, drugged by the intoxicating sensations Cameron aroused in her. How long the kiss went on, Dani had no idea, but it was Cameron's decision to bring it to an end, not hers. Slowly, reluctantly, their lips parted, and when she opened her eyes, she saw a blaze of intent purpose in his.

"Tonight, Dani," he murmured, and there was no mistaking what he meant. The issue of Nicole was cleared away, and Dani couldn't deny that her desire for him was as strong as his for her.

But did Cameron love her?

The question tormented Dani's mind and heart as she watched him return to the dining room. Perhaps it was all a game to him, a game he played with masterly skill to get what he wanted. The greater the challenge, the more he enjoyed it, searching out and finding the right psychological buttons to press, pacing his timing to maximum potential and impact. The dress, the dancing tonight, the intimate smiles at the table, the settlement with Nicole, the kiss . . .

Cameron McFarlane was a man who knew too much about people, how they felt and thought and acted. Maybe that was why he had refused to let her read his books. He didn't want her to know how much he knew. He wanted her responding to him exactly as he planned it, and his timetable was being brought to a close tonight.

What if it was all aimed for a chapter in his next book?

Fear clutched her heart and turmoil reigned in her mind. But she had a dinner to serve, guests who were waiting, and maybe she was confusing herself for no good reason. Perhaps Cameron did truly love her and wanted her to be happy.

She opened the oven door and smoke billowed out at her. Horror seized her for several seconds, then the need for action took over. She removed all the dishes from the oven in frantic haste, closed the door on the smoke, then raced around, throwing every window in the kitchen wide open.

Heart racing, she ran to the oven, bewildered over what had gone wrong. One look at the thermostat told her the awful truth. In her mental distraction over Nicole's presence she had inadvertently turned the temperature up far too high. *Disastrously* high!

With tears pricking her eyes, she examined the results of her ghastly mistake. The honeyed carrots Cameron had liked so much were too burnt to serve. Part of the lamb navarin casserole was stuck to the bottom of its dish. Dani knew that the burnt taste would have permeated the rest of it. The bain-marie had no water left, an ominous sign for the vegetable charlottes, which were to have been masterpieces of colour and taste.

Utter disaster!

So much for one of the world's leading experts!

It was too late to cook anything else. The meal had been delayed too long as it was, what with Nicole and Cameron distracting her from her work. Not that that was any excuse. This was all her fault for not keeping her mind on her job. She had no choice but to serve what she could and hope it wouldn't taste too bad.

In sheer wretched misery Dani took the warmed dinner plates from the second oven and set them out. The vegetable charlottes were stuck to the inside of their moulds. Instead of a beautiful neat mound displaying the three separated colours of white cauliflower, orange sweet potato and green spinach, she had to dig out a mash of them. They were at least edible, although horribly overcooked. What was usable of the lamb navarin only allowed for small portions on each plate. Dani gave herself only one spoonful, hoping no-one would notice. The burnt taste wasn't quite as bad as she anticipated, but it was there for any discerning palate. The carrots were impossible.

People would just have to fill up on bread, Dani thought miserably. They probably had already, since the main course was so long in coming. She felt as though the world was sitting heavily on her shoulders when she wheeled the trolley into the dining room. She served everyone as fast as she could and sat down, her face burning with shame.

No-one said a word about the meal. Dani couldn't look at their faces. She *felt* the quizzical frowns. A professional chef delivering *this?* Finally Nicole made a sisterly remark.

"What did you do with this casserole, Dani? It has a funny taste."

Dani took a deep breath to ease the awful constriction in her chest. "I burnt it," she blurted. Then there was nothing to do but throw an apologetic look at everyone. "Sorry. I hope it isn't too bad."

Polite denials came thick and fast.

"Well, you can't get everything right all the time," was Nicole's consoling comment.

Nicole was in splendid spirits for the rest of the evening. *At least I gave someone pleasure,* Dani thought ruefully. And as Nicole said, not even she could ruin a fresh fruit platter.

Dani consoled herself with the continental cheesecake, which *was* up to her usual standard, but the evening was ruined as far as she was concerned. Cameron couldn't possibly want to keep her on as his personal chef when she made such a mess of things. Particularly for his guests. Although perhaps he had never cared about her cooking. Perhaps that had nothing to do with anything except as a means to an end.

Somehow she couldn't bring herself to look at him to see what he was thinking. It took all her willpower to keep up a hostess face until everyone mercifully took their leave. Cameron slid his arm around her waist as they said goodbye to the last couple, but the moment the door closed behind them, Dani whirled away from him in a fever of confused rejection.

"Dani!" Sharp and urgent.

"You can fire me!" she hurled at him, churning with too many mixed-up feelings to sort anything out.

He started striding around the other side of the fountain, obviously meaning to block her path into the living room from the foyer. "I don't want to fire you. Who cares about one messed-up meal?"

"It was your fault!" she yelled at him across the ornamental pool. She swung towards the front door, determined not to let him near her. "If Nicole hadn't been here I would've got it right. You deliberately invited her for your own ends. And then kissing me in the middle of it! It's definitely all your fault. Definitely!"

Cameron turned, determined on getting to her. "Of course, it's all my fault. You're completely exonerated of any blame. But a man's got a right to clear his name, hasn't he?"

"Not at my expense. If you'd left me alone..."

"That's the problem. I can't leave you alone."

Dani wasn't soothed by these mollifying words. It *was* his fault. And no way was he going to get her tonight! "You planned it all, didn't you?" Dani hotly accused, circling the other way. "The dress..."

"You loved the dress! You wanted to wear it!"

"Bringing Nicole here to show me off in front of her..."

"Why shouldn't I show you off? Aren't I allowed to be proud of the woman I want?"

"That wasn't why you did it!" Dani shouted, changing direction again to keep the fountain between them. "You were softening me up for the kill. It's all one big game to you. But I don't play games, and I won't play your games. Let me tell you, I don't play at making love, Cameron McFarlane, so you'd better think again."

"I was opening Nicole up like an oyster, Dani. Making her confront the woman you are and forcing her to come to terms with it. It was the best way to do it."

"You could have at least warned me!"

"You would have had your guard up and nothing would have been resolved," he argued. "There was something very wrong between you and your sister for Nicole to lie as she did. Shock tactics break down barriers. Truth comes spilling out. That's what happened, wasn't it? You got things sorted out between you, didn't you?"

"That's not the point!"

"It is the point. You said you couldn't take me home on Christmas Day because of her. Why should I let it rest there when I want to be with you?"

"It was devious . . ."

"It was obvious."

Dani kept pacing angrily, yet she was forced to concede that without Cameron as the catalyst, she and Nicole might never have seen each other's point of view. So some good had come out of it. She could no longer feel her old hostility toward Nicole. She didn't even feel jealous of her any more.

But that only proved Cameron knew too much about people. Including her. "I don't think I like you, Cameron McFarlane," she said broodingly.

"Yes, you do. I'm the man you want, Dani Halstead. If you'll only be still long enough, I'll show you how much I want you, and I'll show you how much you want me."

He was right about that, Dani thought feverishly. He could do it. "I'm not going to be forced into anything by you," she hurled at him. "I will not have a time limit put on when I go to bed with you. I'm not even sure I want to go to bed with you. In fact, I'm certain I don't. I make my own decisions, Cameron McFarlane."

"Then stop fooling around and decide! Because I'm not playing any game. I won't be played with, either." He hurled the words at her. "Make up your mind about me, Dani. Here and now!"

The challenge brought Dani to a halt. There was nothing cold or calculated about it. She could see Cameron was every bit as worked up as she was. Suddenly the whole argument seemed stupid because she did want him. He was the only man she wanted. And she was biting off her nose to spite her face.

"All right," she said, pushing aside the turmoil of fear that suddenly welled up in her. If Cameron didn't love her... well, she would soon find out.

"All right, what?" he demanded.

"I'll go to bed with you," she rushed out, sealing her fate with him once and for all.

"At last!" A triumphant grin spread across his face. Cameron, the victor!

It goaded Dani into a last-minute defiance. "But only if you can catch me."

"I've got to what?" he asked incredulously.

"Catch me," Dani said with satisfaction. Cameron needn't start thinking he could have everything his way. She kicked off her shoes, ready to dodge away from him.

He laughed at her, a wild exultant laughter. "I'll catch you." And there was real determination in his voice.

A glorious madness possessed Dani as they faced each other across the ornamental pool, Cameron stalking her like a fever-mad hunter, Dani teasing him over which way she would go next. The fear of the unknown was forgotten in the excitement of the contest.

"I'll get you, Dani Halstead. If it's the last thing I ever do, I'll get you," he declared. "If I have to leap over tall buildings, go faster than a speeding bullet, plunge through boiling rapids..."

He came straight at her, right through the water, shoes and all, slipping on the mossy rocks, barking his shins against the sculptured driftwood, splashing spray everywhere. He gave a yelp of pain, but nothing was going to diminish his ardour or determination.

"Oh, dear!" said Dani. "You've hurt yourself."

He roared like a banshee possessed when he fell over part of the fountain, but he was on his feet again in an instant, coming after her with deadly intent. He made a decisive lunge that Dani evaded.

"I didn't mean you to get hurt, Cameron," she cried, then was off down the hallway to the bedroom wing.

The waiting game was over. She was ready to be caught, but didn't know what Cameron would do once he did catch her. She headed for the master bedroom. Fortunately the door was open and she made a running dive onto Cameron's king-sized bed, laughing and shrieking when Cameron dived after her.

"You're wet! You're wet! You'll ruin my beautiful dress!"

She tumbled off the other side of the bed in a wild froth of silk chiffon. He leapt up and guarded the door against her escaping. He pointed an accusing finger at her.

"You...you are a terrible woman, Dani Halstead."

"Dear Cameron," she said meekly, backing away from him as he advanced on her.

"Nothing on heaven or earth is going to stop me from doing all I've wanted to do since I first met you." He started unbuttoning his shirt.

Dani was half-mesmerised by the action. "I thought you enjoyed all that time with me, Cameron," she protested. Although he had never made any secret of what he wanted, Dani desperately wanted a great deal more from him.

"I did. I surely did," he acknowledged, "but this is the moment I've been waiting for." His shirt hit the floor. He ripped off his wet shoes and socks and started undoing his trousers.

Sheer panic welled up inside her at the thought of what was to be revealed in the next few seconds. "Go towel yourself dry, Cameron."

"No." He was pulling his trousers down.

"Why not?" she asked quickly.

"I haven't got time."

"Yes, you have," she shrieked and leapt onto the bed, bounding across it to the other side.

He was waiting for her at the door, his trousers held up by his hands. "Not this again," he groaned.

"If I get you a towel from your bathroom . . ."

"Okay."

"No tricks."

"Scout's honour."

He was stark naked when she returned. Dani threw him the towel as quickly as she could. He rubbed himself briskly.

"If you want to keep that dress intact, Dani, you'd better take it off now," he warned, his eyes glittering frustration at the delay. No more, they said. Not one damned thing more was going to stop him or get in his way!

This is it, Dani thought. Crunch time. Will he still want me when this is over? Will he think I'm still desirable and sexy and perfect? Will he kiss me tenderly afterwards, and say I love you?

While she had exulted in the thrilling power of making him chase her, she had inadvertently aroused Cameron to fever pitch, and he didn't know she was a virgin, didn't know she had played a childish game because it had helped to lighten what was a frightening moment for her.

Her hands shook as she fumbled with the ties at the back of her neck. They finally fell apart, yet she couldn't bring herself to draw her bodice down. She had never been naked in front of a man before.

Cameron hurled the towel towards the bathroom door. Dani couldn't help staring at him. There was an awesome beauty in his aroused manhood that somehow matched the rest of his physique.

"Dani?"

The soft call of her name wrenched her gaze up to his. Dani didn't know it, but her eyes were swimming with vulnerability, wanting, needing him to show her she was more than a means of satisfying his desire.

"You're embarrassed?" he asked quietly.

"Yes." The word was barely audible. Her heart seemed to be in her mouth. She swallowed hard and finally found voice. "Love me gently, Cameron," she pleaded huskily. "Love me slowly."

"It will be whatever you want, Dani," he promised her, and she saw the deep caring in his eyes, the desire to please her rather than the need to possess, and fear melted into anticipation as, with confident assurance, he closed the last distance that separated them.

CHAPTER ELEVEN

CAMERON TOOK the top of her bodice from Dani's hands and peeled it down her arms, slowly uncovering her breasts, leaving them naked to his view and his touch. Yet his eyes did not leave hers, nor did he touch her, except to lift her hands to his shoulders.

Dani was caught in the thrall of anticipation, every cell in her body yearning to join with his, to feel his flesh against her own. Simply knowing that it was imminent and inevitable was an exquisite feeling in itself.

Cameron's hands moved to her waist. He slid the dress down over her hips, gathering her panties on the way. Her legs felt like jelly but she managed to step clear of her clothes. Her thighs quivered uncontrollably under Cameron's caress as he returned his hands to her waist. His fingers splayed downwards, gently pressuring her towards him.

Dani instinctively arched back, revelling in the first electric contact of stomach and thighs, meeting and savouring the strength of his maleness while reserving the excitement of feeling the soft fullness of her naked breasts press into the firm smooth muscles of his chest. She curled her hands around his shoulders and swayed forward, brushing the bare tips of them against him.

Cameron sucked in a deep breath, seemingly expanding his chest to reach out to her, wanting to feel more, yet wanting the delicious teasing as much as she did. She could see it in the glitter of his eyes, sense it in the expectant tautness of his body. It was as though they had waited all their lives for this moment and there was no need to hurry, only an intense hunger for every possible nuance of feeling they could generate between them.

Dani lifted herself on tiptoe and Cameron supported her, curving his hands around the soft cheeks of her bottom as she moved in a graceful rhythm, caressing him with her breasts.

"Dani..." It was a groan of delight and need, and Dani felt a fierce and primitive exultation in the urgent hardness that pressed against her stomach.

Cameron gathered her closer, crushing her softness to him, winding a hand through her hair, tilting her head back for him to find her mouth with his. It was a wildly passionate kiss, long and deep and avid for all they could give each other... a beautiful madness of caring and needing and wanting and feeling. His hands cupped her face as he rained kisses all over it. He wrapped his arms around her and hugged her tightly to him as he swept his mouth over her hair, hot, feverish, yearning. He sent his tongue delving into her ear, erotically sensual and exciting. Dani found intense pleasure in tasting his flesh wherever her mouth led her. Her hands skimmed over his body in loving discovery. She pressed herself closer and closer, hugging him in an ecstasy of possession . . . her man, so wonderfully, gloriously right for her in every way.

Cameron swept her off her feet and cradled her in his arms, and Dani automatically wound her arms around his neck to hold on. He laughed down at her, a ripple of wild exhilarating joy and deep male triumph.

"I didn't know there was a caveman inside me, Dani. But there is. There most definitely is," he declared as he set her down on the bed and stretched out beside her. His lips moved softly over her lips as he murmured, "But more than anything I want this to feel right for both of us."

And he kissed her with exquisite tenderness while Dani's mind was blissfully echoing his words. She couldn't help herself. Her hands moved instinctively to stroke his shoulders and trace the interplay of the strong muscles on his back. Cameron did not protest. He trailed warm kisses down her throat and circled her breasts with feather-light fingertips. Then he kissed them with such beautiful gentle loving that Dani wanted it to go on and on forever. She barely noticed him gradually increasing the pressure of his mouth, but she was excitingly aware of changes starting inside her, a sweet melting that spread right down her thighs and aroused a quivery sense of anticipation.

Dani floated off into a limbless, boneless world of sensations. She felt as though she were turning into warm liquid. Cameron's caresses and kisses bathed her whole body in streams of pleasure. Her legs instinctively wrapped around him, hugging this wonderful man to her, *her* man. Her body lifted and fell, ululating with the ecstatic rhythm of the waves flowing through her.

Her legs slid down the hard muscular power of his thighs as Cameron prepared to enter her. His blue eyes blazed with a feverish possessiveness. Dani felt the same way. She reached out, and her touch was enough to send his stomach muscles into rippling spasms. He cried out her name, then lowered himself to finally join his body to hers.

The revelation of that moment was like a sunburst through Dani's mind and body. The unbelievable fulfilment of feeling him move inside her, of feeling herself closing around him, of possessing him, deeper and deeper... Oh, yes, Dani cried somewhere in her head. Yes, yes, yes. The words seemed to reverberate through her whole body, an exultation, a knowledge as deep and primitive as any knowledge.

She knew the way to respond to this coming together instinctively, moving her body to the strong beat of his, as graceful as a dance, swinging this way and that, a subtle rolling, closing, sliding, never quite apart, the power and the glory of it sweeping them on and on.

There was the sensation of rushing towards some stormy peak, then Dani felt herself go over the top, out of control. Her thighs were shaking uncontrollably, and there was a moment of release, of gratification, of scintillating satisfaction. Her mind seemed to split in two, to separate her from the real world, and her body floated away on a wave of euphoria.

Cameron enfolded her in his arms and carried her with him as he rolled onto his side. Dani felt his heart pounding madly and his breath rasp through her hair. His flesh was slicked with sweat, but he felt so good to Dani that she hugged him with all the love she felt for him.

She lay still, unable to do otherwise, soaking up peace, contentment and fulfilment. She sensed it spreading through him, too, tension draining away, heartbeat slowing. Eventually he moved a hand, trailing it through her long turbulent hair, circling it around her back. She heard him take a deep breath, but even so, his voice was not at full strength when he spoke.

"Dani..." Somehow he injected her name with all the magic of the world.

She smiled and grazed her lips across the base of his throat, knowing that it had been as good for him as it had been for her.

"Did I hurt you?" he asked tenderly.

"No. You were wonderful," she whispered, her heart too full to find much voice.

"So were you. Unbelievably wonderful." His arm tightened around her and he swept warm kisses over her hair. "You are one very special woman, Dani. Remind me to send Mrs. B a huge Christmas hamper for sending you to me. That was my lucky day."

Mine, too, Dani thought. Maybe her luck was changing for the better. Of course, the best possible stroke of luck would be if Cameron loved her enough to want her with him always. To want marriage and children and grandchildren and all the things that would make their life together really meaningful.

"What do you want, Dani?"

She didn't stop to think he might be asking her what she wanted for Christmas. She answered straight from her heart.

"Marriage. I want you to marry me."

She felt his shock. He went unnaturally still, not even breathing. Dani had an awful feeling that what they had just shared *was* the beginning of the end, and while she could not regret the experience of loving, her heart suddenly went heavy.

Then Cameron slowly exhaled a long breath. "I admire your directness, Dani," he said. "I really do. But..."

With a swift lithe movement, he rolled her onto her back and leaned over her, his eyes blazing straight into hers.

"I will not allow you to take my male prerogatives away from me," he stated emphatically. "I'll decide if I want to marry you. And I'll do the asking. Is that clear?"

"Does that mean no?"

"I didn't say that."

"I'm sorry. I shouldn't have said what I did. I felt so happy..."

"I want you to be happy."

"Forgive me?"

"As long as you never say it again."

"I promise." Cameron was not saying an outright no. Dani smiled at him, her eyes shining with happy hope. "I'm sorry, Cameron. I didn't mean to make your decision for you. Or influence you."

He gave her a stern look. "I'm the man. You're the woman. That's the way it stays. I don't care how screwed up the rest of the world is, I'm running my life as I see fit. And no woman, absolutely no woman, tells me when I get married.''

"Yes, Cameron,'' she said meekly. ''I understand that perfectly. I like to run my life as I see fit, too. And I most definitely don't want a man who doesn't know his own mind.''

He looked suspiciously at her. ''Why do I have a feeling there's a catch in that?''

''Well, it's like you wanting me to come to bed with you, Cameron,'' she explained as sweetly as she could. ''There comes a time when you have to decide. It won't stay open-ended forever. That's not fair. You do have to make up your mind.''

His mouth quirked. ''You want to walk away from me, Dani?''

''No. I was wondering if you were going to walk away from me. Or fly, as the case may be. You said you were flying to the U.S. on Boxing Day.''

''I've postponed the trip.''

''Oh!''

''Indefinitely.''

''Oh!''

''I may never go.''

''Oh?''

''I find myself otherwise occupied.''

''With what?''

''You.''

''Well,'' said Dani, thinking it was a good idea to keep him very occupied. Cameron might not have made up his mind about marrying her, but at present he was definitely obsessed. "Did you hurt yourself, uh, very much when you were chasing me?"

"Terribly," he said sternly. "For which I will need a great deal of tender loving care."

"I'm not as good as Grandma, yet," she said, stroking her fingers lightly down his abdomen. "She has healing hands. But I can practise on you, Cameron, and maybe you'll feel better."

Her feather touch found some erotic spots under his hipbones, and Cameron responded very strongly. "Keep that up and you'll have your grandmother beaten, hands down," he rasped.

"Maybe if I . . ."

"Dani . . ." It was a half-strangled sound.

Cameron didn't need any more healing. He proceeded to show Dani how occupied he could be with her. It took him most of the night. When he woke her the next day after a long languorous sleep, he aroused her to intensely pleasurable consciousness and continued on from where he had left off, demonstrating a dedication to being obsessively occupied for a long time.

CHAPTER TWELVE

CHRISTMAS DAY!

Dani wore a grin a mile wide as she and Cameron set off for her parents' home. This was what she had wanted from her first meeting with Cameron, but she had only envisaged a superficial charade at the time. Now it was the real thing. Cameron McFarlane *was* her man, to all intents and purposes.

Although he hadn't yet come to marriage, Dani felt he might be coming close. He certainly showed no signs of wanting to be apart from her. In fact, it seemed that he really couldn't leave her alone. Or didn't want to. He even drove with one hand so that he could hold hers, his fingers occasionally stroking a possessive caress.

There were other good signs for the future that made Dani feel hopeful. As well as buying Mrs. B a huge hamper, Cameron had bought all her family Christmas presents. That, to Dani, was a clear indication that he wanted to be part of her family. Which, she was sure, would be good for him since he didn't have a family of his own. She did caution herself that Cameron was generous by nature, but that didn't stop her from hoping.

Besides, her luck was changing. It had to be. All three of her disasters had turned into triumphs. She had the best job in the world cooking for Cameron. Mrs. B was in seventh heaven with her Henry. And today was going to be the best Christmas Day ever. It was already the best with Cameron beside her, looking devastatingly handsome in white jeans and a navy blue sports shirt.

Dani's parents lived at Wamberal on the Central Coast, about an hour's journey north of Sydney. Their house was situated on a hill and overlooked the beaches that stretched around the coast as far as the eye could see. It was a good solid comfortable home, nothing luxurious like Cameron's, but the view was lovely, and the veranda overlooking it was wide and spacious. This was where her parents did all their summer relaxing and entertaining. They were seated out there with Grandma when Dani and Cameron pulled up in the driveway.

Although Dani had informed her mother she was bringing Cameron home with her, she had thought it wiser not to spell out their actual relationship. No point in stirring up worries when there might not be any worries at all, she argued to herself. Of course, Nicole could be the fly in the ointment if she had a mind to be, but Dani had decided to give her elder sister the benefit of the doubt. Perhaps they could live and let live this Christmas. Besides, surely Nicole would think twice about saying anything nasty in front of Cameron.

When she and Cameron alighted from the car, Dani saw her mother's eyes open wide and her father's eyebrows lift in startled surprise. Her grandmother simply smiled. Greetings were called out, introductions made, and her father came down to shake Cameron's hand and help carry up the Christmas parcels.

The next half-hour was sheer bliss for Dani. Her parents were completely bowled over by Cameron, who sat holding her hand and throwing her smiles that could only be read as besotted devotion. Which made Dani stand extremely tall in her parents' eyes. They didn't ask one question about her career. Grandma watched, nodding her head occasionally.

The old familiar tension hit Dani when Nicole arrived with her man. She couldn't help worrying whether her sister would be content to let sleeping dogs lie. Yet, much to Dani's pleasant surprise and relief, Nicole seemed happy to accept Cameron's presence and didn't even make a sly dig to Dani about it. In fact, as they sat drinking long glasses of Christmas punch, Nicole actually smiled at her, to which Dani swiftly responded, thinking that her sister had somehow become imbued with real Christmas spirit.

She was even more startled when Nicole engineered a private conversation with her and started it with what seemed to be a sincere apology. "I'm sorry for saying what I did about Cameron, Dani. If you really have something going together..."

"Nicole..." Dani hesitated, but it was a question she felt she had to ask. "Was it because you wanted Cameron for yourself?"

Slowly she shook her head. "Not really. I fancied him. What woman wouldn't? But Barry..."

The look Nicole gave her man sent a flood of relief through Dani.

"We're thinking of getting married."

If only Cameron would think of getting married, Dani thought, but she swiftly stifled the little stab of envy. It was time for her to be generous, too. "How wonderful for you, Nicole."

"Yes, it is." Nicole gave an ironic smile. "Barry doesn't mind about the rules I've broken. It was a kind of rebellion...sleeping with anyone I fancied. But that's not what I want. It was stupid. I ended up not liking myself very much."

"I'm sorry you felt like that," Dani said softly.

Nicole looked at her curiously. "You feel good about yourself, don't you, Dani? You always projected that."

Dani grimaced. "Not always. Two weeks ago I felt like a complete failure, wondering how I was going to face up to the family on Christmas Day. I didn't have a job. My prospects were pretty grim..."

"But now you have Cameron?"

"Yes. Now I have Cameron." More or less, she thought.

"I hope, truly hope you'll be happy with him. Now that I'm happy I want everyone in the world to be happy."

There could be no doubting her sister's sincerity. A dark weight lifted from Dani's heart. She gave her sister a brilliant smile. "Thanks, Nicole. I wish you every happiness, too."

Nicole turned back to Barry, and Dani turned her smile to Cameron, who had made this new harmony with her sister possible. His eyes sparkled knowingly at her, and Dani felt truly grateful that he was so good at psychology. She made up her mind to read all his books now that he could have no objection.

He was talking to Grandma, and Dani was delighted to see that they had established a rapport in no time flat. The liking between them was obviously genuine. Dani could tell by the warmth in Cameron's eyes and the twinkling smiles Grandma kept giving him. Of course, Cameron could charm birds out of trees when he had a mind to, but Grandma was not one to be taken in by superficial charm. She really liked him. No doubt about that.

Eventually Dani's parents declared it was time for the gifts to be opened and they were all ushered into the lounge, where the Christmas tree took pride of place. Dani manoeuvred a private little chat with Grandma on the way.

"Well, now you've met him, Grandma."

"Yes, dear."

"What do you think?"

"I think he has a lot of Irish in him."

"Grandma, you couldn't get a more Scottish name than Cameron McFarlane."

"Gaelic blood. It's all the same."

"Do you think he's like Grandpa?" Dani asked.

Grandma nodded wisely. "He's certainly a man who knows his own mind and fights for what he wants."

Which was fairly spot on, Dani thought appreciatively.

"I think lamb roast would be best," Grandma mused.

Dani looked her bewilderment. "What about lamb roast?"

"Men like him are plain eaters. Plain eaters like lamb roast. He is a plain eater, isn't he?"

"Well, more or less." Dani had been doing her best to teach him better.

"Don't cook fancy," Grandma advised. "He'll say he likes it to please you, but inwardly he'll get indigestion. Give him lamb roast. I always found your grandfather very amenable to any suggestion after I fed him lamb roast."

"Right!" said Dani. "I've got it. Lamb roast. Thank you, Grandma."

The brown eyes twinkled at her and Dani gave her a quick hug. She felt very happy.

Dani's father put an end to any further conversation. "Dani, since you're wearing red and white, you can be Santa Claus this year and give out the presents from under the tree," he announced, beaming more approval at her than he had ever done before.

Cameron grinned at her as he settled on the two-seater sofa with Grandma. "Show some Christmas spirit, Dani," he teased.

She laughed and fossicked through the presents to find one for her mother first. "Happy Christmas, Mum," she said as she handed it to her.

"It is indeed, Dani," she said with a happy smile.

Everyone was happy. Nicole even managed to look delighted with the Lancôme soap. Dani had felt a bit mean about that gift, so she had wrapped the soap in a pair of French lace knickers, which brought a real sparkle to Nicole's eyes, particularly when she looked at Barry.

Cameron laughed delightedly over the collection of things Dani had bought him—a ruler for drawing a straight line, a coffee mug with Good Morning printed on it, a bath towel marked His, a man's kitchen apron depicting a burning barbecue, and a glass-enclosed tableau of a tropical fountain which, when shaken, looked as though spray was going everywhere. Inside it was a little man who tumbled around in the splashing droplets.

Christmas wrapping paper was strewn all over the floor by the time Dani came to the last present. She had deliberately left Cameron's gift to her to the end although she was dying to open it to see what he'd selected for her. It was a rectangular shape, the size of a ladies' purse.

She was conscious of him watching her as she tore off the wrapping, so she threw him a special smile to let him know that whatever it was she would love it. Inside was a velvet box, the kind that would hold an expensive necklace.

Dani took a deep breath, only too aware that Cameron thought nothing of spending a fortune on her. She hoped he hadn't gone terribly wild this time. She unlatched the lid and lifted it up, expecting almost anything except what was there.

In the centre of a groove running across the black velvet was a magnificent solitaire diamond ring. Lying behind it was a card on which Cameron had written, "Will you marry me?"

Her gaze flew up to his—beautiful blue eyes beaming love and commitment straight into her heart. Dani felt too choked with emotion to speak. She got to her feet and carried the box over to him, all the love she felt for him in her eyes. She gave him the box, then held out her left hand for him to put the ring on her finger.

"Say yes," he prompted, his eyes glittering intense and relentless purpose.

"Yes," she whispered.

He pulled her onto his lap and nestled her in the crook of one arm, holding her possessively while he opened the box. He slid the fabulous diamond ring onto the third finger of her left hand with slow deliberate ceremony.

"Marriage," he said decisively. "So now you're well and truly caught."

"Yes," she agreed, finally managing to find her voice. "You caught me, Cameron."

"And there's no getting away."

"Absolutely none."

"Divorce is out."

"Unthinkable."

"Children."

"Yes, children."

"And grandchildren."

"Only if you're capable, dear Cameron."

"I'm *very* capable," he asserted strongly. Then he looked around the assembled family, who were all stunned into silence. "That's it. Dani and I are getting married."

It was definitely the best Christmas Day ever—an impossible dream come true!

When they went to bed together that night, Cameron told Dani again and again how much he loved her. Dani had no compunction whatsoever in impressing on Cameron how much she loved him, too.

A VERY LONG, LONG TIME later, after many things had happened—and this is absolutely true—Dani and Cameron retired to a hobby farm. Dani had her chickens and her fruit trees and her herb and vegetable garden. Cameron took a lively interest in breeding cashmere goats for their wool and Australian silky terriers for the fun of it. It was a good life, full of interesting things happening and sweetened with the contentment of sharing everything together.

Occasionally their children tried to tell them they were getting too old for this kind of life, but Dani and Cameron were determined to live how they wanted to live. After all, that was what they had been doing together all their lives, and they had every right to be stubborn and ornery about it.

Grandchildren came to them for their school holidays, and that was always a lot of fun. Sometimes they whispered together about the mysterious way Grandma knew so much about what they did. They didn't really believe that the birds told her everything. They finally figured out she had some kind of sixth sense that let her know things that even Grandpa didn't know.

Grandma was also wonderful at baking cakes and cookies. They all reckoned she was so good that she could have been a professional cook if she'd wanted to be. Her roast lamb dinners were the best! And her homemade pea and ham soup, which was Grandpa's favourite, was out of this world. The kitchen was always full of delicious smells.

Though whenever anyone got hurt or sick, Grandma was good at that, too. She had soft soothing hands that seemed to comfort all the way inside you. You definitely went to Grandma if you got wounded.

She also had a special part in her brain for wise old sayings. How she knew so many of them was another mystery. She must have been storing them up in her memory ever since she was born. Press a button and out one would come.

It was funny, though, how they seemed to fit whatever was going on. Her fairy stories were like that, too. All the grandchildren agreed it was positively uncanny the way Grandma hit right at the heart of things. She really knew everything.

When anyone wanted some serious advice, the farm was undoubtedly the best place to go. When Danielle McFarlane was fifteen she needed serious advice. Very serious advice. She arrived at the farm on an impromptu visit.

All the grandchildren thought Grandma loved them best, but this one, who had been named after her, was closest to Grandma's heart. Young Dani smiled and chatted, but underneath the surface she was troubled. A very difficult problem weighed on her mind.

Grandpa and Grandma exchanged a knowing look, part of the intimacy that had grown between them over the years. Words weren't necessary between them at times like these. Grandpa excused himself, saying he had to go and see his dogs. Grandma waited for young Dani to tell her the problem that had brought her out of her way today.

"I want to ask you something, Grandma."

"Yes, dear?" Dani threaded her needle, picked up her latest tapestry, then looked at her grand-daughter, who was frowning heavily.

"It's about a boy. Well, not really a boy. He's sixteen. All the girls drool over him because he's so good-looking. I know I'm not the prettiest girl in the school but he seems to like me..."

Dani glanced out the kitchen window. Cameron was still so upright and tall, walking towards the far fence, one of their dogs prancing at his heels. He was almost eighty years old, but he was a fine figure of a man. White-haired, but his eyes were as blue as they ever were, and they hadn't lost their sparkling kindness, nor their wickedness. What a wonderful life they'd had! All these years... and the love they shared was a continual celebration of their life together.

But she mustn't think of that now. She had to help young Dani. She gave her grand-daughter an encouraging smile and went back to her stitching. Bit by bit the problem emerged, and Dani was transported back almost fifty years. When it was time for her to speak, she knew exactly what to say.

"Beauty," she said, "is in the eye of the beholder."

She knew Dani would be disappointed in that answer.

"Well, Grandma, I suppose I'd better be on my way..."

"Before you go, Dani, I think I have to tell you a story. It's a fairy story. But for all it's a fairy story, it's true enough. It happened a long, long time ago. See what you make of it."

She paused, remembering all her own feelings, the beginning of her love for Cameron, his for her. But her grand-daughter was waiting to hear the story, to learn, if she could.

"Once upon a time, there was a young girl..."

As CAMERON DROVE his grand-daughter to the railway station, he grew conscious of young Dani shooting curious glances at him, as though she was appraising him in a new light.

"Something wrong, Dani?" he asked.

"No, Grandpa. Nothing wrong," she denied, and gave him a funny little smile. It held both satisfaction and bemusement. Then she said, "But I would like to know..."

"Know what?"

"Did Grandma really find black lace knickers in your bed when she first met you?"

When Cameron returned to the farm, he found his wife standing dreamily in front of the kitchen window. "Did you have a good day today?" he asked, giving her a hug, their closeness and their love reflected in his twinkling blue eyes.

Since the day they married, Cameron insisted that every woman who was loved should be given three hugs a day. He said it was to show her that no matter what happened, they would always be together. Dani never raised any question about this, but she suspected it had a bit to do with reassuring a man that his woman was well and truly caught.

"Oh, yes, dear," she said. "I had another wonderful day. Everything turned out as it should."

Her mind supplied another thought—all's well that ends well—but she didn't need to voice that to Cameron. His smile said it for her. And when she smiled back he saw no signs of age at all. He saw only the girl who had once come into his bedroom and woke him up to what life could be like ... if he could catch her and keep her with him.

He still had her!

CHRISTMAS MASQUERADE

by

DEBBIE MACOMBER

For Tara
A woman of grace, charm and sensitivity
Thank you

Prologue

The blast of a jazz saxophone that pierced the night was immediately followed by the jubilant sounds of a dixieland band. A shrieking whistle reverberated through the confusion. Singing, dancing, hooting and laughter surrounded Jo Marie Early as she painstakingly made her way down Tulane Avenue. Attracted by the parade, she'd arrived just in time to watch the flambeaux carriers light a golden arc of bouncing flames from one side of the street to the other. Now she was trapped in the milling mass of humanity when she had every intention of going in the opposite direction. The heavy Mardi Gras crowds hampered her progress to a slow crawl. The observation of the "Fat Tuesday" had commenced two weeks earlier with a series of parades and festive balls. Tonight the celebrating culminated in a frenzy of singing, lively dancing and masqueraders who roamed the brilliant streets.

New Orleans went crazy at this time of year, throwing a city-wide party that attracted a million guests. After twenty-three years, Jo Marie thought she would be accustomed to the maniacal behavior in the city she loved. But how could she criticize when she was a participant herself? Tonight, if she ever made it out of this crowd, she was attending a private party dressed as Florence Nightingale. Not her most original costume idea, but the best she could do on such short notice. Just this morning she'd been in a snowstorm in Minnesota and had arrived back this afternoon to hear the news that her roommate, Kelly Beaumont, was in the hospital for a tonsillectomy. Concerned, Joe Marie had quickly donned one of Kelly's nurse's uniforms so she could go directly to the party after visiting Kelly in the hospital.

With a sigh of abject frustration, Jo Marie realized she was being pushed in the direction opposite the hospital.

"Please, let me through," she called, struggling against the swift current of the merrymaking crowd.

"Which way?" a gravelly, male voice asked in her ear. "Do you want to go this way?" He pointed away from the crowd.

"Yes...please."

The voice turned out to be one of three young men who cleared a path for Jo Marie and helped her onto a side street.

Laughing, she turned to find all three were dressed as cavaliers of old. They bowed in gentlemanly fashion, tucking their arms at their waists and sweeping their plumed hats before them.

"The Three Musketeers at your disposal, fair lady."

"Your rescue is most welcome, kind sirs," Jo Marie shouted to be heard above the sound of the boisterous celebration.

"Your destination?"

Rather than try to be heard, Jo Marie pointed toward the hospital.

"Then allow us to escort you," the second offered gallantly.

Jo Marie wasn't sure she should trust three young men wearing red tights. But after all, it was Mardi Gras and the tale was sure to cause Kelly to smile. And that was something her roommate hadn't been doing much of lately.

The three young men formed a protective circle around Jo Marie and led the way down a less crowded side street, weaving in and out of the throng when necessary.

Glancing above to the cast iron balcony railing that marked the outer limits of the French Quarter, Jo Marie realized her heroes were heading for the heart of the partying, apparently more interested in capturing her for themselves than in delivering her to the hospital. "We're headed the wrong way," she shouted.

"This is a short cut," the tallest of the trio explained humorously. "We know of several people this way in need of nursing."

Unwilling to be trapped in their game, Jo Marie broke away from her gallant cavaliers and walked as quickly as her starched white uniform would allow. Dark tendrils of her hair escaped the carefully coiled chignon and framed her small face. Her fingers pushed them aside, uncaring for the moment.

Heavy footsteps behind her assured Jo Marie that the Three Musketeers weren't giving up on her so easily. Increasing her pace, she ran across the street and was within a half block of the hospital parking lot when she collided full speed into a solid object.

Stunned, it took Jo Marie a minute to recover and recognize that whatever she'd hit was warm and lean. Jo Marie raised startled brown eyes to meet the intense gray eyes of the most striking man she had ever seen. His hands reached for her shoulder to steady her.

"Are you hurt?" he asked in a deep voice that was low and resonant, oddly sensuous.

Jo Marie shook her head. "Are you?" There was some quality so mesmerizing about this man that she couldn't move her eyes. Although she was self-consciously staring, Jo Marie was powerless to break eye contact. He wasn't tall—under six feet so that she had only to tip her head back slightly to meet his look. Nor dark. His hair was brown, but a shade no deeper than her own soft chestnut curls. And he wasn't handsome. Not in the urbane sense. Although his look and his clothes spoke of wealth and breeding, Jo Marie knew intuitively that this man worked, played and loved hard. His brow was creased in what looked like a permanent frown and his mouth was a fraction too full.

Not tall, not dark, not handsome, but the embodiment of every fantasy Jo Marie had ever dreamed.

Neither of them moved for a long, drawn-out moment. Jo Marie felt as if she'd turned to stone. All those silly, schoolgirl dreams she'd shelved in the back of her mind as products of a whimsical imagination stood before her. He was the swashbuckling pirate to her captured maiden, Rhett Butler to her Scarlett O'Hara, Heathcliff to her Catherine....

"Are you hurt?" He broke into her thoughts. Eyes as gray as a winter sea narrowed with concern.

"No." She assured him with a shake of her head and forced her attention over her shoulder. Her three gallant heroes had discovered another female attraction and had directed their attention elsewhere, no longer interested in following her.

His hands continued to hold her shoulder. "You're a nurse?" he asked softly.

"Florence Nightingale," she corrected with a soft smile.

His finger was under her chin. Lifting her eyes, she saw his softly quizzical gaze. "Have we met?"

"No." It was on the tip of her tongue to tell him that yes they had met once, a long time ago in her romantic daydreams. But he'd probably laugh. Who wouldn't? Jo Marie wasn't a star-struck teenager, but a woman who had long since abandoned the practice of reading fairy tales.

His eyes were intent as they roamed her face, memorizing every detail, seeking something he couldn't define. He seemed as caught up in this moment as she.

"You remind me of a painting I once saw," he said, then blinked, apparently surprised that he'd spoken out loud.

"No one's ever done my portrait," Jo Marie murmured, frozen into immobility by the breathless bewilderment that lingered between them.

His eyes skidded past her briefly to rest on the fun-seeking Musketeers. "You were running from them?"

The spellbinding moment continued.

"Yes."

"Then I rescued you."

Jo Marie confirmed his statement as a large group of merrymakers crossed the street toward them. But she barely noticed. What captured her attention was the way in which this dream man was studying her.

"Every hero deserves a reward," he said.

Jo Marie watched him with uncertainty. "What do you mean?"

"This." The bright light of the streetlamp dimmed as he lowered his head, blocking out the golden rays. His warm mouth settled over hers, holding her prisoner, kissing her with a hunger as deep as the sea.

In the dark recesses of her mind, Jo Marie realized she should pull away. A man she didn't know was kissing her deeply, passionately. And the sensations he aroused were far beyond anything she'd ever felt. A dream that had become reality.

Singing voices surrounded her and before she could recognize the source the kiss was abruptly broken.

The Three Musketeers and a long line of others were doing a gay rendition of the rumba. Before she could protest, before she was even aware of what was happening, Jo Marie was grabbed from behind by the waist and forced to join in the rambunctious song and dance.

Her dark eyes sought the dream man only to discover that he was frantically searching the crowd for her, pushing people aside. Desperately, Jo Marie fought to break free, but couldn't. She called out, but to no avail, her voice drowned out by the song of the others. The long line of singing pranksters turned the corner, forcing Jo Marie to go with them. Her last sight of the dream man was of him pushing his way through the crowd to find her, but by then it was too late. She, too, had lost him.

Chapter One

You've got that look in your eye again," pixie-faced Kelly Beaumont complained. "I swear every time you pick me up at the hospital something strange comes over you."

Jo Marie forced a smile, but her soft mouth trembled with the effort. "You're imagining things."

Kelly's narrowed look denied that, but she said nothing.

If Jo Marie had felt like being honest, she would have recognized the truth of what her friend was saying. Every visit to the hospital produced a deluge of memories. In the months that had passed, she was certain that the meeting with the dream man had blossomed and grown out of proportion in her memory. Every word, every action had been relived a thousand times until her mind had memorized the smallest detail, down to the musky, spicy scent of him. Jo Marie had never told anyone about that night of the Mardi Gras. A couple of times she'd wanted to confide in Kelly, but the words wouldn't come. Late in the evenings after she'd prepared for bed, it was the dream man's face that drifted into her consciousness as she fell asleep. Jo Marie couldn't understand why this man who had invaded her life so briefly would have such an overwhelming effect. And yet those few minutes had lingered all these months. Maybe in every woman's life there was a man who was meant to fulfill her dreams. And, in that brief five-minute interlude during Mardi Gras, Jo Marie had found hers.

"...Thanksgiving's tomorrow and Christmas is just around the corner." Kelly interrupted Jo Marie's thoughts. The blaring horn of an irritated motorist caused them both to grimace. Whenever possible, they preferred taking the bus, but both wanted an early start on the holiday weekend.

"Where has the year gone?" Jo Marie commented absently. She was paying close attention to the heavy traffic as she merged with the late evening flow that led Interstate 10 through the downtown district. The freeway would deliver them to the two-bedroom apartment they shared.

"I saw Mark today," Kelly said casually.

Something about the way Kelly spoke caused Jo Marie to turn her head. "Oh." It wasn't unnatural that her brother, a resident doctor at Tulane, would run into Kelly. After all, they both worked in the same hospital. "Did World War Three break out?" Jo Marie had never known any two people who could find more things to argue about. After three years, she'd given up trying to figure out why Mark and Kelly couldn't get along. Saying that they rubbed each other the wrong way seemed too trite an explanation. Antagonistic behavior wasn't characteristic of either of them. Kelly was a dedicated nurse and Mark a struggling resident doctor. But when the two were together, the lightning arced between them like a turbulent electrical storm. At one time Jo Marie had thought Kelly and Mark might be interested in each other. But after months of constant bickering she was forced to believe that the only thing between them was her overactive imagination.

"What did Mark have to say?"

Pointedly, Kelly turned her head away and stared out the window. "Oh, the usual."

The low, forced cheerfulness in her roommate's voice didn't fool Jo Marie. Where Kelly was concerned, Mark was merciless. He didn't mean to be cruel or insulting, but he loved to tease Kelly about her family's wealth. Not that money or position was that important to Kelly. "You mean he was kidding you about playing at being a nurse again." That was Mark's favorite crack.

One delicate shoulder jerked in response. "Sometimes I think he must hate me," she whispered, pretending a keen interest in the view outside the car window.

The soft catch in Kelly's voice brought Jo Marie's attention from the freeway to her friend. "Don't mind Mark. He doesn't mean anything by it. He loves to tease. You should hear some of the things he says about my job—you'd think a travel agent did nothing but hand out brochures for the tropics."

Kelly's abrupt nod was unconvincing.

Mentally, Jo Marie decided to have a talk with her big brother. He shouldn't tease Kelly as if she were his sister. Kelly didn't know how to react to it. As the youngest daughter of a large southern candy manufacturer, Kelly had been sheltered and pampered most of her life. Her only brother was years older and apparently the age difference didn't allow for many sibling conflicts. With four brothers, Jo Marie was no stranger to family squabbles and could stand her own against any one of them.

The apartment was a welcome sight after the twenty-minute freeway drive. Jo Marie and Kelly thought of it as their port in the storm. The two-floor apartment buidling resembled the historic mansion from *Gone With the Wind*. It maintained the flavor of the Old South without the problem of constant repairs typical of many older buildings.

The minute they were in the door, Kelly headed for her room. "If you don't mind I think I'll pack."

"Sure. Go ahead." Carelessly, Jo Marie kicked off her low-heeled shoes. Slouching on the love seat, she leaned her head back and closed her eyes. The strain of the hectic rush hour traffic and the tension of a busy day ebbed away with every relaxing breath.

The sound of running bathwater didn't surprise Jo Marie. Kelly wanted to get an early start. Her family lived in an ultramodern home along Lakeshore Drive. The house bordered Lake Pontchartrain. Jo Marie had been inside the Beaumont home only once. That had been enough for her to realize just how good the candy business was.

Jo Marie was sure that Charles Beaumont may have disapproved of his only daughter moving into an apartment with a "nobody" like her, but once he'd learned that she was the great-great granddaughter of Jubal Anderson Early, a Confederate Army colonel, he'd sanctioned the move. Sometime during the Civil

War, Colonel Early had been instrumental in saving the life of a young Beaumont. Hence, a-hundred-and-some-odd years later, Early was a name to respect.

Humming Christmas music softly to herself, Jo Marie wandered into the kitchen and pulled the orange juice from the refrigerator shelf.

"Want a glass?" She held up the pitcher to Kelly who stepped from the bathroom, dressed in a short terry-cloth robe, with a thick towel securing her bouncy blond curls. One look at her friend and Jo Marie set the ceramic container on the kitchen counter.

"You've been crying." They'd lived together for three years, and apart from one sad, sentimental movie, Jo Marie had never seen Kelly cry.

"No, something's in my eye," she said and sniffled.

"Then why's your nose so red?"

"Maybe I'm catching a cold." She offered the weak explanation and turned sharply toward her room.

Jo Marie's smooth brow narrowed. This was Mark's doing. She was convinced he was the cause of Kelly's uncharacteristic display of emotion.

Something rang untrue about the whole situation between Kelly and Mark. Kelly wasn't a soft, southern belle who fainted at the least provocation. That was another teasing comment Mark enjoyed hurling at her. Kelly was a lady, but no shrinking violet. Jo Marie had witnessed Kelly in action, fighting for her patients and several political causes. The girl didn't back down often. After Thanksgiving, Jo Marie would help Kelly fine-tune a few witty comebacks. As Mark's sister, Jo Marie was well acquainted with her brother's weak spots. The only way to fight fire was with fire she mused humorously. Together, Jo Marie and Kelly would teach Mark a lesson.

"You want me to fix something to eat before you head for your parents?" Jo Marie shouted from the kitchen. She was standing in front of the cupboard, scanning its meager contents. "How does soup and a sandwich sound?"

"Boring," Kelly returned. "I'm not really hungry."

"Eight hours of back-breaking work on the surgical ward and you're not interested in food? Are you having problems with your tonsils again?"

"I had them out, remember?"

Slowly, Jo Marie straightened. Yes, she remembered. All too well. It had been outside the hospital that she'd literally run into the dream man. Unbidden thoughts of him crowded her mind and forcefully she shook her head to free herself of his image.

Jo Marie had fixed herself dinner and was sitting in front of the television watching the evening news by the time Kelly reappeared.

"I'm leaving now."

"Okay." Jo Marie didn't take her eyes off the television. "Have a happy Thanksgiving; don't eat too much turkey and trimmings."

"Don't throw any wild parties while I'm away." That was a small joke between them. Jo Marie rarely dated these days. Not since—Mardi Gras. Kelly couldn't understand this change in her friend and affectionately teased Jo Marie about her sudden lack of an interesting social life.

"Oh, Kelly, before I forget—" Jo Marie gave her a wicked smile "—bring back some pralines, would you? After all, it's the holidays, so we can splurge."

At any other time Kelly would rant that she'd grown up with candy all her life and detested the sugary sweet concoction. Pralines were Jo Marie's weakness, but the candy would rot before Kelly would eat any of it.

"Sure, I'll be happy to," she agreed lifelessly and was gone before Jo Marie realized her friend had slipped away. Returning her attention to the news, Jo Marie was more determined than ever to have a talk with her brother.

The doorbell chimed at seven. Jo Marie was spreading a bright red polish on her toenails. She grumbled under her breath and screwed on the top of the bottle. But before she could answer the door, her brother strolled into the apartment and flopped down on the sofa that sat at right angles to the matching love seat.

"Come in and make yourself at home," Jo Marie commented dryly.

"I don't suppose you've got anything to eat around here." Dark brown eyes glanced expectantly into the kitchen. All five of the Early children shared the same dusty, dark eyes.

"This isn't a restaurant, you know."

"I know. By the way, where's money bags?"

"Who?" Confused, Jo Marie glanced up from her toes.

"Kelly."

Jo Marie didn't like the reference to Kelly's family wealth, but decided now wasn't the time to comment. Her brother worked long hours and had been out of sorts lately. "She's left for her parents' home already."

A soft snicker followed Jo Marie's announcement.

"Damn it, Mark, I wish you'd lay off Kelly. She's not used to being teased. It really bothers her."

"I'm only joking," Mark defended himself. "Kell knows that."

"I don't think she does. She was crying tonight and I'm sure it's your fault."

"Kelly crying?" He straightened and leaned forward, linking his hands. "But I was only kidding."

"That's the problem. You can't seem to let up on her. You're always putting her down one way or another."

Mark reached for a magazine, but not before Jo Marie saw that his mouth was pinched and hard. "She asks for it."

Rolling her eyes, Jo Marie continued adding the fire-engine-red color to her toes. It wouldn't do any good for her to argue with Mark. Kelly and Mark had to come to an agreement on their own. But that didn't mean Jo Marie couldn't hand Kelly ammunition now and again. Her brother had his vulnerable points, and Jo Marie would just make certain Kelly was aware of them. Then she could sit back and watch the sparks fly.

Busy with her polish, Jo Marie didn't notice for several minutes how quiet her brother had become. When she lifted her gaze to him, she saw that he had a pained, troubled look. His brow was furrowed in thought.

"I lost a child today," he announced tightly. "I couldn't understand it either. Not medically, I don't mean that. Anything can happen. She'd been brought in last week with a ruptured appendix. We knew from the beginning it was going to be touch and go." He paused and breathed in sharply. "But you know, deep down inside I believed she'd make it. She was their only daughter. The apple of her parents' eye. If all the love in that mother's heart couldn't hold back death's hand, then what good is medical science? What good am I?''

Mark had raised these questions before and Jo Marie had no answers. "I don't know," she admitted solemnly and reached out to touch his hand in reassurance. Mark didn't want to hear the pat answers. He couldn't see that now. Not when he felt like he'd failed this little girl and her parents in some obscure way. At times like these, she'd look at her brother who was a strong, committed doctor and see the doubt in his eyes. She had no answers. Sometimes she wasn't even sure she completely understood his questions.

After wiping his hand across his tired face, Mark stood. "I'm on duty tomorrow morning so I probably won't be at the folks' place until late afternoon. Tell Mom I'll try to make it on time. If I can't, the least you can do is to be sure and save a plate for me.''

Knowing Mark, he was likely to go without eating until tomorrow if left to his own devices. "Let me fix you something now," Jo Marie offered. From his unnatural pallor, Jo Marie surmised that Mark couldn't even remember when he'd eaten his last decent meal, coffee and a doughnut on the run excluded.

He glanced at his watch. "I haven't got time. Thanks anyway." Before she could object, he was at the door.

Why had he come? Jo Marie wondered absently. He'd done a lot of that lately—stopping in for a few minutes without notice. And it wasn't as if her apartment were close to the hospital. Mark had to go out of his way to visit her. With a bemused shrug, she followed him to the front door and watched as he sped away in that run-down old car he was so fond of driving. As he left, Jo Marie mentally questioned if her instincts had been on target all along and Kelly and Mark did hold some deep affection for each other. Mark hadn't come tonight for any specific reason. His first question had been about Kelly. Only later had he mentioned losing the child.

"Jo Marie," her mother called from the kitchen. "Would you mind mashing the potatoes?"

The large family kitchen was bustling with activity. The long white counter top was filled with serving bowls ready to be placed on the linen-covered dining room table. Sweet potato and pecan pies were cooling on the smaller kitchen table and the aroma of spice and turkey filled the house.

"Smells mighty good in here," Franklin Early proclaimed, sniffing appreciatively as he strolled into the kitchen and placed a loving arm around his wife's waist.

"Scat," Jo Marie's mother cried with a dismissive wave of her hand. "I won't have you in here sticking your fingers in the pies and blaming it on the boys. Dinner will be ready in ten minutes."

Mark arrived, red faced and slightly breathless. He kissed his mother on the cheek and when she wasn't looking, popped a sweet pickle into his mouth. "I hope I'm not too late."

"I'd say you had perfect timing," Jo Marie teased and handed him the electric mixer. "Here, mash these potatoes while I finish setting the table."

"No way, little sister." His mouth was twisted mockingly as he gave her back the appliance. "I'll set the table. No one wants lumpy potatoes."

The three younger boys, all in their teens, sat in front of the television watching a football game. The Early family enjoyed sports, especially football. Jo Marie's mother had despaired long ago that her only daughter would ever grow up properly. Instead of playing with dolls, her toys had been cowboy boots and little green army men. Touch football was as much a part of her life as ballet was for some girls.

With Mark out of the kitchen, Jo Marie's mother turned to her. "Have you been feeling all right lately?"

"Me?" The question caught her off guard. "I'm feeling fine. Why shouldn't I be?"

Ruth Early lifted one shoulder in a delicate shrug. "You've had a look in your eye lately." She turned and leaned her hip against the counter, her head tilted at a thoughtful angle. "The last time I saw that look was in your Aunt Bessie's eye before she was married. Tell me, Jo Marie, are you in love?"

Jo Marie hesitated, not knowing how to explain her feelings for a man she had met so briefly. He was more illusion than reality. Her own private fantasy. Those few moments with the dream man were beyond explaining, even to her own mother.

"No," she answered finally, making busy work by placing the serving spoons in the bowls.

"Is he married? Is that it? Save yourself a lot of grief, Jo Marie, and stay away from him if he is. You understand?"

"Yes," she murmured, her eyes avoiding her mother's. For all she knew he could well be married.

Not until late that night did Jo Marie let herself into her apartment. The day had been full. After the huge family dinner, they'd played cards until Mark trapped Jo Marie into playing a game of touch football for old times' sake. Jo Marie agreed and proved that she hadn't lost her "touch."

The apartment looked large and empty. Kelly stayed with her parents over any major holidays. Kelly's family seemed to feel that Kelly still belonged at home and always would, no matter what her age. Although Kelly was twenty-four, the apartment she shared with Jo Marie was more for convenience sake than any need to separate herself from her family.

With her mother's words echoing in her ear, Jo Marie sauntered into her bedroom and dressed for bed. Friday was a work day for her as it was for both Mark and Kelly. The downtown area of New Orleans would be hectic with Christmas shoppers hoping to pick up their gifts from the multitude of sales.

As a travel agent, Jo Marie didn't have many walk-in customers to deal with, but her phone rang continuously. Several people wanted to book holiday vacations, but there was little available that she could offer. The most popular vacation spots had been booked months in advance. Several times her information was accepted with an irritated grumble as if she were to blame. By the time she stepped off the bus outside her apartment, Jo Marie wasn't in any mood for company.

No sooner had the thought formed than she caught sight of her brother. He was parked in the lot outside the apartment building. Hungry and probably looking for a hot meal, she guessed. He knew that their mother had sent a good portion of the turkey and stuffing home with Jo Marie so Mark's appearance wasn't any real surprise.

"Hi," she said and knocked on his car window. The faraway look in his eyes convinced her that after all these years Mark had finally learned to sleep with his eyes open. He was so engrossed in his thoughts that Jo Marie was forced to tap on his window a second time.

"Paging Dr. Early," she mimicked in a high-pitched hospital voice. "Paging Dr. Mark Early."

Mark turned and stared at her blankly. "Oh, hi." He sat up and climbed out of the car.

"I suppose you want something to eat." Her greeting wasn't the least bit cordial, but she was tired and irritable.

The edge of Mark's mouth curled into a sheepish grin. "If it isn't too much trouble."

"No," she offered him an apologetic smile. "It's just been a rough day and my feet hurt."

"My sister sits in an office all day, files her nails, reads books and then complains that her feet hurt."

Jo Marie was too weary to rise to the bait. "Not even your acid tongue is going to get a rise out of me tonight."

"I know something that will," Mark returned smugly.

"Ha." From force of habit, Jo Marie kicked off her shoes and strolled into the kitchen.

"Wanna bet?"

"I'm not a betting person, especially after playing cards with you yesterday, but if you care to impress me, fire away." Crossing her arms, she leaned against the refrigerator door and waited.

"Kelly's engaged."

Jo Marie slowly shook her head in disbelief. "I didn't think you'd stoop to fabrications."

That familiar angry, hurt look stole into Mark's eyes. "It's true, I heard it from the horse's own mouth."

Lightly shaking her head from side to side to clear her thoughts, Jo Marie still came up with a blank. "But who?" Kelly wasn't going out with anyone seriously.

"Some cousin. Rich, no doubt," Mark said and straddled a kitchen chair. "She's got a diamond as big as a baseball. Must be hard for her to work with a rock that size weighing down her hand."

"A cousin?" New Orleans was full of Beaumonts, but none that Kelly had mentioned in particular. "I can't believe it," Jo Marie gasped. "She'd have said something to me."

"From what I understand, she tried to phone last night, but we were still at the folks' house. Just as well," Mark mumbled under his breath. "I'm not about to toast this engagement. First she plays at being nurse and now she wants to play at being a wife."

Mark's bitterness didn't register past the jolt of surprise that Jo Marie felt. "Kelly engaged," she repeated.

"You don't need to keep saying it," Mark snapped.

"Saying what?" A jubilant Kelly walked in the front door.

"Never mind," Mark said and slowly stood. "It's time for me to be going, I'll talk to you later."

"What about dinner?"

"There's someone I'd like you both to meet," Kelly announced.

Ignoring her, Mark turned to Jo Marie. "I've suddenly lost my appetite."

"Jo Marie, I'd like to introduce you to my fiancé, Andrew Beaumont."

Jo Marie's gaze swung from the frustrated look on her brother's face to an intense pair of gray eyes. There was only one man on earth with eyes the shade of a winter sea. The dream man.

Chapter Two

Stunned into speechlessness, Jo Marie struggled to maintain her composure. She took in a deep breath to calm her frantic heartbeat and forced a look of pleasant surprise. Andrew Beaumont apparently didn't even remember her. Jo Marie couldn't see so much as a flicker of recognition in the depth of his eyes. In the last nine months it was unlikely that he had given her more than a passing thought, if she'd been worthy of even that. And yet, she vividly remembered every detail of him, down to the crisp dark hair, the broad, muscular shoulders and faint twist of his mouth.

With an effort that was just short of superhuman, Jo Marie smiled. "Congratulations, you two. But what a surprise."

Kelly hurried across the room and hugged her tightly. "It was to us, too. Look." She held out her hand for Jo Marie to admire the flashing diamond. Mark hadn't been exaggerating. The flawless gem mounted in an antique setting was the largest Jo Marie had ever seen.

"What did I tell you," Mark whispered in her ear.

Confused, Kelly glanced from sister to brother. "Drew and I are celebrating tonight. We'd love it if you came. Both of you."

"No," Jo Marie and Mark declared in unison.

"I'm bushed," Jo Marie begged off.

"...and tired," Mark finished lamely.

For the first time, Andrew spoke. "We insist." The deep, resonant voice was exactly as Jo Marie remembered. But tonight there was something faintly arrogant in the way he spoke that dared Jo Marie and Mark to put up an argument.

Brother and sister exchanged questioning glances, neither willing to be drawn into the celebration. Each for their own reasons, Jo Marie mused.

"Well—" Mark cleared his throat, clearly ill at ease with the formidable fiancé "—perhaps another time."

"You're Jo Marie's brother?" Andrew asked with a mocking note.

"How'd you know?"

Kelly stuck her arm through Andrew's. "Family resemblance, silly. No one can look at the two of you and not know you're related."

"I can't say the same thing about you two. I thought it was against the law to marry a cousin." Mark didn't bother to disguise his contempt.

"We're distant cousins," Kelly explained brightly. Her eyes looked adoringly into Andrew's and Jo Marie felt her stomach tighten. Jealousy. This sickening feeling in the pit of her stomach was the green-eyed monster. Jo Marie had only experienced brief tastes of the emotion; now it filled her mouth until she thought she would choke on it.

"I...had a horribly busy day." Jo Marie sought frantically for an excuse to stay home.

"And I'd have to go home and change," Mark added, looking down over his pale gray cords and sport shirt.

"No, you wouldn't," Kelly contradicted with a provocative smile. "We're going to K-Paul's."

"Sure, and wait in line half the night." A muscle twitched in Mark's jaw.

K-Paul's was a renowned restaurant that was ranked sixth in the world. Famous, but not elegant. The small establishment served creole cooking at its best.

"No," Kelly supplied, and the dip in her voice revealed how much she wanted to share this night with her friends. "Andrew's a friend of Paul's."

Mark looked at Jo Marie and rolled his eyes. "I should have known," he muttered sarcastically.

"What time did you say we'd be there, darling?"

Jo Marie closed her eyes to the sharp flash of pain at the affectionate term Kelly used so freely. These jealous sensations were crazy. She had no right to feel this way. This man...Andrew Beaumont, was a blown-up figment of her imagination. The brief moments they shared should have been forgotten long ago. Kelly was her friend. Her best friend. And Kelly deserved every happiness.

With a determined jut to her chin, Jo Marie flashed her roommate a warm smile. "Mark and I would be honored to join you tonight."

"We would?" Mark didn't sound pleased. Irritation rounded his dark eyes and he flashed Jo Marie a look that openly contradicted her agreement. Jo Marie wanted to tell him that he owed Kelly this much for all the teasing he'd given her. In addition, her look pleaded with him to understand how much she needed his support tonight. Saying as much was impossible, but she hoped her eyes conveyed the message.

Jo Marie turned slightly so that she faced the tall figure standing only a few inches from her. "It's generous of you to include us," she murmured, but discovered that she was incapable of meeting Andrew's penetrating gaze.

"Give us a minute to freshen up and we'll be on our way," Kelly's effervescent enthusiasm filled the room. "Come on, Jo Marie."

The two men remained in the compact living room. Jo Marie glanced back to note that Mark looked like a jaguar trapped in an iron cage. When he wasn't pacing, he stood restlessly shifting his weight repeatedly from one foot to the other. His look was weary and there was an uncharacteristic tightness to his mouth that narrowed his eyes.

"What do you think," Kelly whispered, and gave a long sigh. "Isn't he fantastic? I think I'm the luckiest girl in the world. Of course, we'll have to wait until after the holidays to make our announcement official. But isn't Drew wonderful?"

Jo Marie forced a noncommittal nod. The raw disappointment left an aching void in her heart. Andrew should have been hers. "He's wonderful." The words came out sounding more like a tortured whisper than a compliment.

Kelly paused, lowering the brush. "Jo, are you all right? You sound like you're going to cry."

"Maybe I am." Tears burned for release, but not for the reason Kelly assumed. "It's not every day I lose my best friend."

"But you're not losing me."

Jo Marie's fingers curved around the cold bathroom sink. "But you are planning to get married?"

"Oh yes, we'll make an official announcement in January, but we haven't set a definite date for the wedding."

That surprised Jo Marie. Andrew didn't look like the kind of man who would encourage a long engagement. She would have thought that once he'd made a decision, he'd move on it. But then, she didn't know Andrew Beaumont. Not really.

A glance in the mirror confirmed that her cheeks were pale, her dark eyes haunted with a wounded, perplexed look. A quick application of blush added color to her bloodless face, but there was little she could do to disguise the troubled look in her eyes. She could only pray that no one would notice.

"Ready?" Kelly stood just outside the open door.

Jo Marie's returning smile was frail as she mentally braced herself for the coming ordeal. She paused long enough to dab perfume to the pulse points at the hollow of her neck and at her wrists.

"I, for one, am starved," Kelly announced as they returned to the living room. "And from what I remember of K-Paul's, eating is an experience we won't forget."

Jo Marie was confident that every part of this evening would be indelibly marked in her memory, but not for the reasons Kelly assumed.

Andrew's deep blue Mercedes was parked beside Mark's old clunker. The differences between the two men were as obvious as the vehicles they drove.

Clearly ill at ease, Mark stood on the sidewalk in front of his car. "Why don't Jo Marie and I follow you?"

"Nonsense," Kelly returned, "there's plenty of room in Drew's car for everyone. You know what the traffic is like. We could get separated. I wouldn't want that to happen."

Mark's twisted mouth said that he would have given a weeks' pay to suddenly disappear. Jo Marie studied her brother carefully from her position in the back seat. His displeasure at being included in this evening's celebration was confusing. There was far more than reluctance in his attitude. He might not get along with Kelly, but she would have thought that Mark would wish Kelly every happiness. But he didn't. Not by the stiff, unnatural behavior she'd witnessed from him tonight.

Mark's attitude didn't change any at the restaurant. Paul, the robust chef, came out from the kitchen and greeted the party himself.

After they'd ordered, the small party sat facing one another in stony silence. Kelly made a couple of attempts to start up the conversation, but her efforts were to no avail. The two men eyed each other, looking as if they were ready to do battle at the slightest provocation.

Several times while they ate their succulent Shrimp Remoulade, Jo Marie found her gaze drawn to Andrew. In many ways he was exactly as she remembered. In others, he was completely different. His voice was low pitched and had a faint drawl. And he wasn't a talker. His expression was sober almost to the point of being somber, which was unusual for a man celebrating his engagement. Another word that her mind tossed out was disillusioned. Andrew Beaumont looked as though he was disenchanted with life. From everything she'd learned he was wealthy and successful. He owned a land development firm. Delta Development, Inc. had been in the Beaumont family for three generations. According to Kelly, the firm had expanded extensively under Andrew's direction.

But if Jo Marie was paying attention to Andrew, he was nothing more than polite to her. He didn't acknowledge her with anything more than an occasional look. And since she hadn't directed any questions to him, he hadn't spoken either. At least not to her.

Paul's special touch for creole cooking made the meal memorable. And although her thoughts were troubled and her heart perplexed, when the waitress took Jo Marie's plate away she had done justice to the meal. Even Mark, who had sat uncommunicative and sullen through most of the dinner, had left little on his plate.

After K-Paul's, Kelly insisted they visit the French Quarter. The others were not as enthusiastic. After an hour of walking around and sampling some of the best jazz sounds New Orleans had to offer, they returned to the apartment.

"I'll make the coffee," Kelly proposed as they climbed from the luxury car.

Mark made a show of glancing at his watch. "I think I'll skip the chicory," he remarked in a flippant tone. "Tomorrow's a busy day."

"Come on, Mark—" Kelly pouted prettily "—don't be a spoil sport."

Mark's face darkened with a scowl. "If you insist."

"It isn't every day I celebrate my engagement. And, Mark, have you noticed that we haven't fought once all night? That must be some kind of a record."

A poor facsimile of a smile lifted one corner of his mouth. "It must be," he agreed wryly. He lagged behind as they climbed the stairs to the second-story apartment.

Jo Marie knew her brother well enough to know he'd have the coffee and leave as soon as it was polite to do so.

They sat in stilted silence, drinking their coffee.

"Do you two work together?" Andrew directed his question to Jo Marie.

Flustered she raised her palm to her breast. "Me?"

"Yes. Did you and Kelly meet at Tulane Hospital?"

"No, I'm a travel agent. Mark's the one in the family with the brains." She heard the breathlessness in her voice and hoped that he hadn't.

"Don't put yourself down," Kelly objected. "You're no dummy. Did you know that Jo Marie is actively involved in saving our wetlands? She volunteers her time as an office worker for the Land For The Future organization."

"That doesn't require intelligence, only time," Jo Marie murmured self-consciously and congratulated herself for keeping her voice even.

For the first time that evening, Andrew directed his attention to her and smiled. The effect it had on Jo Marie's pulse was devastating. To disguise her reaction, she raised the delicate china cup to her lips and took a tentative sip of the steaming coffee.

"And all these years I thought the LFTF was for little old ladies."

"No." Jo Marie was able to manage only the one word.

"At one time Jo Marie wanted to be a biologist," Kelly supplied.

Andrew arched two thick brows. "What stopped you?"

"Me," Mark cut in defensively. "The schooling she required was extensive and our parents couldn't afford to pay for us both to attend university at the same time. Jo Marie decided to drop out."

"That's not altogether true." Mark was making her sound noble and self-sacrificing. "It wasn't like that. If I'd wanted to continue my schooling there were lots of ways I could have done so."

"And you didn't?" Again Andrew's attention was focused on her.

She moistened her dry lips before continuing. "No. I plan to go back to school someday. Until then I'm staying active in the causes that mean the most to me and to the future of New Orleans."

"Jo Marie's our neighborhood scientist," Kelly added proudly. "She has a science club for children every other Saturday morning. I swear she's a natural with those kids. She's always taking them on hikes and planning field trips for them."

"You must like children." Again Andrew's gaze slid to Jo Marie.

"Yes," she answered self-consciously and lowered her eyes. She was grateful when the topic of conversation drifted to other subjects. When she chanced a look at Andrew, she discovered that his gaze centered on her lips. It took a great deal of restraint not to moisten them. And even more to force the memory of his kiss from her mind.

Once again, Mark made a show of looking at his watch and standing. "The evening's been—" he faltered looking for an adequate description "—interesting. Nice meeting you, Beaumont. Best wishes to you and Florence Nightingale."

The sip of coffee stuck in Jo Marie's throat, causing a moment of intense pain until her muscles relaxed enough to allow her to swallow. Grateful that no one had noticed, Jo Marie set her cup aside and walked with her brother to the front door. "I'll talk to you later," she said in farewell.

Mark wiped a hand across his eyes. He looked more tired than Jo Marie could remember seeing him in a long time. "I've been dying to ask you all night. Isn't Kelly's rich friend the one who filled in the swampland for that housing development you fought so hard against?"

"And lost." Jo Marie groaned inwardly. She had been a staunch supporter of the environmentalists and had helped gather signatures against the project. But to no avail. "Then he's also the one who bought out Rose's," she murmured thoughtfully as a feeling of dread washed over her. Rose's Hotel was in the French Quarter and was one of the landmarks of Louisiana. In addition to being a part of New Orleans' history, the hotel was used to house transients. It was true that Rose's was badly in need of repairs, but Jo Marie hated to see the wonderful old building destroyed in the name of progress. If annihilating the breeding habitat of a hundred different species of birds hadn't troubled Andrew Beaumont, then she doubted that an old hotel in ill-repair would matter to him either.

Rubbing her temple to relieve an unexpected and throbbing headache, Jo Marie nodded. "I remember Kelly saying something about a cousin being responsible for Rose's. But I hadn't put the two together."

"He has," Mark countered disdainfully. "And come up with megabucks. Our little Kelly has reeled in quite a catch, if you like the cold, heartless sort."

Jo Marie's mind immediately rejected that thought. Andrew Beaumont may be the man responsible for several controversial land acquisitions, but he wasn't heartless. Five minutes with him at the Mardi Gras had proven otherwise.

Mark's amused chuckle carried into the living room. "You've got that battle look in your eye. What are you thinking?"

"Nothing," she returned absently. But already her mind was racing furiously. "I'll talk to you tomorrow."

"I'll give you a call," Mark promised and was gone.

When Jo Marie returned to the living room, she found Kelly and Andrew chatting companionably. They paused and glanced at her as she rejoined them.

"You've known each other for a long time, haven't you?" Jo Marie lifted the half-full china cup, making an excuse to linger. She sat on the arm of the love seat, unable to decide if she should stay and speak her mind or repress her tongue.

"We've known each other since childhood." Kelly answered for the pair.

"And Andrew is the distant cousin you said had bought Rose's."

Kelly's sigh was uncomfortable. "I was hoping you wouldn't put two and two together."

"To be honest, I didn't. Mark figured it out."

A frustrated look tightened Kelly's once happy features.

"Will someone kindly tell me what you two are talking about?" Andrew asked.

"Rose's," they chimed in unison.

"Rose's," he repeated slowly and a frown appeared between his gray eyes.

Apparently Andrew Beaumont had so much land one small hotel didn't matter.

"The hotel."

The unexpected sharpness in his voice caused Jo Marie to square her shoulders. "It may seem like a little thing to you."

"Not for what that piece of land cost me," he countered in a hard voice.

"I don't think Drew likes to mix business with pleasure," Kelly warned, but Jo Marie disregarded the well-intended advice.

"But the men living in Rose's will have nowhere to go."

"They're bums."

A sadness filled her at the insensitive way he referred to these men. "Rose's had housed homeless men for twenty years. These men need someplace where they can get a hot meal and can sleep."

"It's a prime location for luxury condominiums," he said cynically.

"But what about the transients? What will become of them?"

"That, Miss Early, is no concern of mine."

Unbelievably Jo Marie felt tears burn behind her eyes. She blinked them back. Andrew Beaumont wasn't the dream man she'd fantasized over all these months. He was cold and cynical. The only love he had in his life was profit. A sadness settled over her with a weight she thought would be crippling.

"I feel very sorry for you, Mr. Beaumont," she said smoothly, belying her turbulent emotions. "You may be very rich, but there's no man poorer than one who has no tolerance for the weakness of others."

Kelly gasped softly and groaned. "I knew this was going to happen."

"Are you always so opinionated, Miss Early?" There was no disguising the icy tones.

"No, but there are times when things are so wrong that I can't remain silent." She turned to Kelly. "I apologize if I've ruined your evening. If you'll excuse me now, I think I'll go to bed. Good night, Mr. Beaumont. May you and Kelly have many years of happiness together." The words nearly stuck in her throat but she managed to get them out before walking from the room.

"If this offends you in any way I won't do it." Jo Marie studied her roommate carefully. The demonstration in front of Rose's had been planned weeks ago. Jo Marie's wooden picket sign felt heavy in her hand. For the first time in her life, her convictions conflicted with her feelings. She didn't want to march against Andrew. It didn't matter what he'd done, but she couldn't stand by and see those poor men turned into the streets, either. Not in the name of progress. Not when progress was at the cost of the less fortunate and the fate of a once lovely hotel.

"This picket line was arranged long before you met Drew."

"That hasn't got anything to do with this. Drew is important to you. I wouldn't want to do something that will place your relationship with him in jeopardy."

"It won't."

Kelly sounded far more confident than Jo Marie felt.

"In fact," she continued, "I doubt that Drew even knows anything about the demonstration. Those things usually do nothing to sway his decision. In fact, I'd say they do more harm than good as far as he's concerned."

Jo Marie had figured that much out herself, but she couldn't stand by doing nothing. Rose's was scheduled to be shut down the following week...a short month before Christmas. Jo Marie didn't know how anyone could be so heartless. The hotel was to be torn down a week later and new construction was scheduled to begin right after the first of the year.

Kelly paused at the front door while Jo Marie picked up her picket sign and tossed the long strap of her purse over her shoulder.

"You do understand why I can't join you?" she asked hesitatingly.

"Of course," Jo Marie said and exhaled softly. She'd never expected Kelly to participate. This fight couldn't include her friend without causing bitter feelings.

"Be careful." Her arms wrapped around her waist to chase away a chill, Kelly walked down to the parking lot with Jo Marie.

"Don't worry. This is a peaceful demonstration. The only wounds I intend to get are from carrying this sign. It's heavy."

Cocking her head sideways, Kelly read the sign for the tenth time. Save Rose's Hotel. A Piece Of New

Orleans History. Kelly chuckled and slowly shook her head. "I should get a picture of you. Drew would get a real kick out of that."

The offer of a picture was a subtle reminder that Drew wouldn't so much as see the sign. He probably wasn't even aware of the protest rally.

Friends of Rose's and several others from the Land For The Future headquarters were gathered outside the hotel when Jo Marie arrived. Several people who knew Jo Marie raised their hands in welcome.

"Have the television and radio stations been notified?" the organizer asked a tall man Jo Marie didn't recognize.

"I notified them, but most weren't all that interested. I doubt that we'll be given air time."

A feeling of gloom settled over the group. An unexpected cloudburst did little to brighten their mood. Jo Marie hadn't brought her umbrella and was drenched in minutes. A chill caused her teeth to chatter and no matter how hard she tried, she couldn't stop shivering. Uncaring, the rain fell indiscriminately over the small group of protesters.

"You little fool," Mark said when he found her an hour later. "Are you crazy, walking around wet and cold like that?" His voice was a mixture of exasperation and pride.

"I'm making a statement," Jo Marie argued.

"You're right. You're telling the world what a fool you are. Don't you have any better sense than this?"

Jo Marie ignored him, placing one foot in front of the other as she circled the sidewalk in front of Rose's Hotel.

"Do you think Beaumont cares?"

Jo Marie refused to be drawn into his argument. "Instead of arguing with me, why don't you go inside and see what's holding up the coffee?"

"You're going to need more than a hot drink to prevent you from getting pneumonia. Listen to reason for once in your life."

"No!" Emphatically Jo Marie stamped her foot. "This is too important."

"And your health isn't?"

"Not now." The protest group had dwindled down to less than ten. "I'll be all right." She shifted the sign from one shoulder to the other and flexed her stiff fingers. Her back ached from the burden of her message. And with every step the rain water in her shoes squished noisily. "I'm sure we'll be finished in another hour."

"If you aren't, I'm carting you off myself," Mark shouted angrily and returned to his car. He shook his finger at her in warning as he drove past.

True to his word, Mark returned an hour later and followed her back to the apartment.

Jo Marie could hardly drive she was shivering so violently. Her long chestnut hair fell in limp tendrils over her face. Rivulets of cold water ran down her neck and she bit into her bottom lip at the pain caused by gripping the steering wheel. Carrying the sign had formed painful blisters in the palms of her hands. This was one protest rally she wouldn't soon forget.

Mark seemed to blame Andrew Beaumont for the fact that she was cold, wet and miserable. But it wasn't Andrew's fault that it had rained. Not a single forecaster had predicted it would. She'd lived in New Orleans long enough to know she should carry an umbrella with her. Mark was looking for an excuse to dislike Andrew. Any excuse. In her heart, Jo Marie couldn't. No matter what he'd done, there was something deep within her that wouldn't allow any bitterness inside. In some ways she was disillusioned and hurt that her dream man wasn't all she'd thought. But that was as deep as her resentments went.

"Little fool," Mark repeated tenderly as he helped her out of the car. "Let's get you upstairs and into a hot bath."

"As long as I don't have to listen to you lecture all night," she said, her teeth chattering as she climbed the stairs to the second-story apartment. Although she was thoroughly miserable, there was a spark of humor in her eyes as she opened the door and stepped inside the apartment.

"Jo Marie," Kelly cried in alarm. "Good grief, what happened?"

A light laugh couldn't disguise her shivering. "Haven't you looked out the window lately? It's raining cats and dogs."

"This is your fault, Beaumont," Mark accused harshly and Jo Marie sucked in a surprised breath. In her misery, she hadn't noticed Andrew, who was casually sitting on the love seat.

He rose to a standing position and glared at Mark as if her brother were a mad man. "Explain yourself," he demanded curtly.

Kelly intervened, crossing the room and placing a hand on Andrew's arm. "Jo Marie was marching in that rally I was telling you about."

"In front of Rose's Hotel," Mark added, his fists tightly clenched at his side. He looked as if he wanted to get physical. Consciously, Jo Marie moved closer to her brother's side. Fist fighting was so unlike Mark.

He was a healer, not a boxer. One look told Jo Marie that in a physical exchange, Mark would lose.

Andrew's mouth twisted scornfully. "You, my dear Miss Early, are a fool."

Jo Marie dipped her head mockingly. "And you, Mr. Beaumont, are heartless."

"But rich," Mark intervened. "And money goes a long way in making a man attractive. Isn't that right, Kelly?"

Kelly went visibly pale, her blue eyes filling with tears. "That's not true," she cried, her words jerky as she struggled for control.

"You will apologize for that remark, Early." Andrew's low voice held a threat that was undeniable.

Mark knotted and unknotted his fists. "I won't apologize for the truth. If you want to step outside, maybe you'd like to make something of it."

"Mark!" Both Jo Marie and Kelly gasped in shocked disbelief.

Jo Marie moved first. "Get out of here before you cause trouble." Roughly she opened the door and shoved him outside.

"You heard what I said," Mark growled on his way out the door.

"I've never seen Mark behave like that," Jo Marie murmured, her eyes lowered to the carpet where a small pool of water had formed. "I can only apologize." She paused and inhaled deeply. "And, Kelly, I'm sure you know he didn't mean what he said to you. He's upset because of the rally." Her voice was deep with emotion as she excused herself and headed for the bathroom.

A hot bath went a long way toward making her more comfortable. Mercifully, Andrew was gone by the time she had finished. She didn't feel up to another confrontation with him.

"Call on line three."

Automatically Jo Marie punched in the button and reached for her phone. "Jo Marie Early, may I help you?"

"You won."

"Mark?" He seldom phoned her at work.

"Did you hear me?" he asked excitedly.

"What did I win?" she asked humoring him.

"Beaumont."

Jo Marie's hand tightened around the receiver. "What do you mean?"

"It just came over the radio. Delta Development, Inc. is donating Rose's Hotel to the city," Mark announced with a short laugh. "Can you believe it?"

"Yes," Jo Marie closed her eyes to the onrush of emotion. Her dream man hadn't let her down. "I can believe it."

Chapter Three

"But you must come," Kelly insisted, sitting across from Jo Marie. "It'll be miserable without you."

"Kell, I don't know." Jo Marie looked up from the magazine she was reading and nibbled on her lower lip.

"It's just a Christmas party with a bunch of stuffy people I don't know. You know how uncomfortable I am meeting new people. I hate parties."

"Then why attend?"

"Drew says we must. I'm sure he doesn't enjoy the party scene any more than I do, but he's got to go or offend a lot of business acquaintances."

"But I wasn't included in the invitation," Jo Marie argued. She'd always liked people and usually did well at social functions.

"Of course you were included. Both you and Mark," Kelly insisted. "Drew saw to that."

Thoughtfully, Jo Marie considered her roommate's request. As much as she objected, she really would like to go, if for no more reason than to thank Andrew for his generosity regarding Rose's. Although she'd seen him briefly a couple of times since, the opportunity hadn't presented itself to express her appreciation. The party was one way she could do that. New Orleans was famous for its festive balls and holiday parties. Without Kelly's invitation, Jo Marie doubted that there would ever be the chance for her to attend such an elaborate affair.

"All right," she conceded, "but I doubt that Mark will come." Mark and Andrew hadn't spoken since the last confrontation in the girls' living room. The air had hung heavy between them then and Jo Marie doubted that Andrew's decision regarding Rose's Hotel would change her brother's attitude.

"Leave Mark to me," Kelly said confidently. "Just promise me that you'll be there."

"I'll need a dress." Mentally Jo Marie scanned the contents of her closet and came up with zero. Nothing she owned would be suitable for such an elaborate affair.

"Don't worry, you can borrow something of mine," Kelly offered with a generosity that was innate to her personality.

Jo Marie nearly choked on her laughter. "I'm three inches taller than you." And several pounds heavier, but she preferred not to mention that. Only once before had Jo Marie worn Kelly's clothes. The night she'd met Andrew.

Kelly giggled and the bubbly sound was pleasant to the ears. "I heard miniskirts were coming back into style."

"Perhaps, but I doubt that the fashion will arrive in time for Christmas. Don't worry about me, I'll go out this afternoon and pick up some material for a dress."

"But will you have enough time between now and the party to sew it?" Kelly's blue eyes rounded with doubt.

"I'll make time." Jo Marie was an excellent seamstress. She had her mother to thank for that. Ruth Early had insisted that her only daughter learn to sew. Jo Marie had balked in the beginning. Her interests were anything but domestic. But now, as she had been several times in the past, she was grateful for the skill.

She found a pattern of a three-quarter-length dress with a matching jacket. The simplicity of the design made the outfit all the more appealing. Jo Marie could dress it either up or down, depending on the occasion. The silky, midnight blue material she purchased was perfect for the holiday, and Jo Marie knew that shade to be one of her better colors.

When she returned to the apartment, Kelly was gone. A note propped on the kitchen table explained that she wouldn't be back until dinner time.

After washing, drying, and carefully pressing the material, Jo Marie laid it out on the table for cutting. Intent on her task, she had pulled her hair away from her face and had tied it at the base of her neck with a rubber band. Straight pins were pressed between her lips when the doorbell chimed. The neighborhood children often stopped in for a visit. Usually Jo Marie welcomed their company, but she was busy now and interruptions could result in an irreparable mistake. She toyed with the idea of not answering.

The impatient buzz told her that her company was irritated at being kept waiting.

"Damn, damn, damn," she grumbled beneath her breath as she made her way across the room. Extracting the straight pins from her mouth, she stuck them in the small cushion she wore around her wrist.

"Andrew!" Secretly she thanked God the pins were out of her mouth or she would have swallowed them in her surprise.

"Is Kelly here?"

"No, but come in." Her heart was racing madly as he walked into the room. Nervous fingers tugged the rubber band from her chestnut hair in a futile attempt to look more presentable. She shook her hair free, then wished she'd kept it neatly in place. For days Jo Marie would have welcomed the opportunity to thank Andrew, but she discovered as she followed him into the living room that her tongue was tied and her mouth felt gritty and dry. "I'm glad you're here...I wanted to thank you for your decision about Rose's...the hotel."

He interrupted her curtly. "My dear Miss Early, don't be misled. My decision wasn't—"

Her hand stopped him. "I know," she said softly. He didn't need to tell her his reasoning. She was already aware it wasn't because of the rally or anything that she'd done or said. "I just wanted to thank you for whatever may have been your reason."

Their eyes met and held from across the room. Countless moments passed in which neither spoke. The air was electric between them and the urge to reach out and touch Andrew was almost overwhelming. The same breathlessness that had attacked her the night of the Mardi Gras returned. Andrew had to remember, he had to. Yet he gave no indication that he did.

Jo Marie broke eye contact first, lowering her gaze to the wool carpet. "I'm not sure where Kelly is, but she said she'd be back by dinner time." Her hand shook as she handed him the note off the kitchen counter.

"Kelly mentioned the party?"

Jo Marie nodded.

"You'll come?"

She nodded her head in agreement. "If I finish sewing this dress in time." She spoke so he wouldn't think she'd suddenly lost the ability to talk. Never had she been more aware of a man. Her heart was hammering at his nearness. He was so close all she had to do was reach out and touch him. But insurmountable barriers stood between them. At last, after all these months she was alone with her dream man. So many times a similar scene had played in her mind. But Andrew didn't remember her. The realization produced an indescribable ache in her heart. What had been the most profound moment in her life had been nothing to him.

"Would you like to sit down?" she offered, remembering her manners. "There's coffee on if you'd like a cup."

He shook his head. "No, thanks." He ran his hand along the top of the blue cloth that was stretched across the kitchen table. His eyes narrowed and he looked as if his thoughts were a thousand miles away.

"Why don't you buy a dress?"

A smile trembled at the edge of her mouth. To a man who had always had money, buying something as simple as a dress would seem the most logical solution.

"I sew most of my own things," she explained softly, rather than enlightening him with a lecture on economics.

"Did you make this?" His fingers touched the short sleeve of her cotton blouse and brushed against the sensitive skin of her upper arm.

Immediately a warmth spread where his fingers had come into contact with her flesh. Jo Marie's pale cheeks instantly flushed with a crimson flood of color. "Yes," she admitted hoarsely, hating the way her body, her voice, everything about her, was affected by this man.

"You do beautiful work."

She kept her eyes lowered and drew in a steadying breath. "Thank you."

"Next weekend I'll be having a Christmas party at my home for the employees of my company. I would be honored if both you and your brother attended."

Already her heart was racing with excitement; she'd love to visit his home. But seeing where he lived was only an excuse. She'd do anything to see more of him. "I can't speak for Mark," she answered after several moments, feeling guilty for her thoughts.

"But you'll come?"

"I'd be happy to. Thank you." Her only concern was that no one from Delta Development would recognize her as the same woman who was active in the protest against the housing development and in saving Rose's Hotel.

"Good," he said gruffly.

The curve of her mouth softened into a smile. "I'll tell Kelly that you were by. Would you like her to phone you?"

"No, I'll be seeing her later. Goodbye, Jo Marie."

She walked with him to the door, holding onto the knob longer than necessary. "Goodbye, Andrew," she murmured.

Jo Marie leaned against the door and covered her face with both hands. She shouldn't be feeling this eager excitement, this breathless bewilderment, this softness inside at the mere thought of him. Andrew Beaumont was her roommate's fiancé. She had to remember that. But somehow, Jo Marie recognized that her conscience could repeat the information all day, but it would have little effect on her restless heart.

The sewing machine was set up at the table when Kelly walked into the apartment a couple of hours later.

"I'm back," Kelly murmured happily as she hung her sweater in the closet.

"Where'd you go?"

"To see a friend."

Jo Marie thought she detected a note of hesitancy in her roommate's voice and glanced up momentarily from her task. She paused herself, then said, "Andrew was by."

A look of surprise worked its way across Kelly's pixie face. "Really? Did he say what he wanted?"

"Not really. He didn't leave a message." Jo Marie strove for nonchalance, but her fingers shook slightly and she hoped that her friend didn't notice the telltale mannerism.

"You like Drew, don't you?"

For some reason, Jo Marie's mind had always referred to him as Andrew. "Yes." She continued with the mechanics of sewing, but she could feel Kelly's eyes roam over her face as she studied her. Immediately a guilty flush reddened her cheeks. Somehow, some way, Kelly had detected how strongly Jo Marie felt about Andrew.

"I'm glad," Kelly said at last. "I'd like it if you two would fall in..." She hesitated before concluding with, "Never mind."

The two words were repeated in her mind like the dwindling sounds of an echo off canyon walls.

The following afternoon, Jo Marie arrived home from work and took a crisp apple from the bottom shelf of the refrigerator. She wanted a snack before pulling out her sewing machine again. Kelly was working late and had phoned her at the office so Jo Marie wouldn't worry. Holding the apple between her teeth, she lugged the heavy sewing machine out of the bedroom. No sooner had she set the case on top of the table than the doorbell chimed.

Releasing a frustrated sigh, she swallowed the bite of apple.

"Sign here, please." A clipboard was shoved under her nose.

"I beg your pardon," Jo Marie asked.

"I'm making a delivery, lady. Sign here."

"Oh." Maybe Kelly had ordered something without telling her. Quickly, she penned her name along the bottom line.

"Wait here," was the next abrupt instruction.

Shrugging her shoulder, Jo Marie leaned against the door jamb as the brusque man returned to the brown truck parked below and brought up two large boxes.

"Merry Christmas, Miss Early," he said with a sheepish grin as he handed her the delivery.

"Thank you." The silver box was the trademark of New Orleans' most expensive boutique. Gilded lettering wrote out the name of the proprietor, Madame

Renaux Marceau, across the top. Funny, Jo Marie couldn't recall Kelly saying she'd bought something there. But with the party coming, Kelly had apparently opted for the expensive boutique.

Dutifully Jo Marie carried the boxes into Kelly's room and set them on the bed. As she did so the shipping order attached to the smaller box, caught her eye. The statement was addressed to her, not Kelly.

Inhaling a jagged breath, Jo Marie searched the order blank to find out who would be sending her anything. Her parents could never have afforded something from Madame Renaux Marceau.

The air was sucked from her lungs as Jo Marie discovered Andrew Beaumont's name. She fumbled with the lids, peeled back sheer paper and gasped at the beauty of what lay before her. The full-length blue dress was the same midnight shade as the one she was sewing. But this gown was unlike anything Jo Marie had ever seen. A picture of Christmas, a picture of elegance. She held it up and felt tears prickle the back of her eyes. The bodice was layered with intricate rows of tiny pearls that formed a V at the waist. The gown was breathtakingly beautiful. Never had Jo Marie thought to own anything so perfect or so lovely. The second box contained a matching cape with an ornate display of tiny pearls.

Very carefully, Jo Marie folded the dress and cape and placed them back into the boxes. An ache inside her heart erupted into a broken sob. She wasn't a charity case. Did Andrew assume that because she sewed her own clothes that what she was making for the party would be unpresentable?

The telephone book revealed the information she needed. Following her instincts, Jo Marie grabbed a sweater and rushed out the door. She didn't stop until she pulled up in front of the large brick building with the gold plaque in the front that announced that this was the headquarters for Delta Development, Inc.

A listing of offices in the foyer told her where Andrew's was located. Jo Marie rode the elevator to the third floor. Most of the building was deserted, only a few employees remained. Those that did gave her curious stares, but no one questioned her presence.

The office door that had Andrew's name lettered on it was closed, but that didn't dissuade Jo Marie. His receptionist was placing the cover over her typewriter when Jo Marie barged inside.

"I'd like to see Mr. Beaumont," she demanded in a breathless voice.

The gray-haired receptionist glanced at the boxes under Jo Marie's arms and shook her head. "I'm sorry, but the office is closed for the day."

Jo Marie caught the subtle difference. "I didn't ask about the office. I said I wanted to see Mr. Beaumont." Her voice rose with her frustration.

A connecting door between two rooms opened. "Is there a problem, Mrs. Stewart?"

"I was just telling..."

"Jo Marie." Andrew's voice was an odd mixture of surprise and gruffness, yet gentle. His narrowed look centered on the boxes clasped under each arm. "Is there a problem?"

"As a matter of fact there is," she said, fighting to disguise the anger that was building within her to volcanic proportions.

Andrew stepped aside to admit her into his office.

"Will you be needing me further?" Jo Marie heard his secretary ask.

"No, thank you, Mrs. Stewart. I'll see you in the morning."

No sooner had Andrew stepped in the door than Jo Marie whirled on him. The silver boxes from the boutique sat squarely in the middle of Andrew's huge oak desk.

"I think you should understand something right now, Mr. Beaumont," she began heatedly, not bothering to hold back her annoyance. "I am not Cinderella and you most definitely are not my fairy godfather."

"Would I be amiss to guess that my gift displeases you?"

Jo Marie wanted to scream at him for being so calm. She cut her long nails into her palms in an effort to disguise her irritation. "If I am an embarrassment to you wearing a dress I've sewn myself, then I'll simply not attend your precious party."

He looked shocked.

"And furthermore, I am no one's poor relation."

An angry frown deepened three lines across his wide forehead. "What makes you suggest such stupidity?"

"I may be many things, but stupid isn't one of them."

"A lot of things?" He stood behind his desk and leaned forward, pressing his weight on his palms. "You mean like opinionated, headstrong, and impatient."

"Yes," she cried and shot her index finger into the air. "But not stupid."

The tight grip Andrew held on his temper was visible by the way his mouth was pinched until the grooves stood out tense and white. "Maybe not stupid, but incredibly inane."

Her mouth was trembling and Jo Marie knew that if she didn't get away soon, she'd cry. "Let's not argue over definitions. Stated simply, the gesture of buying me a presentable dress was not appreciated. Not in the least."

"I gathered that much, Miss Early. Now if you'll excuse me, I have a dinner engagement."

"Gladly." She pivoted and stormed across the floor ready to jerk open the office door. To her dismay, the door stuck and wouldn't open, ruining her haughty exit.

"Allow me," Andrew offered bitterly.

The damn door! It would have to ruin her proud retreat.

By the time she was in the parking lot, most of her anger had dissipated. Second thoughts crowded her mind on the drive back to the apartment. She could have at least been more gracious about it. Second thoughts quickly evolved into constant recriminations so that by the time she walked through the doorway of the apartment, Jo Marie was thoroughly miserable.

"Hi." Kelly was mixing raw hamburger for meatloaf with her hands. "Did the dress arrive?"

Kelly knew! "Dress?"

"Yes. Andrew and I went shopping for you yesterday afternoon and found the most incredibly lovely party dress. It was perfect for you."

Involuntarily, Jo Marie stiffened. "What made you think I needed a dress?"

Kelly's smile was filled with humor. "You were sewing one, weren't you? Drew said that you were really attending this function as a favor to me. And since this is such a busy time of year he didn't want you spending your nights slaving over a sewing machine."

"Oh." A sickening feeling attacked the pit of her stomach.

"Drew can be the most thoughtful person," Kelly commented as she continued to blend the ground meat. Her attention was more on her task than on Jo Marie. "You can understand why it's so easy to love him."

A strangled sound made its way past the tightness in Jo Marie's throat.

"I'm surprised the dress hasn't arrived. Drew gave specific instructions that it was to be delivered today in case any alterations were needed."

"It did come," Jo Marie announced, more miserable than she could ever remember being.

"It did?" Excitement elevated Kelly's voice. "Why didn't you say something? Isn't it the most beautiful dress you've ever seen? You're going to be gorgeous." Kelly's enthusiasm waned as she turned around. "Jo, what's wrong? You look like you're ready to burst into tears."

"That's...that's because I am," she managed and covering her face with her hands, she sat on the edge of the sofa and wept.

Kelly's soft laugh only made everything seem worse. "I expected gratitude," Kelly said with a sigh and handed Jo Marie a tissue. "But certainly not tears. You don't cry that often."

Noisily Jo Marie blew her nose. "I...I thought I was an embarrassment...to you two...that...you didn't want me...at the party...because I didn't have...the proper clothes...and..."

"You thought what?" Kelly interrupted, a shocked, hurt look crowding her face. "I can't believe you'd even think anything so crazy."

"That's not all. I..." She swallowed. "I took the dress to...Andrew's office and practically...threw it in his face."

"Oh, Jo Marie." Kelly lowered herself onto the sofa beside her friend. "How could you?"

"I don't know. Maybe it sounds ridiculous, but I really believed that you and Andrew would be ashamed to be seen with me in an outfit I'd made myself."

"How could you come up with something so dumb? Especially since I've always complimented you on the things you've sewn."

Miserably, Jo Marie bowed her head. "I know."

"You've really done it, but good, my friend. I can just imagine Drew's reaction to your visit." At the thought Kelly's face grew tight. "Now what are you going to do?"

"Nothing. From this moment on I'll be conveniently tucked in my room when he comes for you..."

"What about the party?" Kelly's blue eyes were rounded with childlike fright and Jo Marie could only speculate whether it was feigned or real. "It's only two days away."

"I can't go, certainly you can understand that."

"But you've got to come," Kelly returned adamantly. "Mark said he'd go if you were there and I need you both. Everything will be ruined if you back out now."

"Mark's coming?" Jo Marie had a difficult time believing her brother would agree to this party idea.

She'd have thought Mark would do anything to avoid another confrontation with Andrew.

"Yes. And it wasn't easy to get him to agree."

"I can imagine," Jo Marie returned dryly.

"Jo Marie, please. Your being there means so much to me. More than you'll ever know. Do this one thing and I promise I won't ask another thing of you as long as I live."

Kelly was serious. Something about this party was terribly important to her. Jo Marie couldn't understand what. In order to attend the party she would need to apologize to Andrew. If it had been her choice she would have waited a week or two before approaching him, giving him the necessary time to cool off. As it was, she'd be forced to do it before the party while tempers continued to run hot. Damn! She should have waited until Kelly was home tonight before jumping to conclusions about the dress. Any halfwit would have known her roommate was involved.

"Well?" Kelly regarded her hopefully.

"I'll go, but first I've got to talk to Andrew and explain."

Kelly released a rush of air, obviously relieved. "Take my advice, don't explain a thing. Just tell him you're sorry."

Jo Marie brushed her dark curls from her forehead. She was in no position to argue. Kelly obviously knew Andrew far better than she. The realization produced a rush of painful regrets. "I'll go to his office first thing tomorrow morning," she said with far more conviction in her voice than what she was feeling.

"You won't regret it," Kelly breathed and squeezed Jo Marie's numb fingers. "I promise you won't."

If that was the case, Jo Marie wanted to know why she regretted it already.

To say that she slept restlessly would be an understatement. By morning, dark shadows had formed under her eyes that even cosmetics couldn't completely disguise. The silky blue dress was finished and hanging from a hook on her cloest door. Compared to the lovely creation Andrew had purchased, her simple gown looked drab. Plain. Unsophisticated. Swallowing her pride had always left a bitter aftertaste, and she didn't expect it to be any different today.

"Good luck," Kelly murmured her condolences to Jo Marie on her way out the door.

"Thanks, I'll need that and more." The knot in her stomach grew tighter every minute. Jo Marie didn't know what she was going to say or even where to begin.

Mrs. Stewart, the gray-haired guardian, was at her station when Jo Marie stepped inside Andrew's office.

"Good morning."

The secretary was too well trained to reveal any surprise.

"Would it be possible to talk to Mr. Beaumont for a few minutes?"

"Do you have an appointment?" The older woman flipped through the calendar pages.

"No," Jo Marie tightened her fists. "I'm afraid I don't."

"Mr. Beaumont will be out of the office until this afternoon."

"Oh." Discouragement nearly defeated her. "Could I make an appointment to see him then?"

The paragon of virtue studied the appointment calendar. "I'm afraid not. Mr. Beaumont has meetings scheduled all week. But if you'd like, I could give him a message."

"Yes, please," she returned and scribbled out a note that said she needed to talk to him as soon as it was convenient. Handing the note back to Mrs. Stewart, Jo Marie offered the woman a feeble smile. "Thank you."

"I'll see to it that Mr. Beaumont gets your message," the efficient woman promised.

Jo Marie didn't doubt that the woman would. What she did question was whether Andrew would respond.

By the time Jo Marie readied for bed that evening, she realized that he wouldn't. Now she'd be faced with attending the party with the tension between them so thick it would resemble an English fog.

Mark was the first one to arrive the following evening. Dressed in a pin-stripe suit and a silk tie he looked exceptionally handsome. And Jo Marie didn't mind telling him so.

"Wow." She took a step in retreat and studied him thoughtfully. "Wow," she repeated.

"I could say the same thing. You look terrific."

Self-consciously, Jo Marie smoothed out an imaginary wrinkle from the skirt of her dress. "You're sure?"

"Of course, I am. And I like your hair like that."

Automatically a hand investigated the rhinestone combs that held the bouncy curls away from her face and gave an air of sophistication to her appearance.

"When will money bags be out?" Mark's gaze drifted toward Kelly's bedroom as he took a seat.

"Any minute."

Mark stuck a finger in the collar of his shirt and ran it around his neck. "I can't believe I agreed to this fiasco."

Jo Marie couldn't believe it either. "Why did you?"

Her brother's shrug was filled with self-derision. "I don't know. It seemed to mean so much to Kelly. And to be honest, I guess I owe it to her for all the times I've teased her."

"How do you feel about Beaumont?"

Mark's eyes narrowed fractionally. "I'm trying not to feel anything."

The door opened and Kelly appeared in a red frothy creation that reminded Jo Marie of Christmas and Santa and happy elves. She had seen the dress, but on Kelly the full-length gown came to life. With a lissome grace Jo Marie envied, Kelly sauntered into the room. Mark couldn't take his eyes off her as he slowly rose to a standing position.

"Kelly." He seemed to have difficulty speaking. "You...you're lovely."

Kelly's delighted laughter was filled with pleasure. "Don't sound so shocked. You've just never seen me dressed up is all."

For a fleeting moment Jo Marie wondered if Mark had ever really seen her roommate.

The doorbell chimed and three pairs of eyes glared at the front door accusingly. Jo Marie felt her stomach tighten with nervous apprehension. For two days she'd dreaded this moment. Andrew Beaumont had arrived.

Kelly broke away from the small group and answered the door. Jo Marie watched her brother's eyes narrow as Kelly stood on her tiptoes and lightly brushed her lips across Andrew's cheek. The involuntary reaction stirred a multitude of questions in Jo Marie about Mark's attitude toward Kelly. And her own toward Andrew.

When her gaze drifted from her brother, Jo Marie discovered that Andrew had centered his attention on her.

"You look exceedingly lovely, Miss Early."

"Thank you. I'm afraid the dress I should have worn was mistakenly returned." She prayed he understood her message.

"Let's have a drink before we leave," Kelly suggested. She'd been in the kitchen earlier mixing a concoction of coconut milk, rum, pineapple and several spices.

The cool drink helped relieve some of the tightness in Jo Marie's throat. She sat beside her brother, across from Andrew. The silence in the room was interrupted only by Kelly, who seemed oblivious to the terrible tension. She chattered all the way out to the car.

Again Mark and Jo Marie were relegated to the back seat of Andrew's plush sedan. Jo Marie knew that Mark hated this, but he submitted to the suggestion without comment. Only the stiff way he held himself revealed his discontent. The party was being given by an associate of Andrew's, a builder. The minute Jo Marie heard the name of the firm she recognized it as the one that had worked on the wetlands project.

Mark cast Jo Marie a curious glance and she shook her head indicating that she wouldn't say a word. In some ways, Jo Marie felt that she was fraternizing with the enemy.

Introductions were made and a flurry of names and faces blurred themselves in her mind. Jo Marie recognized several prominent people, and spoke to a few. Mark stayed close by her side and she knew without asking that this whole party scene made him uncomfortable.

In spite of being so adamant about needing her, Kelly was now nowhere to be seen. A half hour later, Jo Marie noticed that Kelly was sitting in a chair against the wall, looking hopelessly lost. She watched amazed as Mark delivered a glass of punch to her and claimed the chair beside her roommate. Kelly brightened immediately and soon the two were smiling and chatting.

Scanning the crowded room, Jo Marie noticed that Andrew was busy talking to a group of men. The room suddenly felt stuffy. An open glass door that led to a balcony invited her outside and into the cool evening air.

Standing with her gloved hands against the railing, Jo Marie glanced up at the starlit heavens. The night was clear and the black sky was adorned with a thousand glittering stars.

"I received a message that you wanted to speak to me." The husky male voice spoke from behind her.

Jo Marie's heart leaped to her throat and she struggled not to reveal her discomfort. "Yes," she said with a relaxing breath.

Andrew joined her at the wrought-iron railing. His nearness was so overwhelming that Jo Marie closed her eyes to the powerful attraction. Her long fingers tightened their grip.

"I owe you an apology. I sincerely regret jumping to conclusions about the dress. You were only being kind."

An eternity passed before Andrew spoke. "Were you afraid I was going to demand a reward, Florence Nightingale?"

Chapter Four

Jo Marie's heart went still as she turned to Andrew with wide, astonished eyes. "You do remember." They'd spent a single, golden moment together so many months ago. Not once since Kelly had introduced Andrew as her fiancé had he given her the slightest inkling that he remembered.

"Did you imagine I could forget?" he asked quietly.

Tightly squeezing her eyes shut, Jo Marie turned back to the railing, her fingers gripping the wrought iron with a strength she didn't know she possessed.

"I came back every day for a month," he continued in a deep, troubled voice. "I thought you were a nurse."

The color ebbed from Jo Marie's face, leaving her pale. She'd looked for him, too. In all the months since the Mardi Gras she'd never stopped looking. Every time she'd left her apartment, she had silently searched through a sea of faces. Although she'd never known his name, she had included him in her thoughts every day since their meeting. He was her dream man, the stranger who had shared those enchanted moments of magic with her.

"It was Mardi Gras," she explained in a quavering voice. "I'd borrowed Kelly's uniform for a party."

Andrew stood beside her and his wintry eyes narrowed. "I should have recognized you then," he said with faint self-derision.

"Recognized me?" Jo Marie didn't understand. In the short time before they were separated, Andrew had said she reminded him of a painting he'd once seen.

"I should have known you from your picture in the newspaper. You were the girl who so strongly protested the housing development for the wetlands."

"I...I didn't know it was your company. I had no idea." A stray tendril of soft chestnut hair fell forward as she bowed her head. "But I can't apologize for demonstrating against something which I believe is very wrong."

"To thine own self be true, Jo Marie Early." He spoke without malice and when their eyes met, she discovered to her amazement that he was smiling.

Jo Marie responded with a smile of her own. "And you were there that night because of Kelly."

"I'd just left her."

"And I was on my way in." Another few minutes and they could have passed each other in the hospital corridor without ever knowing. In some ways Jo Marie wished they had. If she hadn't met Andrew that night, then she could have shared in her friend's joy at the coming marriage. As it was now, Jo Marie was forced to fight back emotions she had no right to feel.

Andrew belonged to Kelly and the diamond ring on her finger declared as much.

"And...and now you've found Kelly," she stammered, backing away. "I want to wish you both a life filled with much happiness." Afraid of what her expressive eyes would reveal, Jo Marie lowered her lashes which were dark against her pale cheek. "I should be going inside."

"Jo Marie."

He said her name so softly that for a moment she wasn't sure he'd spoken. "Yes?"

Andrew arched both brows and lightly shook his head. His finger lightly touched her smooth cheek, following the line of her delicate jaw. Briefly his gaze darkened as if this was torture in the purest sense. "Nothing. Enjoy yourself tonight." With that he turned back to the railing.

Jo Marie entered the huge reception room and mingled with those attending the lavish affair. Not once did she allow herself to look over her shoulder toward the balcony. Toward Andrew, her dream man, because he wasn't hers, would never be hers. Her mouth ached with the effort to appear happy. By the time she made it to the punch bowl her smile felt brittle and was decidedly forced. All these months she'd hoped to find the dream man because her heart couldn't forget him. And now that she had, nothing had ever been more difficult. If she didn't learn to curb the strong sensual pull she felt toward him, she could ruin his and Kelly's happiness.

Soft Christmas music filled the room as Jo Marie found a plush velvet chair against the wall and sat down, a friendly observer to the party around her. Forcing herself to relax, her toe tapped lightly against the floor with an innate rhythm. Christmas was her favorite time of year—no, she amended, Mardi Gras was. Her smile became less forced.

"You look like you're having the time of your life," Mark announced casually as he took the seat beside her.

"It is a nice party."

"So you enjoy observing the life-style of the rich and famous." The sarcastic edge to Mark's voice was less sharp than normal.

Taking a sip of punch, Jo Marie nodded. "Who wouldn't?"

"To be honest I'm surprised at how friendly everyone's been," Mark commented sheepishly. "Obviously no one suspects that you and I are two of the less privileged."

"Mark," she admonished sharply. "That's a rotten thing to say."

Her brother had the good grace to look ashamed. "To be truthful, Kelly introduced me to several of her friends and I must admit I couldn't find anything to dislike about them."

"Surprise, surprise." Jo Marie hummed the Christmas music softly to herself. "I suppose the next thing I know, you'll be playing golf with Kelly's father."

Mark snorted derisively. "Hardly."

"What have you got against the Beaumonts anyway? Kelly's a wonderful girl."

"Kelly's the exception," Mark argued and stiffened.

"But you just finished telling me that you liked several of her friends that you were introduced to tonight."

"Yes. Well, that was on short acquaintance."

Standing, Jo Marie set her empty punch glass aside. "I think you've got a problem, brother dearest."

A dark look crowded Mark's face, and his brow was furrowed with a curious frown. "You're right, I do." With an agitated movement he stood and made his way across the room.

Jo Marie mingled, talking with a few women who were planning a charity benefit after the first of the year. When they asked her opinion on an important point, Jo Marie was both surprised and pleased. Although she spent a good portion of the next hour with these older ladies, she drifted away as they moved toward the heart of the party. If Andrew had recognized her as the girl involved in the protest against the wetlands development, others might too. And she didn't want to do anything that would cause him and Kelly embarrassment.

Kelly, with her blue eyes sparkling like sapphires, rushed up to Jo Marie. "Here you are!" she exclaimed. "Drew and I have been looking for you."

"Is it time to leave?" Jo Marie was more than ready, uncomfortably aware that she could be recognized at any moment.

"No...no, we just wanted to be certain some handsome young man didn't cart you away."

"Me?" Jo Marie's soft laugh was filled with incredulity. Few men would pay much attention to her, especially since she'd gone out of her way to remain unobtrusively in the background.

"It's more of a possibility than you realize," Andrew spoke from behind her, his voice a gentle rasp against her ear. "You're very beautiful tonight."

"Don't blush, Jo Marie," Kelly teased. "You really are lovely and if you'd given anyone half a chance, they'd have told you so."

Mark joined them and murmured something to Kelly. As he did so, Andrew turned his head toward Jo Marie and spoke so that the other two couldn't hear him. "Only Florence Nightingale could be more beautiful."

A tingling sensation raced down Jo Marie's spine and she turned so their eyes could meet, surprised that he would say something like that to her with Kelly present. Silently, she pleaded with him not to make this any more difficult for her. Those enchanted moments they had shared were long past and best forgotten for both their sakes.

Jo Marie woke to the buzz of the alarm early the next morning. She sat on the side of the bed and raised her arms high above her head and yawned. The day promised to be a busy one. She was scheduled to work in the office that Saturday morning and then catch a bus to LFTF headquarters on the other side of the French Quarter. She was hoping to talk to Jim Rowden, the director and manager of the conservationists' group. Jim had asked for additional volunteers during the Christmas season. And after thoughtful consideration, Jo Marie decided to accept the challenge. Christmas was such a busy time of year that many of the other volunteers wanted time off.

The events of the previous night filled her mind. Lowering her arms, Jo Marie beat back the unexpected rush of sadness that threatened to overcome her. Andrew hadn't understood any of the things she'd tried to tell him last night. Several times she found him watching her, his look brooding and thoughtful as if she'd displeased him. No matter where she went during the course of the evening, when she looked up she found Andrew studying her. Once their eyes had met and held and everyone between them had seemed to disappear. The music had faded and it was as if only the two of them existed in the party-filled crowd. Jo Marie had lowered her gaze first, frightened and angry with them both.

Andrew and Mark had been sullen on the drive home. Mark had left the apartment almost immediately and Jo Marie had fled to the privacy of her room, unwilling to witness Andrew kissing Kelly goodnight. She couldn't have borne it.

Now, in the light of the new day, she discovered that her feelings for Andrew were growing stronger. She wanted to banish him to a special area of her life, long past. But he wouldn't allow that. It had been in his eyes last night as he studied her. Those moments at the Mardi Gras were not to be forgotten by either of them.

At least when she was at the office, she didn't have to think about Andrew or Kelly or Mark. The phone buzzed continually. And because they were short-staffed on the weekends, Jo Marie hardly had time to think about anything but airline fares, bus routes and train schedules the entire morning.

She replaced the telephone receiver after talking with the Costa Lines about booking a spring Caribbean cruise for a retired couple. Her head was bowed as she filled out the necessary forms. Jo Marie didn't hear Paula Shriver, the only other girl in the office on Saturday, move to her desk.

"Mr. Beaumont's been waiting to talk to you," Paula announced. "Lucky you," she added under her breath as Andrew took the seat beside Jo Marie's desk.

"Hello, Jo Marie."

"Andrew." Her hand clenched the ballpoint pen she was holding. "What can I do for you?"

He crossed his legs and draped an arm over the back of the chair giving the picture of a man completely at ease. "I was hoping you could give me some suggestions for an ideal honeymoon."

"Of course. What did you have in mind?" Inwardly she wanted to shout at him not to do this to her, but she forced herself to smile and look attentive.

"What would you suggest?"

She lowered her gaze. "Kelly's mentioned Hawaii several times. I know that's only place she'd enjoy visiting."

He dismissed her suggestion with a short shake of his head. "I've been there several times. I was hoping for something less touristy."

"Maybe a cruise then. There are several excellent lines operating in the Caribbean, the Mediterranean or perhaps the inside passage to Alaska along the Canadian west coast."

"No." Again he shook his head. "Where would *you* choose to go on a honeymoon?"

Jo Marie ignored his question, not wanting to answer him. "I have several brochures I can give you that could spark an idea. I'm confident that any one of these places would thrill Kelly." As she pulled out her bottom desk drawer, Jo Marie was acutely conscious of Andrew studying her. She'd tried to come across with a strict business attitude, but her defenses were crumbling.

Reluctantly, he accepted the brochures she gave him. "You didn't answer my question. Shall I ask it again?"

Slowly, Jo Marie shook her head. "I'm not sure I'd want to go anywhere," she explained simply. "Not on my honeymoon. Not when the most beautiful city in the world is at my doorstep. I'd want to spend that time alone with my husband. We could travel later." Briefly their eyes met and held for a long, breathless moment. "But I'm not Kelly, and she's the one you should consider while planning this trip."

Paula stood and turned the sign in the glass door, indicating that the office was no longer open. Andrew's gaze followed her movements. "You're closing."

Jo Marie's nod was filled with relief. She was uncomfortable with Andrew. Being this close to him was a test of her friendship to Kelly. And at this moment, Kelly was losing...they both were. "Yes. We're only open during the morning on Saturdays."

He stood and placed the pamphlets on the corner of her desk. "Then let's continue our discussion over lunch."

"Oh, no, really that isn't necessary. We'll be finished in a few minutes and Paula doesn't mind waiting."

"But I have several ideas I want to discuss with you and it could well be an hour or so."

"Perhaps you could return another day."

"Now is the more convenient time for me," he countered smoothly.

Everything within Jo Marie wanted to refuse. Surely he realized how difficult this was for her. He was well aware of her feelings and was deliberately ignoring them.

"Is it so difficult to accept anything from me, Jo Marie?" he asked softly. "Even lunch?"

"All right," she agreed ungraciously, angry with him and angrier with herself. "But only an hour. I've got things to do."

A half smile turned up one corner of his mouth. "As you wish," he said as he escorted her to his Mercedes.

Jo Marie was stiff and uncommunicative as Andrew drove through the thick traffic. He parked on a narrow street outside the French Quarter and came around to her side of the car to open the door for her.

"I have reservations at Chez Lorraine's."

"Chez Lorraine's?" Jo Marie's surprised gaze flew to him. The elegant French restaurant was one of New Orlean's most famous. The food was rumored to be exquisite, and expensive. Jo Marie had always dreamed of dining there, but never had.

"Is it as good as everyone says?" she asked, unable to disguise the excitement in her voice.

"You'll have to judge for yourself," he answered, smiling down on her.

Once inside, they were seated almost immediately and handed huge oblong menus featuring a wide variety of French cuisine. Not having sampled several of the more traditional French dishes, Jo Marie toyed with the idea of ordering the calf's sweetbread.

"What would you like?" Andrew prompted after several minutes.

"I don't know. It all sounds so good." Closing the menu she set it aside and lightly shook her head. "I think you may regret having brought me here when

I'm so hungry." She'd skipped breakfast, and discovered now that she was famished.

Andrew didn't look up from his menu. "Where you're concerned, there's very little I regret." As if he'd made a casual comment about the weather, he continued. "Have you decided?"

"Yes...yes," she managed, fighting down the dizzying effect of his words. "I think I'll try the salmon, but I don't think I should try the French pronunciation."

"Don't worry, I'll order for you."

As if by intuition, the waiter reappeared when they were ready to place their order. "The lady would like *les mouilles à la crème de saumon fumé,* and I'll have the *le canard de rouen braise.*"

With a nod of approval the red-jacketed waiter departed.

Self-consciously, Jo Marie smoothed out the linen napkin on her lap. "I'm impressed," she murmured, studying the old world French provincial decor of the room. "It's everything I thought it would be."

The meal was fabulous. After a few awkward moments Jo Marie was amazed that she could talk as freely to Andrew. She discovered he was a good listener and she enjoyed telling him about her family.

"So you were the only girl."

"It had its advantages. I play a mean game of touch football."

"I hope you'll play with me someday. I've always enjoyed a rousing game of touch football."

The fork was raised halfway to her mouth and Jo Marie paused, her heart beating double time. "I...I only play with my brothers."

Andrew chuckled. "Speaking of your family, I find it difficult to tell that you and Mark are related. Oh, I can see the family resemblance, but Mark's a serious young man. Does he ever laugh?"

Not lately, Jo Marie mused, but she didn't admit as much. "He works hard, long hours. Mark's come a long way through medical school." She hated making excuses for her brother. "He doesn't mean to be rude."

Andrew accepted the apology with a wry grin. "The chip on his shoulder's as big as a California redwood. What's he got against wealth and position?"

"I don't know," she answered honestly. "He teases Kelly unmercifully about her family. I think Kelly's money makes him feel insecure. There's no reason for it; Kelly's never done anything to give him that attitude. I never have understood it."

Pushing her clean plate aside, Jo Marie couldn't recall when she'd enjoyed a meal more—except the dinner they'd shared at K-Paul's the night Kelly and Andrew had announced their engagement. Some of the contentment faded from her eyes. Numbly, she folded her hands in her lap. Being here with Andrew, sharing this meal, laughing and talking with him wasn't right. Kelly should be the one sitting across the table from him. Jo Marie had no right to enjoy his company this way. Not when he was engaged to her best friend. Pointedly, she glanced at her watch.

"What's wrong?"

"Nothing." She shook her head slightly, avoiding his eyes, knowing his look had the ability to penetrate her soul.

"Would you care for some dessert?"

Placing her hand on her stomach, she declined with a smile. "I couldn't," she declared, but her gaze fell with regret on the large table display of delicate French pastries.

The waiter reappeared and a flurry of French flew over her head. Like everything else Andrew did, his French was flawless.

Almost immediately the waiter returned with a plate covered with samples of several desserts which he set in front of Jo Marie.

"Andrew," she objected, sighing his name, "I'll get fat."

"I saw you eyeing those goodies. Indulge. You deserve it."

"But I don't. I can't possibly eat all that."

"You can afford to put on a few pounds." His voice deepened as his gaze skimmed her lithe form.

"Are you suggesting I'm skinny?"

"My, my," he said, slowly shaking his head from side to side. "You do like to argue. Here, give me the plate. I'll be the one to indulge."

"Not on your life," she countered laughingly, and dipped her fork into the thin slice of chocolate cheesecake. After sampling three of the scrumptious desserts, Jo Marie pushed her plate aside. "Thank you, Andrew," she murmured as her fingers toyed with the starched, linen napkin. "I enjoyed the meal and...and the company, but we can't do this again." Her eyes were riveted to the tabletop.

"Jo Marie—"

"No. Let me finish," she interrupted on a rushed breath. "It...it would be so easy...to hurt Kelly and I won't do that. I can't. Please, don't make this so difficult for me." With every word her voice grew weaker and shakier. It shouldn't be this hard, her heart cried, but it was. Every womanly instinct was reaching out to him until she wanted to cry with it.

"Indulge me, Jo Marie," he said tenderly. "It's my birthday and there's no one else I'd rather share it with."

No one else...his words reverberated through her mind. They were on treacherous ground and Jo Marie felt herself sinking fast.

"Happy birthday," she whispered.

"Thank you."

They stood and Andrew cupped her elbow, leading her to the street.

"Would you like me to drop you off at the apartment?" Andrew asked several minutes later as they walked toward his parked car.

"No. I'm on my way to the LFTF headquarters." She stuck both hands deep within her sweater pockets.

"Land For The Future?"

She nodded. "They need extra volunteers during the Christmas season."

His wide brow knitted with a deep frown. "As I recall, that building is in a bad part of town. Is it safe for you to—"

"Perfectly safe." She took a step in retreat. "Thank you again for lunch. I hope you have a wonderful birthday," she called just before turning and hurrying along the narrow sidewalk.

Jo Marie's pace was brisk as she kept one eye on the darkening sky. Angry gray thunderclouds were rolling in and a cloud burst was imminent. Everything looked as if it was against her. With the sky the color of Andrew's eyes, it seemed as though he was watching her every move. Fleetingly she wondered if she'd ever escape him...and worse, if she'd ever want to.

The LFTF headquarters were near the docks. Andrew's apprehensions were well founded. This was a high crime area. Jo Marie planned her arrival and departure times in daylight.

"Can I help you?" The stocky man with crisp ebony hair spoke from behind the desk. There was a speculative arch to his bushy brows as he regarded her.

"Hello." She extended her hand. "I'm Jo Marie Early. You're Jim Rowden, aren't you?" Jim had recently arrived from the Boston area and was taking over the manager's position of the nonprofit organization.

Jim stepped around the large oak desk. "Yes, I remember now. You marched in the demonstration, didn't you?"

"Yes, I was there."

"One of the few who stuck it out in the rain, as I recall."

"My brother insisted that it wasn't out of any sense of purpose, but from a pure streak of stubbornness." Laughter riddled her voice. "I'm back because you mentioned needing extra volunteers this month."

"Do you type?"

"Reasonably well. I'm a travel agent."

"Don't worry I won't give you a time test."

Jo Marie laughed. "I appreciate that more than you know."

The majority of the afternoon was spent typing personal replies to letters the group had received after the demonstration in front of Rose's. In addition, the group had been spurred on by their success, and was planning other campaigns for future projects. At four-thirty, Jo Marie slipped the cover over the typewriter and placed the letters on Jim's desk for his signature.

"If you could come three times a week," Jim asked, "it would be greatly appreciated."

She left forty minutes later feeling assured that she was doing the right thing by offering her time. Lending a hand at Christmas seemed such a small thing to do. Admittedly, her motives weren't pure. If she could keep herself occupied, she wouldn't have to deal with her feelings for Andrew.

A lot of her major Christmas shopping was completed, but on her way to the bus stop, Jo Marie stopped in at a used-book store. Although she fought it all afternoon, her thoughts had been continually on Andrew. Today was his special day and she desperately wanted to give him something that would relay her feelings. Her heart was filled with gratitude. Without him, she may never have known that sometimes dreams can come true and that fairy tales aren't always for the young.

She found the book she was seeking. A large leather-bound volume of the history of New Orleans. Few cities had a more romantic background. Included in the book were hundreds of rare photographs of the city's architecture, courtyards, patios, ironwork and cemeteries. He'd love the book as much as she. Jo Marie had come by for weeks, paying a little bit each pay day. Not only was this book rare, but extremely expensive. Because the proprietor knew Jo Marie, he had made special arrangements for her to have this volume. But Jo Marie couldn't think of anything else Andrew would cherish more. She wrote out a check for the balance and realized that she would probably be short on cash by the end of the month, but that seemed a small sacrifice.

Clenching the book to her breast, Jo Marie hurried home. She had not right to be giving Andrew gifts, but this was more for her sake than his. It was her thank you for all that he'd given her.

The torrential downpour assaulted the pavement just as Jo Marie stepped off the bus. Breathlessly, while holding the paper-wrapped leather volume to her stomach, she ran to the apartment and inserted her key into the dead bolt. Once again she had barely escaped a thorough drenching.

Hanging her Irish knit cardigan in the hall closet, Jo Marie kicked off her shoes and slid her feet into fuzzy, worn slippers.

Kelly should arrive any minute and Jo Marie rehearsed what she was going to say to Kelly. She had to have some kind of explanation to be giving her friend's fiancé a birthday present. Her thoughts came back empty as she paced the floor, wringing her hands. It was important that Kelly understand, but finding a plausible reason without revealing herself was difficult. Jo Marie didn't want any ill feelings between them.

When her roommate hadn't returned from the hospital by six, Jo Marie made herself a light meal and turned on the evening news. Kelly usually phoned if she was going to be late. Not having heard from her friend caused Jo Marie to wonder. Maybe Andrew had picked her up after work and had taken her out to dinner. It was, after all, his birthday; celebrating with his fiancé would only be natural. Unbidden, a surge of resentment rose within her and caused a lump of painful hoarseness to tighten her throat. Mentally she gave herself a hard shake. *Stop it,* her mind shouted. *You have no right to feel these things. Andrew belongs to Kelly, not you.*

A mixture of pain and confusion moved across her smooth brow when the doorbell chimed. It was probably Mark, but for the first time in recent memory, Jo Marie wasn't up to a sparring match with her older brother. Tonight she wanted to be left to her own thoughts.

But it wasn't Mark.

"Andrew." Quickly she lowered her gaze, praying he couldn't read her startled expression.

"Is Kelly ready?" he asked as he stepped inside the entryway. "We're having dinner with my mother."

"She isn't home from work yet. If you'd like I could call the hospital and see what's holding her up." So they were going out tonight. Jo Marie successfully managed to rein in her feelings of jealousy, having dealt with them earlier.

"No need, I'm early. If you don't mind, I'll just wait."

"Please, sit down." Self-consciously she gestured toward the love seat. "I'm sure Kelly will be here any minute."

Impeccably dressed in a charcoal-gray suit that emphasized the width of his muscular shoulders, Andrew took a seat.

With her hands linked in front of her, Jo Marie fought for control of her hammering heart. "Would you like a cup of coffee?"

"Please."

Relieved to be out of the living room, Jo Marie hurried into the kitchen and brought down a cup and saucer. Spending part of the afternoon with Andrew was difficult enough. But being alone in the apartment with him was impossible. The tension between them was unbearable as it was. But to be separated by only a thin wall was much worse. She yearned to touch him. To hold him in her arms. To feel again, just this once, his mouth over hers. She had to know if what had happened all those months ago was real.

"Jo Marie," Andrew spoke softly from behind her.

Her pounding heart leaped to her throat. Had he read her thoughts and come to her? Her fingers dug unmercifully into the kitchen counter top. Nothing would induce her to turn around.

"What's this?" he questioned softly.

A glance over her shoulder revealed Andrew holding the book she'd purchased earlier. Her hand shook as she poured the coffee. "It's a book about the early history of New Orleans. I found it in a used-book store and..." Her voice wobbled as badly as her hand.

"There was a card on top of it that was addressed to me."

Jo Marie set the glass coffeepot down. "Yes...I knew you'd love it and I wanted you to have it as a birthday present." She stopped just before admitting that she wanted him to remember her. "I also heard on the news tonight that...that Rose's Hotel is undergoing some expensive and badly needed repairs, thanks to you." Slowly she turned, keeping her hands behind her. "I realize there isn't anything that I could ever buy for you that you couldn't purchase a hundred times over. But I thought this book might be the one thing I could give you...." She let her voice fade in midsentence.

A slow faint smile touched his mouth as he opened the card and read her inscription. "To Andrew, in appreciation for everything." Respectfully he opened the book, then laid it aside. "Everything, Jo Marie?"

"For your generosity toward the hotel, and your thoughtfulness in giving me the party dress and..."

"The Mardi Gras?" He inched his way toward her.

Jo Marie could feel the color seep up her neck and tinge her cheeks. "Yes, that too." She wouldn't deny how speical those few moments had been to her. Nor could she deny the hunger in his hard gaze as he concentrated on her lips. Amazed, Jo Marie watched as Andrew's gray eyes darkened to the shade of a stormy Arctic sea.

No pretense existed between them now, only a shared hunger that could no longer be repressed. A surge of intense longing seared through her so that when Andrew drew her into his embrace she gave a small cry and went willingly.

"Haven't you ever wondered if what we shared that night was real?" he breathed the question into her hair.

"Yes, a thousand times since, I've wondered." She gloried in the feel of his muscular body pressing against the length of hers. Freely her hands roamed his back. His index finger under her chin lifted her face and her heart soared at the look in his eyes.

"Jo Marie," he whispered achingly and his thumb leisurely caressed the full curve of her mouth.

Her soft lips trembled in anticipation. Slowly, deliberately, Andrew lowered his head as his mouth sought hers. Her eyelids drifted closed and her arms reached up and clung to him. The kiss was one of hunger and demand as his mouth feasted on hers.

The feel of him, the touch, the taste of his lips filled her senses until Jo Marie felt his muscles strain as he brought her to him, riveting her soft form to him so tightly that she could no longer breathe. Not that she cared.

Gradually the kiss mellowed and the intensity eased until he buried his face in the gentle slope of her neck. "It was real," he whispered huskily. "Oh, my sweet Florence Nightingale, it was even better than I remembered."

"I was afraid it would be." Tears burned her eyes and she gave a sad little laugh. Life was filled with ironies and finding Andrew now was the most painful.

Tenderly he reached up and wiped the moisture from her face. "I shouldn't have let this happen."

"It wasn't your fault." Jo Marie felt she had to accept part of the blame. She'd wanted him to kiss her so badly. "I...I won't let it happen again." If one of them had to be strong, then it would be her. After years of friendship with Kelly she owed her roommate her loyalty.

Reluctantly they broke apart, but his hands rested on either side of her neck as though he couldn't bear to let her go completely. "Thank you for the book," he said in a raw voice. "I'll treasure it always."

The sound of the front door opening caused Jo Marie's eyes to widen with a rush of guilt. Kelly would take one look at her and realize what had happened. Hot color blazed in her cheeks.

"Jo Marie!" Kelly's eager voice vibrated through the apartment.

Andrew stepped out of the kitchen, granting Jo Marie precious seconds to compose herself.

"Oh, heavens, you're here already, Drew. I'm sorry I'm so late. But I've got so much to tell you."

With her hand covering her mouth to smother the sound of her tears, Jo Marie leaned against the kitchen counter, suddenly needing its support.

Chapter Five

"Are you all right?" Andrew stepped back into the kitchen and brushed his hand over his temples. He resembled a man driven to the end of his endurance, standing with one foot in heaven and the other in hell. His fingers were clenched at his side as if he couldn't decide if he should haul her back into his arms or leave her alone. But the tortured look in his eyes told Jo Marie how difficult it was not to hold and reassure her.

"I'm fine." Her voice was eggshell fragile. "Just leave. Please. I don't want Kelly to see me." Not like this, with tears streaming down her pale cheeks and her eyes full of confusion. Once glance at Jo Marie and the astute Kelly would know exactly what had happened.

"I'll get her out of here as soon as she changes clothes," Andrew whispered urgently, his stormy gray eyes pleading with hers. "I didn't mean for this to happen."

"I know." With an agitated brush of her hand she dismissed him. "Please, just go."

"I'll talk to you tomorrow."

"No." Dark emotion flickered across her face. She didn't want to see him. Everything about today had been wrong. She should have avoided Andrew, feeling as she did. But in some ways, Jo Marie realized that the kiss had been inevitable. Those brief magical moments at the Mardi Gras demanded an exploration of the sensation they'd shared. Both had hoped to dismiss that February night as whimsy—a result of the craziness of the season. Instead, they had discovered how real it had been. From now on, Jo Marie vowed, she would shun Andrew. Her only defense was to avoid him completely.

"I'm sorry to keep you waiting." Kelly's happy voice drifted in from the other room. "Do I look okay?"

"You're lovely as always."

Jo Marie hoped that Kelly wouldn't catch the detached note in Andrew's gruff voice.

"You'll never guess who I spent the last hour talking to."

"Perhaps you could tell me on the way to mother's?" Andrew responded dryly.

"Drew." Some of the enthusiasm drained from Kelly's happy voice. "Are you feeling ill? You're quite pale."

"I'm fine."

"Maybe we should cancel this dinner. Really, I wouldn't mind."

"There's no reason to disappoint my mother."

"Drew?" Kelly seemed hesitant.

"Are you ready?" His firm voice brooked no disagreement.

"But I wanted to talk to Jo Marie."

"You can call her after dinner," Andrew responded shortly, his voice fading as they moved toward the entryway.

The door clicked a minute later and Jo Marie's fingers loosened their death grip against the counter. Weakly, she wiped a hand over her face and eyes. Andrew and Kelly were engaged to be married. Tonight was his birthday and he was taking Kelly to dine with his family. And Jo Marie had been stealing a kiss from him in the kitchen. Self-reproach grew in her breast with every breath until she wanted to scream and lash out with it.

Maybe she could have justified her actions if Kelly hadn't been so excited and happy. Her roommate had come into the apartment bursting with enthusiasm for life, eager to see and talk to Andrew.

The evening seemed interminable and Jo Marie had a terrible time falling asleep, tossing and turning long past the time Kelly returned. Finally at the darkest part of the night, she flipped on the beside lamp and threw aside the blankets. Pouring herself a glass of milk, Jo Marie leaned against the kitchen counter and drank it with small sips, her thoughts deep and dark. She couldn't ask Kelly to forgive her for what had happened without hurting her roommate and perhaps ruining their friendship. The only person there was to confront and condemn was herself.

Once she returned to bed, Jo Marie lay on her back, her head clasped in her hands. Moon shadows fluttered against the bare walls like the flickering scenes of a silent movie.

Unhappy beyond words, Jo Marie avoided her roommate, kept busy and occupied her time with other friends. But she was never at peace and always conscious that her thoughts never strayed from Kelly and Andrew. The episode with Andrew wouldn't happen again. She had to be strong.

Jo Marie didn't see her roommate until the following Monday morning. They met in the kitchen where Jo Marie was pouring herself a small glass of grapefruit juice.

"Morning." Jo Marie's stiff smile was only slightly forced.

"Howdy, stranger. I've missed you the past couple of days."

Jo Marie's hand tightened around the juice glass as she silently prayed Kelly wouldn't ask her about Saturday night. Her roommate must have known Jo Marie was in the apartment, otherwise Andrew wouldn't have been inside.

"I've missed you," Kelly continued. "It seems we hardly have time to talk anymore. And now that you're going to be doing volunteer work for the foundation, we'll have even less time together. You're spreading yourself too thin."

"There's always something going on this time of year." A chill seemed to settle around the area of Jo Marie's heart and she avoided her friend's look.

"I know, that's why I'm looking forward to this weekend and the party for Drew's company. By the way, he suggested that both of us stay the night on Saturday."

"Spend the night?" Jo Marie repeated like a recording and inhaled a shaky breath. That was the last thing she wanted.

"It makes sense, don't you think? We can lay awake until dawn the way we used to and talk all night." A distant look came over Kelly as she buttered the hot toast and poured herself a cup of coffee. "Drew's going to have enough to worry about without dragging us back and forth. From what I understand, he goes all out for his company's Christmas party."

Hoping to hide her discomfort, Jo Marie rinsed out her glass and deposited it in the dishwasher, but a gnawing sensation attacked the pit of her stomach. Although she'd promised Kelly she would attend the lavish affair, she had to find a way of excusing herself without arousing suspicion. "I've been thinking about Andrew's party and honestly feel I shouldn't go—"

"Don't say it. You're going!" Kelly interrupted hastily. "There's no way I'd go without you. You're my best friend, Jo Marie Early, and as such I want you with me. Besides, you know how I hate these things."

"But as Drew's wife you'll be expected to attend a lot of these functions. I won't always be around."

A secret smile stole over her friend's pert face. "I know, that's why it's so important that you're there now."

"You didn't seem to need me Friday night."

Round blue eyes flashed Jo Marie a look of disbelief. "Are you crazy? I would have been embarrassingly uncomfortable without you."

It seemed to Jo Marie that Mark had spent nearly as much time with Kelly as she had. In fact, her brother had spent most of the evening with Kelly at his side. It was Mark whom Kelly really wanted, not her. But convincing her roommate of that was a different matter. Jo Marie doubted that Kelly had even admitted as much to herself.

"I'll think about going," Jo Marie promised. "But I can't honestly see that my being there or not would do any good."

"You've got to come," Kelly muttered, looking around unhappily. "I'd be miserable meeting and talking to all those people on my own." Silently, Kelly's bottomless blue eyes pleaded with Jo Marie. "I promise never to ask anything from you again. Say you'll come. Oh, please, Jo Marie, do this one last thing for me."

An awkward silence stretched between them and a feeling of dread settled over Jo Marie. Kelly seemed so genuinely distraught that it wasn't in Jo Marie's heart to refuse her. As Kelly had pointedly reminded her, she was Kelly's best friend. "All right, all right," she agreed reluctantly. "But I don't like it."

"You won't be sorry, I promise." A mischievous gleam lightened Kelly's features.

Jo Marie mumbled disdainfully under her breath as she moved out of the kitchen. Pausing at the closet, she took her trusted cardigan from the hanger. "Say, Kell, don't forget this is the week I'm flying to Mazatlán." Jo Marie was scheduled to take a familiarization tour of the Mexican resort town. She'd be flying with ten other travel agents from the city and staying at the Riviera Del Sol's expense. The luxury hotel was sponsoring the group in hopes of having the agents book their facilities for their clients. Jo Marie usually took the "fam" tours only once or twice a year. This one had been planned months before and she mused that it couldn't have come at a better time. Escaping from Andrew and Kelly was just the thing she needed. By the time she returned, she prayed, her life could be back to normal.

"This is the week?" Kelly stuck her head around the kitchen doorway. "Already?"

"You can still drive me to the airport, can't you?"

"Sure," Kelly answered absently. "But if I can't, Drew will."

Jo Marie's heart throbbed painfully. "No," she returned forcefully.

"He doesn't mind."

But I do, Jo Marie's heart cried as she fumbled with the buttons of her sweater. If Kelly wasn't home when it came time to leave for the airport, she would either call Mark or take a cab.

"I'm sure Drew wouldn't mind," Kelly repeated.

"I'll be late tonight," she answered, ignoring her friend's offer. She couldn't understand why Kelly would want her to spend time with Andrew. But so many things didn't make sense lately. Without a backward glance, Jo Marie went out the front door.

Joining several others at the bus stop outside the apartment building en route to the office, Jo Marie fought down feelings of guilt. She'd honestly thought she could get out of attending the party with Kelly. But there was little to be done, short of offending her friend. These constant recriminations regarding Kelly and Andrew were disrupting her neatly ordered life, and Jo Marie hated it.

Two of the other girls were in the office by the time Jo Marie arrived.

"There's a message for you," Paula announced. "I think it was the same guy who stopped in Saturday morning. You know, I'm beginning to think you've been holding out on me. Where'd you ever meet a hunk like that?"

"He's engaged," she quipped, seeking a light tone.

"He is?" Paula rolled her office chair over to Jo Marie's desk and handed her the pink slip. "You could have fooled me. He looked on the prowl, if you want my opinion. In fact, he was eyeing you like a starving man looking at a cream puff."

"Paula!" Jo Marie tried to toss off her co-worker's observation with a forced laugh. "He's engaged to my roommate."

Paula lifted one shoulder in a half shrug and scooted the chair back to her desk. "If you say so." But both her tone and her look were disbelieving.

Jo Marie read the message, which listed Andrew's office number and asked that she call him at her earliest convenience. Crumbling up the pink slip, she tossed it in the green metal wastebasket beside her desk. She might be attending this party, but it was under duress. And as far as Andrew was concerned, she had every intention of avoiding him.

Rather than rush back to the apartment after work, Jo Marie had dinner in a small café near her office. From there she walked to the Land For The Future headquarters.

She was embarrassingly early when she arrived outside of the office door. The foundation's headquarters were on the second floor of an older brick building in a bad part of town. Jo Marie decided to arrive earlier than she'd planned rather than kill time by walking around outside. From the time she'd left the travel agency, she'd wandered around with little else to do. Her greatest fear was that Andrew would be waiting for her at the apartment. She hadn't returned his call and he'd want to know why.

Jim Rowden, the office manager and spokesman, was busy on the telephone when Jo Marie arrived.

Quietly she slipped into the chair at the desk opposite him and glanced over the letters and other notices that needed to be typed. As she pulled the cover from the top of the typewriter, Jo Marie noticed a shadowy movement from the other side of the milky white glass inset of the office door.

She stood to investigate and found a dark-haired man with a worn felt hat that fit loosely on top of his head. His clothes were ragged and the faint odor of cheap wine permeated the air. He was curling up in the doorway of an office nearest theirs.

His eyes met hers briefly and he tugged his thin sweater around his shoulders. "Are you going to throw me out of here?" The words were issued in subtle challenge.

Jo Marie teetered with indecision. If she did tell him to leave he'd either spend the night shivering in the cold or find another open building. On the other hand if she were to give him money, she was confident it wouldn't be a bed he'd spend it on.

"Well?" he challenged again.

"I won't say anything," she answered finally. "Just go down to the end of the hall so no one else will find you."

He gave her a look of mild surprise, stood and gathered his coat before turning and ambling down the long hall in an uneven gait. Jo Marie waited until he was curled up in another doorway. It was difficult to see that he was there without looking for him. A soft smile of satisfaction stole across her face as she closed the door and returned to her desk.

Jim replaced the receiver and smiled a welcome at Jo Marie. "How'd you like to attend a lecture with me tonight?"

"I'd like it fine," she agreed eagerly.

Jim's lecture was to a group of concerned city businessmen. He relayed the facts about the dangers of thoughtless and haphazard land development. He presented his case in a simple, straightforward fashion without emotionalism or sensationalism. In addition, he confidently answered their questions, defining the difference between building for the future and preserving a link with the past. Jo Marie was impressed and from the looks on the faces of his audience, the businessmen had been equally affected.

"I'll walk you to the bus stop," Jim told her hours later after they'd returned from the meeting. "I don't like the idea of you waiting at the bus stop alone. I'll go with you."

Jo Marie hadn't been that thrilled with the prospect herself. "Thanks, I'd appreciate that."

Jim's hand cupped her elbow as they leisurely strolled down the narrow street, chatting as they went. Jim's voice was drawling and smooth and Jo Marie mused that she could listen to him all night. The lamplight illuminated little in the descending fog and would have created an eerie feeling if Jim hadn't been at her side. But walking with him, she barely noticed the weather and instead found herself laughing at his subtle humor.

"How'd you ever get into this business?" she queried. Jim Rowden was an intelligent, warm human being who would be a success in any field he chose to pursue. He could be making twice and three times the money in the business world that he collected from the foundation.

At first introduction, Jim wasn't the kind of man who would bowl women over with his striking good looks or his suave manners. But he was a rare, dedicated man of conscience. Jo Marie had never known anyone like him and admired him greatly.

"I'm fairly new with the foundation," he admitted, "and it certainly wasn't what I'd been expecting to do with my life, especially since I struggled through college for a degree in biology. Afterward I went to work for the state, but this job gives me the opportunity to work first hand with saving some of the—well, you heard my speech."

"Yes, I did, and it was wonderful."

"You're good for my ego, Jo Marie. I hope you'll stick around."

Jo Marie's eyes glanced up the street, wondering how long they'd have to wait for a bus. She didn't want their discussion to end. As she did, a flash of midnight blue captured her attention and her heart dropped to her knees as the Mercedes pulled to a stop alongside the curb in front of them.

Andrew practically leaped from the driver's side. "Just what do you think you're doing?" The harsh anger in his voice shocked her.

"I beg your pardon?" Jim answered on Jo Marie's behalf, taking a step forward.

Andrew ignored Jim, his eyes cold and piercing as he glanced over her. "I've spent the good part of an hour looking for you."

"Why?" Jo Marie demanded, tilting her chin in an act of defiance. "What business is it of yours where I am or who I'm with?"

"I'm making it my business."

"Is there a problem here, Jo Marie?" Jim questioned as he stepped forward.

"None whatsoever," she responded dryly and crossed her arms in front of her.

"Kelly's worried sick," Andrew hissed. "Now I suggest you get in the car and let me take you home before...." He let the rest of what he was saying die. He paused for several tense moments and exhaled a sharp breath. "I apologize, I had no right to come at you like that." He closed the car door and moved around the front of the Mercedes. "I'm Andrew Beaumont," he introduced himself and extended his hand to Jim.

"From Delta Development?" Jim's eyes widened appreciatively. "Jim Rowden. I've been wanting to meet you so that I could thank you personally for what you did for Rose's Hotel."

"I'm pleased I could help."

When Andrew decided to put on the charm it was like falling into a jar of pure honey, Jo Marie thought. She didn't know of a man, woman or child who couldn't be swayed by his beguiling showmanship. Having been under his spell in the past made it all the more recognizable now. But somehow, she realized, this was different. Andrew hadn't been acting the night of the Mardi Gras, she was convinced of that.

"Jo Marie was late coming home and luckily I remembered her saying something about volunteering for the foundation. Kelly asked that I come and get her. We were understandably worried about her taking the bus alone at this time of night."

"I'll admit I was a bit concerned myself," Jim returned, taking a step closer to Jo Marie. "That's why I'm here."

As Andrew opened the passenger's side of the car, Jo Marie turned her head to meet his gaze, her eyes fiery as she slid into the plush velvet seat.

"I'll see you Friday," she said to Jim.

"Enjoy Mexico," he responded and waved before turning and walking back toward the office building. A fine mist filled the evening air and Jim pulled up his collar as he hurried along the sidewalk.

Andrew didn't say a word as he turned the key in the ignition, checked the rearview mirror and pulled back onto the street.

"You didn't return my call." He stopped at a red light and the full force of his magnetic gray eyes was turned on her.

"No," she answered in a whisper, struggling not to reveal how easily he could affect her.

"Can't you see how important it is that we talk?"

"No." She wanted to shout the word. When their eyes met, Jo Marie was startled to find that only a few inches separated them. Andrew's look was centered on her mouth and with a determined effort she averted her gaze and stared out the side window. "I don't want to talk to you." Her fingers fumbled with the clasp of her purse in nervous agitation. "There's nothing more we can say." She hated the husky emotion-filled way her voice sounded.

"Jo Marie." He said her name so softly that she wasn't entirely sure he'd spoken.

She turned back to him, knowing she should pull away from the hypnotic darkness of his eyes, but doing so was impossible.

"You'll come to my party?"

She wanted to explain her decision to attend—she hadn't wanted to go—but one glance at Andrew said that he understood. Words were unnecessary.

"It's going to be difficult for us both for a while."

He seemed to imply things would grow easier with time. Jo Marie sincerely doubted that they ever would.

"You'll come?" he prompted softly.

Slowly she nodded. Jo Marie hadn't realized how tense she was until she exhaled and felt some of the coiled tightness leave her body. "Yes, I'll...be at the party." Her breathy stammer spoke volumes.

"And wear the dress I gave you?"

She ended up nodding again, her tongue unable to form words.

"I've dreamed of you walking into my arms wearing that dress," he added on a husky tremor, then shook his head as if he regretted having spoken.

Being alone with him in the close confines of the car was torture. Her once restless fingers lay limp in her lap. Jo Marie didn't know how she was going to avoid Andrew when Kelly seemed to be constantly throwing them together. But she must for her own peace of mind...she must.

All too quickly the brief respite of her trip to Mazatlán was over. Saturday arrived and Kelly and Jo Marie were brought to Andrew's home, which was a faithful reproduction of an antebellum mansion.

The dress he'd purchased was hanging in the closet of the bedroom she was to share with Kelly. Her friend threw herself across the canopy bed and exhaled on a happy sigh.

"Isn't this place something?"

Jo Marie didn't answer for a moment, her gaze falling on the dress that hung alone in the closet. "It's magnificent." There was little else that would describe this palace. The house was a three-story structure with huge white pillars and dark shutters. It faced the Mississippi River and had a huge garden in the back. Jo Marie learned that it was his mother who took an avid interest in the wide variety of flowers that grew in abundance there.

The rooms were large, their walls adorned with paintings and works of art. If Jo Marie was ever to doubt Andrew's wealth and position, his home would prove to be a constant reminder.

"Drew built it himself," Kelly explained with a proud lilt to her voice. "I don't mean he pounded in every nail, but he was here every day while it was being constructed. It took months."

"I can imagine." And no expense had been spared from the look of things.

"I suppose we should think about getting ready," Kelly continued. "I don't mind telling you that I've had a queasy stomach all day dreading this thing."

Kelly had! Jo Marie nearly laughed aloud. This party had haunted her all week. Even Mazatlán hadn't been far enough away to dispel the feeling of dread.

Jo Marie could hear the music drifting in from the reception hall by the time she had put on the finishing touches of her makeup. Kelly had already joined Andrew. A quick survey in the full-length mirror assured her that the beautiful gown was the most elegant thing she would ever own. The reflection that came back to her of a tall, regal woman was barely recognizable as herself. The dark crown of curls was styled on top of her head with a few stray tendrils curling about her ears. A lone strand of pearls graced her neck.

Self-consciously she moved from the room, closing the door. From the top of the winding stairway, she looked down on a milling crowd of arriving guests. Holding in her breath, she placed her gloved hand on the polished bannister, exhaled, and made her descent. Keeping her eyes on her feet for fear of tripping, Jo Marie was surprised when she glanced down to find Andrew waiting for her at the bottom of the staircase.

As he gave her his hand, their eyes met and held in a tender exchange. "You're beautiful."

The deep husky tone in his voice took her breath away and Jo Marie could do nothing more than smile in return.

Taking her hand, Andrew tucked it securely in the crook of his elbow and led her into the room where the other guests were mingling. Everyone was meeting for drinks in the huge living room and once the party was complete they would be moving up to the ballroom on the third floor. The evening was to culminate in a midnight buffet.

With Andrew holding her close by his side, Jo Marie had little option but to follow where he led. Moving from one end of the room to the other, he introduced her to so many people that her head swam trying to remember their names. Fortunately, Kelly and Andrew's engagement hadn't been officially announced and Jo Marie wasn't forced to make repeated explanations. Nonetheless, she was uncomfortable with the way he was linking the two of them together.

"Where's Kelly?" Jo Marie asked under her breath. "She should be the one with you. Not me."

"Kelly's with Mark on the other side of the room."

Jo Marie faltered in midstep and Andrew's hold tightened as he dropped his arm and slipped it around her slim waist. "With Mark?" She couldn't imagine her brother attending this party. Not feeling the way he did about Andrew.

Not until they were upstairs and the music was playing did Jo Marie have an opportunity to talk to her brother. He was sitting against the wall in a high-backed mahogany chair with a velvet cushion. Kelly was at his side. Jo Marie couldn't recall a time she'd seen her brother dress so formally or look more handsome. He'd had his hair trimmed and was clean shaven. She'd never dreamed she'd see Mark in a tuxedo.

"Hello, Mark."

Her brother looked up, guilt etched on his face. "Jo Marie." Briefly he exchanged looks with Kelly and stood, offering Jo Marie his seat.

"Thanks," she said as she sat and slipped the high-heeled sandals from her toes. "My feet could use a few moments' rest."

"You certainly haven't lacked for partners," Kelly observed happily. "You're a hit, Jo Marie. Even Mark was saying he couldn't believe you were his sister."

"I've never seen you look more attractive," Mark added. "But then I bet you didn't buy that dress out of petty cash either."

If there was a note of censure in her brother's voice, Jo Marie didn't hear it. "No." Absently her hand smoothed the silk skirt. "It was a gift from Andrew...and Kelly." Hastily she added her roommate's name. "I must admit though, I'm surprised to see you here."

"Andrew extended the invitation personally," Mark replied, holding his back ramrod stiff as he stared straight ahead.

Not understanding, Jo Marie glanced at her roommate. "Mark came for me," Kelly explained, her voice soft and vulnerable. "Because I...because I wanted him here."

"We're both here for you, Kelly," Jo Marie reminded her and punctuated her comment by arching her brows.

"I know, and I love you both for it."

"Would you care to dance?" Mark held out his hand to Kelly, taking her into his arms when they reached the boundary of the dance floor as if he never wanted to let her go.

Confused, Jo Marie watched their progress. Kelly was engaged to be married to Andrew, yet she was gazing into Mark's eyes as if he were her knight in shining armor who had come to slay dragons on her behalf. When she'd come upon them, they'd acted as if she had intruded on their very private party.

Jo Marie saw Andrew approach her, his brows lowered as if something had displeased him. His strides were quick and decisive as he wove his way through the throng of guests.

"I've been looking for you. In fact, I was beginning to wonder if I'd ever get a chance to dance with you." The pitch of his voice suggested that she'd been deliberately avoiding him. And she had.

Jo Marie couldn't bring herself to meet his gaze, afraid of what he could read in her eyes. All night she'd been pretending it was Andrew who was holding her and yet she'd known she wouldn't be satisfied until he did.

"I believe this dance is mine," he said, presenting her with his hand.

Peering up at him, a smile came and she paused to slip the strap of her high heel over her ankle before standing.

Once on the dance floor, his arms tightened around her waist, bringing her so close that there wasn't a hair's space between them. He held her securely as if challenging her to move. Jo Marie discovered that she couldn't. This inexplicable feeling was beyond argument. With her hands resting on his muscular shoulders, she leaned her head against his broad chest and sighed her contentment.

She spoke first. "It's a wonderful party."

"You're more comfortable now, aren't you?" His fingers moved up and down her back in a leisurely exercise, drugging her with his firm caress against her bare skin.

"What do you mean?" She wasn't sure she understood his question and slowly lifted her gaze.

"Last week, you stayed on the outskirts of the crowd afraid of joining in or being yourself."

"Last week I was terrified that someone would recognize me as the one who had once demonstrated against you. I didn't want to do anything that would embarrass you," she explained dryly. Her cheek was pressed against his starched shirt and she thrilled to the uneven thump of his heart.

"And this week?"

"Tonight anyone who looked at us would know that we've long since resolved our differences."

She sensed more than felt Andrew's soft touch. The moment was quickly becoming too intimate. Using her hands for leverage, Jo Marie straightened, creating a space between them. "Does it bother you to have my brother dance with Kelly?"

Andrew looked back at her blankly. "No. Should it?"

"She's your fiancée." To the best of Jo Marie's knowledge, Andrew hadn't said more than a few words to Kelly all evening.

A cloud of emotion darkened his face. "She's wearing my ring."

"And...and you care for her."

Andrew's hold tightened painfully around her waist. "Yes, I care for Kelly. We've always been close." His eyes darkened to the color of burnt silver. "Perhaps too close."

The applause was polite when the dance number finished.

Jo Marie couldn't escape fast enough. She made an excuse and headed for the powder room. Andrew wasn't pleased and it showed in the grim set of his mouth, but he didn't try to stop her. Things weren't right. Mark shouldn't be sitting like an avenging angel at Kelly's side and Andrew should at least show some sign of jealousy.

When she returned to the ballroom, Andrew was busy and Jo Marie decided to sort through her thoughts in the fresh night air. A curtained glass door that led to the balcony was open, and unnoticed she slipped silently into the dark. A flash of white captured her attention and Jo Marie realized she wasn't alone. Inadvertently, she had invaded the private world of two young lovers. With their arms wrapped around each other they were locked in a passionate embrace. Smiling softly to herself, she turned to escape as silently as she'd come. But something stopped her. A sickening knot tightened her stomach.

The couple so passionately embracing were Kelly and Mark.

Chapter Six

Jo Marie woke just as dawn broke over a cloudless horizon. Standing at the bedroom window, she pressed her palms against the sill and surveyed the beauty of the landscape before her. Turning, she glanced at Kelly's sleeping figure. Her hands fell limply to her side as her face darkened with uncertainty. Last night while they'd prepared for bed, Jo Marie had been determined to confront her friend with the kiss she'd unintentionally witnessed. But when they'd turned out the lights, Kelly had chatted happily about the success of the party and what a good time she'd had. And Jo Marie had lost her nerve. What Mark and Kelly did wasn't any of her business, she mused. In addition, she had no right to judge her brother and her friend when she and Andrew had done the same thing.

The memory of Andrew's kiss produce a breathlessness, and surrendering to the feeling, Jo Marie closed her eyes. The infinitely sweet touch of his

mouth seemed to have branded her. Her fingers shook
as she raised them to the gentle curve of her lips. Jo
Marie doubted that she would ever feel the same
overpowering rush of sensation at another man's
touch. Andrew was special, her dream man. Whole
lifetimes could pass and she'd never find anyone she'd
love more. The powerful ache in her heart drove her
to the closet where a change of clothes were hanging.

Dawn's light was creeping up the stairs, awaking a
sleeping world, when Jo Marie softly clicked the bedroom door closed. Her overnight bag was clenched
tightly in her hand. She hated to sneak out, but the
thought of facing everyone over the breakfast table
was more than she could bear. Andrew and Kelly
needed to be alone. Time together was something they
hadn't had much of lately. This morning would be the
perfect opportunity for them to sit down and discuss
their coming marriage. Jo Marie would only be an
intruder.

Moving so softly that no one was likely to hear her,
Jo Marie crept down the stairs to the wide entry hall.
She was tiptoeing toward the front door when a voice
behind her interrupted her quiet departure.

"What do you think you're doing?"

Releasing a tiny, startled cry, Jo Marie dropped the
suitcase and held her hand to her breast.

"Andrew, you've frightened me to death."

"Just what are you up to?"

"I'm...I'm leaving."

"That's fairly easy to ascertain. What I want to
know is why." His angry gaze locked with hers, refusing to allow her to turn away.

"I thought you and Kelly should spend some time
together and...and I wanted to be gone this morning

before everyone woke." Regret crept into her voice. Maybe sneaking out like this wasn't such a fabulous idea, after all.

He stared at her in the dim light as if he could examine her soul with his penetrating gaze. When he spoke again, his tone was lighter. "And just how did you expect to get to town. Walk?"

"Exactly."

"But it's miles."

"All the more reason to get an early start," she reasoned.

Andrew studied her as though he couldn't believe what he was hearing. "Is running away so important that you would sneak out of here like a cat burglar and not tell anyone where you're headed?"

How quickly her plan had backfired. By trying to leave unobtrusively she'd only managed to offend Andrew when she had every reason to thank him. "I didn't mean to be rude, although I can see now that I have been. I suppose this makes me look like an ungrateful house guest."

His answer was to narrow his eyes fractionally.

"I want you to know I left a note that explained where I was going to both you and Kelly. It's on the nightstand."

"And what did you say?"

"That I enjoyed the party immensely and that I've never felt more beautiful in any dress."

A brief troubled look stole over Andrew's face. "Once," he murmured absently. "Only onece have you been more lovely." There was an unexpectedly gentle quality to his voice.

Her eyelashes fluttered closed. Andrew was reminding her of that February night. He too hadn't been able to forget the Mardi Gras. After all this time, after everything that had transpired since, neither of them could forget. The spell was as potent today as it had been those many months ago.

"Is that coffee I smell?" The question sought an invitation to linger with Andrew. Her original intent had been to escape so that Kelly could have the opportunity to spend this time alone with him. Instead, Jo Marie was seeking it herself. To sit in the early light of dawn and savor a few solitary minutes alone with Andrew was too tempting to ignore.

"Come and I'll get you a cup." Andrew led her toward the back of the house and his den. The room held a faint scent of leather and tobacco that mingled with the aroma of musk and spice.

Three walls were lined with leather-bound books that reached from the floor to the ceiling. Two wing chairs were angled in front of a large fireplace.

"Go ahead and sit down. I'll be back in a moment with the coffee."

A contented smile brightened Jo Marie's eyes as she sat and noticed the leather volume she'd given him lying open on the ottoman. Apparently he'd been reading it when he heard the noise at the front of the house and had left to investigate.

Andrew returned and carefully handed her the steaming earthenware mug. His eyes followed her gaze which rested on the open book. "I've been reading it. This is a wonderful book. Where did you ever find something like this?"

"I've known about it for a long time, but there were only a few volumes available. I located this one about three months ago in a used-book store."

"It's very special to me because of the woman who bought it for me."

"No." Jo Marie's eyes widened as she lightly tossed her head from side to side. "Don't let that be the reason. Appreciate the book for all the interesting details it gives of New Orleans' colorful past. Or admire the pictures of the city architects' skill. But don't treasure it because of me."

Andrew looked for a moment as if he wanted to argue, but she spoke again.

"When you read this book ten, maybe twenty, years from now, I'll only be someone who briefly passed through your life. I imagine you'll have trouble remembering what I looked like."

"You'll never be anyone who flits in and out of my life."

He said it with such intensity that Jo Marie's fingers tightened around the thick handle of the mug. "All right," she agreed with a shaky laugh. "I'll admit I barged into your peaceful existence long before Kelly introduced us but—"

"But," Andrew interrupted on a short laugh, "it seems we were destined to meet. Do you honestly believe that either of us will ever forget that night?" A faint smile touched his eyes as he regarded her steadily.

Jo Marie knew that she never would. Andrew was her dream man. It had been far more than mere fate that had brought them together, something almost spiritual.

"No," she answered softly. "I'll never forget."

Regret moved across his features, creasing his wide brow and pinching his mouth. "Nor will I forget," he murmured in a husky voice that sounded very much like a vow.

The air between them was electric. For months she'd thought of Andrew as the dream man. But coming to know him these past weeks had proven that he wasn't an apparition, but real. Human, vulnerable, proud, intelligent, generous—and everything that she had ever hoped to find in a man. She lowered her gaze and studied the dark depths of the steaming coffee. Andrew might be everything she had ever wanted in a man, but Kelly wore his ring and her roommate's stake on him was far more tangible than her own romantic dreams.

Taking an exaggerated drink of her coffee, Jo Marie carefully set aside the rose-colored mug and stood. "I really should be leaving."

"Please stay," Andrew requested. "Just sit with me a few minutes longer. It's been in this room that I've sat and thought about you so often. I'd always hoped that someday you would join me here."

Jo Marie dipped her head, her heart singing with the beauty of his words. She'd fantasized about him too. Since their meeting, her mind had conjured up his image so often that it wouldn't hurt to steal a few more moments of innocent happiness. Kelly would have him for a lifetime. Jo Marie had only today.

"I'll stay," she agreed and her voice throbbed with the excited beat of her heart.

"And when the times comes, I'll drive you back to the city."

She nodded her acceptance and finished her coffee. "It's so peaceful in here. It feels like all I need to do is lean my head back, close my eyes and I'll be asleep."

"Go ahead," he urged in a whispered tone.

A smile touched her radiant features. She didn't want to fall asleep and miss these precious moments alone with him. "No." She shook her head. "Tell me about yourself. I want to know everything."

His returning smile was wry. "I'd hate to bore you."

"Bore me!" Her small laugh was incredulous. "There's no chance of that."

"All right, but lay back and close your eyes and let me start by telling you that I had a good childhood with parents who deeply loved each other."

As he requested, Jo Marie rested her head against the cushion and closed her eyes. "My parents are wonderful too."

"But being raised in an ideal family has its drawbacks," Andrew continued in a low, soothing voice. "When it came time for me to think about a wife and starting a family there was always a fear in the back of my mind that I would never find the happiness my parents shared. My father wasn't an easy man to love. And I won't be either."

In her mind, Jo Marie took exception to that, but she said nothing. The room was warm, and slipping off her shoes, she tucked her nylon-covered feet under her. Andrew continued speaking, his voice droning on as she tilted her head back.

"When I reached thirty without finding a wife, I became skeptical about the women I was meeting. There were some who never saw past the dollar signs and others who were interested only in themselves. I wanted a woman who could be soft and yielding, but one who wasn't afraid to fight for what she believes, even if it meant standing up against tough opposition. I wanted someone who would share my joys and divide my worries. A woman as beautiful on the inside as any outward beauty she may possess."

"Kelly's like that." The words nearly stuck in Jo Marie's throat. Kelly was everything Andrew was describing and more. As painful as it was to admit, Jo Marie understood why Andrew had asked her roommate to marry him. In addition to her fine personal qualities, Kelly had money of her own and Andrew need never think that she was marrying him for any financial gains.

"Yes, Kelly's like that." There was a doleful timbre to his voice that caused Jo Marie to open her eyes.

Fleetingly she wondered if Andrew had seen Mark and Kelly kissing on the terrace last night. If he had created the picture of a perfect woman in his mind, then finding Kelly in Mark's arms could destroy him. No matter how uncomfortable it became, Jo Marie realized she was going to have to confront Mark about his behavior. Having thoughtfully analyzed the situation, Jo Marie believed it would be far better for her to talk to her brother. She could speak more freely with him. It may be the hardest thing she'd ever do, but after listening to Andrew, Jo Marie realized that she must talk to Mark. The happiness of too many people was at stake.

Deciding to change the subject, Jo Marie shifted her position in the supple leather chair and looked to Andrew. "Kelly told me that you built the house yourself."

Grim amusement was carved in his features. "Yes, the work began on it this spring."

"Then you've only been living in it a few months?"

"Yes. The construction on the house kept me from going insane." He held her look, revealing nothing of his thoughts.

"Going insane?" Jo Marie didn't understand.

"You see, for a short time last February, only a matter of moments really, I felt my search for the right woman was over. And in those few, scant moments I thought I had met that special someone I could love for all time."

Jo Marie's heart was pounding so fast and loud that she wondered why it didn't burst right out of her chest. The thickening in her throat made swallowing painful. Each breath became labored as she turned her face away, unable to meet Andrew's gaze.

"But after those few minutes, I lost her," Andrew continued. "Ironically, I'd searched a lifetime for that special woman, and within a matter of minutes, she was gone. God knows I tried to find her again. For a month I went back to the spot where I'd last seen her and waited. When it seemed that all was lost I discovered I couldn't get the memory of her out of my mind. I even hired a detective to find her for me. For months he checked every hospital in the city, searching for her. But you see, at the time I thought she was a nurse."

Jo Marie felt moisture gathering in the corner of her eyes. Never had she believed that Andrew had looked for her to the extent that he hired someone.

"For a time I was convinced I was going insane. This woman, whose name I didn't even know, filled my every waking moment and haunted my sleep. Building the house was something I've always wanted to do. It helped fill the time until I could find her again. Every room was constructed with her in mind."

Andrew was explaining that he'd built the house for her. Jo Marie had thought she'd be uncomfortable in such a magnificent home. But she'd immediately felt the welcome in the walls. Little had she dreamed the reason why.

"Sometimes," Jo Marie began awkwardly, "people build things up in their minds and when they're confronted with reality they're inevitably disappointed." Andrew was making her out to be wearing angel's wings. So much time had passed that he no longer saw her as flesh and bone, but a wonderful fantasy his mind had created.

"Not this time," he countered smoothly.

"I wondered where I'd find the two of you." A sleepy-eyed Kelly stood poised in the doorway of the den. There wasn't any censure in her voice, only her usual morning brightness. "Isn't it a marvelous morning? The sun's up and there's a bright new day just waiting for us."

Self-consciously, Jo Marie unwound her feet from beneath her and reached for her shoes. "What time is it?"

"A quarter to eight." Andrew supplied the information.

Jo Marie was amazed to realize that she'd spent the better part of two hours talking to him. But it would be time she'd treasure all her life.

"If you have no objections," Kelly murmured and paused to take a wide yawn, "I thought I'd go to the hospital this morning. There's a special...patient I'd like to stop in and visit."

A patient or Mark, Jo Marie wanted to ask. Her brother had mentioned last night that he was going to be on duty in the morning. Jo Marie turned to Andrew, waiting for a reaction from him. Surely he would say or do something to stop her. Kelly was his fiancée and both of them seemed to be regarding their commitment to each other lightly.

"No problem." Andrew spoke at last. "In fact I thought I'd go into the city myself this morning. It is a beautiful day and there's no better way to spend a portion of it than in the most beautiful city in the world. You don't mind if I tag along with you, do you, Jo Marie?"

Half of her wanted to cry out in exaltation. If there was anything she wished to give of herself to Andrew it was her love of New Orleans. But at the same time she wanted to shake both Andrew and Kelly for the careless attitude they had toward their relationship.

"I'd like you to come." Jo Marie spoke finally, answering Andrew.

It didn't take Kelly more than a few moments to pack her things and be ready to leave. In her rush, she'd obviously missed the two sealed envelopes Jo Marie had left propped against the lamp on Kelly's nightstand. Or if she had discovered them, Kelly chose not to mention it. Not that it mattered, Jo Marie decided as Andrew started the car. But Kelly's actions revealed what a rush she was in to see Mark. If it was Mark that she was indeed seeing. Confused emotions flooded Jo Marie's face, pinching lines around her nose and mouth. She could feel Andrew's caressing gaze as they drove toward the hospital.

"Is something troubling you?" Andrew questioned after they'd dropped Kelly off in front of Tulane Hospital. Amid protests from Jo Marie, Kelly had assured them that she would find her own way home. Standing on the sidewalk, she'd given Jo Marie a happy wave, before turning and walking toward the double glass doors that led to the lobby of the hospital.

"I think Kelly's going to see Mark," Jo Marie ventured in a short, rueful voice.

"I think she is too."

Jo Marie sat up sharply. "And that doesn't bother you?"

"Should it?" Andrew gave her a bemused look.

"Yes," she said and nodded emphatically. She would never have believed that Andrew could be so blind. "Yes, it should make you furious."

He turned and smiled briefly. "But it doesn't. Now tell me where you'd like to eat breakfast. Brennan's?"

Jo Marie felt trapped in a labyrinth in which no route made sense and from which she could see no escape. She was thoroughly confused by the actions of the three people she loved.

"I don't understand any of this," she cried in frustration. "You should be livid that Kelly and Mark are together."

A furrow of absent concentration darkened Andrew's brow as he drove. Briefly he glanced in her direction. "The time will come when you do understand," he explained cryptically.

Rubbing the side of her neck in agitation, Jo Marie studied Andrew as he drove. His answer made no sense, but little about anyone's behavior this last month had made sense. She hadn't pictured herself as being obtuse, but obviously she was.

Breakfast at Brennan's was a treat known throughout the south. The restaurant was built in the classic Vieux Carre style complete with courtyard. Because they didn't have a reservation, they were put on a waiting list and told it would be another hour before there would be a table available. Andrew eyed Jo

Marie, who nodded eagerly. For all she'd heard, the breakfast was worth the wait.

Taking her hand in his, they strolled down the quiet streets that comprised the French Quarter. Most of the stores were closed, the streets deserted.

"I was reading just this morning that the French established New Orleans in 1718. The Spanish took over the 3,000 French inhabitants in 1762, although there were so few Spaniards that barely anyone noticed until 1768. The French Quarter is like a city within a city."

Jo Marie smiled contentedly and looped her hand through his arm. "You mean to tell me that it takes a birthday present for you to know about your own fair city?"

Andrew chuckled and drew her closer by circling his arm around her shoulders. "Are you always snobbish or is this act for my benefit?"

They strolled for what seemed far longer than a mere hour, visiting Jackson Square and feeding the pigeons. Strolling back, with Andrew at her side, Jo Marie felt she would never be closer to heaven. Never would she want for anything more than today, this minute, with this man. Jo Marie felt tears mist her dusty eyes. A tremulous smile touched her mouth. Andrew was here with her. Within a short time he would be married to Kelly and she must accept that, but for now, he was hers.

The meal was everything they'd been promised. Ham, soft breads fresh from the bakery, eggs and a fabulous chicory coffee. A couple of times Jo Marie found herself glancing at Andrew. His expression revealed little and she wondered if he regretted having decided to spend this time with her. She prayed that wasn't the case.

When they stood to leave, Andrew reached for her hand and smiled down on her with shining gray eyes.

Jo Marie's heart throbbed with love. The radiant light of her happiness shone through when Andrew's arm slipped naturally around her shoulder as if branding her with his seal of protection.

"I enjoy being with you," he said and she couldn't doubt the sincerity in his voice. "You're the kind of woman who would be as much at ease at a formal ball as you would fishing from the riverside with rolled-up jeans."

"I'm not Huck Finn," she teased.

"No," he smiled, joining in her game. "Just my Florence Nightingale, the woman who has haunted me for the last nine months."

Self-consciously, Jo Marie eased the strap of her leather purse over her shoulder. "It's always been my belief that dreams have a way of fading, especially when faced with the bright light of the sun and reality."

"Normally, I'd agree with you," Andrew responded thoughtfully, "but not this time. There are moments so rare in one's life that recognizing what they are can sometimes be doubted. Of you, of that night, of us, I have no doubts."

"None?" Jo Marie barely recognized her own voice.

"None," he confirmed.

If that were so, then why did Kelly continue to wear his ring? How could he look at her with so much emotion and then ask another woman to share his life?

The ride to Jo Marie's apartment was accomplished in a companionable silence. Andrew pulled into the parking space and turned off the ignition. Jo Marie's gaze centered on the dashboard. Silently she'd hoped that he wouldn't come inside with her. The atmosphere when they were alone was volatile. And with everything that Andrew had told her this morning, Jo Marie doubted that she'd have the strength to stay out of his arms if he reached for her.

"I can see myself inside." Gallantly, she made an effort to avoid temptation.

"Nonsense," Andrew returned, and opening the car door, he removed her overnight case from the back seat.

Jo Marie opened her side and climbed out, not waiting for him to come around. A feeling of doom settled around her heart.

Her hand was steady as she inserted the key into the apartment lock, but that was the only thing that was. Her knees felt like rubber as the door swung open and she stepped inside the room, standing in the entryway. The drapes were pulled, blocking out the sunlight, making the apartment's surroundings all the more intimate.

"I have so much to thank you for," she began and nervously tugged a strand of dark hair behind her ear. "A simple thank you seems like so little." She hoped Andrew understood that she didn't want him to come any farther into the apartment.

The door clicked closed and her heart sank. "Where would you like me to put your suitcase?"

Determined not to make this situation any worse for them, Jo Marie didn't move. "Just leave it here."

A smoldering light of amused anger burned in his eyes as he set the suitcase down. "There's no help for this," he whispered as his hand slid slowly, almost unwillingly along the back of her waist. "Be angry with me later."

Any protests died the moment his mouth met hers in a demanding kiss. An immediate answering hunger seared through her veins, melting all resistance until she was molded against the solid wall of his chest. His caressing fingers explored the curve of her neck and shoulders and his mouth followed, blazing a trail that led back to her waiting lips.

Jo Marie rotated her head, giving him access to any part of her face that his hungry mouth desired. She offered no protest when his hands sought the fullness of her breast, then sighed with the way her body responded to the gentleness of his fingers. He kissed her expertly, his mobile mouth moving insistently over hers, teasing her with light, biting nips that made her yearn for more and more. Then he'd change his tactics and kiss her with a hungry demand. Lost in a mindless haze, she clung to him as the tears filled her eyes and ran unheeded down her cheeks. Everything she feared was happening. And worse, she was powerless to stop him. Her throat felt dry and scratchy and she uttered a soft sob in a effort to abate the flow of emotion.

Andrew went still. He cupped her face in his hands and examined her tear-streaked cheeks. His troubled expression swam in and out of her vision.

"Jo Marie," he whispered, his voice tortured. "Don't cry, darling, please don't cry." With an infinite tenderness he kissed away each tear and when he reached her trembling mouth, the taste of salt was on his lips. A series of long, drugging kisses only confused her more. It didn't seem possible she could want him so much and yet that it should be so wrong.

"Please." With every ounce of strength she possessed Jo Marie broke from his embrace. "I promised myself this wouldn't happen again," she whispered feeling miserable. Standing with her back to him, her hands cradled her waist to ward off a sudden chill.

Gently he pressed his hand to her shoulder and Jo Marie couldn't bring herself to brush it away. Even his touch had the power to disarm her.

"Jo Marie." His husky tone betrayed the depths of his turmoil. "Listen to me."

"No, what good would it do?" she asked on a quavering sob. "You're engaged to be married to my best friend. I can't help the way I feel about you. What I feel, what you feel, is wrong as long as Kelly's wearing your ring." With a determined effort she turned to face him, tears blurring her sad eyes. "It would be better if we didn't see each other again...at least until you're sure of what you want..or who you want."

Andrew jerked his hand through his hair. "You're right. I've got to get this mess straightened out."

"Promise me, Andrew, please promise me that you won't make an effort to see me until you know in your own mind what you want. I can't take much more of this." She wiped the moisture from her cheekbones with the tips of her fingers. "When I get up in the morning I want to look at myself in the mirror. I don't want to hate myself."

Andrew's mouth tightened with grim displeasure. He looked as if he wanted to argue. Tense moments passed before he slowly shook his head. "You deserve to be treated so much better than this. Someday, my love, you'll understand. Just trust me for now.''

"I'm only asking one thing of you," she said unable to meet his gaze. "Don't touch me or make an effort to see me as long as Kelly's wearing your ring. It's not fair to any one of us." Her lashes fell to veil the hurt in her eyes. Andrew couldn't help but know that she was in love with him. She would have staked her life that her feelings were returned full measure. Fresh tears misted her eyes.

"I don't want to leave you like this."

"I'll be all right," she murmured miserably. "There's nothing that I can do. Everything rests with you, Andrew. Everything."

Dejected, he nodded and added a promise. "I'll take care of it today."

Again Jo Marie wiped the wetness from her face and forced a smile, but the effort was almost more than she could bear.

The door clicked, indicating that Andrew had gone and Jo Marie released a long sigh of pent-up emotion. Her reflection in the bathroom mirror showed that her lips were parted and trembling from the hungry possession of his mouth. Her eyes had darkened from the strength of her physical response.

Andrew had asked that she trust him and she would, with all her heart. He loved her, she was sure of it. He wouldn't have hired a detective to find her or built a huge home with her in mind if he didn't feel something strong toward her. Nor could he have held her and kissed her the way he had today without loving and needing her.

While she unpacked the small overnight bag a sense of peace came over her. Andrew would explain everything to Kelly, and she needn't worry. Kelly's interests seemed to be centered more on Mark lately, and maybe...just maybe, she wouldn't be hurt or upset and would accept that neither Andrew nor Jo Marie had planned for this to happen.

Time hung heavily on her hands and Jo Marie toyed with the idea of visiting her parents. But her mother knew her so well that she'd take one look at Jo Marie and want to know what was bothering her daughter. And today Jo Marie wasn't up to explanations.

A flip of the radio dial and Christmas music drifted into the room, surrounding her with its message of peace and love. Humming the words softly to herself, Jo Marie felt infinitely better. Everything was going to be fine, she felt confident.

A thick Sunday paper held her attention for the better part of an hour, but at the slightest noise, Jo Marie's attention wandered from the printed page and she glanced up expecting Kelly. One look at her friend would be enough to tell Jo Marie everything she needed to know.

Setting the paper aside, Jo Marie felt her nerves tingle with expectancy. She felt weighted with a terrible guilt. Kelly obviously loved Andrew enough to agree to be his wife, but she showed all the signs of falling in love with Mark. Kelly wasn't the kind of girl who would purposely hurt or lead a man on. She was too sensitive for that. And to add to the complications were Andrew and Jo Marie who had discovered each other again just when they had given up all hope. Jo Marie loved Andrew, but she wouldn't find her own happiness at her friend's expense. But Andrew was going to ask for his ring back, Jo Marie was sure of it. He'd said he'd clear things up today.

The door opened and inhaling a calming breath, Jo Marie stood.

Kelly came into the apartment, her face lowered as her gaze avoided her friend's.

"Hi," Jo Marie ventured hesitantly.

Kelly's face was red and blotchy; tears glistened in her eyes.

"Is something wrong?" Her voice faltered slightly.

"Drew and I had a fight, that's all." Kelly raised her hand to push back her hair and as she did so the engagement ring Andrew had given her sparkled in the sunlight.

Jo Marie felt the knot tighten in her stomach. Andrew had made his decision.

Chapter Seven

Somehow Jo Marie made it through the following days. She didn't see Andrew and made excuses to avoid Kelly. Her efforts consisted of trying to get through each day. Once she left the office, she often went to the LFTF headquarters, spending long hours helping Jim. Their friendship had grown. Jim helped her laugh when it would have been so easy to cry. A couple of times they had coffee together and talked. But Jim did most of the talking. This pain was so all-consuming that Jo Marie felt like a newly fallen leaf tossed at will by a fickle wind.

Jim asked her to accompany him on another speaking engagement which Jo Marie did willingly. The talk was on a stretch of wetlands Jim wanted preserved and it had been well received. Silently, Jo Marie mocked herself for not being attracted to someone as wonderful as Jim Rowden. He was everything a woman could want. In addition, she was convinced that he was interested in her. But it was Andrew who continued to fill her thoughts, Andrew who haunted her dreams, Andrew whose soft whisper she heard in the wind.

Lost in the meandering trail of her musing, Jo Marie didn't hear Jim's words as they sauntered into the empty office. Her blank look prompted him to repeat himself. "I thought it went rather well tonight, didn't you?" he asked, grinning boyishly. He brushed the hair from his forehead and pulled out the chair opposite hers.

"Yes," Jo Marie agreed with an absent shake of her head. "It did go well. You're a wonderful speaker." She could feel Jim's gaze watching her and in an effort to avoid any questions, she stood and reached for her purse. "I'd better think about getting home."

"Want some company while you walk to the bus stop?"

"I brought the car tonight." She almost wished she was taking the bus. Jim was a friendly face in a world that had taken on ragged, pain-filled edges.

Kelly had been somber and sullen all week. Half the time she looked as if she were ready to burst into tears at the slightest provocation. Until this last week, Jo Marie had always viewed her roommate as an emotionally strong woman, but recently Jo Marie wondered if she really knew Kelly. Although her friend didn't enjoy large parties, she'd never known Kelly to be intimidated by them. Lately, Kelly had been playing the role of a damsel in distress to the hilt.

Mark had stopped by the apartment only once and he'd resembled a volcano about to explode. He'd left after fifteen minutes of pacing the living-room carpet when Kelly didn't show.

And Andrew—yes, Andrew—by heaven's grace she'd been able to avoid a confrontation with him. She'd seen him only once in the last five days and the look in his eyes had seared her heart. He desperately wanted to talk to her. The tormented message was clear in his eyes, but she'd gently shaken her head, indicating that she intended to hold him to his word.

"Something's bothering you, Jo Marie. Do you want to talk about it?" Dimples edged into Jim's round face. Funny how she'd never noticed them before tonight.

Sadness touched the depths of her eyes and she gently shook her head. "Thanks, but no. Not tonight."

"Venturing a guess, I'd say it had something to do with Mr. Delta Development."

"Oh?" Clenching her purse under her arm, Jo Marie feigned ignorance. "What makes you say that?"

Jim shook his head. "A number of things." He rose and tucked both hands in his pants pockets. "Let me walk you to your car. The least I can do is see that you get safely outside."

"The weather's been exceptionally cold lately, hasn't it?"

Jim's smile was inviting as he turned the lock in the office door. "Avoiding my questions, aren't you?"

"Yes." Jo Marie couldn't see any reason to lie.

"When you're ready to talk, I'll be happy to listen." Tucking the keys in his pocket, Jim reached for Jo Marie's hand, placing it at his elbow and patting it gently.

"Thanks, I'll remember that."

"Tell me something more about you," Jo Marie queried in a blatant effort to change the subject. Briefly Jim looked at her, his expression thoughtful.

They ventured onto the sidewalk. The full moon was out, its silver rays clearing a path in the night as they strolled toward her car.

"I'm afraid I'd bore you. Most everything you already know. I've only been with the foundation a month."

"LFTF needs people like you, dedicated, passionate, caring."

"I wasn't the one who gave permission for a transient to sleep in a doorway."

Jo Marie softly sucked in her breath. "How'd you know?"

"He came back the second night looking for a handout. The guy knew a soft touch when he saw one."

"What happened?"

Jim shrugged his shoulder and Jo Marie stopped walking in mid-stride. "You gave him some money!" she declared righteously. "And you call me a soft touch."

"As a matter of fact, I didn't. We both knew what he'd spend it on."

"So what did you do?"

"Took him to dinner."

A gentle smile stole across her features at the picture that must have made. Jim dressed impeccably in his business suit and the alcoholic in tattered, ragged clothes.

"It's sad to think about." Slowly, Jo Marie shook her head.

"I got in touch with a friend of mine from a mission. He came for him afterward so that he'll have a place to sleep at least. To witness, close at hand like that, a man wasting his life is far worse to me than..." he paused and held her gaze for a long moment, looking deep into her brown eyes. Then he smiled faintly and shook his head. "Sorry, I didn't mean to get so serious."

"You weren't," Jo Marie replied, taking the car keys from her purse. "I'll be back Monday and maybe we could have a cup of coffee."

The deep blue eyes brightened perceptively. "I'd like that and listen, maybe we could have dinner one night soon."

Jo Marie nodded, revealing that she'd enjoy that as well. Jim was her friend and she doubted that her feelings would ever go beyond that, but the way she felt lately, she needed someone to lift her from the doldrums of self-pity.

The drive home was accomplished in a matter of minutes. Standing otuside her apartment building, Jo Marie heaved a steadying breath. She dreaded walking into her own home—what a sad commentary on her life! Tonight, she promised herself, she'd make an effort to clear the air between herself and Kelly. Not knowing what Andrew had said to her roommate about his feelings for her, if anything, or the details of the argument, had put Jo Marie in a precarious position. The air between Jo Marie and her best friend was like the stillness before an electrical storm. The problem was that Jo Marie didn't know what to say to Kelly or how to go about making things right.

She made a quick survey of the cars in the parking lot to assure herself that Andrew wasn't inside. Relieved, she tucked her hands inside the pockets of her cardigan and hoped to give a nonchalant appearance when she walked through the front door.

Kelly glanced up from the book she was reading when Jo Marie walked inside. The red, puffy eyes were a testimony of tears, but Kelly didn't explain and Jo Marie didn't pry.

"I hope there's something left over from dinner," she began on a forced note of cheerfulness. "I'm starved."

"I didn't fix anything," Kelly explained in an ominously quiet voice. "In fact I think I'm coming down with something. I've got a terrible stomachache."

Jo Marie had to bite her lip to keep from shouting that she knew what was wrong with the both of them. Their lives were beginning to resemble a three-ring circus. Where once Jo Marie and Kelly had been best friends, now they rarely spoke.

"What I think I'll do is take a long, leisurely bath and go to bed."

Jo Marie nodded, thinking Kelly's sudden urge for a hot soak was just an excuse to leave the room and avoid the problems that faced them.

While Kelly ran her bathwater, Jo Marie searched through the fridge looking for something appetizing. Normally this was the time of the year that she had to watch her weight. This Christmas she'd probably end up losing a few pounds.

The radio was playing a series of spirited Christmas carols and Jo Marie started humming along. She took out bread and cheese slices from the fridge. The cupboard offered a can of tomato soup.

By the time Kelly came out of the bathroom, Jo Marie had set two places at the table and was pouring hot soup into deep bowls.

"Dinner is served," she called.

Kelly surveyed the table and gave her friend a weak, trembling smile. "I appreciate the effort, but I'm really not up to eating."

Exhaling a dejected sigh, Jo Marie turned to her friend. "How long are we going to continue pretending like this? We need to talk, Kell."

"Not tonight, please, not tonight."

The doorbell rang and a stricken look came over Kelly's pale features. "I don't want to see anyone," she announced and hurried into the bedroom, leaving Jo Marie to deal with whoever was calling.

Resentment burned in her dark eyes as Jo Marie crossed the room. If it was Andrew, she would simply explain that Kelly was ill and not invite him inside.

"Merry Christmas." A tired-looking Mark greeted Jo Marie sarcastically from the other side of the door.

"Hi." Jo Marie watched him carefully. Her brother looked terrible. Tiny lines etched about his eyes revealed lack of sleep. He looked as though he was suffering from both mental and physical exhaustion.

"Is Kelly around?" He walked into the living room, sat on the sofa and leaned forward, roughly rubbing his hands across his face as if that would keep him awake.

"No, she's gone to bed. I don't think she's feeling well."

Briefly, Mark stared at the closed bedroom door and as he did, his shoulder hunched in a gesture of defeat.

"How about something to eat? You look like you haven't had a decent meal in days."

"I haven't." He moved lackadaisically to the kitchen and pulled out a chair.

Lifting the steaming bowls of soup from the counter, Jo Marie brought them to the table and sat opposite her brother.

As Mark took the soup spoon, his tired eyes held a distant, unhappy look. Kelly's eyes had revealed the same light of despair. "We had an argument," he murmured.

"You and Kell?"

"I said some terrible things to her." He braced his elbow against the table and pinched the bridge of his nose. "I don't know what made me do it. The whole time I was shouting at her I felt as if it was some stranger doing this. I know it sounds crazy but it was almost as if I were standing outside myself watching, and hating myself for what I was doing."

"Was the fight over something important?"

Defensively, Mark straightened. "Yeah, but that's between Kelly and me." He attacked the toasted cheese sandwich with a vengeance.

"You're in love with Kelly, aren't you?" Jo Marie had yet to touch her meal, more concerned about what was happening between her brother and her best friend than about her soup and sandwich.

Mark hesitated thoughtfully and a faint grimness closed off his expression. "In love with Kelly? I am?"

"You obviously care for her."

"I care for my cat, too," he returned coldly and his expression hardened. "She's got what she wants—money. Just look at who she's marrying. It isn't enough that she's wealthy in her own right. No, she sets her sights on J. Paul Getty."

Jo Marie's chin trembled in a supreme effort not to reveal her reaction to his words. "You know Kelly better than that." Averting her gaze, Jo Marie struggled to hold back the emotion that tightly constricted her throat.

"Does either one of us really know Kelly?" Mark's voice was taut as a hunter's bow. Cyncism drove deep grooved lines around his nose and mouth. "Did she tell you that she and Drew have set their wedding date?" Mark's voice dipped with contempt.

A pain seared all the way through Jo Marie's soul. "No, she didn't say." With her gaze lowered, she struggled to keep her hands from shaking.

"Apparently they're going to make it official after the first of the year. They're planning on a spring wedding."

"How...nice." Jo Marie nearly choked on the words.

"Well, all I can say is that those two deserve each other." He tossed the melted cheese sandwich back on the plate and stood. "I guess I'm not very hungry, after all."

Jo Marie rose with him and glanced at the table. Neither one of them had done more than shred their sandwiches and stir their soup. "Neither am I," she said, and swallowed at the tightness gripping her throat.

Standing in the living room, Mark stared for a second time at the closed bedroom door.

"I'll tell Kelly you were by." For a second it seemed that Mark hadn't heard.

"No," he murmured after a long moment. "Maybe it's best to leave things as they are. Good night, sis, thanks for dinner." Resembling a man carrying the weight of the world on his shoulders, Mark left.

Leaning against the front door, Jo Marie released a bitter, pain-filled sigh and turned the dead bolt. Tears burned for release. So Andrew and Kelly were going to make a public announcement of their engagement after Christmas. It shouldn't shock her. Kelly had told her from the beginning that they were. The wedding plans were already in the making. Wiping the salty dampness from her cheek, Jo Marie bit into the tender skin inside her cheek to hold back a sob.

"There's a call for you on line one," Paula called to Jo Marie from her desk.

"Thanks." With an efficiency born of years of experience, Jo Marie punched in the telephone tab and lifted the receiver to her ear. "This is Jo Marie Early, may I help you?"

"Jo Marie, this is Jim. I hope you don't mind me calling you at work."

"No problem."

"Good. Listen, you, ah, mentioned something the other night about us having coffee together and I said something about having dinner."

If she hadn't known any better, Jo Marie would have guessed that Jim was uneasy. He was a gentle man with enough sensitivity to campaign for the future. His hesitancy surprised her now. "I remember."

"How would you feel about this Wednesday?" he continued. "We could make a night of it."

Jo Marie didn't need to think it over. "I'd like that very much." After Mark's revelation, she'd realized the best thing to do was to put the past and Andrew behind her and build a new life for herself.

"Good." Jim sounded pleased. "We can go Wednesday night...or would you prefer Friday?"

"Wednesday's fine." Jo Marie doubted that she could ever feel again the deep, passionate attraction she'd experienced with Andrew, but Jim's appeal wasn't built on fantasy.

"I'll see you then. Goodbye, Jo Marie."

"Goodbye Jim, and thanks."

The mental uplifting of their short conversation was enough to see Jo Marie through a hectic afternoon. An airline lost her customer's reservations and the tickets didn't arrive in time. In addition the phone rang repeatedly.

By the time she walked into the apartment, her feet hurt and there was a nagging ache in the small of her back.

"I thought I heard you." Kelly sauntered into the kitchen and stood in the doorway dressed in a robe and slippers.

"How are you feeling?"

She lifted one shoulder in a weak shrug. "Better."

"You stayed home?" Kelly had still been in bed when Jo Marie left for work. Apparently her friend had phoned in sick.

"Yeah." She moved into the living room and sat on the sofa.

"Mark was by last night." Jo Marie mentioned the fact casually, waiting for a response from her roommate. Kelly didn't give her one. "He said that the two of you had a big fight," she continued.

"That's all we do anymore—argue."

"I don't know what he said to you, but he felt bad about it afterward."

A sad glimmer touched Kelly's eyes and her mouth formed a brittle line that Jo Marie supposed was meant to be a smile. "I know he didn't mean it. He's exhausted. I swear he's trying to work himself to death."

Now that her friend mentioned it, Jo Marie realized that she hadn't seen much of her brother lately. It used to be that he had an excuse to show up two or three times a week. Except for last night, he had been to the apartment only twice since Thanksgiving.

"I don't think he's eaten a decent meal in days," Kelly continued. "He's such a good doctor, Jo Marie, because he cares so much about his patients. Even the ones he knows he's going to lose. I'm a nurse, I've seen the way the other doctors close themselves off from any emotional involvement. But Mark's there, always giving." Her voice shook uncontrollably and she paused to bite into her lip until she regained her composure. "I wanted to talk to him the other night, and do you know where I found him? In pediatrics holding a little boy who's suffering with terminal cancer. He was rocking this child, holding him in his arms and telling him the pain wouldn't last too much longer. From the hallway, I heard Mark talk about heaven and how there wouldn't be any pain for him there. Mark's a wonderful man and wonderful doctor."

And he loves you so much it's tearing him apart, Jo Marie added silently.

"Yesterday he was frustrated and angry and he took it out on me. I'm not going to lie and say it didn't hurt. For a time I was devastated, but I'm over that now."

"But you didn't go to work today." They both knew why she'd chosen to stay home.

"No, I felt Mark and I needed a day away from each other."

"That's probably a good idea." There was so much she wanted to say to Kelly, but everything sounded so inadequate. At least they were talking, which was a major improvement over the previous five days.

The teakettle whistled sharply and Jo Marie returned to the kitchen bringing them both back a steaming cup of hot coffee.

"Thanks." Kelly's eyes brightened.

"Would you like me to talk to Mark?" Jo Marie's offer was sincere, but she wasn't exactly sure what she'd say. And in some ways it could make matters worse.

"No. We'll sort this out on our own."

The doorbell chimed and the two exchanged glances. "I'm not expecting anyone," Kelly murmured and glanced down self-consciously at her attire. "In fact I'd rather not be seen, so if you don't mind I'll vanish inside my room."

The last person Jo Marie expected to find on the other side of the door was Andrew. The welcome died in her eyes as their gazes met and clashed. Jo Marie quickly lowered hers. Her throat went dry and a rush of emotion brought a flood of color to her suddenly pale cheeks. A tense air of silence surrounded them. Andrew raised his hand as though he wanted to reach out and touch her. Instead he clenched his fist and lowered it to his side, apparently having changed his mind.

"Is Kelly ready?" he asked after a breathless moment. Jo Marie didn't move, her body blocking the front door, refusing him admittance.

She stared up at him blankly. "Ready?" she repeated.

"Yes, we're attending the opera tonight. Bizet's *Carmen*," he added as if in an afterthought.

"Oh, dear." Jo Marie's eyes widened. Kelly had obviously forgotten their date. The tickets for the elaborate opera had been sold out for weeks. Her roommate would have to go. "Come in, I'll check with Kelly."

"Andrew's here," Jo Marie announced and leaned against the wooden door inside the bedroom, her hands folded behind her.

"Drew?"

"Andrew to me, Drew to you," she responded cattily. "You have a date to see *Carmen*."

Kelly's hand flew to her forehead. "Oh, my goodness, I completely forgot."

"What are you going to do?"

"Explain, what else is there to do?" she snapped.

Jo Marie followed her friend into the living room. Andrew's gray eyes widened at the sight of Kelly dressed in her robe and slippers.

"You're ill?"

"Actually, I'm feeling better. Drew, I apologize, I completely forgot about tonight."

As Andrew glanced at his gold wristwatch, a frown marred his handsome face.

"Kelly can shower and dress in a matter of a few minutes," Jo Marie said sharply, guessing what Kelly was about to suggest.

"I couldn't possibly be ready in forty-five minutes," she denied. "There's only one thing to do. Jo Marie, you'll have to go in my place."

Andrew's level gaze crossed the width of the room to capture Jo Marie's. Little emotion was revealed in the impassive male features, but his gray eyes glinted with challenge.

"I can't." Her voice was level with hard determination.

"Why not?" Two sets of eyes studied her.

"I'm...." Her mind searched wildly for an excuse. "I'm baking cookies for the Science Club. We're meeting Saturday and this will be our last time before Christmas."

"I thought you worked Saturdays," Andrew cut in sharply.

"Every other Saturday." Calmly she met this gaze. Over the past couple of weeks, Kelly had purposely brought Jo Marie and Andrew together, but Jo Marie wouldn't fall prey to that game any longer. She'd made an agreement with him and refused to back down. As long as he was engaged to another woman she wouldn't...couldn't be with him. "I won't go," she explained in a steady voice which belied the inner turmoil that churned her stomach.

"There's plenty of time before the opening curtain if you'd care to change your mind."

Kelly tossed Jo Marie an odd look. "It looks like I'll have to go," she said with an exaggerated sigh. "I'll be as fast as I can." Kelly rushed back inside the bedroom leaving Jo Marie and Andrew separated by only a few feet.

"How have you been?" he asked, his eyes devouring her.

"Fine," she responded on a stiff note. The lie was only a little one. The width of the room stood between them, but it might as well have been whole light-years.

Bowing her head, she stared at the pattern in the carpet. When she suggested Kelly hurry and dress, she hadn't counted on being left alone with Andrew. "If you'll excuse me, I'll get started on those cookies."

To her dismay Andrew followed her into the kitchen.

"What are my chances of getting a cup of coffee?" He sounded pleased with himself, his smile was smug.

Wordlessly Jo Marie stood on her tiptoes and brought down a mug from the cupboard. She poured in the dark granules, stirred in hot water and walked past him to carry the mug into the living room. All the while her mind was screaming with him to leave her alone.

Andrew picked up the mug and followed her back into the kitchen. "I've wanted to talk to you for days."

"You agreed."

"Jo Marie, believe me, talking to Kelly isn't as easy as it seems. There are some things I'm not at liberty to explain that would resolve this whole mess."

"I'll just bet there are." The bitter taste of anger filled her mouth.

"Can't you trust me?" The words were barely audible and for an instant Jo Marie wasn't certain he'd spoken.

Everything within her yearned to reach out to him and be assured that the glorious times they'd shared had been as real for him as they'd been for her. Desperately she wanted to turn and tell him that she would trust him with her life, but not her heart. She couldn't, not when Kelly was wearing his engagement ring.

"Jo Marie." A faint pleading quality entered his voice. "I know how all this looks. At least give me a chance to explain. Have dinner with me tomorrow. I swear I won't so much as touch you. I'll leave everything up to you. Place. Time. You name it."

"No." Frantically she shook her head, her voice throbbing with the desire to do as he asked. "I can't."

"Jo Marie." He took a step toward her, then another, until he was so close his husky voice breathed against her dark hair.

Forcing herself into action, Jo Marie whirled around and backed out of the kitchen. "Don't talk to me like that. I realized last week that whatever you feel for Kelly is stronger than any love you have for me. I've tried to accept that as best I can."

Andrew's knuckles were clenched so tightly that they went white. He looked like an innocent man facing a firing squad, his eyes resigned, the line of his jaw tense, anger and disbelief etched in every rugged mark of his face.

"Just be patient, that's all I'm asking. In due time you'll understand everything."

"Will you stop?" she demanded angrily. "You're talking in puzzles and I've always hated those. All I know is that there are four people who—"

"I guess this will have to do," Kelly interrupted as she walked into the room. She had showered, dressed and dried her hair in record time.

Jo Marie swallowed the taste of jealousy as she watched the dark, troubled look dissolve from Andrew's eyes. "You look great," was all she could manage.

"We won't be too late," Kelly said on her way out.

"Don't worry," Jo Marie murmured and breathed in a sharp breath. "I won't be up; I'm exhausted."

Who was she trying to kid? Not until the key turned in the front door lock five hours later did Jo Marie so much as yawn. As much as she hated herself for being so weak, the entire time Kelly had been with Andrew, Jo Marie had been utterly miserable.

The dinner date with Jim the next evening was the only bright spot in a day that stretched out like an empty void. She dressed carefully and applied her makeup with extra care, hoping to camouflage the effects of a sleepless night.

"Don't fix dinner for me, I've got a date," was all she said to Kelly on her way out the door to the office.

As she knew it would, being with Jim was like stumbling upon an oasis in the middle of a sand-tossed desert. He made her laugh, teasing her affectionately. His humor was subtle and light and just the antidote for a broken heart. She'd known from the moment they'd met that she was going to like Jim Rowden. With him she could relax and be herself. And not once did she have to look over her shoulder.

"Are you going to tell me what's been troubling you?" he probed gently over their dessert.

"What? And cry all over my lime-chiffon pie?"

Jim's returning smile was one of understanding and encouragement. Again she noted the twin dimples that formed in his cheeks. "Whenever you're ready, I'm available to listen."

"Thanks." She shook her head, fighting back an unexpected swell of emotion. "Now what's this surprise you've been taunting me with most of the evening?'' she questioned, averting the subject from herself.

"It's about the wetlands we've been crusading for during the last month. Well, I talked to a state senator today and he's going to introduce a bill that would make the land into a state park." Lacing his hands together, Jim leaned toward the linen-covered table. "From everything he's heard, George claims from there it should be a piece of cake."

"Jim, that's wonderful." This was his first success and he beamed with pride over the accomplishment.

"Of course, nothing's definite yet, and I'm not even sure I should have told you, but you've heard me give two speeches on the wetlands and I wanted you to know."

"I'm honored that you did."

He acknowledged her statement with a short nod. "I should know better than to get my hopes up like this, but George—my friend—sounded so confident."

"Then you should be too. We both should."

Jim reached for her hand and squeezed it gently. "It would be very easy to share things with you, Jo Marie. You're quite a woman."

Flattery had always made her uncomfortable, but Jim sounded so sincere. It cost her a great deal of effort to simply smile and murmur her thanks.

Jim's arm rested across her shoulder as they walked back toward the office. He held open her car door for her and paused before lightly brushing his mouth over hers. The kiss was both gentle and reassuring. But it wasn't Andrew's kiss and Jim hadn't the power to evoke the same passionate response Andrew seemed to draw so easily from her.

On the ride home, Jo Marie silently berated herself for continuing to compare the two men. It was unfair to them both to even think in that mode.

The apartment was unlocked when Jo Marie let herself inside. She was hanging up her sweater-coat when she noticed Andrew. He was standing in the middle of the living room carpet, regarding her with stone cold eyes.

One glance and Jo Marie realized that she'd never seen a man look so angry.

"It's about time you got home." His eyes were flashing gray fire.

"What right is it of yours to demand what time I get in?"

"I have every right." His voice was like a whip lashing out at her. "I suppose you think you're playing a game. Every time I go out with Kelly, you'll pay me back by dating Jim?"

Stunned into speechlessness, Jo Marie felt her voice die in her throat.

"And if you insist on letting him kiss you the least you can do is look for someplace more private than the street." The white line about his mouth became more pronounced as his eyes filled with bitter contempt. "You surprise me, Jo Marie, I thought you had more class than that."

Chapter Eight

How dare you...how dare you say such things to me!" Jo Marie's quavering voice became breathless with rage. Her eyes were dark and stormy as she turned around and jerked the front door open.

"What do you expect me to believe?" Andrew rammed his hand through his hair, ruffling the dark hair that grew at his temple.

"I expected a lot of things from you, but not that you'd follow me or spy on me. And then...then to have the audacity to confront and insult me." The fury in her faded to be replaced with a deep, emotional pain that pierced her heart.

Andrew's face was bloodless as he walked past her and out the door. As soon as he was through the portal, she slammed it closed with a sweeping arc of her hand.

Jo Marie was so furious that the room wasn't large enough to contain her anger. Her shoulders rose and sagged with her every breath. At one time Andrew had been her dream man. Quickly she was learning to separate the fantasy from the reality.

Pacing the carpet helped relieve some of the terrible tension building within her. Andrew's behavior was nothing short of odious. She should hate him for saying those kinds of things to her. Tears burned for release, but deep, concentrated breaths held them at bay. Andrew Beaumont wasn't worth the emotion. Staring sightlessly at the ceiling, her damp lashes pressed against her cheek.

The sound of the doorbell caused her to whirl around. Andrew. She'd stake a week's salary on the fact. In an act of defiance, she folded her arms across her waist and stared determinedly at the closed door. He could rot in the rain before she'd open that door.

Again the chimes rang in short, staccato raps. "Come on, Jo Marie, answer the damn door."

"No," she shouted from the other side.

"Fine, we'll carry on a conversation by shouting at each other. That should amuse your neighbors."

"Go away." Jo Marie was too upset to talk things out. Andrew had hurt her with his actions and words.

"Jo Marie." The appealing quality in his voice couldn't be ignored. "Please, open the door. All I want is to apologize."

Hating herself for being so weak, Jo Marie turned the lock and threw open the solid wood door. "You have one minute."

"I think I went a little crazy when I saw Jim kiss you," he said pacing the area in front of the door. "Jo Marie, promise me that you won't see him again. I don't think I can stand the thought of any man touching you."

"This is supposed to be an apology?" she asked sarcastically. "Get this, Mr. Beaumont," she said, fighting to keep from shouting at him as her finger punctuated the air. "You have no right to dictate anything to me."

His tight features darkened. "I can make your life miserable."

"And you think you haven't already?" she cried. "Just leave me alone. I don't need your threats. I don't want to see you again. Ever." To her horror, her voice cracked. Shaking her head, unable to talk any longer, she shut the door and clicked the lock.

Almost immediately the doorbell chimed, followed by continued knocking. Neither of them were in any mood to discuss things rationally. And perhaps it was better all the way around to simply leave things as they were. It hurt, more than Jo Marie wanted to admit, but she'd recover. She'd go on with her life and put Andrew, the dream man and all of it behind her.

Without glancing over her shoulder, she ignored the sound and moved into her bedroom.

The restaurant was crowded, the luncheon crowd filling it to capacity. With Christmas only a few days away the rush of last-minute shoppers filled the downtown area and flowed into the restaurants at lunch time.

Seeing Mark come through the doors, Jo Marie raised her hand and waved in an effort to attract her brother's attention. He looked less fatigued than the last time she'd seen him. A brief smile momentarily brightened his eyes, but faded quickly.

"I must admit this is a surprise," Jo Marie said as her brother slid into the upholstered booth opposite her. "I can't remember the last time we met for lunch."

"I can't remember either." Mark picked up the menu, decided and closed it after only a minute.

"That was quick."

"I haven't got a lot of time."

Same old Mark, always in a rush, hurrying from one place to another. "You called me, remember?" she taunted softly.

"Yeah, I remember." His gaze was focused on the paper napkin which he proceeded to fold into an intricate pattern. "This is going to sound a little crazy so promise me you won't laugh."

The edge of her mouth was already twitching. "I promise."

"I want you to attend the hospital Christmas party with me Saturday night."

"Me?"

"I don't have time to go out looking for a date and I don't think I can get out of it without offending half the staff."

In the past three weeks, Jo Marie had endured enough parties to last her a lifetime. "I guess I could go."

"Don't sound so enthusiastic."

"I'm beginning to feel the same way about parties as you do."

"I doubt that," he said forcefully and shredded the napkin in half.

The waitress came for their order and delivered steaming mugs of coffee almost immediately afterward.

Jo Marie lifted her own napkin, toying with the pressed paper edge. "Will Kelly and...Drew be there?"

"I doubt it. Why should they? There won't be any ballroom dancing or a midnight buffet. It's a pot luck. Can you picture old 'money bags' sitting on a folding chair and balancing a paper plate on her lap? No. Kelly goes more for the two-hundred-dollar-a-place-setting affairs."

Jo Marie opened her mouth to argue, but decided it would do little good. Discussing Andrew—Drew, her mind corrected—or Kelly with Mark would be pointless.

"I suppose Kelly's told you?"

"Told me what?" Jo Marie glanced up curious and half-afraid. The last time Mark had relayed any information about Drew and Kelly it had been that they were going to publicly announce their engagement.

"She's given her two-week notice."

"No," Jo Marie gasped. "She wouldn't do that. Kelly loves nursing; she's a natural." Even more surprising was the fact that Kelly hadn't said a word to Jo Marie about leaving Tulane Hospital.

"I imagine with the wedding plans and all that she's decided to take any early retirement. Who can blame her, right?"

But it sounded very much like Mark was doing exactly that. His mouth was tight and his dark eyes were filled with something akin to pain. What a mess this Christmas was turning out to be.

"Let's not talk about Kelly or Drew or anyone for the moment, okay. It's Christmas next week." She forced a bit of yuletide cheer into her voice.

"Right," Mark returned with a short sigh. "It's almost Christmas." But for all the enthusiasm in his voice he could have been discussing German measles.

Their soup and sandwiches arrived and they ate in strained silence. "Well, are you coming or not?" Mark asked, pushing his empty plate aside.

"I guess." No need to force any enthusiasm into her voice. They both felt the same way about the party.

"Thanks, sis."

"Just consider it your Christmas present."

Mark reached for the white slip the waitress had placed on their table, examining it. "And consider this lunch yours," he announced and scooted from his seat. "See you Saturday night."

"Mark said you've given the hospital your two-week notice?" Jo Marie confronted her roommate first thing that evening.

"Yes," Kelly replied lifelessly.

"I suppose the wedding will fill your time from now on."

"The wedding?" Kelly gave her an absent look. "No," she shook her head and an aura of dejected defeat hung over her, dulling her responses. "I've got my application in at a couple of other hospitals."

"So you're going to continue working after you're married."

For a moment it didn't look as if Kelly had heard her. "Kell?" Jo Marie prompted.

"I'd hoped to."

Berating herself for caring how Kelly and Andrew lived their lives, Jo Marie picked up the evening paper and pretended an interest in the front page. But-if

Kelly had asked her so much as what the headline read she couldn't have answered.

Saturday night Jo Marie dressed in the blue dress that she'd sewn after Thanksgiving. It fit her well and revealed a subtle grace in her movements. Although she took extra time with her hair and cosmetics, her heart wasn't up to attending the party.

Jo Marie had casually draped a lace shawl over her shoulder when the front door opened and Kelly entered with Andrew at her side.

"You're going out," Kelly announced, stopping abruptly inside the living room. "You...you didn't say anything."

Jo Marie could feel Andrew's gaze scorching her in a slow, heated perusal, but she didn't look his way. "Yes, I'm going out; don't wait up for me."

"Drew and I have plans too."

Reaching for her evening bag, Jo Marie's mouth curved slightly upward in a poor imitation of a smile. "Have a good time."

Kelly said something more, but Jo Marie was already out the door, grateful to have escaped without another confrontation with Andrew.

Mark had given her the address of the party and asked that she meet him there. He didn't give any particular reason he couldn't pick her up. He didn't need an excuse. It was obvious he wanted to avoid Kelly.

She located the house without a problem and was greeted by loud music and a smoke-filled room. Making her way between the dancing couples, Jo Marie delivered the salad she had prepared on her brother's behalf to the kitchen. After exchanging pleasantries with the guests in the kitchen, Jo Marie went back to the main room to search for Mark.

For all the noisy commotion the party was an orderly one and Jo Marie spotted her brother almost immediately. He was sitting on the opposite side of the room talking to a group of other young men, who she assumed were fellow doctors. Making her way across the carpet, she was waylaid once by a nurse friend of Kelly's that she'd met a couple of times. They chatted for a few minutes about the weather.

"I suppose you've heard that Kelly's given her notice," Julie Frazier said with a hint of impatience. "It's a shame, if you ask me."

"I agree," Jo Marie murmured.

"Sometimes I'd like to knock those two over the head." Julie motioned toward Mark with the slight tilt of her head. "Your brother's one stubborn male."

"You don't need to tell me. I'm his sister."

"You know," Julie said and glanced down at the cold drink she was holding in her hand. "After Kelly had her tonsils out I could have sworn those two were headed for the altar. No one was more surprised than me when Kell turns up engaged to this mystery character."

"What do you mean about Kelly and Mark?" Kelly's tonsils had come out months ago during the Mardi Gras. No matter how much time passed, it wasn't likely that Jo Marie would forget that.

"Kelly was miserable—adult tonsillectomies are seldom painless—anyway, Kelly didn't want anyone around, not even her family. Mark was the only one who could get close to her. He spent hours with her, coaxing her to eat, spoon-feeding her. He even read her to sleep and then curled up in the chair beside her bed so he'd be there when she woke.''

Jo Marie stared back in open disbelief. "Mark did that?'' All these months Mark had been in love with Kelly and he hadn't said a word. Her gaze sought him now and she groaned inwardly at her own stupidity. For months she'd been so caught up in the fantasy of those few precious moments with Andrew that she'd been blind to what was right in front of her own eyes.

"Well, speaking of our friend, look who's just arrived.''

Jo Marie's gaze turned toward the front door just as Kelly and Andrew came inside. From across the length of the room, her eyes clashed with Andrew's. She watched as the hard line of his mouth relaxed and he smiled. The effect on her was devastating; her heart somersaulted and color rushed up her neck, invading her face. These were all the emotions she had struggled against from the beginning. She hated herself for being so vulnerable when it came to this one man. She didn't want to feel any of these emotions toward him.

"Excuse me—'' Julie interrupted Jo Marie's musings "—there's someone I wanted to see.''

"Sure.'' Mentally, Jo Marie shook herself and joined Mark, knowing she would be safe at his side.

"Did you see who just arrived?'' Jo Marie whispered in her brother's ear.

Mark's dusty dark eyes studied Kelly's arrival and Jo Marie witnessed an unconscious softening in his gaze. Kelly did look lovely tonight, and begrudgingly Jo Marie admitted that Andrew and Kelly were the most striking couple in the room. They belonged together—both were people of wealth and position. Two of a kind.

"I'm surprised that she came," Mark admitted slowly and turned his back to the pair. "But she's got as much right to be here as anyone."

"Of course she does."

One of Mark's friends appointed himself as disc jockey and put on another series of records for slow dancing. Jo Marie and Mark stood against the wall and watched as several couples began dancing on the makeshift dance floor. When Andrew turned Kelly into his arms, Jo Marie diverted her gaze to another section of the room, unable to look at them without being affected.

"You don't want to dance, do you?" Mark mumbled indifferently.

"With you?"

"No, I'd get one of my friends to do the honors. It's bad enough having to invite my sister to a party. I'm not about to dance with you, too."

Jo Marie couldn't prevent a short laugh. "You really know how to sweet talk a woman don't you, brother dearest?"

"I try," he murmured and his eyes narrowed on Kelly whose arms were draped around Andrew's neck as she whispered in his ear. "But obviously not hard enough," he finished.

Standing on the outskirts of the dancing couples made Jo Marie uncomfortable. "I think I'll see what I can do to help in the kitchen," she said as an excuse to leave.

Julie Frazier was there, placing cold cuts on a round platter with the precision of a mathematician.

"Can I help?" Jo Marie offered, looking around for something that needed to be done.

Julie turned and smiled her appreciation. "Sure. Would you put the serving spoons in the salads and set them out on the dining room table?"

"Glad to." She located the spoons in the silverware drawer and carried out a large glass bowl of potato salad. The Formica table was covered with a vinyl cloth decorated with green holly and red berries.

"And now ladies and gentleman—" the disc jockey demanded the attention of the room "—this next number is a ladies' choice."

With her back to the table, Jo Marie watched as Kelly whispered something to Andrew. To her surprise, he nodded and stepped aside as Kelly made her way to the other side of the room. Her destination was clear—Kelly was heading directly to Mark. Jo Marie's pulse fluttered wildly. If Mark said or did anything cruel to her friend, Jo Marie would never forgive him.

Her heart was in her eyes as Kelly tentatively tapped Mark on the shoulder. Engrossed in a conversation, Mark apparently wasn't aware he was being touched. Kelly tried again and Mark turned, surprise rounding his eyes when he saw her roommate.

Jo Marie was far enough to the side so that she couldn't be seen by Mark and Kelly, but close enough to hear their conversation.

"May I have this dance?" Kelly questioned, her voice firm and low.

"I thought it was the man's prerogative to ask." The edge of Mark's mouth curled up sarcastically. "And if you've noticed, I haven't asked."

"This number is ladies' choice."

Mark tensed visibly as he glared across the room, eyeing Andrew. "And what about Rockefeller over there?"

Slowly, Kelly shook her head, her inviting gaze resting on Mark. "I'm asking you. Don't turn me down, Mark, not tonight. I'll be leaving the hospital in a little while and then you'll never be bothered with me again."

Jo Marie doubted that her brother could have refused Kelly anything in that moment. Wordlessly he approached the dance floor and took Kelly in his arms. A slow ballad was playing and the soft, melodic sounds of Billy Joel filled the room. Kelly fit her body to Mark's. Her arms slid around his neck as she pressed her temple against his jaw. Mark reacted to the contact by closing his eyes and inhaling as his eyes drifted closed. His hold, which had been loose, tightened as he knotted his hands at the small of Kelly's back, arching her body closer.

For the first time that night, her brother looked completely at ease. Kelly belonged with Mark. Jo Marie had been wrong to think that Andrew and Kelly were meant for each other. They weren't, and their engagement didn't make sense.

Her eyes sought out the subject of her thoughts. Andrew was leaning against the wall only a few feet from her. His eyes locked with hers, refusing to release her. He wanted her to come to him. She couldn't. His gaze seemed to drink her in as it had the night of the Mardi Gras. She could almost feel him reaching out to her, imploring her to come, urging her to cross the room so he could take her in his arms.

With unconscious thought Jo Marie took one step forward and stopped. No. Being with Andrew would only cause her more pain. With a determined effort she lightly shook her head, effectively breaking the spell. Her heart was beating so hard that breathing was difficult. Her steps were marked with decision as she returned to the kitchen.

A sliding glass door led to a lighted patio. A need to escape for a few moments overtook her and silently she slipped past the others and escaped into the darkness of the night.

A chill ran up her arms and she rubbed her hands over her forearms in an effort to warm her blood. The stars were out in a dazzling display and Jo Marie tilted her face toward the heavens, gazing at the lovely sight.

Jo Marie stiffened as she felt more than heard someone join her. She didn't need to turn around to realize that it was Andrew.

He came and stood beside her, but he made no effort to speak, instead focusing his attention on the dark sky.

Whole eternities seemed to pass before Andrew spoke. "I came to ask your forgiveness."

All the pain of his accusation burned in her breast. "You hurt me," she said on a breathless note after a long pause.

"I know, my love, I know." Slowly he removed his suit jacket and with extraordinary concern, draped it over her shoulders, taking care not to touch her.

"I'd give anything to have those thoughtless words back. Seeing Jim take you in his arms was like waving a red flag in front of an angry bull. I lashed out at you, when it was circumstances that were at fault."

Something about the way he spoke, the emotion that coated his words, the regret that filled his voice made her feel that her heart was ready to burst right out of her breast. She didn't want to look at him, but somehow it was impossible to keep her eyes away. With an infinite tenderness, he brushed a stray curl from her cheek.

"Can you forgive me?"

"Oh, Andrew." She felt herself weakening.

"I'd go on my knees if it would help."

The tears felt locked in her throat. "No, that isn't necessary."

He relaxed as if a great burden had been lifted from his shoulders. "Thank you."

Neither moved, wanting to prolong this tender moment. When Andrew spoke it was like the whisper of a gentle breeze and she had to strain to hear him.

"When I first came out here you looked like a blue sapphire silhouetted in the moonlight. And I was thinking that if it were in my power, I'd weave golden moonbeams into your hair."

"Have you always been so poetic?"

His mouth curved upward in a slow, sensuous smile. "No." His eyes were filled with an undisguised hunger as he studied her. Ever so slowly, he raised his hand and placed it at the side of her neck.

The tender touch of his fingers against her soft skin caused a tingling sensation to race down her spine. The feeling was akin to pain. Jo Marie loved this man as she would never love again and he was promised to another woman.

"Jo Marie," he whispered and his warm breath fanned her mouth. "There's mistletoe here. Let me kiss you."

There wasn't, of course, but Jo Marie was unable to pull away. She nodded her acquiescence. "One last time." She hadn't meant to verbalize her thoughts.

He brought her into his arms and she moistened her lips anticipating the hungry exploration of his mouth over hers. But she was to be disappointed. Andrew's lips lightly moved over hers like the gentle brush of the spring sun on a hungry earth. Gradually the kiss deepened as he worked his way from one corner of her mouth to another—again like the earth long starved from summer's absence.

"I always knew it would be like this for us, Florence Nightingale," he whispered against her hair. "Even when I couldn't find you, I felt a part of myself would never be the same."

"I did too. I nearly gave up dating."

"I thought I'd go crazy. You were so close all these months and yet I couldn't find you."

"But you did." Pressing her hands against the strong cushion of his chest she created a space between them. "And now it's too late."

Andrew's eyes darkened as he seemed to struggle within himself. "Jo Marie." A thick frown marred his face.

"Shh." She pressed her fingertips against his lips. "Don't try to explain. I understand and I've accepted it. For a long time it hurt so much that I didn't think I'd be able to bear it. But I can and I will."

His hand circled her wrist and he closed his eyes before kissing the tips of her fingers. "There's so much I want to explain and can't."

"I know." With his arm holding her close, Jo Marie felt a deep sense of peace surround her. "I'd never be the kind of wife you need. Your position demands a woman with culture and class. I'm proud to be an Early and proud of my family, but I'm not right for you."

The grip on her wrist tightened. "Is that what you think?" The frustrated anger in his voice was barely suppressed. "Do you honestly believe that?"

"Yes," she answered him boldly. "I'm at peace within myself. I have no regrets. You've touched my heart and a part of me will never be the same. How can I regret having loved you? It's not within me."

He dropped her hand and turned from her, his look a mixture of angry torment. "You honestly think I should marry Kelly."

It would devastate Mark, but her brother would need to find his own peace. "Or someone like her." She removed his suit jacket from her shoulders and handed it back to him, taking care to avoid touching him. "Thank you," she whispered with a small catch to her soft voice. Unable to resist any longer, she raised her hand and traced his jaw. Very lightly, she brushed her mouth over his. "Goodbye, Andrew."

He reached out his hand in an effort to stop her, but she slipped past him. It took her only a moment to collect her shawl. Within a matter of minutes, she was out the front door and on her way back to the apartment. Mark would never miss her.

Jo Marie spent Sunday with her family, returning late that evening when she was assured Kelly was asleep. Lying in bed, studying the darkness around her, Jo Marie realized that she'd said her final goodbye to Andrew. Continuing to see him would only make it difficult for them both. Avoiding him had never succeeded, not when she yearned for every opportunity to be with him. The best solution would be to leave completely. Kelly would be moving out soon and Jo Marie couldn't afford to pay the rent on her own. The excuse would be a convenient one although Kelly was sure to recognize it for what it was.

After work Monday afternoon, before she headed for the LFTF office, Jo Marie stopped off at the hospital, hoping to talk to Mark. With luck, she might be able to convince her brother to let her move in with him. But only until she could find another apartment and another roommate.

Julie Frazier, the nurse who worked with both Kelly and Mark, was at the nurses' station on the surgical floor when Jo Marie arrived.

"Hi," she greeted cheerfully. "I don't suppose you know where Mark is?"

Julie glanced up from a chart she was reading. "He's in the doctors' lounge having a cup of coffee."

"Great. I'll talk to you later." With her shoes making clicking sounds against the polished floor, Jo Marie mused that her timing couldn't have been more perfect. Now all she needed was to find her brother in a good mood.

The doctors' lounge was at the end of the hall and was divided into two sections. The front part contained a sofa and a couple of chairs. A small kitchen area was behind that. The sound of Mark's and Kelly's voices stopped Jo Marie just inside the lounge.

"You can leave," Mark was saying in a tight, pained voice. "Believe me I have no intention of crying on your shoulder."

"I didn't come here for that," Kelly argued softly.

Jo Marie hesitated, unsure of what she should do. She didn't want to interrupt their conversation which seemed intense, nor did she wish to intentionally stay and listen in either.

"That case with the Randolph girl is still bothering you, isn't it?" Kelly demanded.

"No, I did everything I could. You know that."

"But it wasn't enough, was it?"

Jo Marie had to bite her tongue not to interrupt Kelly. It wasn't like her roommate to be unnecessarily cruel. Jo Marie vividly recalled her brother's doubts after the young child's death. It had been just before Thanksgiving and Mark had agonized that he had lost her.

"No," Mark shouted, "it wasn't enough."

"And now you're going to lose the Rickard boy." Kelly's voice softened perceptively.

Fleetingly Jo Marie wondered if this child was the one Kelly had mentioned who was dying of cancer.

"I've known that from the first." Mark's tone contained the steel edge of anger.

"Yes, but it hasn't gotten any easier, has it?"

"Listen, Kelly, I know what you're trying to do, but it isn't going to work."

"Mark," Kelly murmured his name on a sigh, "sometimes you are so blind."

"Maybe it's because I feel so inadequate. Maybe it's because I'm haunted with the fact that there might have been something more I could have done."

"But there isn't, don't you see?" Kelly's voice had softened as if her pain was Mark's. "Now won't you tell me what's really bothering you?"

"Maybe it's because I don't like the odds with Tommy. His endless struggle against pain. The deck was stacked against him from the beginning and now he hasn't got a bettor's edge. In the end, death will win."

"And you'll have lost, and every loss is a personal one."

Jo Marie didn't feel that she could eavesdrop any longer. Silently she slipped from the room.

The conversation between Mark and Kelly played back in her mind as she drove toward the office and Jim. Mark would have serious problems as a doctor unless he came to terms with these feelings. Kelly had recognized that and had set personal relationships aside to help Mark settle these doubts within himself. He'd been angry with her and would probably continue to be until he fully understood what she was doing.

Luckily Jo Marie found a parking space within sight of the office. With Christmas just a few days away the area had become more crowded and finding parking was almost impossible.

Her thoughts were heavy as she climbed from the passenger's side and locked her door. Just as she turned to look both ways before crossing the street she caught a glimpse of the dark blue Mercedes. A cold chill raced up her spine. Andrew was inside talking to Jim.

Chapter Nine

I**s everything all right?''** Wearily Jo Marie eyed Jim,
looking for a telltale mannerism that would reveal the
reason for Andrew's visit. She'd avoided bumping into
him by waiting in a small antique shop across the street
from the foundation. After he'd gone, she sauntered
around for several additional minutes to be certain he
was out of the neighborhood. Once assured it was
safe, she crossed the street to the foundation's office.

"Should anything be wrong?'' Jim lifted two thick
brows in question.

"You tell me. I saw Andrew Beaumont's car parked
outside.''

"Ah, yes.'' Jim paused and smiled fleetingly. "And
that concerns you?''

"No.'' She shook her head determinedly. "All right,
yes!'' She wasn't going to be able to fool Jim, who was
an excellent judge of human nature.

A smile worked its way across his round face. "He came to meet the rest of the staff at my invitation. The LFTF Foundation is deeply indebted to your friend."

"My friend?"

Jim chuckled. "Neither one of you has been successful at hiding your feelings. Yes, my dear, sweet, Jo Marie, *your* friend."

Any argument died on her tongue.

"Would you care for a cup of coffee?" Jim asked, walking across the room and filling a Styrofoam cup for her.

Jo Marie smiled her appreciation as he handed it to her and sat on the edge of her desk, crossing his arms. "Beaumont and I had quite a discussion."

"And?" Jo Marie didn't bother to disguise her curiosity.

The phone rang before Jim could answer her. Jim reached for it and spent the next ten minutes in conversation. Jo Marie did her best to keep occupied, but her thoughts were doing a crazy tailspin. Andrew was here on business. She wouldn't believe it.

"Well?" Jo Marie questioned the minute Jim replaced the receiver.

His expression was empty for a moment. "Are we back to Beaumont again?"

"I don't mean to pry," Jo Marie said with a rueful smile, "but I'd really like to know why he was here."

Jim was just as straightforward. "Are you in love with him?"

Miserably, Jo Marie nodded. "A lot of good it's done either of us. Did he mention me?"

A wry grin twisted Jim's mouth. "Not directly, but he wanted to know my intentions."

"He didn't!" Jo Marie was aghast at such audacity.

Chuckling, Jim shook his head. "No, he came to ask me about the foundation and pick up some of our literature. He's a good man, Jo Marie."

She studied the top of the desk and typewriter keys. "I know."

"He didn't mention you directly, but I think he would have liked to. I had the feeling he was frustrated and concerned about you working here so many nights, especially in this neighborhood."

"He needn't worry, you escort me to my car or wait at the bus stop until the bus arrives."

Jim made busy work with his hands. "I had the impression that Beaumont is deeply in love with you. If anything happened to you while under my protection, he wouldn't take it lightly."

Even hours later when Jo Marie stepped into the apartment the echo of Jim's words hadn't faded. Andrew was concerned for her safety and was deeply in love with her. But it was all so useless that she refused to be comforted.

Kelly was sitting up, a blanket wrapped around her legs and torso as she paid close attention to a television Christmas special.

"Hi, how'd it go tonight?" Kelly greeted, briefly glancing from the screen.

Her roommate looked pale and slightly drawn, but Jo Marie attributed that to the conversation she'd overheard between her brother and her roommate. She wanted to ask how everything was at the hospital, but doubted that she could adequately disguise her interest.

"Tonight...oh, everything went as it usually does...fine."

"Good." Kelly's answer was absentminded, her look pinched.

"Are you feeling all right, Kell?"

Softly, she shook her head. "I've got another stomachache."

"Fever?"

"None to speak of. I think I might be coming down with the flu."

Tilting her head to one side, Jo Marie mused that Kelly had been unnaturally pale lately. But again she had attributed that to painfully tense times they'd all been through in the past few weeks.

"You know, one advantage of having a brother in the medical profession is that he's willing to make house calls."

Kelly glanced her way, then turned back to the television. "No, it's nothing to call Mark about."

But Kelly didn't sound as convincing as Jo Marie would have liked. With a shrug, she went into the kitchen and poured herself a glass of milk.

"Want one?" She raised her glass to Kelly for inspection.

"No thanks," Kelly murmured and unsuccessfully tried to disguise a wince. "In fact, I think I'll head for bed. I'll be fine in the morning, so don't worry about me."

But Jo Marie couldn't help doing just that. Little things about Kelly hadn't made sense in a long time—like staying home because of an argument with Mark. Kelly wasn't a shy, fledgling nurse. She'd stood her ground with Mark more than once. Even her behavior at the Christmas parties had been peculiar. Nor was Kelly a shrinking violet, yet she'd behaved like one. Obviously it was all an act. But her reasons remained unclear.

In the morning, Kelly announced that she was going to take a day of sick leave. Jo Marie studied her friend with worried eyes. Twice during the morning she phoned to see how Kelly was doing.

"Fine," Kelly answered impatiently the second time. "Listen, I'd probably be able to get some decent rest if I didn't have to get up and answer the phone every fifteen minutes."

In spite of her friend's testiness, Jo Marie chuckled. "I'll try to restrain myself for the rest of the day."

"That would be greatly appreciated."

"Do you want me to bring you something back for dinner?"

"No," she answered emphatically. "Food sounds awful."

Mark breezed into the office around noon, surprising Jo Marie. Sitting on the corner of her desk, he dangled one foot as she finished a telephone conversation.

"Business must be slow if you've got time to be dropping in here," she said, replacing the receiver.

"I come to take you to lunch and you're complaining?"

"You've come to ask about Kelly?" She wouldn't hedge. The time for playing games had long passed.

"Oh?" Briefly he arched a brow in question. "Is that so?"

"She's got the flu. There, I just saved you the price of lunch." Jo Marie couldn't disguise her irritation.

"You didn't save me the price of anything," Mark returned lazily. "I was going to let you treat."

Unable to remain angry with her brother for long, Jo Marie joined him in a nearby café a few minutes later, but neither of them mentioned Kelly again. By unspoken agreement, Kelly, Andrew, and Kelly's unexpected resignation were never mentioned.

Jo Marie's minestrone soup and turkey sandwich arrived and she unwrapped the silverware from the paper napkin. "How would you feel about a roommate for a while?" Jo Marie broached the subject tentatively.

"Male or female?" Dusky dark eyes so like her own twinkled with mischief.

"This may surprise you—female."

Mark laid his sandwich aside. "I'll admit my interest has been piqued."

"You may not be as keen once you find out that it's me."

"You?"

"Well I'm going to have to find someplace else to move sooner or later and—"

"And you're interested in the sooner," he interrupted.

"Yes." She wouldn't mention her reasons, but Mark was astute enough to figure it out for himself.

Peeling open his sandwich, Mark removed a thin slice of tomato and set it on the beige plate. "As long as you do the laundry, clean, and do all the cooking I won't object."

A smile hovered at the edges of her mouth. "Your generosity overwhelms me, brother dearest."

"Let me know when you're ready and I'll help you cart your things over."

"Thanks, Mark."

Briefly he looked up from his meal and grinned. "What are big brothers for?"

Andrew's car was in the apartment parking lot when Jo Marie stepped off the bus that evening after work. The darkening sky convinced her that waiting outside for him to leave would likely result in a drenching. Putting aside her fears, she squared her shoulders and tucked her hands deep within her pockets. When Kelly was home she usually didn't keep the door locked so Jo Marie was surprised to discover that it was. While digging through her purse, she was even more surprised to hear loud voices from the other side of the door.

"This has to stop," Andrew was arguing. "And soon."

"I know," Kelly cried softly. "And I agree. I don't want to ruin anyone's life."

"Three days."

"All right—just until Friday."

Jo Marie made unnecessary noise as she came through the door. "I'm home," she announced as she stepped into the living room. Kelly was dressed in her robe and slippers, slouched on the sofa. Andrew had apparently been pacing the carpet. She could feel his gaze seek her out. But she managed to avoid it, diverting her attention instead to the picture on the wall behind him. "If you'll excuse me I think I'll take a hot shower."

"Friday," Andrew repeated in a low, impatient tone.

"Thank you, Drew," Kelly murmured and sighed softly.

Kelly was in the same position on the sofa when Jo Marie returned, having showered and changed clothes. "How are you feeling?"

"Not good."

For Kelly to admit to as much meant that she'd had a miserable day. "Is there anything I can do?"

Limply, Kelly laid her head back against the back of the couch and closed her eyes. "No, I'm fine. But this is the worst case of stomach flu I can ever remember?"

"You're sure it's the flu?"

Slowly Kelly opened her eyes. "I'm the nurse here."

"Yes, your majesty." With a dramatic twist to her chin, Jo Marie bowed in mock servitude. "Now would you like me to fix you something for dinner?"

"No."

"How about something cool to drink?"

Kelly nodded, but her look wasn't enthusiastic. "Fine."

As the evening progressed, Jo Marie studied her friend carefully. It could be just a bad case of the stomach flu, but Jo Marie couldn't help but be concerned. Kelly had always been so healthy and full of life. When a long series of cramps doubled Kelly over in pain, Jo Marie reached for the phone.

"Mark, can you come over?" She tried to keep the urgency from her voice.

"What's up?"

"It's Kelly. She's sick." Jo Marie attempted to keep her voice low enough so her roommate wouldn't hear. "She keeps insisting it's the flu, but I don't know. She's in a lot of pain for a simple intestinal virus."

Mark didn't hesitate. "I'll be right there."

Ten minutes later he was at the door. He didn't bother to knock, letting himself in. "Where's the patient?"

"Jo Marie." Kelly's round eyes tossed her a look of burning resentment. "You called Mark?"

"Guilty as charged, but I wouldn't have if I didn't think it was necessary."

Tears blurred the blue gaze. "I wish you hadn't," she murmured dejectedly. "It's just the flu."

"Let me be the judge of that." Mark spoke in a crisp professional tone, kneeling at her side. He opened the small black bag and took out the stethoscope.

Not knowing what else to do, Jo Marie hovered at his side for instructions. "Should I boil water or something?"

"Call Drew," Kelly insisted. "He at least won't overreact to a simple case of the flu."

Mark's mouth went taut, but he didn't rise to the intended gibe.

Reluctantly Jo Marie did as she was asked. Andrew answered on the third ring. "Beaumont here."

"Andrew, this is—"

"Jo Marie," he finished for her, his voice carrying a soft rush of pleasure.

"Hi," she began awkwardly and bit into the corner of her bottom lip. "Mark's here. Kelly's not feeling well and I think she may have something serious. She wanted to know if you could come over."

"I'll be there in ten minutes." He didn't take a breath's hesitation.

As it was, he arrived in eight and probably set several speed records in the process. Jo Marie answered his hard knock. "What's wrong with Kelly? She seemed fine this afternoon." He directed his question to Mark.

"I'd like to take Kelly over to the hospital for a couple of tests."

Jo Marie noted the way her brother's jaw had tightened as if being in the same room with Andrew was a test of his endurance. Dislike exuded from every pore.

"No," Kelly protested emphatically. "It's just the stomach flu."

"With the amount of tenderness in the cecum?" Mark argued, shaking his head slowly from side to side in a mocking gesture.

"Mark's the doctor," Andrew inserted and Jo Marie could have kissed him for being the voice of reason in a room where little evidence of it existed.

"You think it's my appendix?" Kelly said with shocked disbelief.

"It isn't going to hurt to run a couple of tests," Mark countered, again avoiding answering a direct question.

"Why should you care?" Kelly's soft voice wavered uncontrollably. "After yesterday I would have thought..."

"After yesterday," Mark cut in sharply, "I realized that you were right and that I owe you an apology." His eyes looked directly into Kelly's and the softness Jo Marie had witnessed in his gaze at the hospital Christmas party returned. He reached for Kelly's hand, folding it in his own. "Will you accept my apology? What you said yesterday made a lot of sense, but at the time I was angry at the world and took it out on you. Forgive me?"

With a trembling smile, Kelly nodded. "Yes, of course I do."

The look they shared was both poignant and tender, causing Jo Marie to feel like an intruder. Briefly, she wondered what Andrew was thinking.

"If it does turn out that I need surgery would you be the one to do it for me?"

Immediately Mark lowered his gaze. "No."

His stark response was cutting and Kelly flinched. "There's no one else I'd trust as much as you."

"I said I wouldn't." Mark pulled the stethoscope from his neck and placed it inside his bag.

"Instead of fighting about it now, why don't we see what happens?" Jo Marie attempted to reason. "There's no need to argue."

"There's every reason," Andrw intervened. "Tell us, Mark, why wouldn't you be Kelly's surgeon if she needed one?"

Jo Marie stared at Andrew, her dark eyes filled with irritation. Backing Mark into a corner wouldn't help the situation. She wanted to step forward and defend her brother, but Andrew stopped her with an abrupt motion of his hand, apparently having read her intent.

"Who I chose as my patients is my business." Mark's tone was dipped in acid.

"Isn't Kelly one of your patients?" Andrew questioned calmly. "You did hurry over here when you heard she was sick."

Coming to a standing position, Mark ignored the question and the man. "Maybe you'd like to change clothes." He directed his comment to Kelly.

Shaking her head she said, "No, I'm not going anywhere."

"Those tests are important." Mark's control on his anger was a fragile thread. "You're going to the hospital."

Again, Kelly shook her head. "No, I'm not."

"You're being unreasonable." Standing with his feet braced apart, Mark looked as if he was willing to take her to the hospital by force if necessary.

"Why not make an agreement," Andrew suggested with cool-headed resolve. "Kelly will agree to the tests, if you agree to be her doctor."

Tiredly, Mark rubbed a hand over his jaw and chin. "I can't do that."

"Why not?" Kelly implored.

"Yes, Mark, why not?" Andrew taunted.

Her brother's mouth thinned grimly as he turned aside and clenched his fists. "Because it isn't good practice to work on the people you're involved with emotionally."

The corners of Kelly's mouth lifted in a sad smile. "We're not emotionally involved. You've gone out of your way to prove that to me. If you have any emotion for me it would be hate."

Mark's face went white and it looked for an instant as if Kelly had physically struck him. "Hate you?" he repeated incredulously. "Maybe," he replied in brutal honesty. "You're able to bring out every other emotion in me. I've taken out a lot of anger on you recently. Most of which you didn't deserve and I apologize for that." He paused and ran a hand through his hair, mussing it. "No, Kelly," he corrected, "I can't hate you. It would be impossible when I love you so much," he announced with an impassive expression and pivoted sharply.

A tense silence engulfed the room until Kelly let out a small cry. "You love me? All these months you've put me through this torment and you love me?" She threw back the blanket and stood, placing her hands defiantly on her hips.

"A lot of good it did me." Mark's angry gaze crossed the width of the room to hold hers. "You're engaged to Daddy Warbucks over there so what good would it do to let you know?"

Jo Marie couldn't believe what she was hearing and gave a nervous glance to Andrew. Casually standing to the side of the room, he didn't look the least disturbed by what was happening. If anything, his features were relaxed as if he were greatly relieved.

"And if you cared for me then why didn't you say something before now?" Kelly challenged.

Calmly he met her fiery gaze. "Because he's got money, you've got money. Tell me what can I offer you that could even come close to the things he can give you."

"And you relate love and happiness with things?" Her low words were scathing. "Let me tell you exactly what you can offer me, Mark Jubal Early. You have it in your power to give me the things that matter most in my life: your love, your friendship, your respect. And...and...if you turn around and walk out that door, by heaven I'll never forgive you."

"I have no intention of leaving," Mark snapped in return. "But I can't very well ask you to marry me when you're wearing another man's ring."

"Fine." Without hesitating Kelly slipped Andrew's diamond from her ring finger and handed it back to him. Lightly she brushed her mouth over his cheeks. "Thanks, Drew."

His hands cupped her shoulders as he kissed her back. "Much happiness, Kelly," he whispered.

Brother and sister observed the scene with open-mouthed astonishment.

Turning, Kelly moved to Mark's side. "Now," she breathed in happily, "if that was a proposal, I accept."

Mark was apprently too stunned to answer.

"Don't tell me you've already changed your mind?" Kelly muttered.

"No, I haven't changed my mind. What about the hospital tests?" he managed finally, his voice slightly raw as his eyes devoured her.

"Give me a minute to change." Kelly left the room and the three were left standing, Jo Marie and Mark staring blankly at each other. Everything was happening so fast that it was like a dream with dark shades of unreality.

Kelly reappeared and Mark tucked her arm in his. "We should be back in an hour," Mark murmured, but he only had eyes for the pert-faced woman on his arm. Kelly's gaze was filled with a happy radiance that brought tears of shared happiness to Jo Marie's eyes.

"Take your time and call if you need us," Andrew said as the happy couple walked toward the door.

Jo Marie doubted that either Kelly or Mark heard him. When she turned her attention to Andrew she discovered that he was already walking toward her. With eager strides he eliminated the distance separating them.

"As I recall, our agreement was that I wouldn't try to see you or contact you again while Kelly wore my engagement ring."

Her dark eyes smiled happily into his. "That's right."

"Then let's be rid of this thing once and for all." He led her into the kitchen where he carelessly tossed the diamond ring into the garbage.

Jo Marie gasped. Andrew was literally throwing away thousands of dollars. The diamond was the largest she had ever seen.

"The ring is as phony as the engagement."

Still unable to comprehend what he was saying, she shook her head to clear her thoughts. "What?"

"The engagement isn't any more real than that so-called diamond."

"Why?" Reason had escaped her completely.

His hands brought Jo Marie into the loving circle of his arms. "By Thanksgiving I'd given up every hope of ever finding you again. I'd convinced myself that those golden moments were just a figment of my imagination and that some quirk of fate had brought us together, only to pull us apart."

It seemed the most natural thing in the world to have his arms around her. Her eyes had filled with moisture so that his features swam in and out of her vision. "I'd given up hope of finding you, too," she admitted in an achingly soft voice. "But I couldn't stop thinking about you."

Tenderly he kissed her, briefly tasting the sweetness of her lips. As if it was difficult to stop, he drew in an uneven breath and rubbed his jaw over the top of her head, mussing her hair. "I saw Kelly at her parents' house over the Thanksgiving holiday and she was miserable. We've always been close for second cousins and we had a long talk. She told me that she'd been in love with Mark for months. The worst part was that she was convinced that he shared her feelings, but his pride was holding him back. Apparently your brother has some strange ideas about wealth and position.''

"He's learning," Jo Marie murmured, still caught in the rapture of being in Andrew's arms. "Give him time." She said this knowing that Kelly was willing to devote the rest of her life to Mark.

"I told Kelly she should give him a little competition and if someone showed an interested in her, then Mark would step forward. But apparently she'd already tried that."

"My brother can be as stubborn as ten men."

"I'm afraid I walked into this phony engagement with my eyes wide open. I said that if Mark was worth his salt, he wouldn't stand by and let her marry another man. If he loved her, really loved her, he'd step in.''

"But he nearly didn't."

"No," Andrew admitted. "I was wrong. Mark loved Kelly enough to sacrifice his own desires to give her what he thought she needed. I realized that the night of my Christmas party. By that time I was getting desperate. I'd found you and every minute of this engagement was agony. In desperation, I tried to talk to Mark. But that didn't work. He assumed I was warning him off Kelly and told me to make her happy or I'd pay the consequences."

The irony of the situation was almost comical. "You were already suffering the consequences. Why didn't you say something? Why didn't you explain?"

"Oh, love, if you'd been anyone but Mark's sister I would have." Again his mouth sought hers as if he couldn't get enough of her kisses. "Here I was trapped in the worst set of circumstances I've ever imagined. The woman who had haunted me for months was within my grasp and I was caught in a steel web."

"I love you, Andrew. I've loved you from the moment you held me all those months ago. I knew then that you were meant to be someone special in my life."

"This has taught me the most valuable lesson of my life." He arched her close. So close it was impossible to breath normally. "I'll never let you out of my arms again. I'm yours for life, Jo Marie, whether you want me or not. I've had to trust again every instinct that you would wait for me. Dear Lord, I had visions of you falling in love with Jim Rowden, and the worst part was I couldn't blame you if you did. I can only imagine what kind of man you thought me."

Lovingly, Jo Marie spread kisses over his face. "It's going to take me a lifetime to tell you."

"Oh, love." His grip tightened against the back of her waist, arching her closer until it was almost painful to breathe. Not that Jo Marie cared. Andrew was holding her and had promised never to let her go again.

"I knew something was wrong with you and Kelly from the beginning," she murmured between soft, exploring kisses. Jo Marie couldn't have helped but notice.

"I've learned so much from this," Andrew confessed. "I think I was going slowly mad. I want more than to share my life with you, Jo Marie. I want to see our children in your arms. I want to grow old with you at my side."

"Oh, Andrew." Her arms locked around his neck and the tears of happiness streamed down her face.

"I love you, Florence Nightingale."

"And you, Andrew Beaumont, will always be my dream man."

"Forever?" His look was skeptical.

She lifted her mouth to his. "For all eternity," she whispered in promise.

"An ulcer?" Jo Marie shook her head slowly.

"Well, with all the stress I was under in the past few weeks, it's little wonder," Kelly defended herself.

The four sat in the living room sipping hot cocoa. Kelly was obediently drinking plain heated milk and hating it. But her eyes were warm and happy as they rested on Mark who was beside her with an arm draped over her shoulders.

"I've felt terrible about all this, Jo Marie," Kelly continued. "Guilt is a horrible companion. I didn't know exactly what was going on with you and Andrew. But he let it be known that he was in love with you and wanted this masquerade over quickly."

"You felt guilty?" Mark snorted. "How do you think I felt kissing another man's fiancée?"

"About the same way Jo Marie and I felt," Andrew returned with a chuckle.

"You know, Beaumont. Now that you're marrying my sister, I don't think you're such a bad character after all."

"That's encouraging."

"I certainly hope you get along since you're both going to be standing at the altar at the same time."

Three pairs of blank eyes stared at Kelly. "Double wedding, silly. It makes sense, doesn't it? The four of us have been through a lot together. It's only fitting we start our new lives at the same time."

"But soon," Mark said emphatically. "Sometime in January."

Everything was moving so fast, Jo Marie barely had time to assimilate the fact that Andrew loved her and she was going to share his life.

"Why not?" she agreed with a small laugh. "We've yet to do anything else conventionally."

Her eyes met Andrew's. They'd come a long way, all four of them, but they'd stuck it out through the doubts and the hurts. Now their whole lives stretched before them filled with promise.

Ann Charlton wanted to be a commercial artist but became a secretary. She wanted to play the piano but plays guitar instead, and she never planned to be a writer. From time to time she abseils which surprises her because she is afraid of heights. She would like to do more tapestry work and paint miniatures.

Born in Sydney, Ann now lives in Brisbane. Since her first book was published by Mills & Boon® in 1984, Ann has had more than 7 million copies of her books distributed worldwide.

STEAMY DECEMBER
by
ANN CHARLTON

In memory of my father, Ted Flower
1901-1992

CHAPTER ONE

UNTIL the two, large, uniformed officers showed up there was nothing about the job to actually alarm her.

'Just a few hours, that's all I'm asking,' her mother had said. 'Standing on a street, asking questions, with a tape-recorder in your bag.' Her mother ran a part-time employment agency and was always looking for students and out-of-work actors for all manner of odd jobs. As she had forged a new career in theatrical make-up and special effects, it was some time since Ami had been an out-of-work actor but she hadn't yet figured a way to remove her name from her mother's files.

'What kind of questions—and isn't that illegal? Recording people's answers without their knowledge?'

'Only if you record their names as well, darling,' her mother had said impatiently. 'It's for my freelance writer, who's doing research for a book and he's got a list of questions to ask—nothing dreadful, just "excuse me, have you got the time" and "do you know where I can catch a bus to Balmain" and so on. He wants a young, attractive woman who has no nerves about chatting to strangers, so naturally I thought of you. I'm trying to talk him into coming to the charity art show next week. Did I mention he's thirtyish, good-looking and divorced?'

'What kind of book?' Ami asked, picking her way through the minefield of Lenore Winterburn's marital aspirations for her only child.

'It's a long story,' her mother had said, not noticing her own pun as usual. 'Look, darling, I just don't have anyone else on the books at the moment who can do it

5

and you know how I hate letting clients down. Let Helen run the shop without you and do this little job for me and you won't be sorry.'

But Ami was feeling her first real twinge of regret when one of the large, uniformed men planted himself on the pavement in front of her and said, 'Afternoon, madam. We'd like a word.'

Ami glanced at the insignia on his sleeve. Not a policeman but a private security guard. She relaxed. 'Which word would you like?' she asked breezily and got a humourless stare.

'Perhaps we could talk inside?' A beefy hand indicated the glittering, glassed foyer of the near-completed Avalon Hotel, outside which workmen were laying marble on a walkway rimming the semicircular concourse. The hotel motto, *Come home to heaven*, was scripted in gold and white by the doors. Several life-sized bronzes of voluptuous women torchbearers on plinths lined the pathway to heaven. A sign informed passersby that these had been reclaimed from the nineteenth-century hotel demolished to make way for this new one, a token piece of conservation that had not impressed those who had protested against the change.

Ami frowned. 'Talk about what?'

'Come along now, don't play dumb. You've been warned once. We don't want any trouble, do we?' the second guard said, holding out a hand as if to take her arm.

Suddenly glad there were plenty of people around, Ami sidestepped and raised her voice. 'I don't know what you mean. Please go away.'

They seemed sensitive to the attention of bypassers, for the two men took a long look at her, then retreated in the direction of the hotel. Uneasily aware of the tape-recorder in her bag, she considered moving away but then, why should she? Ami turned and saw the guards in conversation with someone inside the Avalon's glass doors before passing pedestrians blocked her view. Next time she turned around, she came face to face with exactly the kind of man she was supposed to approach for her mother's writer client.

Thirty to forty age group. The cut of the suit indicated upper income bracket, businessman or professional. He met her eyes very directly and Ami blurted out the opening question she'd asked all the others.

'Excuse me, can you tell me the time?'

She assessed him with quickening interest. Tall, wide-shouldered, a lean body and a lean face, coal-black hair, near black brows dead straight as if drawn with a ruler. Wide mouth, almost as straight as the brows but unexpectedly full at the corners as if his lips had been drawn in by someone who hadn't wanted to stop. A face designed by an architect with a longing to paint. He had grey eyes, thickly and darkly lashed and in another man this might have produced a boyish, smiling impression. But the eyes were shrewd, assured, coolly calculating and cancelled out any mellowing effect from their lush framing.

'You must be a non-smoker,' he said easily.

'I'm sorry?'

'Isn't the standard gambit to hold out a cigarette and ask for a light?'

It conjured up a somewhat tawdry image. 'Maybe I really *do* just want to know the time,' she suggested gently, showing her wrists bare of a watch.

'If you really *did* just want the time, you would have noticed the hotel clock,' he said mockingly and turned a hawkish profile toward the unfinished hotel lobby where an art clock was clearly visible through the glass. He looked at her, lowered his chin and raised his brows, as if to say, 'Your move.'

Challenged, Ami promptly shaded her eyes and squinted. 'Oh, is there a clock? I haven't got my glasses,' she improvised, giving him a brilliant smile.

He blinked, looked deep in her eyes like an eye specialist diagnosing the exact nature of her vision impairment. Then he scrutinised her from her heeled boots all the way up her jeans to the jumble of blue alphabet letters knitted into her cream cotton sweater. His gaze lingered, as if he suspected there might be a complete word to be found there on her chest.

He consulted an expensive watch. 'Six-fifteen,' he said. 'Are you—waiting for someone in particular or...?'

Her heartbeat quickened. Was he going to try to pick her up? She was conscious of a dual excitement and repugnance at the idea. He waited with intense interest for her answer and she began to feel she was playing in some kind of competition. Or was being played with. Unsettled, she fell back on another of the routine questions she'd been asking. 'Do you know where the Bondi Junction buses leave?'

Whatever he'd been expecting her to say, that wasn't it. His eyebrows shot up. 'Lost your nerve?' he asked softly. 'Maybe you know who you're dealing with?'

Puzzled, Ami said again, 'Sorry?'

He beckoned her to follow, walked past a sculptured torchbearer to point to the bus terminal less than half a block away on the opposite side of York Street. 'If it's a Bondi bus you want,' he said sardonically, 'there's one.'

'No, that's going to Clovelly,' she said, easily reading the destination on the distant bus.

'It's a miracle,' he drawled.

'What is?'

'Your eyesight restored after mere moments in my company. And without me even laying hands on you.'

She felt a decided frisson at that. Involuntarily she looked at his hands. One was relaxed, by his side. The other was spread casually on the voluptuous, bronzed leg of the statue on the dais beside him. His thumb rubbed at the cast impression of a sandal strap.

'I've been watching you. From my office up there,' he said. Startled, Ami looked up at the mirrored blankness of the glass he indicated.

'My security thought at first that you might be casing the place for a robbery or terrorist action,' he went on conversationally.

My office, my security. His fingers flexed on the lavish curves of the torchbearer's calf muscle as if he relished the smooth perfection of the surface. Ami found it immensely annoying.

'I'm North Kendrick,' he went on smoothly. 'I own this place—more or less.'

And that included the statues, Ami thought, dragging her eyes from the proprietarial hand on the bronze. North? Was that a name or a compass bearing? A woman emerged from the hotel doors and signalled to him with a portable phone. Kendrick made a peremptory gesture that said, 'Wait.'

'Did you say terrorists?' Ami said, distracted.

'A bit extreme, I agree, although we had our troubles with SOPS during demolition of the old Avalon.' At her blank expression he said blandly, 'Save Old Pubs Society. Sometimes security overreacts.'

'Obviously. I'm no threat to your security.' She smiled, made a palms-up, hands to the side gesture that said, 'Look—no weapons,' in case he had his armed guards about to close in on her.

'I'm not so sure about that,' he murmured, eyes narrowed on her expansive gesture and smile. 'But then they realised you'd been here before. Working alone this time, are you? Isn't that unusual?'

'Why would that be unusual—what do you mean, *this time*?'

'There's a description of you on file, right down to the alphabet sweater.'

'A *description*? Well, it isn't of me! I've never seen your security men before.'

'They weren't the ones on duty before. And the probability of two long-legged women with blonde hair, pants and an alphabet sweater choosing my hotel as a, shall we say rendezvous is very slight.'

Ami's eyes flashed. There was clearly some confusion, and she could explain why she was here easily enough. But, she thought stubbornly, why should she have to explain herself to a series of officious, self-important, patronising males? 'First your guards, now you. This is verging on harassment, you realize.'

He looked admiring. 'You've got class, they didn't mention that in the files. Nor did they mention your eyes.'

Ami blinked. 'What?'

'I suppose you're wearing coloured lenses—that aquamarine colour can't be the real thing.'

'Can't it, indeed?' she said coldly.

For a moment he looked dubious, but his eyes flicked down to the letters on her sweater and whatever they spelled out for him restored his cool assurance. 'The thing is, I can't have prospective customers being—ah, canvassed right outside my doors. It might give the Avalon a bad name and my investors wouldn't like it. Spread the word, there's a good girl.'

'I haven't been a girl for at least ten years,' she snapped.

'I won't ask how long it is since you've been good.' His mouth twitched at his own wit. He took her arm in a deceptively casual grip.

'Now, just one minute!' Ami pulled back in alarm, but failed to dislodge him.

He raised a hand to the woman waiting at the doors for him. The woman said something into the phone. He nodded to the commissionaire. The man walked out and signalled a cab. 'I want you to let go of my arm,' she said, but the traffic surged and her voice was diminished and the summoned taxi swept in alongside. Ami couldn't believe it when Kendrick guided her strongly toward it.

'I don't *want* a cab, thank you,' she said loudly. 'I don't exactly know what you're talking about but if you at least let me—'

'Have it your way,' he said, not relinquishing his hold on her. 'You're probably just a nice girl selling magazine subscriptions but I'd prefer you didn't do it here. Or inside my hotel once it opens, for that matter. It's been most enjoyable, but I'm pressed for time so why don't we just leave it at that? No hard feelings, hm?'

'This is a public space—you have no right to hustle me away.'

'There might be some argument as to who's doing the hustling, sweetheart,' he said, amused. He crooked his index finger. The woman hurried over to hand him the phone. He turned his head and nodded. A limousine crept into view.

'Hustling?' she said frostily. The finger crooked again. The doorman hurried over, straightening his tie, adjusting the flower in his lapel. Without taking his eyes off her or releasing his hold, Kendrick spoke over his shoulder to the doorman. 'This lady has made a mistake, Morgan. She finds herself in the wrong place. Should she lose her way again, you will be good enough to show her into a cab.'

'Yes, Mr. Kendrick.' The doorman studied Ami. 'I never forget a face.'

'This is ridiculous!' Scarlet-faced, she tried to open her bag to show him the tape-recorder and her business card but Kendrick took her by the wrist and steered her into the cab while he spoke into the phone. The grip had all the charm of a handcuff, as she found when she tried to shake it off. The driver gawped insolently, the workmen stopped to watch as she was deposited in the cab. Her face flamed in humiliation. The man called Kendrick handed back the phone and leaned in. His eyes were piercing, intense, and Ami found the cab's interior suddenly suffocating.

'Sydney's a big place. Don't come back. I'm being nice about it this time but I don't like complications, understand?' He hesitated, eyes roaming over her face and hair. 'Life's tough, I know,' he said. 'It's nothing personal, sweetheart.' Then he turned and plucked the gardenia from Morgan's lapel. Ami recoiled as he leaned in again, a knee on the seat. The scent of the single flower was as overpowering as the looming presence of the man. He tucked the flower behind her ear. His fingers brushed against her cheek, and softly down the length of her hair. His gaze went to her mouth and he moved forward, tilted his head. Ami's mouth parted, she stared at him, held in a trance state as his breath mingled with hers. But he drew back a fraction just when she was certain he was about to kiss her. His hand curved around her jaw, his thumb stroked across her lower lip in a substitute kiss. Under his breath, he said, 'What a pity.' With that he closed the door and slapped twice on the roof of the taxi, which pulled away in slavish obedience. Kendrick got into the limousine and the two cars were briefly alongside each other before they entered the York Street traffic and she had one last glimpse of Kendrick's black hair and hawkish profile. She snatched the gardenia from her hair, ground it into a fragrant pulp with her heel, cursing that she'd left it too late for Kendrick to see what she thought of his patronising gesture.

'What a pity!' Ami mimicked to her best friend nearly two weeks later as she pulled off her grey wig in one of the Shoelace Theatre's dressing rooms. 'As if I was a— nice bit of sculpture he wouldn't mind putting with his half-naked bronzes, if only he hadn't found out it was flawed. Supercilious swine.'

'Well, if anyone can set a supercilious swine straight, it's you,' Emma said as she stacked up the metal chairs recently vacated by a dozen students. 'That was a terrific class. My workshop people were quite inspired.'

Ami didn't answer. That was the trouble. She hadn't set him straight at all. She thought of the spineless way she'd just sat there in the taxi and let that man tuck the flower in her hair, touch her face...every bit as inanimate as one of his bronze torchbearers, she thought, hating herself.

'Are you intending to drive home in full make-up?' Emma enquired. 'You look older than my grandmother. I'm having second thoughts about you being my bridesmaid.'

She indicated Ami's face, used to demonstrate her latex ageing effects, which had turned her into a seventy-year-old woman in around ninety minutes. But Ami looked broodingly in the mirror, not seeing her own made-up reflection. If it hadn't been for the gardenia, she thought, she would have forgotten the whole thing by now. She doubted she would ever again be able to smell the perfume of a gardenia without triggering off the memory of her humiliation. If only she had thrown the flower at him, she would feel so much better.

'Ami?'

Ruefully, she smiled. Emma was back from a brief reunion with her fiancé at his place out west, glowing with happiness and confidence, serene about her wedding plans and keen to talk about material samples and designs. 'Sorry to sound off but I just cannot abide that smug, superior kind of male. Didn't give me a chance to explain, just hustled me into a cab saying it had been "most enjoyable". And there was the gardenia and I thought for a moment he was going to... I should have bitten his thumb off,' she said blackly.

'His *thumb*?'

'His sniffy doorman studied me as if I was on the ten most wanted list and I'm banned from going inside that fancy hotel of his—can you believe it? ''Sydney's a big place,"' she said in mimicry of Kendrick's deep voice. '"Don't come back."' She swept up an armful of used tissues and cotton-wool pads to toss them in the waste-bin and looked reflectively at Emma. 'When I was a kid, if someone told me I wasn't allowed to walk on the grass, I just *had* to go and put at least one foot on it.'

Emma's brows went up. 'You're not thinking of putting a foot on Kendrick's turf, are you?'

Ami grinned. 'I just might, at that.'

Her friend looked suddenly alert. 'North Kendrick? CKC? Electronics and transport and all the rest? I've heard about him. Hard as nails and twice as sharp. I'd sleep on the idea if I were you. Your pride might not withstand being thrown out a second time and I wouldn't gamble on the doorman not recognising you. Come on, take off your wrinkles. I keep thinking I'm talking to a stranger.'

Ami focused at last on her reflection. She blinked to centre the cloudy contact lenses that turned her eyes from aquamarine to an indeterminate grey-blue. The slight ir-ritation they caused gave her eyes a convincing watery look. With professional pride she prodded at the lifelike folds on her neck, the pliable, sagging jawline unde-tectable from real skin even for close television camera work. 'It *is* good, isn't it?' she said, pleased with her creation.

'Your own mother wouldn't know you. I'm going to lock up.'

'I hate to simply take it all off after so much work,' Ami complained, raising her voice as her friend disap-peared to check the exits and alarms of her theatre. 'It seems such a waste of effort.'

Ami sat, a finger teasing at the pins holding her long, blonde hair close to her scalp. Then, thoughtfully, she put on the grey wig again and adjusted it, leaning close to scrutinize the countenance her own mother wouldn't recognize.

Don't come back.
I never forget a face.
There's a description of you on file.

Ami's eyes gleamed. A smile played around her mouth. Such a *terrible* waste to simply dismantle ninety minutes of work. Waste not, want not, she thought virtuously.

'Emma,' she yelled, unzipping her cranberry jumpsuit. 'Can I borrow some gear from your costume department?'

The Avalon was open for business, its semicircular drive completed and lined with a row of potted, pollarded fig trees that looked like three-dimensional lollipops. Sydney's pigeons had discovered the torchbearers; there was a spattering of white on the smooth, bronze breasts and shoulders.

The suave watchdog, Morgan, once again wore a gardenia on his lapel. The man who never forgot a face looked blankly at her as she approached, and Ami felt the flush of elation she always got from a convincing piece of work. Emma's theatre costume department had yielded a floral dress and a cheap pink cardigan, support shoes, a vinyl handbag and white gloves. 'I shouldn't be helping you with this—it's a mad idea,' Emma had said, but she had been in theatre even longer than Ami and hadn't been able to resist the professional challenge of transformation. Body pads and a hunch had modified Ami's tall, dancer's body into a shorter, dumpier shape. Morgan had no more luck identifying her figure than her face.

'Can I help you, madam?' he said.

'I'm going to have a look at your lovely new hotel,' she confided cosily, taking pleasure in looking him right in the eye. 'And have a cup of coffee in your coffee shop.'

Morgan quickly reviewed her weathered wrinkles, her modest clothes, and his manner became more familiar. 'It's not a good time for that tonight, dear. It's an official opening, you see, for VIPs and the press—'

'That's all right, I don't mind a few officials,' she said broad-mindedly, suspecting that Morgan was trying to keep her out for an entirely new reason. She felt a jolt at the information. Kendrick was bound to be here if the place was crawling with VIPs and press. Just for a moment, she hung back. Emma was right, it was a mad idea. But the scent of Morgan's gardenia wafted to her nostrils and when he turned away with a toothy welcome for better-dressed people, Ami slipped through the doors.

Amongst the guests she recognized a media sports celebrity and a retired politician whose make-up she'd done once for a TV talk show. With the sports celebrity was a girlfriend wearing glamour-punk black and glitter, and with the politician a bow-tied, distinguished husband. All the beautiful people.

Morgan and his boss, she thought, would no doubt prefer not to have impoverished old ladies in pink cardies tottering around the lavish foyer spoiling the classiness of the place while the VIPs were present. Too bad. She intercepted a waiter who dubiously gave her a glass of champagne.

Through a gap in the crowd, she saw Kendrick. His tall, lean figure was distinguished in the black and white of a dinner suit. Were his shoulders really so broad? Probably overstuffed shoulder pads. A very elegant brunette, wearing fuchsia pink and pearls, stayed close by him as he greeted guests and journalists. He smiled and made an expansive gesture as he related some anecdote to his immediate audience. They all laughed. Well, they would, wouldn't they, she thought, remembering the obedient leap of the taxi when Kendrick had signalled it to go.

Kendrick, she had read since he had sent her packing, was success personified. He was into electronics, transport, property and a multitude of profitable ventures that had sprung from an unlikely start as an engineer with a handful of patented designs. He was one of just a few of the young turks who had avoided the financial quicksand of the past decade, known for a combination of flair, ruthlessness and a formidable patience for long-term investment. The only extravagant mistake he might have made, according to the financial pages, was to build this hotel. But a man with his resources could afford a mistake. Being on his turf seemed suddenly not only childish but dangerous. Ami couldn't have explained it, but she usually went with her intuition, so she was already plotting her course to the door through the cocktail dresses and the dinner suits when a young man wearing a hotel badge took her elbow and said softly, 'Good evening, madam. Allow me to call you a cab.'

Leaving was exactly what she'd intended but when she found herself being inexorably assisted to do so, she was nettled. When she glanced over and saw North Kendrick frowning in her direction, no doubt watching to see that she was removed, her temper flared. One way or another, he was always throwing her out. 'Oh, but I don't want to go yet,' she said in a quavering voice that nevertheless projected nicely in the soaring vestibule. 'I want to have a look around your lovely hotel.'

The young man beside her pasted an embarrassed smile on his face and moved her through the guests. She raised her voice a bit.

'Young man, you're hurting my arm. I don't understand why I'm being treated like a criminal just because I wanted to have a look around.'

Kendrick was looking over now with sharpened interest. So were several members of the press. Australians loved an underdog. Ami warmed to her role.

'Do you have to be rich and famous to come in to look at this hotel?' she asked the nearest guests. 'I couldn't stay here—couldn't afford that, not on the pension. But just to *look*—' The sentence remained pathetically unfinished. By now there was a decided pall over the celebrations. Kendrick had stopped smiling. Ami was beginning to enjoy herself. 'Tossed on the scrap heap,' she said with perfect clarity and a hint of tears because the contact lenses were hurting. 'That's all right. I'll go,' she said with a sniff. She was rather keen to make that exit now because Kendrick was approaching through the crowd, a frown deeply etched on his brow. He was perturbed, embarrassed because his guests were embarrassed. Good. Ami felt justice had been done and moved to the door with a vigour that took her escort by surprise.

It was Kendrick who stopped her, just as the massive glass doors slid apart. He carried with him an almost full glass of champagne but must have moved like greased lightning without spilling a drop, a fact that doubled her apprehension. 'Just a moment.' He gave her a clean white handkerchief, took her arm and handed the glass to the young man. 'Get someone to collect the current batch of champagne and replace it with properly chilled bottles. I like my champagne *cold*,' he said. The young man vanished on the command. Ami's glass of champagne had felt positively icy through her gloves. Kendrick was either a perfectionist or just liked throwing his weight around. 'I'm North Kendrick,' he said, bending toward her as she shrank into the hanky. 'I own this hotel and I apologise for any unpleasantness you might have encountered. The hotel management staff may have overinterpreted their instructions—'

What a lovely man, she thought. Dropping the blame on the staff who couldn't answer back. Ami felt the first real pangs of alarm as he led her inside the hotel as inexorably as his employee had been trying to lead her out. Wouldn't you know it, she thought furiously. The man wasn't going to risk the press writing up something unpleasant about a pensioner being ejected from the Avalon. Clasped to Kendrick's side, she felt near to panic.

'Will you tell us your name?' Kendrick bent persuasively over her. His beautiful brunette companion came over and introduced herself as Francesca quite loudly to Ami, assuming that deafness automatically went with wrinkles.

Ami saw that there was no way out of this. She could hardly take off her wig and admit she was a fraud. His gung-ho security guards would probably clap her in irons as a SOPS infiltrator. She would simply have to improvise until an opportunity to escape presented itself. 'My name is Amelia,' she said, giving the full version of her name she never used. She was rather disconcerted to find Kendrick's well-groomed head tilted an inch from her mouth. His skin was tan and rather rough-grained, his thick hair gleaming a Celtic black. Her gaze locked onto a single grey hair, shining like a tiny silver arrow just above his ear. Shifting her eyes from a close-up of his hair to a close-up of his resolute jaw, she almost gave him her real last name and hastily substituted an alias. 'Amelia Anderson,' she said. As soon as she said the name, she started concocting a personality for Amelia Anderson and she felt better. Safer. Or was that because North Kendrick had moved slightly farther away?

'Mrs. Anderson—it *is* Mrs?' he asked, glancing at her gloved left hand.

'I'm a widow,' Ami said cautiously.

'May I call you Amelia? You realise you've gate-crashed our opening celebrations, Amelia,' he said on a playful, yet chiding note.

If I really was seventy years old, she thought, I would strenuously object to being treated like a nincompoop. 'I didn't see any sign saying the public couldn't come in. I'm a gatecrasher because I'm not rich and important, isn't that what you mean, young man?'

Kendrick looked taken aback, an expression she felt was surely alien to him and that gave her some intense satisfaction. 'You are important, Amelia. In fact—' He paused and she could almost see the wheels turning as he assessed the situation. 'To mark our opening and your keen interest in the hotel—' It was said with the barest trace of dryness. 'We want you to be our guest for a weekend—absolutely free—in one of our best suites.'

Ami's horror was genuine. 'Oh, no,' she cried, as journalists took notes and photographers took pictures. 'I couldn't!'

Kendrick smiled slightly at this response. 'Of course you could. The doorman said you wanted to come in for a cup of coffee. Well, Amelia, you shall have all the coffee you can drink, on the house.'

It was clear that any little old lady in support shoes and a pink cardie should be jumping for joy at such largesse. As she acted overcome and flustered, her panic subsided. The whole thing had got out of hand, but why was she worried? Nobody knew who she was, the lighting was discreet enough for her latex to pass muster and people weren't looking all that closely at her. She was an old lady and everyone already thought they knew just what an old lady looked like so there was no need for close scrutiny. She would go along with this and simply fade away at the first opportunity.

The opportunity to escape didn't present itself. When she excused herself to go, ostensibly to the ladies room, Francesca went with her. Kendrick wasn't going to risk the now high-profile widow Anderson falling and breaking her hip on his premises. Fortunately, Francesca was too absorbed in touching up her own lovely face to notice that the widow Anderson didn't take off her gloves.

With relentless generosity, Kendrick included her in the tour of the grand new building. The press liked the quirky notion of the stray old pensioner being given the keys to a luxury suite. They demanded details. Where did she live? Was she alone in the world? Had she ever stayed in a luxury hotel before? She was shakily vague about her address and voluble about her family. 'Then there's my youngest son Bernard and my daughter-in-law, Brenda,' she waffled as the eyes of the press glazed over. 'And the grandkiddies...the twins, lovable, cheeky little devils.'

The party went up in the elevators, to tour the hotel's impressive function rooms, the ballroom, the restaurant and coffee shop. Champagne, spirits and canapés were offered at every stop. Ami, who had somehow been elevated to guest of honour, kept up a steady flow of appreciation.

'What a nice, *cosy* feel it has,' she said, of the stand-offish chrome and marble interior of the coffee shop where the widow Anderson was destined to whoop it up during her stay. What would Kendrick do when the widow failed to turn up for her free holiday? 'But you know I can't help thinking a little lamp on every table would have just been the finishing touch. With a little, pleated shade on each of them, and maybe a tiny posy of artificial flowers. I make them, you know.' She beamed at a bemused North Kendrick who must surely be regretting his decision to include her in the party. 'Lamp shades. I must have made—oh, hundreds of lamp shades in my time.'

With this impressive feat to mull over, they moved on to the empty ballroom where, to Ami's dismay, chandeliers blazed. But, at a barely perceptible nod of Kendrick's handsome head, the lights dimmed and the great waltz from *Der Rosenkavalier* swelled through hidden speakers. No wonder Kendrick thought highly of himself—his passage through life was smoothed by

people who just stood about waiting to do what he
wanted, when he wanted, at a quirk of his eyebrow. The
widow Anderson must have come as a nasty surprise,
she thought maliciously.

'Oh, my,' said Ami clasping her gloved hands. 'How
I used to love to waltz. I used to be quite a dancer in
my time, but I don't suppose you believe that, Mr.
Kendrick—or may I call you North?' she said roguishly.

'Waltz with me, Amelia,' North Kendrick said, holding
out his arms. All the cameras went up in readiness.
Francesca, who was a fashion designer, wearing her own
creation, looked disappointed that this prime piece of
exposure was going to someone with nothing to promote.

Ami's roguish smile disappeared. 'Oh, I couldn't—
my *legs* aren't what they used to be. Dance with
Francesca.'

'Just one circuit.' He smiled. What very good teeth
he had, she thought, staring at him and cursing her im-
pulsiveness. He moved in and there was nowhere to go
but into his arms.

He was a reasonably good dancer. As one who had
trained in ballet since four years old, she was inclined
to judge harshly. Even so, he was very stylish, very crisp,
very purposeful. It would be interesting to dance properly
with him instead of this measured, sedate circuit of the
floor suitable for a dowager. As the heady music swelled,
quickened into a whirling pace, Ami wondered what
would happen if she straightened out of her stoop, threw
back her head and slid her hand around that rather
interesting angle of his neck. The thought so startled her
that she stumbled. His arm tightened in support and she
was drawn up onto her toes through several bars of frolicking music, her false matronly bosom and the pink
cardigan crushed to his chest, her mouth narrowly
missing his bow tie.

'Are you all right, Amelia?'

Genuine concern had such an amazing effect on his uncompromising features that she stared unguardedly for a moment. His eyes narrowed. Ami's head filled with the drumbeat of her pulse. Had her contact lenses slipped? Oh, lord, why had she let herself get so carried away? The man would tear her limb from limb.

But he smiled and said, 'I'll bet you never lacked partners when you were a girl.'

'Well...' she said modestly, almost sagging in relief.

'Did your husband like to dance?'

'No,' she said, unwilling to complicate matters with a dancing husband. 'Most men don't have the first idea of dancing. Now *you*, North,' she said truthfully, 'you're a very good dancer. You know how to lead. So many men don't.'

He laughed. 'It's the age of equality, Amelia. A lot of women don't appreciate men who take control. Consequently men are less confident about taking the lead in anything lest they be labelled chauvinist pigs.'

Balderdash, she thought. 'Dear me. Well, I can see you don't let the age of equality bother you, North.'

His brows went up. She smiled seraphically though the strain of disguising her height, the heat of the wig and the padding and the latex were getting to her. Her heartbeat was galloping along at a pace that would surely make him call an ambulance if he felt the vibrations. But moments later, smiling as the guests applauded, he led her from the floor. She ought to send him a bill considering the public relations value he was getting out of Amelia Anderson, she thought sourly.

A man in a wheelchair had joined the guests while she was dancing, Ami noticed. He was elderly and very thin, with a face like a creased leather satchel and large hands with knobby knuckles and wrists. A superb dark suit sat awkwardly on him, as if he was done up in someone else's Sunday best. North Kendrick looked displeased at the man's presence and went to him at once, bending over him to say a few words. The old man shook his head and settled into the chair with an air of stubbornness. If he'd been asked to leave, he wasn't going, either. Kendrick had his share of out-of-place senior citizens tonight, Ami thought, catching the eye of the invalid. He looked tired but his gaze was unexpectedly sharp, and she nodded and turned away quickly, unwilling to be examined by a genuine elder. Ami found those eyes focused steadily on her as she was held in conversation by various people and forced to expand on her family life. She exhausted Bernard and the twins and launched her eldest son, Duncan, who lived in Canada. Something about the watchful old man was disturbingly familiar, and she felt a new urgency to get away. But no sooner the thought than North Kendrick was there, taking her arm again and steering her to the disabled man. Were old women always bundled around in this bossy manner?

'Amelia, meet my father,' he said. 'Harry Kendrick.'

His father? She was taken aback but the sense of familiarity was explained. The man's eyes were like his son's except there was a gleam in them to suggest humour to match the shrewdness.

'How do you do, Mr. Kendrick,' she said carefully.

The old man listened as his son explained Amelia's presence and her expected stay in a penthouse suite as a guest of the management. 'Is that so?' Harry said, raising shaggy eyebrows. 'And is there a Mr. Anderson?'

'Amelia is widowed, too, Harry,' North said.

Ami had the sudden crazy thought that Kendrick might be matching her up with his dad. She almost burst into hysterical laughter. Harry was asking her about her family, and she went into her patter about her elder son, Duncan, who lived in New Zealand. As soon as she said it she knew she'd made a slip. Duncan lived in Canada. She started to feel a bit desperate.

'Nice place, New Zealand. A lot like Canada, I believe,' Harry said blandly and gave her a wink. Just then there was a concerted move to another location and he patted a chair alongside him and said, 'Sit down and take a load off your feet for a while, Mrs. Anderson.'

It was an ideal opportunity to escape. She sat down, not certain whether she'd been rumbled. When Kendrick and the crowd disappeared, she counted to ten, but instead of leaving, she turned to meet Harry's watery, blue-grey eyes. They were crinkled up in silent laughter.

'If you're a pensioner, I'm the prime minister,' he said.

CHAPTER TWO

SHE could have gone then. Kendrick might come back at any moment. But professional curiosity delayed her. 'What gave me away?'

Harry drew a handkerchief from his suit pocket and wiped his eyes. 'Oh, never mind. You're not one of those SOPS people, are you? Is there a bomb in that handbag?'

'Good heavens, is everyone in this place paranoid about bombs?' she said lightly, opening her bag to show him that it contained no explosives. She spun him a tale about wanting to test out her special effects in public, which was, after all, close to the truth. 'They were so good,' she said modestly, 'that one thing led to another and—here I am.'

'And North doesn't have a clue!' Harry went off into wheezy laughter again. 'Ah, this is a rare treat. He's a smart lad, you see, smarter than me. I never had much education, worked with my hands all my life, on building sites around the city. Nowadays people like my boy knock down things I helped to build and replace them with fancy towers like this,' he said with a sigh as he squinted out the window at the glittering city. 'North, now—he was brainy right from the start, was rich before he turned thirty. People have been bowing and scraping to him, treating him like a god for so long, it's no wonder he thinks he knows everything.' He went off again, gasping and heaving. 'My poor boy! I think he was hoping to do a bit of matchmaking between me and the widow!' He mopped up again and she was watching him stuff the handkerchief in his top pocket when his other hand flashed out and plucked the wallet from her open bag.

It was unfolded and he was reading her business card before she gathered her wits.

'Ami Winterburn,' he read out loud. 'Performing Arts, Special Effects, Peruke Maker, Illusion—Theatrical Supplies. Busy girl, aren't you? What's a peruke?'

'A wig,' she said, swiping her wallet from him.

'And what's Illusion? A shop or something?'

She took the card and tucked it away, not answering.

He had retained her driver's licence and now checked her date of birth. 'Hm. Twenty-six. Single?'

'Yes. You're a nosy old man,' she said, dismayed that he'd seen her real name. Amelia Anderson could just fade into the blue. Ami Winterburn, failed actress, make-up artist and wigmaker, was listed in bold type in the phone book.

'And you're a fraudulent old bag,' he guffawed, surrendering the licence. 'It's my birthday today. I'm seventy-one.'

'Well, happy birthday.'

He grinned at her tension. 'Don't worry. I won't tell North your real name,' he said and as she relaxed, added, 'but only if you stay and come to the penthouse in that get-up to celebrate my birthday.'

'That's blackmail,' she squeaked.

'That's right, Mrs. Anderson.'

Head flung back, she stalked to the door, forgetting the frock and the pink cardigan and the stout shoes. Harry looked on with appreciation.

'Bet you're a good-looking woman under all that. But that won't cut any ice with North if he finds out what a fool you've made of him. He's not a man who likes to be messed about.'

'You wouldn't tell him?'

But Harry just grinned, and she'd passed up her chance at escape because North Kendrick came back just then, with Francesca and the others following in the high good humour generated by alcohol and pampered egos.

'North, my boy—Mrs. Anderson's got a surprise for you,' Harry announced, with a provocative look at Ami. Horrified, she thought he really did intend to get his birthday kicks by exposing her in front of everyone. She imagined peeling off her disguise to stand before Kendrick, imagined those grey eyes on her real face. Her nerve broke.

'I'm, er, Harry kindly invited me to celebrate his birthday with you tonight,' she twittered. 'Unless of course I would be intruding on a family occasion—'

North broke in quite eagerly to assure her she wouldn't be intruding. Francesca wouldn't be staying for dinner, but would escort them up and he would join them when his guests had gone. Ami thought she saw the whites of Francesca's eyes at this, but the woman accompanied them dutifully.

The penthouse was sheer luxury. In the mellow light of table lamps, a pale lake of marble stretched out with clustered furniture on islands of rugs. Sculptures in bronze and stone, mirrored in the marble, looked like ancient monuments stranded in water. A clump of pre-historic palm-like cycads flourished beneath a domed skylight. Softly lit shelves set into the walls housed a host of art treasures. A table was set for dinner with candelabra and on a trolley was a large, perfect birthday cake covered in candles. Ami thought there would be exactly seventy-one. It was all tasteful, perfect, elegant. It had the touch of the hotel's catering department on it. Impersonally yours, she thought, remembering that brief glimpse of irritation tonight when North Kendrick had first seen his father. She wondered what he had given Harry for his birthday. A diamond-studded tie clip or something equally fabulous, she supposed.

Francesca was drawn to a panoramic mirror where she anxiously surveyed her lovely face.

'Mirror, mirror on the wall,' Harry muttered with a grimace. 'You don't think he'd marry her, do you?'

Ami studied Francesca anew at this idea. She wasn't sure which one she would pity most in such a liaison. But she didn't answer, and Harry reached out and touched the wrinkles at the corner of her eyes, smiling smugly at the success of his manouvres.

'Dirty Harry,' she whispered from the corner of her mouth. 'I'm not accustomed to being blackmailed into doing things.'

'Ah, my days as a blackmailer are numbered. Can't count on another birthday after this one.'

She was disconcerted. 'You mean that you're...?'

Harry gave a philosophical shrug and a gaunt grin that cut to the heart of her. She must be mad but in spite of everything, she liked this reprehensible old man who seemed so lonely in this elevated bastion of good taste. 'Well,' she said. 'Just keep your part of the bargain. And make sure that the lights stay down low. I don't want to be unmasked over the birthday cake.'

North Kendrick arrived then, emerging suddenly from behind the clump of cycads, shedding his dinner jacket, satisfaction tilting his mouth, a gleam in his eyes. He had turned a potential difficulty into an advantage, the evening had been a success and he had the look of a winner. There was a symbolic warning here somewhere, Ami thought, that in this haven of sophistication the man should appear, triumphant, from behind a lush growth of plants that dated back to primitive times. He tossed the jacket onto a couch, and rolled up the sleeves of his evening shirt. The overall impression was of broad-shouldered athleticism. Of course, his leanness could be mere skinniness. Under that loose, expensive shirt he was probably thin as a rake, his ribs sticking out.

'Amelia,' he said, stretching his hands toward her. 'I can't tell you how pleased I am you're joining us.' His warmth made her uneasy, guilty. But she thought of his enthusiasm to have a complete stranger join in a family affair and wondered if it was relief. Maybe, she speculated, North Kendrick just didn't want to be alone with his father. Her gloved hands were held in his and he stooped toward her, lingered for a moment, and she felt the draw of his attraction as his eyes crinkled with a smile. Old ladies, apparently, brought out a certain sweetness in Kendrick. He closed his eyes briefly, took a deep breath and Ami found herself gazing at him, fascinated by this uninhibited boyishness.

'That reminds me of my grandmother,' he said with a nostalgic sad-sweet smile that caught at her.

'What does?'

'That scent. What is it?'

'Oh. Just some talc,' she said weakly. At the theatre, she'd shaken some apple blossom talc on to disguise the smell of adhesive, and she was jolted that her fraud had brought back an intimate memory to him. It seemed a very refined form of cheating. Ami felt terrible.

North joined Francesca to fetch some drinks.

'The best birthday present of them all,' Harry said, watching his son. 'It's the first time since he was about fifteen that I know something he doesn't.' He positively glowed with his secret knowledge. Ami couldn't decide which was sadder—Harry's malicious pleasure at her presence, or his son's patent relief at it. She looked over at Francesca who appeared to be mixing more than drinks with North. The brunette rested her fingertips on the junction of his neck and shoulder, to emphasise some point. There must be something about that part of his neck that women liked. Ami thought of her own ridiculous fixation on it when she'd danced with him. Her fingertips tingled.

'What did you get for your birthday, Harry?' she said abruptly as she noticed the old man keenly observing her interest. 'Other than Amelia Anderson, I mean.'

Harry guffawed silently, reached down the side of the wheelchair and produced some birthday cards, made by his grandchildren. 'Here's a card from my neighbour—she's looking after my house while I'm staying here. North wants me to sell it, so I hope it will still be mine when I want to go back,' he said dryly.

She looked at him askance. 'You're joking, aren't you?'

'North likes to get his way,' the old man said with a stubborn set of his jaw that suggested where North's trait might have come from. 'He gave me this for my birthday,' he said, pushing back his shirt cuff and holding out his left hand. There was a gold Rolex watch on his knobby wrist. 'Shockproof,' the old man said, looking at the beautiful timepiece. 'And waterproof down as far as two hundred metres.' There was some gentle humour in his eyes as he raised them to Ami. 'Better make sure I don't lose my head and go diving deeper than that, eh?'

They were laughing when North brought the drinks. Francesca made some polite, expert small talk in a loud voice for the benefit of the old folks, then said goodbye and North saw her to the elevator. Through the cycad's palm-like fronds Ami caught a glimpse of Francesca clasped in his arms, or him being clasped in Francesca's, it was hard to tell. The goodbye kiss was brief, anything but passionate, probably because they had no privacy at present. As he came back Ami wondered what that was like—being kissed by North Kendrick. The adolescent speculation annoyed her.

Through dinner, Harry continued to extract the maximum enjoyment from the situation. Ami couldn't help feeling that although Harry might not have the money and power of his son, he was far from the helpless, pitiful old man he'd portrayed to her.

'North. Such an unusual name,' Ami said curiously.

'We named him Connaught—his mother's maiden name. Always intended to call him Connor, but as soon as he could talk he called himself Nort . . . it kind of grew into North. He insisted on it, refused to answer to Connor. Stubborn as a mule even when he was three,' Harry said in mingled irritation and pride.

Connaught. Ami glanced at North, who was taking all this chitchat about his babyhood with surprising tolerance. She pictured him a chubby child lisping his own name, insisting on his version of it. Harry produced baby pictures after dinner, passing them to Ami with a dry commentary guaranteed to wreck the image of a grown-up, successful son. There was one of a near-naked toddler on a beach, concentrating fiercely on shovelling sand into a bucket. There was a family shot of a dark-haired woman with North and an older girl, decorating a Christmas tree. 'We had one every year,' Harry said. 'There was this place we used to get our trees—don't suppose it's there anymore. Ah, take a look at this one.' It was a later photograph of North, sitting on the pillion seat of a Ducati motorbike clinging to a dashing, leather-clad Harry. At eight or nine, he was a thin boy showing little signs of the compelling looks he would have in maturity. His intelligent face bore an expression of mingled pride, confidence and anxiety. Ami wondered if the confidence had driven out all uncertainties or if the grown man had simply become more adept at disguising his inner doubts. A quick comparison with the adult North convinced her that this latter idea was unlikely. North Kendrick had the air of a man who had the answers and never doubted himself, whether he was buying a company or clearing the streets of unsuitable women.

'I used to race Cats. Ducati bikes,' Harry explained. 'Won quite a bit, too.' To his son Harry said gruffly, 'I don't suppose you remember much about that.'

North looked startled. 'Of course I remember, Harry,' he said so emphatically that Ami thought he was putting

on a front and had in fact consigned Harry's racing days
to the forgotten files. Ami wondered at what age North
stopped calling his father Dad, or if he ever had.

The birthday candles were lit and extinguished, the
cake cut and Ami said her goodbyes.

'I'll come down with you,' North said, steering her
into the lift. Her heart thumped.

'No, there's no need,' she said, desperate to escape at
last. But he pressed buttons and the lift doors closed on
Harry in his wheelchair, and she was alone with his son.

'Can you spare another few minutes, Amelia?' North
said as the elevator stopped on the mezzanine floor. He
gave her no time to answer, but guided her from the lift
and along a hushed, carpeted corridor to an office. Her
pulse was all but deafening now. He must know, and it
was even worse now, because she was beginning to quite
like him, and her guilt was killing her. Kendrick flicked
a switch, which turned on a desk lamp, an uplighter and
several discreet lights that illuminated paintings and an
elegant sculpture on a marble base. More like a miniature
art gallery than an office, she thought, bracing herself
as he stood before her, frowning, hands on hips. How
long had he known?

'I want your advice, Amelia,' he said.

She gaped at him.

'About Harry.'

He guided her into a low chair alongside a coffee table
and she leaned back, weak with relief, wondering how
much of this kind of stress she could take. He talked
about Harry's stubborn wish to go back to managing
alone in his own house instead of moving into more
suitable surroundings. It became clear that it wasn't
advice he wanted so much as simply to talk. It also
became clear that Harry had deliberately tugged at her
heartstrings with hints that he wasn't long for this earth.
He wasn't even permanently confined to a wheelchair,
according to his son, but recovering from an operation

on his knees. She gritted her teeth, remembering how
moved she'd been by his assertions that there would be
no more birthdays. That old phoney, she thought furiously. The irony of that hit her a moment later and she
almost laughed.

'I haven't seen him so animated in weeks. He's been
very—depressed, in fact, since the operations. You're
good for him, Amelia. I hoped, if I could tell you the
way things are, you might be able to get my point across
to him when you see him again. You're his contemporary and I think he'd listen to you. After all, you must
know many people whose health has forced them to re-
consider their way of life.'

'Oh. Hm,' she murmured. So that explained North's
affection for poor old Amelia. She might come in useful
to bring Harry around to North's way of thinking. He
certainly knew how to get a benefit out of everything
that came his way. She liked him less and her conscience
eased a little.

He waved his hand at a hotplate where a jug of coffee
simmered. 'Coffee?'

She demurred and said, 'I really must go.'

'Just a few minutes, please,' he said with a natural
smile of great charm. She studied him while he took a
china cup from a cupboard and milk from a small refrigerator. When he was talking to her, believing her to
be old, he seemed more relaxed, less guarded. She shifted
a little to ensure that the lamp alongside did not illuminate her face. Her attention was drawn to a
notebook and some invoices on the side table. All bore
the imprint of Monica's Executive Gifts and a slogan
that promised that Monica could take all the hassle out
of gift buying for busy executives. Monica, it seemed,
could 'personalise' the gifts so that the receivers would
never know the giver hadn't set eyes on them. Maybe
Monica had selected Harry's birthday present, she
thought cynically.

North seated himself in his magnificent chair, a study of male rakishness as he lounged, drinking coffee, his hair black as night, his white shirt carelessly open and catching the light, his skin a burnished gold in the mellow highlights thrown by the lamp. Ami wondered just how busy he kept Monica's gift-buying service.

'My sister lives in Melbourne and has her hands full with four children and two stepchildren. Ideally, I should get married and have Harry live with me,' he said. 'As his contemporary, what do you think about that?'

'Married? To Francesca?' she asked, finding an awful fascination in the scenario. Sophisticated, ambitious North Kendrick, the narcissistic Francesca—and Harry?

His now rather heavy-lidded eyes settled on her. He smiled, more mellow than ever, and Ami remembered that he'd had two brandies after dinner. Alcohol certainly took the harsh edge off him. He looked sleepy and relaxed and almost cuddly. 'Do I detect a note of disapproval, Amelia?'

'Oh, goodness me. It's not my place to pass comment,' she said, genuinely flustered. 'But—'

He lifted his brows in query. 'But?'

'Well—I mean, does Francesca like that idea? Of having Harry living with you?'

'I haven't actually discussed it with her.'

'Have you proposed?' she asked, feeling a curious sympathy suddenly for the ornamental Francesca.

He let his head drop back on the chair and closed his eyes. 'Not yet. I'm only thinking about it.'

'Do you love her?' she said before she could stop herself.

His chest heaved with a silent laugh. 'Does that seem important to you, Amelia?'

'It helps,' she said tartly.

'I suppose I thought that eventually love would come my way, but...it hasn't.' He sighed. 'I'm thirty-five, Amelia. When I was young I was always ahead of my contemporaries, and now I'm still out of step. All my friends are married. I meet a lot of women but they are usually too young or too old, or ready to settle for any man with money. If they're not married they're divorced and neurotic, or they're feminist academics.' He finished with a shudder.

Poor man. The whole female sex was unsatisfactory.

'Francesca suits me in many ways. She's quite beautiful—as I'm sure you noticed. I frankly admit I prefer my women to be beautiful.'

Ami took some deep breaths. He preferred his women to be beautiful and his champagne cold.

'I've known Francesca and her husband a long time. She's separated and possibly faced with a messy divorce and she's happy to have an uncomplicated relationship, someone to be seen with. Her husband had an affair,' he explained. Ami wondered if that was the reason Francesca checked her appearance so often, with that slightly dazed air, wondering what she didn't have that the other woman had. 'We enjoy similar things—she likes entertaining and I have to do a lot of that. She comes to me for financial advice—I often find her contacts useful—'

A sort of corporate affair, Ami thought. They probably claimed each other as a tax deduction.

'You don't approve, I can see. You're a romantic, Amelia. Maybe you'd prefer to know that I can, and do, fall for the wrong kind of woman. I just don't allow it to develop.'

'A bit like frostbite stunting the growth of a new, little plant?' she said, with gentle spite.

He laughed. 'No point in letting something start when you know it can only be trouble in the long term. There was a case in point not so long ago, a woman who caught my eye...'

A woman who caught his eye, like a flashy car, or a nice sports jacket, Ami thought. 'But she was the wrong kind of woman? Tch, tch. Neurotic? Feminist? Or just not beautiful enough, North dear?'

He seemed amused and entertained by her sarcasm. 'She was lovely. I was instantly attracted to her.' He got up and went to the window. 'I saw her from here, in fact, not so long ago, but when I went down to talk to her...'

'She had a voice like a crow?' Amelia said before she registered what he'd said. Her eyes widened. *I saw her from here. I went down to talk to her.* She froze, looking at his back as he stood staring over the hotel forecourt and the street. He must mean *her*. The knowledge touched her vanity for a fleeting moment. *I was instantly attracted to her.* A flare of triumph was followed by distaste. In desperation, she cast around for escape, a trapped eavesdropper.

'Her voice was good, too. I doubt the colour of her eyes and hair was real, but apart from that there were no apparent flaws in her at all—but her circumstances were, shall we say, unsavoury.'

Ami's nostrils quivered. No *apparent* flaws, indeed. Her self-loathing was considerably reduced by this breathtaking arrogance.

'A pity. It might have been interesting.'

'She might not have fancied *you*, North, dear, have you thought of that?' she said.

He had not. 'Without wishing to sound conceited, Amelia, I can tell when a woman is interested,' he said with a smile of reminiscence. 'She was, and it wasn't just business.' He glanced at her then, as if regretting such a frank reference to an old lady, presumably sheltered from the knowledge of such things as prostitution.

'You can tell! Dear *me*,' she said, gripping her bag tightly. 'What a very handy knack that must be. How does it work?'

He blinked and gave a boyish, rueful laugh. 'I couldn't even attempt to explain it, Amelia. But let's just say, I had it on good authority that she was not the kind of girl Harry would like me to bring home to dinner, so I—passed up the opportunity.'

Ami clutched her handbag and resisted the urge to hit him with it. So, he thought she'd been interested but *he'd* passed up the opportunity because she wasn't up to snuff! The self-opinionated stuffed shirt. His phone buzzed and he went over to the desk.

'Yes?' he said, snapping out of his nostalgic mood. There were some curt monosyllables and she got up, seeing her chance to get away. North Kendrick looked over and she made fluttery little gestures of thanks and farewell.

But he said, 'Hold on,' laid the receiver on the desk and came over. Taking her by the arm again, he walked to the lift with her, asking if she required a car to take her home. Ami said hastily that she had her own, which surprised him a little. 'There have been a few incidents around here,' he said. 'I'll have Morgan walk you to your car.'

'Thank you.' She beamed. He was letting her go alone. Thank heavens. The elevator door closed. He was gone. She was safe.

Morgan was at the concierge's desk taking a call and she slipped out before he saw her. Ami let out a great sigh of relief. One more minute and she would have hit Kendrick. *I can tell when a woman is interested.* She realised she was swinging her handbag in a furious arc and hoisted it over her arm. Up there in his office Kendrick might be watching her now, wondering why the widow Anderson wasn't tamely being escorted to her car by Morgan. She walked a little faster, anxious to get to the intersection so that she could abandon her elderly pace and get out of here. She heard footsteps overtaking her and for a moment her guilty conscience made her think it might be Kendrick, about to unmask her.

She upped her pace a fraction but the footsteps gained on her just before she turned the corner, and with the accelerated sound came the first prickle of apprehension. She glanced around and saw a youth break into a run toward her. He grabbed her handbag, but the handle caught on her wrist and tightened painfully as he tried to bolt with it. She couldn't get away, so she jabbed him with her elbow and landed a kick on his legs.

'Ow! Let go, you old bag! What do you think you're doing?' There was a note of injury in his voice, as if she was breaking some unwritten code by hitting back at her attacker. He saw that her wrist was entwined with the handle and brutally jerked the handbag free. The force might have broken the arm of a seventy-year-old woman. But Ami Winterburn was twenty-six and strong from years of ballet training and she saw red.

'You horrible little creep!' she yelled, loping around the corner after him. 'Attacking old women! Coward!'

The purse snatcher looked around with disbelief as this particular old woman sprinted alongside and gave him a vigorous push. Alarmed at the aged virago snarling at him, he stopped and raised a clenched fist at her. Ami delivered a high ballet kick that ripped her skirt and connected just below his elbow. His mouth dropped open in pain and shock. He flung down the handbag and fled. 'Just think twice before you pick on old ladies, you coward!' she yelled after him and shakily bent to pick up a few things that had spilled from her bag. Still kneeling, she looked along the street and saw a man coming to her rescue, slowing now as it was obvious the danger was past.

She blinked. It was North Kendrick. As her pulse crashed thunderously faster in her ears, his steps grew slower still. She closed her handbag, stood up. From his window he must have seen the youth follow her. How much had he seen and heard of what came after that?

'Oh dear,' she said breathlessly enough, clutching the ripped skirt over her thigh, trying to shrug her body pads back into place. 'My dress—torn to shreds, that awful boy, thank goodness you're here, Mr. Kendrick. North.'

His dead straight eyebrows crammed together in a deep frown. 'Amelia?' he said. She made a move away but he snapped his arm around her, reflectively spread his hand at her waist as if remembering when he danced with her. Ami tried to lean away from him, and his eyes narrowed at the youthful flex of muscle he could feel between the displaced body pads.

'Oh, it was terrible, that awful boy—I'm shaking all over,' she said truthfully. 'And I've skinned my knee.'

She bit her lip, wishing she hadn't directed his attention there. His head tilted, he took a torn edge of her skirt and lifted it aside like a curtain. Even in the black support shoes her legs were the firm, shapely legs of a dancer.

'Who are you?' he said softly. He took her arm in a grip less tender than she'd been used to from him and hauled her up close. Her hands braced against his upper arms. It was a bad time to discover he was anything but thin. Hard muscle rippled beneath her fingers and Ami tried to console herself that North Kendrick was sure to have a sense of humour over this. He was bound to see how ridiculous the whole thing was and enjoy a good laugh. Given time, he might even appreciate just how good her make-up job was. And there was Harry. She'd made his father very happy on his seventy-first birthday, hadn't she?

Ami looked at his set jaw and the muscle twitching in his cheek and decided not to rely on his sense of humour.

'Oh, dear, dear,' she said in a flustered, distressed voice.

It was enough to shift the balance of power. North's reason was telling him one thing, but she could see he was hampered by the visual signals his brain was interpreting. Confused, he relaxed for a moment and didn't expect the strength behind the shove she gave him. Kendrick sprawled on the footpath, the second man that night she'd floored in that spot, she thought in panicky humour, and Ami sprinted past some baffled bystanders and turned the next corner into the back street where she'd parked her car. Panting, she took several stabs with the key and finally got the door open. Just in time, she got inside, closed the door and sank down below the dashboard as Kendrick appeared at the corner, looking for her fleeing figure. After maybe thirty seconds, she cautiously raised one eye and saw him walk a little way down, then back again as if he'd given up, and quite suddenly the street corner was deserted.

Ami breathed deeply, waited a good ten minutes for safety then started the car. She was so rattled, she took two wrong turns in the city and added a frustrating half hour to her journey. At home, she pulled off the ripped dress, the body pads, the support shoes and stockings, wrapped herself in a short, silk robe and made herself some strong coffee. Her dog, barricaded inside the back garden, barked a welcome and a demand for release and Ami yelled, 'Just a minute, Spritz.'

She put an adhesive strip over her skinned knee then pulled off the wig and tossed it on her dresser. When the doorbell rang, she jumped, sat frozen for a moment. 'Fool,' she muttered, going to answer the door. It would be Emma with sample fabrics for the wedding, wondering why she'd taken so long to drink a cup of coffee at Kendrick's hotel. She opened the door, talking as she unfastened the chain. 'You'll have to talk to me while I get this stuff off my face. My skin is absolutely—' She stopped with her mouth open.

It wasn't Emma. It was North Kendrick.

CHAPTER THREE

'IF IT isn't the widow Anderson,' he drawled, looking at her long, smooth legs displayed beneath the robe. 'Been paddling in the fountain of youth, Amelia?'

She tried to close the door, which was mad, because now that he knew where she lived, it was much too late. But he stuck his foot in the opening, laid one hand flat against the door and pushed it open, then walked past her.

'How did you—?'

'Find you?' he finished, walking over to peer into her kitchen, thrust aside the curtain of the dining nook. Coming back to her, he reached past and gave the door the merest nudge. It slammed behind her and once again she jumped. 'You left your card, Ms. A. Winterburn.' He tweaked a credit card from his shirt pocket and flicked it at her feet. Ami clutched the robe closer to her breasts and bent to pick up the card.

'It dropped from your purse during your free-for-all with the bag snatcher. At least Amelia appears to be your real name. That's something, I suppose.'

She licked her lips. 'Most people call me Ami. Look, I can explain—'

His mouth thinned and he turned a glacial look on her. When he was sure he'd frozen her to the spot he walked away, down the narrow hallway, looking into her bathroom, bedroom, her spare room with her make-up dresser and work-table with several partly finished wigs on forms. She wondered what he expected to find—a covey of old ladies? As he came back, he picked up one

42

of the matronly shoes that she had discarded in the living room.

'The hotel has very good facilities for checking out suspect credit cards. You'd be surprised what I know about you now. Your business partnership, what you earn. What you *owe*.' He strolled all the way back, turning over the shoe and inspecting it closely before he tossed it onto a chair. Ami thought she should have heeded that warning earlier when he'd appeared from behind the primitive plant life in his apartment. 'Everything I need to know,' he went on. 'Except what you really look like.'

And when he knew that, he would be angrier still.

'So let's get the sweet, old wrinkles off, shall we?' he snapped, gesturing towards her spare room.

'You're not going to watch?' she said, aghast.

He looked at her bare legs and feet and the clinging silk robe and gave a grim smile. 'I don't intend to take my eyes off you, sweetheart.'

Ami walked to her spare room, conscious of him following close behind. *Sweetheart.* Perhaps he wouldn't remember her real face when he saw it. Perhaps it wasn't *her* he'd meant when he spoke of instant attractions. It was probably some other woman who'd caught his eye, the arrogant swine. The man was so damned sexist that he probably couldn't remember one woman from another.

Ami sat at her make-up mirror and watched him manhandle a chair to sit astride it, facing her over its back. He reached for the wig, studied it intently, a muscle flickering in his cheek. He slapped it a couple of times against the edge of the table.

'Be careful,' Ami protested. 'That's a very expensive item. Real European hair on the best imported lace base, and it has to go back into stock at the shop—'

She met his eyes and her protest stuck in her throat. Using tweezers, she peeled off the tissue-thin edges of the foam latex prosthetics one by one. The neck pieces, the forehead, the eye pouches all moulded to the cast of her own face. 'Latex. I make them myself,' she said nervously, for something to say, but it was clear North Kendrick was not interested in the technical process that had hoodwinked him. Coldly he regarded each piece of trickery, slapping the expensive wig against his hand from time to time, saying nothing, speaking volumes. Ami moved slowly, unwilling to be revealed to North Kendrick. It was as embarrassing as doing a striptease. She bent and smothered her face with white cleansing cream to remove the remaining bits of adhesive and stippled colour. 'In Elizabethan days,' she said, aware that time was running out as she wiped the last traces of her disguise away, 'actors used to use chunks of pig fat to remove their make-up. It's the origin of the nickname "hams" for actors.'

'Fascinating,' he growled.

Her face was a little pink, but back to normal. She raised her head and looked at him in the mirror. North Kendrick stiffened. The rhythmic slapping of the grey wig stopped sharply.

'What the hell—*you!*'

Ami experienced a vain satisfaction that he *had* remembered her face. Slowly she removed the ageing yellow stain from her teeth, took out the contact lenses that had clouded her aquamarine eyes. She brushed her flattened hair. It crackled with static electricity, flying out from her scalp, strands clinging to her face. He grasped her chin, jerked her around to him, and she whirled on her swivel stool. The hard, grey eyes looked into hers, blinked rapidly. His nostrils distended as he subjected her to a long, intense scrutiny.

'All colours guaranteed natural,' she said dryly.

She felt the angry flex of his fingers on her chin, the short gusts of his breath. Abruptly, he transferred his hand to the back of her chair, and the move inched the castors forward so that she was propelled closer to him.

'Just what is your game?'

'Not the one you thought it was,' she retorted.

'You're not from SOPS, I checked. Some kind of scam, then,' he said slowly, suspicion squinting his thick-lashed eyes into slits. 'A confidence trick, maybe. Now what are you after? Money, naturally, but—'

'No. The first time I saw you I was just doing a job for my mother,' she said.

He gave a snort of incredulity. 'Ah, a job on the streets for your *mother*. And what do we call her—*Madam* Winterburn?'

Ami glowered at him, thinking in other circumstances it would have been hilarious. 'I was doing some research for her agency, as it happens, but that's none of your business. You and your guards confused me with someone else,' she said shortly. 'I'd never been near your hotel until that day. I'm a make-up artist, not a confidence trickster.'

'There's a difference?' he sneered.

'I'm not interested in your money. Nor am I interested in *you*.'

'Did I say that?'

'"Without wishing to sound conceited, I can tell when a woman is interested—and she was,"' she said, mimicking his voice. 'Well, here it is, straight from the horse's mouth. She *wasn't*.'

His nostrils flared and there was a flush of colour high on his cheeks. North was still having trouble remembering that everything he'd said to harmless, grandmotherly Amelia had actually been said to Ami Winterburn. She shifted slightly, her skin prickling with the heat from the light bulbs around her make-up mirror.

'I don't believe you,' he murmured. 'I'm good at reading signals.' There was a moment when she could have run for cover but it had already passed when he leaned forward and the reflection of a dozen lights glittered in his eyes as he clamped a hand to her nape and kissed her. She made a muffled sound of outrage that he would choose this way to express his anger. And he was angry, she could feel the rage shimmering around him, feel it in the imprisoning grasp of his large hand on her neck and the fierce pressure of his mouth on hers.

Abruptly, he stopped, and Ami dragged a hand ostentatiously across her mouth. 'Yuck,' she said with great deliberation.

Unexpectedly, he laughed without making a sound. 'It was good for me.'

Her pulses clamoured. 'It was a power play, so it would be, wouldn't it?' He had not released her and she felt the flex of his hand at the nape of her neck, the merest touch of his breath on her face. Her knees touched his and she was hotly aware of the intimate contact.

'I should have known you couldn't be on the game,' he said, almost to himself. 'Because all the men you approached walked away from you again.' He paused a moment, gazing into her eyes. 'That's a compliment.'

Ami glared. 'Do you really think so?'

He looked at her mouth and touched it with his thumb, the way he had that day in the cab. Her heart hammered away in her chest, her throat felt dry.

'Shall we try it again?' he said.

'I can't think of anything I'd like less.'

'Liar. You criticised my technique. That's practically a challenge to me to do it again.'

And this time it was a different kind of power play. Not a display of strength, but one of persuasion. He moved his head slightly, from side to side, rubbing his lips across hers. Ami kept her eyes open, fiercely gazing into his to show him that his expertise was wasted. He smiled and took it as another challenge. She saw the sudden answering gleam in his eyes as his fingers slid into her hair and his mouth parted hers in a quick, confident demand. Her eyelids drooped. Kisses, in her experience, were inclined to be sloppy, disappointing things. North, she thought distractedly, was a virtuoso. Authority with gentleness, sensuality with restraint. She had wondered what it would be like to be kissed by him but the reality rocked her. His tongue dipped inside, languorously withdrew and his mouth slid across her cheek to the sensitive skin of her temple and down beneath her ear. Her hand, set against him in rejection, now curved to the shape of his arm and she felt the bulk of muscle and the texture of fine wool beneath her fingers.

'Ami Winterburn,' he said against her mouth as if he was completing his identification of her.

She inched back, mortified that she could be seduced by physical magnetism and a slick technique. Abruptly she turned her chair on its swivel, came face to face with herself in the mirror. Her cheeks were flushed, and there was a moist shine to her lips. She tore a tissue from the box and wiped the wanton look from her mouth as she met his eyes in the mirror.

'Like I said,' North murmured, a complacent smile curving his mouth. 'I rarely get it wrong.'

'You got everything wrong the *first* time you saw me,' she reminded him, tossing the used tissue into a bin and the traces of his kiss with it. 'You got everything wrong the *second* time. So maybe you've got it wrong yet again, have you thought of that?'

He looked hard at her, the way he had when he'd first seen her face with the disguise removed, as if he didn't quite trust the apparent genuineness of it. For a man who had hardly put a foot wrong in fifteen years, it must be galling to be fooled.

'I've thought a great many things tonight,' he said in a soft, biting tone. 'Most of them punishable by long sentences in maximum security jails.'

He got up and went into the hall. She looked at the wig and bit her lip. The man was awful, but she supposed she did owe him an apology to conclude this stupid business.

Ami hurried after him, catching him as he reached for the front door. 'Mr. Kendrick—North—at least let me apologise for, um, Amelia and explain how—'

She grabbed his arm and he spun around, shoving her hand off as if it was a contaminant. 'How the hell are you going to *explain* why you duped my guests, involved me in some kind of—of sick joke!'

She threw her arms out and said, 'All right! I'm sorry. It escalated into something I never intended, I admit,' she said. 'But it was your own fault, basically.'

'My fault? *My* fault that an important night of my life was dominated by a—a phoney pensioner gibbering about bloody *lamp shades*?' he roared. 'And the worst of it is—I *liked* her!'

He stood very still, hands on hips, looking at the ceiling for twenty seconds. His chest rose and fell as he took deep, calming breaths. Ami crossed her fingers that it would work. She looked around for a weapon in case it didn't. Maybe she should let Spritz inside. The dog was making a racket at the back door. She inched toward it.

'I just wanted to get into your hotel,' she said reasonably, using her most soothing voice. 'You'd thrown me out on the strength of some second-hand description, insulted me. *Banned* me, told Morgan never to let me darken your door again. So naturally I had to go inside just *once*. To restore my self-esteem.'

His eyes came down from the ceiling to fix, incredulously, on her. 'Your self-esteem.'

'I just happened to have the aged make-up on, so I thought—Morgan would never recognise me like this.' She turned her head and shouted through the door. 'Be quiet, Spritz!'

'You just *happened* to look like someone's grand-mother!'

'I'd given a special-effects demonstration to some students,' she said, slowly and carefully so as not to enrage him further. 'It takes a good ninety minutes to apply and I'd done such a good job it seemed a pity to waste it.' His mouth actually hung open for a moment. He closed it with a snap of his jaw worthy of a fresh-water crocodile and she judged that it was too late to soothe him. Frankly she went on, 'Look, I would have been into the coffee shop and out again and no-one the wiser if I hadn't been treated like a second-class citizen—yet again.'

'Don't you dare try to justify this fraud!'

'*Come home to heaven*—but not if you don't look right for the occasion. Not if you're old and don't match the furnishings and look powerless enough to just be shoved off. Morgan had the nerve to tell me to run along home and come back another time, *you* sent that young man to show me the door—'

'I did no such thing,' he snapped.

'Oh, well, then Morgan must have, so he thought he was only interpreting *your* wishes. And *you* patronised me—yet again.'

'What the hell are you talking about?' he yelled over Spritz's escalating yelps.

'"You shall have *all* the coffee you can drink,"' she mimicked, patting the nearest lounge chair in imitation of his consoling manner with Amelia.

It was the wrong thing to say on several counts. His eyes glittered and she was reminded that it was not much more than an hour since she was sitting in his office while he poured out coffee and confidences.

'You have the gall to talk about social injustice when I was photographed by the press, waltzing with an old woman who is actually twenty-six years old! *Waltzing*,' he repeated and his head went back as if he was only now collating the many separate grudges he had against her. Was he thinking of that moment when she'd slipped and ended up close in his arms?

'Well, you shouldn't have asked Amelia to dance, should you? I tried to refuse but you were just too masterful for your own good. Considering the public relations value you got from waltzing with poor old Amelia, it's churlish of you to resent it now.'

'Churlish!' he shouted. 'You unprincipled little— You let Harry innocently invite her—*you* to dinner, you accepted my hospitality, made fools of an old man and me and you dare to criticise *me*!' Spritz was going crazy in the back garden, and half the neighbourhood dogs were barking in sympathy. North strode to the back door, flung it open and bellowed, 'Be *quiet*!'

The racket stopped. He slammed the door and Ami jumped. His jaw gritted and Ami thought it highly likely that he was grinding his teeth. A continuing, obedient silence from outside enhanced her wariness. Spritz seemed hardly reliable as a secret weapon if she could be silenced so readily. It didn't seem the time to tell North that only he had been the fool, that innocent old Harry had been in on the joke all along. He would realise that soon enough.

'What can I say? I'm not sorry I did it because you drove me to it, but I *am* sorry it went so far,' she said again, her arms spread wide in apology. North Kendrick stared at her in the oddest way. 'There is no real harm done, is there? I didn't give the agency the tape-recording. It wouldn't be ethical because you gave your name and—'

'Tape-recording!' He seized her, his thumbs pressing into the soft flesh inside her elbows. She was no featherweight but the pressure lifted her forward, onto the balls of her feet and too close inside the range of his hard, grey eyes. 'What tape-recording? When? Where the hell did you plant a microphone? Who are you working for?'

'You're hurting me,' she said, wincing at the bruising strength of his hands. The pressure eased slightly, not enough. 'Look, I'm not some kind of corporate spy, if that's what you're thinking. Are all businessmen so paranoid? I thought actors were bad enough. It was in my handbag. Do you want it? The tape, I mean.'

'Well, I don't want your bloody handbag,' he said between his teeth.

Ami hurried to fetch the tape from her living room. 'You can have it. Naturally, it all ends here. You have my word that I won't tell anyone about it—my disguise, I mean, and how successful it was.'

'Your word,' he said, curling his lip.

'Yes. My word!' She slapped the tape into his hand and he took a few moments to consider it before he tucked it into his inside pocket. It cost her dearly, but Ami held out her hand to him in a staunch gesture of goodwill. Anything to make an end to this awful business. 'No hard feelings, I hope?' Too late she realised that it sounded like a mocking mimicry of his own words to her the day of the gardenia.

North looked her over as if she was an alien life form. He opened the door and stepped outside then looked back at her. His voice was very low, very controlled. 'You're the one who has it all wrong, Miss Winterburn, if you think this is where it ends.'

He closed the door behind him and she braced herself for another slam. Instead, it made a small, sinister snick. Ami listened for the sound of a car departing and it, too, was moderate, controlled. It would have made her feel less anxious had he slammed a few doors and revved his motor.

Ami phoned Emma with a much edited version of the evening's activities and made a date to see her the following evening. She fed Spritz and did some chores and failed to relax in a deep, warm bath. North Kendrick. Less like a man's name and more like an address. Where are you going? To North Kendrick.

It was unfortunate that Kendrick seemed to be associated with so many powerful sensual triggers. Smell. The heavy scent of gardenia. Hearing. The insistent sound of the waltz that echoed in her head. Touch. His kiss. She touched her lips, recalling the sensation of his mouth on hers, and her body reacted with a primitive thrill. I hardly know him, she thought, shocked. I don't *want* to know him. Ami clambered from the bath and wrapped herself tightly in a towelling robe. Just where, she wondered, *would* it all end?

CHAPTER FOUR

'WE MUST decide on Christmas decorations for the shop,' her partner said the next day when Ami had farewelled her weekly make-up students, all wearing scars and bruises of their own creation.

Ami groaned. 'Helen—September's only just finished!'

'Time slips away and the Christmas cards are already out in the supermarket,' Helen said with a hunted air. 'I've started my Christmas shopping. This year I am *not*, absolutely *not* going to get stuck with last-minute shopping.'

Ami straightened some eye-shadow palettes and fantasy eyelashes. Using the shelf as a *barre*, she performed a few ballet stretches to get out the kinks from an hour of close work bending over fake wounds and contusions. 'You're not going to insist on artificial snow on the windows this year, are you?'

'Why not?'

'It's ridiculous. Here we are, sweltering in a hot south land full of gums and palm trees and we spray fake snow on our windows and stick blobs of cotton wool on fir trees and try to make the sub-tropics look like Victorian England in winter.'

Helen looked shocked. 'But you must have a pine tree for Christmas, and snow. And stars. We always put gold stars on our front window at home for Christmas. Everyone in the street expects it.'

Ami dipped low, arching her arm down so that her fingers skimmed the floor. 'All those portly men sweating away on city streets in Santa suits. Even when I was a

53

little kid, I wondered why so many Santas sweated. He never did in story books. By the way, I've ordered in some Santa beards for Christmas.'

Helen said something she didn't hear. 'Ami,' she added, louder, to get her attention.

As she straightened, Ami saw there was a customer in the shop. She was smiling her dazzling smile of welcome before she saw who it was. The smile switched off. By daylight he looked more tanned and physical, even in the precise drape of a pin-striped double-breasted suit. Eyeing his width of shoulder, she wondered how she had ever thought he might be skinny. Pure wishful thinking, trying to cut him down to size.

'Ami,' Helen said, 'this is Mr. Kendrick. He came in earlier, about make-up for a promotion, while you were with the class. This is Ami Winterburn, our principal and genius with make-up and special effects.' Helen smiled rather archly at North Kendrick. 'Perhaps you'd like to see some of Ami's work—'

'I've already seen some of Miss Winterburn's work.' He took a long, measuring look at Ami's svelte figure in shirt, vest and black pants tucked into short boots, her streaky blonde hair twitched casually into a bunch on one side of her head. 'Genius might be an exaggeration, but I think she's quite good,' he said to Helen, keeping his eyes on Ami.

'I'm almost sure it would take a genius to fool *you*, Mr. Kendrick,' Ami said with false admiration.

His ruler-straight mouth crimped a bit at that.

'You might like to see our design samples,' Helen said, frowning at Ami's lack of enthusiasm for a prospective customer. Crouching down, Helen sorted through their photo collection of make-up designs, sliding folders onto the counter surface.

North Kendrick walked away, looking around the small space at the displays of stock. After a slight hesitation, Ami followed him. He studied a wig made entirely of curled silver foil strips, took a jaundiced view of a display board of false noses. 'What could the queen of illusion possibly have against fake snow at Christmas?' he said sardonically.

'I just don't like pretend snow in summer.'

'But you're ordering in Santa beards.'

Ami shrugged, flashed the palms of her hands. 'That's business.'

He held up a bottle of artificial tears and perspiration. 'I find it contradictory—not at all what I would expect.'

'I must be awfully complex, then,' she said with gentle sarcasm.

He smiled. 'I see your partner doesn't know about your escapade. Didn't she see your sweet little old face alongside mine in the newspaper this morning?'

Guilt made Ami flush. The picture had been a large one, of her and North, waltzing. *Gatecrashing Granny*, the inane caption went. She had looked fantastic—old enough to be his mother. Her thrill of professional pride had only lasted until Emma phoned her to ask her if she was out of her mind and to offer the name of a very good lawyer. 'I haven't told Helen yet. But if that's what it takes to satisfy you, go ahead and tell her yourself.'

Turning a small pot in his hand, he glanced at her, said ambiguously, 'That isn't what it will take to satisfy me.'

Ami snorted. 'Am I supposed to be thrown into maidenly confusion by that?'

'Are you ever thrown into maidenly confusion?'

By him she was, she thought, but he would be the last to know it.

He held up the tiny pot. 'What's this?'

'Congealed blood,' she said feelingly.

He put it down, lifted a make-up palette and viewed the assortment of yellows, greens and purples. 'And you'd use these colours for?'

'Bruises,' she said, picking out a perfect site for one on the arrogant line of his jaw.

His eyes went to a realistic bruise on her wrist, where she'd demonstrated for her students. 'More of your work?' he asked, looking at it with genuine interest. Ami was tempted to say that she had some real bruises just emerging, from his brutish handling the night before. 'Very realistic. I want to talk to you. Come to the hotel tomorrow.'

A command, not an invitation. 'Tomorrow? Thursday?' she said in dismay.

'One-thirty sharp. Come as yourself—if you know what that is. The widow Anderson is not required.'

'I'm tied up with a make-up class tomorrow. I can't be back by one-thirty.'

'More lessons in illusion?' he said derisively. 'Teaching others how to appear what they aren't? Cancel it.'

She was tempted. If he only knew, every week she wished for a legitimate reason to cancel this particular class. And that was why she never did. 'Absolutely not.'

He studied her with such care that Ami wondered when someone had last said no to him. 'You know I could ruin you if I chose to?' he said softly.

Her heart gave a bump. Ruin? In their current state of business, that wouldn't take much doing. With his resources he could buy the building, put up their rent. That alone would be enough to finish them off. Guardedly, Ami met his eyes. 'I suppose you could,' she said, picturing herself and Helen as the puny target of a multimillion-dollar enterprise. 'I can make it by two-thirty. If I don't arrive on time, then you've still got all afternoon to ruin me.'

He laughed, the sudden flash of teeth taking her by surprise. 'All right, two-thirty.' North inclined his head by way of concession but Ami had a feeling that she had just been outmanouvred by an expert. While she'd been busy asserting herself over *which* time, she had quite forgotten that she should have refused to go at all. She tried to disguise a moue of vexation.

Smiling, he thrust the palette into her hand. 'Your bruises, Miss Winterburn.'

The door closed behind him. Ami let out a deep breath. Helen had followed the final folder upwards and leaned on the desk, dismayed at the customer who'd got away.

'Ami, what's going on? Why were you so *aggressive* with the man? He was the *good* news!'

Ami laughed so much that in the end she had to explain to Helen why North Kendrick couldn't be considered good news. 'His talk about a make-up job was just a ploy to take a closer look at the shop, have a sniff around. The man isn't going to let me get away with making a fool of him.'

Dazed by Ami's quick-fire confession about her disguise, she said, 'Are you sure he didn't guess? He looks too shrewd to be fooled by anything or anyone.'

'About money, maybe, about numbers and percentages, but Mr. Kendrick isn't so hot when it comes to people.' She paused, thinking of the fragile state of North's relationship with his father, wondered why she felt so sad about it when he hardly deserved sympathy.

'And the press took photographs?'

Ami squirmed. She braced herself for recriminations, for a perfectly justified bawling out by her partner, for juvenile behaviour. But when Helen had been shown the newspaper photo and assimilated the story, what she said was, 'What was he like to dance with?'

Ami went to the hotel the next day at two-thirty. Let him call the shots and waste her time if it made him feel better. He was entitled to his anger, she admitted grudgingly. She kept her sunglasses on as she entered and overrode her depressed Thursday mood with some semblance of breeziness for the sake of pride.

Morgan was on the door. He looked swiftly over her black pants, baggy lilac cotton sweater, short boots and three inches of silver bangles and gave her a sheepish smile to show that his instructions had been reversed since the day of the gardenia.

'Never forget a face, Mr. Morgan? Or should I say, a face or two?' she added, unable to resist reminding him that she'd got past him in her disguise.

The doorman looked blankly at her and Ami realised he didn't know that she and the old lady who had caused a fuss were one and the same.

'Mr. Kendrick will be down in a moment, Miss Winterburn.'

She sat down and felt very ill-used when he kept her waiting fifteen minutes. He arrived at last, not a hair out of place, not a pucker on his charcoal suit jacket. Silk tie and matching pocket handkerchief. It was an intimidating picture he made, the handsome, successful man, striding across his marble floor with his vast hotel foyer as a backdrop, staff members all but tugging their forelocks and women guests ogling him.

'You haven't told Morgan about my stint as the widow,' she said breezily, to deny the feeling of intimidation.

'Not yet. You can apologise to Morgan another time. Right now you have a more important apology to make.'

She frowned over this as they entered his private lift. 'I've already apologised but if you want me to grovel, let me do it now to save time.'

He didn't answer, just silently reviewed her appearance and when the lift opened on his foyer, took her elbow to urge her into the lake-and-island living room.

'You can grovel to me later. I thought we'd have lunch and preliminary grovelling first—with Harry.'

'Harry?' she said, faltering at the steely, significant look he bestowed on her.

'He was asleep when I returned last night so I haven't told him yet, either. *You* can have that pleasure,' he said.

Ami's eyes opened wide. 'Oh, but—I mean, Harry—'

He misread her dismay, gave a sardonic smile. 'I'm glad to see even you have some conscience. I'll be most interested to see how you tell my father that the widow Anderson is a fraud.' He gestured ahead to the terrace where Harry sat in his wheelchair, studying the city through a pair of binoculars. Ami looked at Harry, licked her lips and once again he mistook the reason for her dismay. She'd thought by now that Harry would have been gloating about the deception. Surely, when North had reflected on it he would have *guessed* Harry knew? Taking in his glacial smile of satisfaction, she felt a sudden shaft of pity. Clever, shrewd, arrogant North Kendrick hadn't even considered that his father was in on the joke. It was an appealing blind spot in such a clever man. But she felt terrible, privy to a humiliating knowledge. Impulsively, she grabbed his sleeve, held back his relentless forward progress. 'Look, I don't think you—could you stop for a minute—*North*!' She dragged on his arm and he stopped suddenly, sliding an arm around her waist to steady them both.

'*Ami*!' he said, mocking her urgent tone. His breath swept across her cheek, and his arm tightened around her in extravagant, loverlike fashion. 'Didn't you say that's what your friends call you?' he said in her ear, as if it was an endearment rather than a rhetorical question.

Ami was disconcerted, shaken by the heat generated by his voice and the touch of his arm hard around her. *I was attracted to her*... She pulled back, aware of a tiny flare of triumph that the attraction was still active, feeling the force of the earthy nature of it. Her heart thumped, her breath seemed strangled in her throat. It was some kind of chemistry but surely she was only receptive to it because she was in her emotional Thursday afternoon state.

'You asked me what would satisfy me,' he murmured, stroking an index finger down her hair. 'Now you know.'

Her silver bracelets jangled as she batted his hand away and glared at him. He laughed, lifted her sunglasses off and regarded her quizzically. 'Red eyes. Tch, tch, have I made you cry, Ami?'

Taking back the glasses, Ami said, 'I only cry about important things. I've just been demonstrating for students again.'

'It's a very subtle effect,' he said, frowning.

'Of course. All my work is very good. That's why I'm here, isn't it?' she mocked.

'Are all make-up girls so conceited?'

'Are all chief executives so patronising?'

He looked enquiringly at her.

'If I were twenty-six and male, would you refer to me as a make-up *boy*?' she said, warming to her theme. 'I am a make-up *artist*. I am not a girl. I am a *woman*.'

'I hear you roar,' he said blandly.

Taking her elbow again, he marched her toward the terrace. A small table was set to look like a cookery-book lunch illustration. Starched napkins, a basket of crusty bread rolls, a glass-domed cheese platter. Green and purple grapes in a high-stemmed goblet. Chilled glasses and a bottle of wine in an ice bucket. Even Kendrick's lunch looked like a work of art.

Harry lowered his binoculars and in just a moment would look their way. 'North, I'm trying to tell you that, um, Harry, well, Harry—' She licked her lips and rushed to finish as the old man turned his wheelchair. 'Harry already knows.'

North stopped dead, looked at Harry and his eyes flew open wide as if someone had clashed cymbals in his ear. For a moment he looked as oddly vulnerable as he had in that photo of him as a boy. Ami felt a rush of tenderness for him, an astonishing wish to put her arms around the arrogant, complacent man.

The wheelchair came humming over. Harry inspected Ami from head to toe with intense appreciation. A wheezing laugh broke from him. 'I *said* you'd be a good-looking woman under those wrinkles, didn't I?'

Beside her North stiffened. Harry guffawed and took a white handkerchief from his pocket to wipe his eyes. Ami stood miserably in the drawn-out silence broken only by Harry's wheezing laughter and the muffled sound of city traffic below.

'And what made you think she wasn't what she seemed?' North said harshly.

'It was her joints that gave her away.'

'Joints?' North Kendrick said, biting down on the word as if it was indeed a bone. A flush of colour appeared high on the younger man's cheeks. His jaw clenched so hard, a muscle twitched in his cheek. 'And the birthday dinner? That was cooked up between you?' he said, grinding out the pun. 'All that cosy chitchat about my misdemeanors as a kid, the baby photographs, the double entendres...' His voice rose and cut off abruptly before he said to Ami, 'You even had me rambling on about how you reminded me of my grandmother.'

'Oh, I know that's unforgivable,' she said, distressed. 'And quite unintended. I felt a terrible cheat—'

'That's because you *are* a cheat.'

'You weren't supposed ever to know,' she said, colour surging into her face. 'It was just a joke Harry was going to enjoy privately.' North's nostrils flared and she was reminded that it was only a short time ago that she was telling him about her own private joke that had gone wrong. 'If it hadn't been for that purse snatcher you never *would* have known. Amelia would have disappeared and you none the wiser.'

The idea of being none the wiser seemed to have no appeal for him, either. 'And did it entertain you?' he asked, in a low, dangerous voice that sent shivers down her spine. Harry went off into paroxysms again.

'Is all this sniggering good for you, Harry?' North bit out.

'Oh, come on, boy. Where's your sense of humour? You seem to have lost it since you've become so high and mighty. You always were a bit too serious for your own good but you're getting to be a real stuffed shirt these days.'

Genuine amazement broke up the ice on North's face. 'A stuffed shirt?' He seemed startled, even hurt by the criticism but recovered quickly. 'I don't appreciate you conniving with a total stranger and raking over private family matters with her. How dare you abuse my privacy by inviting a conscienceless, malicious fraud into my home to ridicule me!' His voice had risen to a shout. In awful fascination, Ami saw that his control was almost broken. Anger tensed every line of his body. The flickering muscle in his cheek quickened. He made a rageful sweep with one fist and she winced, half expecting the still-life lunch to go flying.

'Yeah, well, I'm not too thrilled, either,' Harry said in a tone quite different from his usual geniality. It was surprisingly like his son's. 'You know why you're in such a temper? Because you can't believe your dumb old man could work something out that fooled *you*, the genius!'

Once again North was visibly affected by the attack from his father, and Ami wished passionately that she wasn't here to witness it. He already held so many grudges against her. After a moment he turned away.

'That's right—just turn your back on me. It doesn't matter what I think, does it?' Harry roared. 'I'm just a sick old man you picked up from the hospital because you thought it was your duty.'

'That's enough, Harry,' North said through gritted teeth. 'I don't intend to discuss private matters in front of this—' His jaw worked as he searched without success for a word to describe her. 'As for you, Miss Winterburn—you have ten minutes to say your goodbyes and be out on the street.'

Where you belong. The unspoken phrase resounded. Thrown out again. Ami turned scarlet.

'If my friends aren't welcome here, I won't be staying, either,' Harry bellowed as North strode away. This time North didn't stop. He disappeared inside, until his progress was a mere movement behind the walls of glass that reflected towers and shifting cloud. Ami couldn't stand the man, but she wouldn't wish the situation on her worst enemy. Sympathy for him warred with her fury at his high-handed, insulting manner. She was angry with both of them, sad for both of them. Her own family life might be chaotic at times but never like this. There was a solid affection that underpinned her relationship with her parents, and this stormy exchange left her feeling shaky and battered.

The old man said gruffly, 'Stay a minute, have a grape.' He offered her the fruit then held out the binoculars to her and it wouldn't have made her stay except that his hand trembled. She took the glasses and looked where he directed, at a building he had worked on in his youth. 'The old Century Hotel. I did a nice bit of panelling in the dining room. Wonder if it's still there?' he said to himself. 'I thought, if I let him bring me here after the operation, we'd maybe work out how to get along together at last, North and me,' he said sadly. 'But I suppose it's too late for that now.'

When she left, he wheeled alongside her to the elevator, gave her a slip of paper with his address and phone number on it. 'Come and see me when I'm back in my own place, Ami.'

She kissed his cheek, thinking it was unlikely she would visit Harry. Where Harry was, North might be and it was a risk she would rather not take. The sooner she got the Kendrick men out of her life, the better.

A week passed without a sign of North Kendrick. CKC was finalising the purchase of a well-known electronics chain and business writers were hinting that North Kendrick would soon turn his attention to buying into the media. Shrewd, clever, realistic, a consummate player, they called him. Yet shrewd, clever North Kendrick had displayed a naive faith in his father's loyalty, had even been outraged on his father's behalf when he thought Ami had deceived Harry, too. There was nothing so savage as righteous outrage discovered to be unnecessary. Nothing so humiliating as blind faith shattered. After such a colossal loss of face North Kendrick probably wouldn't seek her out again, even for revenge. It was a cause for celebration that left her feeling curiously flat.

'Ami, dear, I've got a job that's right up your street— walking two Borzoi dogs one hour a day. It needs someone who can sing.'

'Sing? Why?'

'The dogs like to be sung to during their walk. The owner's lost her voice. I thought of you at once, you sing so nicely.'

'Mother—' Ami groaned into the phone, turning over in bed to peer at her clock. It was barely seven on Friday morning. 'No—not another job that's right up my street. Please take my name off your books.'

'Ami, my love, you must know that a daughter's name will always be on a mother's books,' her mother said affectionately. 'But all right, if you don't want the Borzoi job, I won't hound you,' she went on with her unfaltering flair for words. 'Don't forget the art exhibition tonight. It's a marvellous nineteenth-century private collection, I understand, and this is the only chance to see it in Sydney. The owner's grown tired of it and is donating it to a gallery in Melbourne, I believe. Pre-Raphaelite, art nouveau—I've got your ticket. Do come. We're trying to persuade the collector to donate a work of art to us for a fundraiser, and a good turn-up would make a strong argument.'

Ami wrinkled her nose. 'I hate nineteenth-century art. All those listless women with peekaboo breasts and red hair, languishing over bowls of fruit and sheafs of wheat.'

'That's all right, dear. It's *art*. You don't have to like it.'

But, in fact, Ami had to admit even if she didn't like the style it was a fine collection, shown to curious advantage in a modern house that occupied several levels on a steep, rocky site overlooking Pittwater. A solo violinist played to the viewers of paintings, posters, sculptures, lamps, glassware, all of which incorporated dragons, deities, anguished maidens, voluminous robes and lilies. There was even a fountain, fully operational and mossy in a sheltered courtyard, spouting water from the open mouths of several fish that clustered around a brace of underdressed women. Looking at the eight ripe, bare breasts pointing in an angle identical to that of the fishes, Ami thought it was a mercy that the water was gushing where it was.

'Wonderful, isn't it?' Lenore Winterburn said to her.

'Hideous, but beautifully executed,' she allowed. Ami stopped abruptly to eye a row of sculpted nymphs that wouldn't look out of place outside the Avalon. She could almost imagine North Kendrick alongside one of them, a hand proprietarially on a perfect white marble thigh. 'Does this owner have any furniture other than collector's items?' Ami asked, looking around at the open spaces between exhibits.

'He doesn't live here anymore, actually. Too many stairs for him now, Erica said, so I suppose the poor man must have trouble with his mobility. There's just his collection and the security people here, which is why he agreed to the exhibition, because it doesn't interfere with his privacy anymore. I believe the house is to be rented out soon, and the collection will all be packed up and sent to Melbourne.' She looked speculatively at the quartet of garlanded female figures. 'I wonder if he would give the society one of those nymphs to raffle.'

Ami laughed. 'You can't raffle a nymph. It's disrespectful.'

But her mother had turned to look behind her for the committee president who was doing the rounds with various charity VIPs, making introductions. 'I suppose that must be the owner with Erica—the one in the wheelchair,' Lenore murmured in Ami's ear.

'Wheelchair?' Ami said, feeling a prickling sensation between her shoulder-blades. She turned. North Kendrick was behind her, no more than a nymph away.

CHAPTER FIVE

HER pulse, grown sluggish at the prospect of yet more sculptures and small talk with her mother's charity committee friends, raced into a hectic rhythm. He was in profile by a sculpture giving its provenance to three very attentive women. As they made comments, he bent his dark head and nodded. He placed a hand on the sculptured knee of a nymph and Ami heard him say, 'Exquisite.'

As if her gaze had alerted him, he turned his head. He didn't recognise her instantly, probably because it was the last place he expected to see her. Also probably because she had made a concession to her mother's favourite charity and dressed in an elegant, thin-strapped dress of caramel silk and oiled back her long hair into a classic dancer's knot. A delicate, beaded plait hung each side of her face. Her skirt was above the knee and her long legs looked longer still in high heels, a fact that Kendrick appeared to be noting. His hand withdrew from the nymph's white thigh when he realised whose legs he was admiring. A thunderous look transformed him, to the dismay of the charity committee, for whom all had been going so well.

He excused himself and walked forward. 'Miss Winterburn, we meet yet again.'

She smiled with a great deal more composure than she felt as he eyed her intently. 'Mr. Kendrick.'

'What do you think of the show?'

'The violinist is very good,' she said earnestly.

A sardonic smile tilted his mouth. He raked another look over her sleek, oil-darkened hair, her bare shoulders and the hint of cleavage showing at her neckline. 'Disguised again? Do you ever look the same twice?'

Ami determined to keep her temper. Her mother, summoned away by the committee president, would never forgive her if she made a scene with the committee's benevolent art collector.

'Harry's with you, I see,' she said, looking hopefully in Harry's direction, but he hadn't seen her yet.

North's eyes narrowed. 'Yes, he is, no thanks to you.'

She bit her lip to hold back a sharp retort, resentful that he should try to blame her for widening a rift in a relationship that was already in trouble. 'This is your collection then?' she went on doggedly. 'I didn't know.'

'Really? You keep turning up in my life, Miss Winterburn. You can't expect me to believe it's sheer coincidence. What are you doing here?'

Ami's good intentions slipped away. 'Oh, I'm casing the joint,' she mocked. 'I thought I might nick a nymph or two.'

His mouth smiled but his eyes remained cool and watchful. He glanced around quickly, as if searching for conspirators.

'I'm working alone again,' she drawled, reminding him of previous errors of judgement.

'You're good value, I'll give you that,' he said, laughing. 'Come with me.'

He took her arm and walked her through the scattered crowd and she could hardly make a fuss without ruining the occasion. Everyone took an interest. Ami raised a hand to Harry, who waved cheerfully at her and, to her chagrin, didn't even attempt to come after her. And her mother, who never hesitated to butt in where she wasn't wanted, now failed to butt in exactly where she *was* wanted.

Red-faced, she said, 'Where are you taking me? Going to hand me over to your gung-ho security officers for interrogation?'

'Why should they have all the fun?' He guided her into a room mercifully free of the whiplash curves of art nouveau. It was furnished with a large, plain desk, a couple of chairs and a drinks cabinet. A green-shaded table lamp was switched on, illuminating some paperwork. He went to the drinks cabinet, took out two glasses and a bottle of champagne from an ice bucket. He poured the wine, came back to hand her a glass.

'This is a very civilised interrogation,' she said lightly, taking a sip. He drank from his glass, watching her as he did so, and a silence stretched out in the room. The collective hum of voices wafted through from the exhibition. Down the rocky slope, trees shushed in the salt breeze, the sound a mimesis of that other rhythmic rush of water on sand below. The violin played an English folk song, a descant over the mellow murmurings.

Ami grew uneasy. His hard-eyed look reminded her that she had been privy to his humiliation on Thursday. 'I am sorry about Thursday,' she said sincerely. 'If I'd realised earlier that you didn't know that Harry knew— I could have saved you the, er, embarrassment.'

His jaw hardened and his head went back to an arrogant angle. 'Don't patronise me, Miss Winterburn. And don't make the mistake of thinking I'm any kind of fool just because you and my father pulled a fast one on me.'

'I don't think that makes you a fool at all,' she said, shrugging. 'I think it's rather sweet and trusting that it didn't occur to you that your father would engineer a joke at your expense.'

'*Sweet?*' he said, choking on a mouthful of good, dry champagne as if it was pure saccharine. 'Good God, I think I'd prefer you thought me a fool.'

'Well, whatever you prefer, North,' she said demurely.

He laughed silently, finding her good value again, she supposed. One day, she thought maliciously, watching his shoulders heave, he would probably have one of those awful, wheezy laughs like Harry.

'Now—tell me what's going on,' he said.

'Going on? Where?'

'I wasn't born yesterday, Ami. You hang about outside my hotel, you turn up a couple of weeks later in disguise and insinuate your way into a private function, then into my private quarters. Now you turn up again at my former home. If it isn't some con game you're playing, what the hell is it?'

'Insinuate? I've told you how that happened. There is no game, do you understand? My mother invited me here tonight—'

'Ah, your *mother* again! Your inventiveness is growing threadbare.'

Ami eyed him with dislike. 'Look, think what you like. I didn't want to come here, even when I didn't know it was your place. I am not fond of the pre-Raphaelites or art nouveau, but it was for a deserving charity and I promised my mother.'

'Ami Winterburn, philanthropist, dutiful daughter,' he marvelled. 'Widow, grandmother, cheat. My God, when I said you were the kind of girl Harry wouldn't like me to take home to dinner, I might not have got it quite right but I wasn't wrong, either.'

Ami compressed her mouth. 'What's bugging you is that it was *Harry* who asked me to dinner.'

The shaft went home. His eyes glittered. 'Yes, that does bug me,' he said softly. 'But I can live with it. The question is, what am I going to do about you?'

Ami backed up a step, suddenly apprehensive so far from the crowd. Common sense told her that it was unlikely North Kendrick would do anything violent with a houseful of guests just a scream away. Ami took another step back.

'It's happened before,' he told her.

'What has?'

'A woman, turning up at odd times again and again when I least expected it. It went on for months.'

'That's the price you pay for being so irresistible,' she snapped. 'Such a bore—wait a minute! Are you implying that I am—that I am *chasing* you like t⁰⁰° other poor, misguided woman?'

'You fit the profile. Attention-seeking behaviour, tape-recorders and disguises, insinuating your way into my private life, coming to functions I'll be attending. You make a career of fooling people,' he said thoughtfully.

'I don't fit any profile, you pompous, conceited oaf.'

'I could be wrong,' he admitted, coming toward her.

'You are.' She backed off again, then turned and strode out as best she could in high heels on the thick carpet. Heeding a warning crack in her weaker ankle, she stopped and took off her shoes. North regarded with some wariness the two metal-tipped spiked heels pointing at him.

He put his hands up in mock surrender. 'I'm unarmed.'

Ami eyed him dispassionately. 'Men like you are never unarmed.'

'Disarmed, then.' He smiled. 'If I'm suspicious it's because I never know what to make of you. I'm forced to consider the wildest possibilities.'

Her heart thumped. He stood there with a stripe of light just missing his eyes, casting a glitter in them.

'That bag snatcher might not have been unarmed,' he said softly. 'Did you think of that when you chased him?'

'It always crosses a woman's mind, I suppose, but I was so furious that he would attack an old lady I just—' She lifted one shoulder. 'He could easily have broken an arm on an elderly woman with arthritis, or osteoporosis.'

'But you weren't an elderly woman with arthritis,' he said in a curious tone.

'What's that got to do with it?' she asked, throwing her arms out. '*He* didn't know that, little creep.'

'He might be a reformed little creep now. That high kick really connected.'

'Yes, it did, didn't it?' she said with ghoulish satisfaction.

'Ballet lessons?' he enquired.

'Since I was four.'

They walked to the next doorway.

'Were you any good?'

'Yes,' she said without false modesty. 'My ambition was to join a classical ballet company but it is very competitive and I grew too tall and acquired a weak ankle, so—' She shrugged.

'And what does a failed ballet dancer do?'

Irritated at the phrase, she said airily, 'Oh—teach, join a modern dance company or do cabaret. Or,' she added with a glint in her eye, 'become an exotic dancer.'

'And which did *you* do?'

'What do you think?'

'Like I said—I always consider wild possibilities where you're concerned.'

'Are you actually entertaining ideas of me stripping in some sleazy nightclub?' she challenged, a hand on her hip.

'Mm. I, er, hadn't got as far as the sleazy nightclub,' he murmured, slanting her a look that said exactly how far he had got.

Ami mistimed her next step to the doorway and collided with North as he leaned past her to nudge the partly closed door aside. She jerked away but the doorframe was directly behind her and brought her up with a jolt no farther from him than before. The room had the chill of emptiness and she felt the radiation of heat from North's body on her shoulders and through the thin dress. He laid his hand on her bare arm and she shivered with the warmth of it.

'North—'

'Ami,' he said in the mocking way he'd said it the other day. And he bent and put his mouth to her bare shoulder, nudging aside a silk shoestring strap with his fingertips. She drew in a sharp breath and he straightened to look at the effect he'd had on her. Whatever he saw pleased him.

'I want to go back to your awful nymphs,' she said huskily.

'I'm not stopping you,' he said, breathing the words on her temple. 'But I wish you'd stay.'

He waited a moment, perhaps to give her time to leave, and when she didn't, his eyes glinted in triumph and he bent again, kissed her neck below her ear, nuzzled in so that the tiny plait swayed, its beads making small clinking noises that seemed somehow linked with the soft sounds of North's lips on her skin. The fabric of his jacket brushed against her bare skin, pleasantly abrasive. The smell of him, citron and champagne, rose in her nostrils and she reached out with her free hand to his hair. Thick, springy hair. Her fingers pushed through it, urgently. North made a throaty sound and put his hands to her waist, lifted her clear of the doorway and set her down, hauling her close against him. Her breath escaped in a startled sigh. Her hands slid beneath his jacket until her arms were around him and she felt the heat of his skin through the fine fabric of his shirt. North tilted his head and looked blazingly at her for a few seconds and she was already rising on her toes towards him when he kissed her. Her lips parted beneath his persuasive, fleeting caresses. She pressed close to him, craving more, wanting the teasing, nomadic touch to settle and deepen. She turned her head so that she captured his wandering mouth with her own, kissing him wildly, excitement trembling in her body. It had never been like this. She heard her own breathy sigh just a moment before the other voice.

'Ami, dear, where are you?'

It was her mother, butting in where she wasn't wanted.

Ami bolted from North's arms, looping her strap, smoothing her dress with trembling fingers as she amended the traitorous thought. It was her mother, butting in exactly where she was wanted for once. Ami ran her tongue over her lips. Out of the corner of her eye, she saw North quickly smooth his hair that she had ruffled so passionately. Was she crazy? She knew what kind of game he was playing, but she didn't have to make it easy for him. Lenore cast a thoughtful look over her daughter's stockinged feet, the shoes tucked under one arm, the flush on her cheeks. Then she turned her attention to North. Ami cursed silently as she saw the gleam in her mother's eyes.

'Well, I know he's not a kissing cousin,' Lenore said, removing any doubts that she might have arrived too late to see them in a clinch. 'Introduce me, Ami, my love.'

'Mum, meet North Kendrick. My mother, Lenore Winterburn.'

At least that appeared to shake him—the mythical mother so close at hand and so obviously genuine. Only a mother had such immaculate timing.

'*Madam* Winterburn,' Ami added dryly in an undertone.

Colour appeared high on his cheekbones as he courteously shook her mother's hand and weathered a scrutiny almost as thorough as any he had given Ami. North put a hand to his tie and flexed his neck. Even his superb self-confidence was rocked by the prospect of maternal criticism. Not, she noted sourly, that her mother appeared to be finding much to criticise.

'North is the owner of the collection—all those wonderful nymphs that he's grown tired of,' she said with sly malice. It would serve Mr. North Kendrick right, to get the third degree from her mother, a veritable tigress when it came to raising money for disadvantaged children. Ami put on her shoes and beat a hasty retreat from the empty rooms where she almost fancied the echo of her own sigh of pleasure hung on the air for everyone to hear.

As it happened, Lenore Winterburn spent a good twenty minutes with North, during which time even Francesca, stunning in black and silver mesh, had to take a back seat. Every now and then, North looked thoughtfully in Ami's direction and she couldn't help feeling that the donation of a nymph was not the only subject under discussion.

Her mother looked mightily pleased with herself when she rejoined Ami. 'What a charming man,' she said. 'And so modest. He makes nothing of the fact that he was a boy genius.'

'Oh, was he?' Ami said flatly, eyeing the boy genius. He was strikingly handsome in a light grey double-breasted suit of finest wool. A wolf in sheep's clothing.

'Erica told me. He was a prodigy—was inventing things when he was only fifteen and one of his school-masters fortunately had the wit to take out patents for him. He won all sorts of scholarships and went into high school and university years ahead of his peers, because he was so clever.'

That must have been what he meant, Ami decided, when he'd said he was always ahead of his contemporaries. *Out of step.* She pondered the significance of a boyhood spent, not with other kids his own age, but in the company of older people. Instead of carefree years at primary school, he went early into high school. When his peers were messing about in high school musicals and sneaking into nightclubs with falsified IDs, he was already at university. And the boy genius might very well have been intellectually mature, but there was every chance he had been emotionally still a little kid. It occurred to Ami that being intellectually advanced might have been a lonely business.

'Yes, he was brilliant at mathematics and science,' her mother was saying, 'and once he got into finance, he was brilliant at that, too.'

'Mathematics and science,' Ami said dryly, looking around at the languishing maidens, dragons and arum lily motifs. 'That explains a lot.'

Harry sought her out eventually. He seemed out of sorts, saying that he'd only come tonight to get away from the hotel prison. 'I don't know why he moved there. To be in the limelight when the hotel opened, I suppose,' he said pettishly.

Ami frowned at his tone. 'Isn't that a bit ungrateful, Harry? From what I can gather, North moved out of this place because all the levels and stairs were going to be a problem for you while you recovered from your op. This is a lovely house with a fabulous view. I don't suppose he particularly wanted to leave it. At least at the hotel, he can be near you with an office in the same building, and you have to admit it is easier for you with the lifts and staff when he's away.'

Harry cast her a look of such cunning that she wondered if she'd missed something. But it was gone in an instant and he was asking if she would drive him back to the hotel. 'North's going to be here for a while and I'm a bit weary.'

'I don't think your son would like that.'

'He'll like it. Let him and Francesca have some time alone—they might want to stop off somewhere and park, eh?' A suggestive wink went with this.

'Don't you think they're too old for hanky-panky in the back seat of a car?' she snapped, with a mental image of Francesca and North straightening their clothes, smoothing ruffled hair. Her cheeks burned.

'Never too old,' the old man said, giving his wheezy laugh.

'Anyway, I got the impression you weren't in favour of a match between North and Francesca,' she went on spikily.

'North's ready to settle down, I can read the signs. I'm starting to think I might have to face the inevitable,' Harry said with a sigh and a sharp look at her.

Inevitable. Ami glanced at the two prospective partners, wondering if the merger was to go ahead after all. She thought again of North, kissing her in his empty house tonight, and her temper flared. What kind of man could contemplate a union of marriage with one woman while fancying another? A collector, that's who, she thought, her eyes ranging over the exhibits. She had the panicky feeling that she must not stand still or she might join the row of nymphs. She had a vision of herself, cast in bronze standing on a plinth in a frozen pose, with North's hand possessively on her thigh.

'Well, all right then. I'll drive you,' she said to Harry. At his request, Ami dropped Harry in the hotel car park rather than the front concourse. She unfolded the wheelchair, helped him into it and, at Harry's insistence, left him waiting by the elevator. She waved, wondering if she would see him again. The idea of losing touch dismayed her. But, unless she could be certain North Kendrick was safely out of the country, she wouldn't be calling on his father.

He wasn't out of the country the next day when Ami jogged back from a run to the park with Spritz. She saw a large, pale car parked near her house, its outline fuzzed by sunshine. The footpath was a long strait ahead of her, patched with bright strips of sun and the lacy shade of arching cotoneaster branches. Ami leaped in the air to touch a branch and Spritz yelped and leaped with her as they covered the last few yards to the front gate. Laughing, exhilarated by the exercise, Ami spun into a high pirouette, taking with her the blurred impression of a man leaning on the car. She was in the air when some intuition told her who it was.

Panting, heart pounding, feet firmly on the ground, she adjusted her damp headband and stared at him.

'Very carefree,' he said sardonically, eyeing her track shoes, gym shorts and sweatshirt. 'Ami Winterburn, fitness enthusiast.' He announced it as if it was another role she was playing, another disguise she was wearing.

He didn't look carefree at all but baggy-eyed and bad-tempered and raffishly unshaven. He wore jeans and a light cotton sweater that called attention to his shoulders. His arms were crossed and the fingers of one hand tapped out a fast rhythm on his biceps. Spritz failed to absorb these antisocial signals and leaped up to lick his hand as if he was a long-lost friend instead of the barbarian who had bellowed at her on Tuesday night.

'Marvellous! My life's in chaos and you're frolicking with the dog.'

'I always frolic with the dog on Saturday,' she said. 'What's the matter? One of your languishing redheads gone missing? Lost a dryad?' She opened her eyes wide. 'You've decided art theft is the reason I *insinuated* myself into your life.'

'Always so chirpy. Doesn't it bother you that I could turn nasty and lay charges against you?' he said, and there was less threat than curiosity in the gaze that settled on her.

Ami grinned. 'Turn *nasty*? *You*?'

'It's been known,' he said without shame.

'I'm sure. Anyway, what charges could you bring against me?'

'Let's see.' He straightened and slotted his hands into his back jeans pockets, a strategy that added unnecessary inches to his shoulder span. 'Fraud? False pretences? I'd have to put it before my lawyers.'

She laughed. 'You wouldn't. You'd look ridiculous.'

North looked at the sky to compose a news item. 'Hotel magnate sues theatrical artist for false pretences. In court today, failed actress, dancer and make-up artist, Ms. Ami Winterburn, pleaded guilty to charges of false pretences—'

'You'd have to admit that Kendrick the infallible was totally taken in by a mere make-up *girl*,' she pointed out. 'Wouldn't that send share prices in CKC plummeting?'

'Hotel magnate sues theatrical company, Illusion, for false pretences. In court today, peruke maker, failed dancer and failed actress Ami Winterburn and her partner, Helen—'

Ami waved her hands urgently. 'This has nothing to do with Helen or the shop.'

'—answered charges that they practiced a malicious hoax on Connaught Kendrick, as a publicity stunt for their enterpise.'

'That's not true and you know it!'

He shrugged. 'That doesn't matter. Everyone could believe you show-biz types will do anything for publicity.'

'It's only your ego that's hurt. I truly don't believe you'd be so petty.'

'Men fight wars for their ego,' he said dryly. 'Why don't we talk inside?'

He shoved the garden gate open and waved her through, trying to establish his dominance on her own territory. And as if he needed any help, Spritz leaped alongside him and licked his hand.

'Sycophant,' she muttered. 'Heel, Spritz.'

Instead, Spritz rushed ahead, up the front patio stairs, to fetch a gnawed tennis ball in her jaws.

'Good boy,' North said, crouching as the dog brought the ball to him.

'It's a she. A good girl,' Ami said dryly. He tossed the ball and Spritz galloped to bring it back and lay it at his feet with a slavish look. 'I'll have to take her back to obedience school for a refresher course. She thinks just *anyone* is a friend.'

He slanted a look upwards at her, his eyes crinkled against the sun. 'They say animals and children can always tell. Do you think that's true?'

'I don't know. What are you like with children?'

'They dote on me.'

'Oh, really?' she said sceptically. 'Which children are these?'

'Three nieces, a nephew and two step-nephews in Melbourne. I'm godfather to two of them and to four other kids besides.'

'Six godchildren?' she said, surprised, trying to imagine him holding a baby at a christening font. Unclipping her jogger's drink bottle from her shorts waistband, Ami adjusted the plastic straw and took a cooling draught of water.

'Married people always try to find some role for their single friends—best man at the wedding, godfather at the christening, Santa Claus at Christmas. You must have experienced the same thing.'

She spluttered a little on the drink, failing miserably to imagine him in a Santa beard and red suit. 'I'm generally thought to be too tall to be in people's wedding photos.'

'Never the bridesmaid?' he quipped.

'Oh, yes, once, years ago. And I'm to be bridesmaid again soon for the same friend. Her second marriage. Emma's the same height as me,' she said in explanation, smiling at the thought of Emma's wedding.

He reviewed her height consideringly from his kneeling position. 'Two of you,' he said and gave a low whistle. 'I hope the groom is the assertive type. He might disappear without a trace.'

Ami gave a gurgle of laughter at the thought of the bearlike Mackenzie sinking without a trace. 'No, no.

Matt's a lot like you—people might hate him, or love him, but they'll never overlook him.'

'And which is it you feel for me?'

She snorted. 'What do you think?'

'If that was hate last night, then hate me some more, Ami Winterburn.'

The blood rose to her face. It was only a kiss, for heaven's sake, she thought in annoyance. But she wasn't in the habit of getting into clinches with unsuitable men, however attractive, and it was the second time it had happened. She averted her eyes from North Kendrick's self-satisfied smile, finding it very easy to hate him.

'Your friend Emma is either very confident or very beautiful,' he commented, running his hand in a long caress down Spritz's back. Without meaning to, Ami followed the motion, registering a tingle down her own spine.

'She's both. Why?'

His eyes came back to her, roamed from ankles to the top of her head. 'You would make a—distracting feature in anyone's wedding pictures.'

Ami blinked, not entirely pleased. A 'distracting feature' could just as well be a chandelier or a flower arrangement. His compliments always roused this dual pleasure and aversion. It was as if his very admiration was a trap.

His admiration was certainly getting a warm response from Spritz. The dog drooled and grinned at a smiling North, in the unqualified affection that can exist between a human and an animal. The man looked suddenly more relaxed. 'I used to have a dog. A sheepdog. He was very intelligent,' North said, giving Spritz a last pat before he stood up.

'What did you call him?'

'Meg.'

'A boy dog called Meg?'

'Short for Megabyte,' he said, with a faint smile of reminiscence. 'I was precocious and keen on computers.'

'Yes, I heard. The boy genius,' she said, leading the way into the house.

Inside, she dumped her drink bottle down and pulled the elastic from her hair. She shook her head, rubbed at it with a towel. Scowling at North, she said, 'Just for the record, I am not a failed actress.'

'That stung, did it?'

'I've had several good parts.'

'Years ago. In soup commercials. And party turns as a singing telegram girl, whatever that entails. Exotic dancing, perhaps?'

'Even the best performers have back-up careers because it can be hard to stay in work. I got into make-up and special effects as a sideline and it became more fascinating than acting and dancing. It often happens.'

His grey eyes didn't waver. Liar, they seemed to say. 'After all, *you* started off inventing things and now you sit at a desk adding noughts to numbers on paper.'

He frowned at this and she went on curiously, 'What kind of things did you invent?'

North shoved his hands into his pockets. 'Nothing you would recognize. Small electronics components. Inventions are worth nothing unless you get them into production. I spent a couple of years just getting investment funds and finding production partners and the whole thing blew up into a huge operation.'

'And you never did get back to inventing. Do you miss it?'

'Why should I? It was merely a springboard to better things.'

But Ami looked levelly at him and his eyes flicked away to a table that held a head form with a wig foundation partly tufted with black hair. He fingered the hair and grimaced. 'What is this stuff you're sewing on?'

'Not sewing, ventilating,' she said. 'I'm ventilating synthetic hair onto the lace foundation. It's to be an Egyptian pharaoh wig—cheap—for an amateur theatre group I help out now and then. Look, you didn't come to ask questions about wig making.'

Grey eyes held hers. 'No.'

Ami waited a moment and when he remained silent, she spread her hands in a silent invitation to go on. North followed her hand movements as he always seemed to and something in his eyes made her heartbeat quicken. Now that the glow of exercise was diminishing, she felt a chill tingle along her spine and down between her breasts. 'Well?' she prompted, huskily.

'Do you know where Harry is?'

Ami blinked in surprise. 'No. Don't you?'

His mouth compressed. 'Has he phoned you?'

'No,' she said. Then, flippantly, 'Don't tell me Harry has run away from home?'

His head went back and he looked down his nose. 'Harry told me he was going home by cab last night, but my information is that it was you who dropped him off at the hotel. So you were the last person to speak to him. I ask again, have you seen him or heard from him?'

My information. Hands on hips, she said, 'And I'm telling you again, no, I have not. I left him at the car park elevator.'

'But then, you are a first-class liar. You won't mind if I look around?'

He headed off down the hall, pushing wide the doors the way he had that other time. Ami followed indignantly. 'Yes, I do mind. Harry's not hiding in my wardrobe!'

He looked suspiciously around her bedroom before his gaze came to rest on her unmade double bed. Any other day of the week it would be chastely made up and smoothed by now, but it was Saturday, the day she changed the sheets, and the pillows were awry and the bedclothes in the rumpled state occasioned by her sprawling sleeping habits. Her bed always looked as if two people, not one, had slept in it, a fact not lost on North Kendrick.

'Heavy night?' he drawled.

Ami flushed. She looked him in the eye and reached past him to close her door with an eloquent little snap. 'Harry's not here.'

'I want you to let me know if he contacts you.'

A vague alarm on Harry's behalf, but she dismissed it. After all, that day on the roof, the old man had shouted that he wouldn't stay where his friends weren't welcome. At present, Harry had no choice but to stay, but he was probably hiding out with a friend somewhere in token independence, to worry North a little, make him feel guilty, even. Harry, she thought without any illusions, was a manipulative old devil. Ami surveyed North's appearance and wondered if it was guilt or concern that had put the bags under his eyes and prevented him from shaving. 'When did you notice he was missing?'

'I got home after two this morning and stopped by his room, found his bed hadn't been slept in. There was no note.'

After two, she thought. The bags and the bristles were more likely the aftermath of some serious socialising in that case. With Francesca, she wondered? In the back seat of that magnolia Jaguar? Ami dismissed the idea. The man owned a hotel full of magnificent rooms. He would not need to resort to the back seat of a car if Francesca tired of an uncomplicated love life while her divorce came through. 'Someone must have seen him leave the hotel. Your paranoid security people? The hawk-eyed Morgan?'

He shook his head. 'He didn't go to his own house, so... I want you to ring me if you hear from him.'

I want again. Deliberately she shrugged one shoulder as she walked into the kitchen. 'I'll think about it.' She snatched up her drink bottle from the counter and tipped it up to drink from it.

'You'd be wise to cooperate unless you want to hear from my lawyers,' he said harshly.

Ami spun around, arms outflung. A few drops of barley water flew from the drink bottle. 'What is it about you Kendrick men? Harry threatens to tell you my real name if I don't perform my pensioner act for his birthday, you threaten to take me to court if I don't cooperate!'

'Ah—he forced your hand, did he? The cunning old devil,' North said, a gleam in his eyes. 'Serves you right.'

'You *admire* that, don't you?' she said incredulously. 'By forcing my hand, he made a complete idiot of you, but even so you can't help admiring him for getting the better of me. *Men!*'

'You might lose the game, but you have to appreciate the skill of the other players,' he said with what he clearly believed was inarguable logic.

Ami shook her head, baffled by the ability of males to fight with each other yet at the same time remain their own greatest fans.

'Well, I don't find blackmail and manipulation admirable. Don't either of you ever just *ask* people to do things for you—say "would you please" instead of "I want"? But then, maybe you both like the buzz of making people jump through hoops!'

'It worked. You did stay for his birthday,' he pointed out mockingly as if the blackmail was justified by the result. 'It can only have been sympathy for him or fear of me that did the trick. And even Harry couldn't have commanded your sympathy in such a short time.'

Ami laughed. '*Fear*? Don't imagine there is anything about you personally that I fear, North. Only your influence. You have power and like most men you abuse it. I fear *that*.' North didn't like that, she noticed.

He sneered. 'On the other hand, maybe you did it because you enjoyed it. As part of your varied career, have you often dressed up to entertain men for their birthdays? Or even,' he added, flicking an insolent glance over her body, 'dressed down?'

Ami drew in an audible breath and let it out in a hiss. She jerked her hand towards him and liquid from her drink bottle shot out in an arc over his face and chest.

CHAPTER SIX

BARLEY water dripped from his hair. It ran in rivulets over the concave planes of his cheeks, along his bristly jaw to drip from his chin. Impassively, he looked down at his drenched sweater, tweaked the fabric between finger and thumb.

'Oh,' she said lamely. 'Here—have my towel.' She dragged it from around her neck and thrust it at him and he flinched, as if this might be some new attack. Regarding her through spiky lashes, he took the towel, mopped his face.

'That was inexcusable,' he said at last.

'Don't you lecture *me* on behaviour,' she said heatedly out of combined pique and guilt.

'I mean, what I said was inexcusable.'

Ami opened and shut her mouth. With a lopsided smile, he added, 'I wonder why we seem to bring out the worst in each other.'

And while she was still adjusting to this philosophical reaction to having a drink flung in his face, he looped the towel over her shoulder, crossed his arms and pulled off his sweater so that she was suddenly confronted with a half-naked North Kendrick. She had an impression of a wide, deep chest with a spattering of dark hair on tan skin as he turned away. Perfunctorily, he said, 'Do you mind?' and proceeded to wring his wet sweater over the basin. In the course of her mixed career Ami had seen a great many men without their shirts, some of them famous for their physique. So why she should find the sight of this man, performing a homely task at her kitchen sink, so riveting, she couldn't say. It was true, he was very nicely built. Without clothes, he looked much bigger, more muscular. She watched the flex and play of muscle in his upper back as he shook out the sweater. His shoulders rose and fell with the action, and, with his arms held up as he inspected the sweater for damage, made one of those irresistible contour lines so persuasively male. Power and beauty together, she thought, frankly admiring the bulge of biceps and his smooth, lightly tanned skin.

He flipped the wet sweater over one shoulder and took up a leaning stance against the counter. Pure James Dean, she thought derisively. The charismatic drifter look. If he had seemed formidable in his high-priced suit in his high-priced hotel foyer, now he looked positively dangerous with his unshaven jaw and his damp hair hanging over his forehead. From one kind of power to another, she thought. It was so unfair.

'I apologize,' he said.

For a confused moment she thought he was apologizing for his sex appeal. In the few blank moments when she stared at him, he gave a cat-got-the-cream smile, nodded at the drink bottle on the counter. 'I hope there's no drink left in that thing. I'm getting nervous with you staring at me like that.'

Which was as good a way as any to let her know that he knew she was gaping at him. 'You're safe,' she said ambivalently. 'Unless you insult me again.'

'I suppose I should apologize for that other comment, too—prompted by the state of your bed.'

'I suppose you should,' she said tightly. 'It's none of your business whether I've had a heavy night or not.'

'Put it down to jealousy,' he said. 'I wish it was me who had rumpled your sheets.'

She might have thought she hadn't heard right, except that his expression confirmed his words. Ami felt the attraction, the magnetism of the man, the flutter of her own pleasure at his earthy statement of desire. He was handsome, wealthy, powerful and many women probably lost their head when such a man announced his intentions. Ami made a concerted effort to keep hers as he turned to leave, and she followed him to the door, unable to avoid the sight of his lovely bare back and his rear, jauntily encased in denim. A weakness made her knees waver. I want him, she thought in astonishment, and she imagined herself laying her hands on that broad back, sliding them into the back pockets of his jeans... So compelling was it, that she rushed, breathless, to get him out, reaching past him for the door. He looked at her arm.

'You give lessons in illusion on a Saturday?' he mocked, indicating the four-day-old bruise inside her elbow. 'Or can't you bear to wash off your own work?'

'Your work, actually,' she said, before she thought.

'What?' Startled, he took her arm and looked closer at the real bruise inside her elbow. 'I didn't see this last night.'

'I'm a make-up *girl*,' she mocked, intensely conscious of his touch. 'I can make a bruise go where there isn't one, and I can conceal a real one. You didn't see it because I didn't want it seen.'

As he assimilated how and when he might have done it, he took her other arm and found the matching mark there. A dull flush settled on his cheekbones and he stood there holding her arms, his thumbs circling gently on the discolourations as if he might erase them. The sensation reached beyond the skin he touched, rippled down her spine, zipped along her temples to the top of her head. Ami touched her tongue to her lower lip and, as if he was waiting for some such signal, North raised her left arm and bent to put his mouth to the bruise. He didn't take his eyes off her, and she stared at him, bemused, her eyelids flickering in response to the warm, delicate touch of his lips on her skin. Ami jumped at the sly touch of his tongue. Low down in her body she felt again that pang of desire. Still holding her gaze, confident now and deliberate, he reached for her other arm and Ami backed away in alarm, wondering if she'd been hypnotized. She felt vaguely disappointed that the glimpse of sincerity in him had been so soon eclipsed by opportunism.

North smiled. 'If it's any consolation, you gave me a bruise, too, that night, when you felled me.'

Oh, good, she thought. 'Well, I won't offer to kiss it better.'

He laughed softly, showing his very nice teeth. 'I should be so lucky.' He rubbed one lean flank, to indicate the position of the bruise, and Ami felt another jolt of sensation at the earthiness of it. She had vastly underestimated North Kendrick, she realized, as she opened her front door and let him out to a joyous welcome from Spritz. His lack of people skills did not prevent him being expert at seduction. But then seduction didn't actually come under people skills. More an exercise in appreciation, like the expertise of the wine connoisseur or the art collector. North Kendrick wanted her for the same reason that she had needed to get through his glass doors. They both wanted to restore their self-esteem by making their mark on the other's territory. But for her, the territory had been his hotel. For him, *she* was the territory.

Marvellous, she thought, as she got on with her chores when he was gone. He had accused her of insinuating herself into his life, but the man had insinuated himself into hers. The kitchen wasn't quite the same now that he'd stripped half naked in it, and as for the bedroom... Ami ripped the old sheets from the bed for washing, and replaced them with fresh ones. *I wish it was me who'd rumpled your sheets.* 'Huh!' she said out loud, energetically smoothing rumples from the clean sheets to erase any images of him in her bed. Then she had another, irrelevant vision of North, coming in at two in the morning and stopping by Harry's room. Did he always stop by his father's room when he came home? Did he tiptoe? Sneak the door ajar so as not to disturb the old man? North as the concerned, caring son? She slid the pillows into new cases and bashed them into a huddled group. She smoothed the quilt cover, catching sight of the bruises on her arms with every move. Later, when she'd hung out her washing and showered, she used some flesh-coloured concealer over the bruises. When she'd finished, she viewed the results with professional satisfaction. No one would know there were bruises there. No one except her and North Kendrick.

North swivelled his chair to look down at the hotel concourse. He waited for the thrill of possession, of fulfilled ambition but it was wearing off already. He grimaced. Even a year ago, he'd still experienced an intense pleasure from bringing off new deals, making new acquisitions, fulfilling ambitions that had once seemed laughable. This hotel was one of them. A foolish venture in some ways, when he could have simply bought a profitable existing hotel and management package, or pumped funds into an unprofitable one. Plenty of those around at present. But it was a long time since his inventive days and he'd wanted to build something he could actually see, so he had, against all advice. Not with his own hands, of course, but with his brain and acumen and powers of persuasion with his investors. He'd expected it to be the greatest thrill of his life, but somehow it was falling rather flat. Maybe he should take up parachuting—an adrenalin-high sport—as an antidote to boredom.

The phone buzzed and he flicked a switch. 'Mr. Kendrick,' a harried female voice said. 'I'm from room service. I just took some of your father's favourite cake up for morning tea and—I'm sorry, but he's gone.'

North felt the sting of anxiety. 'Gone? Again?' He sighed. 'All right. Thank you. Leave it with me.'

He went through the routine again. Checked for a note, checked with floor staff, with Morgan. Someone in the kitchens remembered an 'old geezer' passing through with walking sticks. No-one knew where Harry had gone this time. No-one, North thought grimly, knew where he'd been last time. He'd arrived back two days later and said he'd been looking up a few friends he hadn't seen since the old days, and chances were that's where he'd gone again. North didn't know who they were. A fear that hadn't finished growing gnawed at his insides, but he refused to give it a name. Instead, he applied himself to the problem. Harry must have told someone where he'd been. He was a talker and it wasn't natural for Harry to be so close-lipped. So who would he confide in? He thought of confidences and inevitably thought of Ami who had heard so many of his own. He knew Harry had phoned her. Yes. Ami Winterburn would know something. Logically, he should wait a little longer in case Harry turned up, but he convinced himself he should speak to Ami as soon as possible. It was nearly two weeks since he'd seen her, leaping along the footpath with her dog.

North felt a rush of exhilaration, as if he'd been pumped full of a stimulant or parachuted out the hatch. He felt the challenge as if she'd looked right through him with those fey aquamarine eyes, taunted him with one of those extravagant hand movements. Right now, she was probably out in her back room at her shop, creating a scar on the back of her hand or showing someone how to look bald.

But Ami wasn't at the shop. Ami was conducting her Thursday class, Helen said dubiously, but when he worked on her a little, she gave him the address. With a new surge of energy, he ordered his car to be brought to the hotel entrance.

The class was being held in an office building at North Sydney. There was a double foyer, the outer one a small jungle of potted plants. Through the glass door, he saw Ami walk into this outer foyer. She rounded the doorway and stepped back against the partition where she was out of sight of her students, whose heads North could just about make out, bobbing beyond a screen. Ami's head went back, her eyes closed and for a few seconds her body sagged before she took a deep breath, gathered herself up. Smiling, she made light-hearted comments as her students passed into the foyer on their way out. Her Thursday class that she had adamantly refused to cancel. He remembered that other Thursday weeks ago, and her reddened eyes that might have been a tribute to her make-up skill, but then again, might not.

The students came through the outer door, and North saw why this was one make-up class she wouldn't cancel even under threat of ruin. That they came out laughing told him more about Ami Winterburn than he'd ever gleaned from his computer enquiries or even from her mother.

The last time he'd seen faces like these had been in a hospital. There were six students, five women, one man, casualties of accident and disease. North had to control the urge to drop his eyes as they glanced at him. He stood there a while, watching them walk away, thinking of different kinds of courage. Thinking of his shallow assumptions about Ami's profession, about Ami herself. His considerable achievements suddenly seemed to shrink compared to this small group of maimed people who could leave Ami Winterburn's class smiling. 'Teaching others to appear what they aren't,' he'd said in lofty ignorance. He cringed at the memory.

He found her as he'd never expected to find the flippant, happy-go-lucky Ami Winterburn. Hunched over her partly packed make-up kit, weeping into a tissue. She turned at the sound of his approach and her eyes widened in surprise. She made no attempt to hide her tears. 'Special effects,' she said with a sniff. 'I'll bet you can't tell them from genuine tears.'

'I saw your students,' he said softly, making short work of that little bit of bravado. She suppressed a hiccup and looked balefully at him. Why had he turned up suddenly out of the blue? North looked at her steadily, the way he had that night when she'd taken off her wrinkles and he'd wanted to know what lay beneath. Well, the man who liked his women beautiful wasn't seeing anyone he would fancy this time, she thought, with fierce satisfaction. Her nose always reddened when she cried, her skin turned blotchy and her eyelids swelled.

Here I am, she thought, facing him squarely, a real, hurting person—not an attractive piece of female merchandise—see how you like this, Mr. North Kendrick. He held her gaze, fished in his pocket and found a folded handkerchief, which he offered to her.

'You can have my shoulder to cry on if you prefer,' he said, when she didn't take the handkerchief.

Ami looked at both his shoulders, outlined in tailored fine wool. She might have admired them but hadn't considered them as anchors in a storm, hadn't thought of North Kendrick as someone she might lean on in a moment of weakness. Her heart beat faster. She plucked the handkerchief from him and he gave a sardonic smile at her choice.

Ami dabbed her eyes and blew her nose noisily. 'I run several cosmetic therapy courses each year. Every time I start a six-week course, I think, this time I can handle it, and most times I can. I've made it through to the fifth week this time without—' She waggled her fingers at her teary face. 'They don't want sympathy, just practical solutions.' She turned away to slot tubes and jars into their allotted places in her fold-out make-up case.

She swallowed hard, busied herself with fastening the case. But this time the tears wouldn't stop coming.

'You can't drive in that state,' North said and took her arm. 'There's a deli across the road. I'm buying you a coffee.'

The delicatessen had an alcove with low lights and canvas chairs. The air was steamily warm, scented by ground coffee beans, fresh bread and the bunches of drying rosemary and thyme that hung over their marble-topped table. North ordered coffee and sandwiches. He took off his jacket, loosened his tie and sat back, saying nothing as Ami blew her nose again.

'Tell me,' he said.

Ami blinked at the bald invitation. 'One of my students. Miranda. Eighteen. She was in a car accident and her face was badly scarred. Her boyfriend saw her in hospital when the bandages came off and never came back. Her father cries when he sees her. She's a bright kid with heaps of personality and humour and courage but people are treating her as if she's lost the only thing that matters... her *looks*. Suddenly she's the invisible woman. She keeps talking about how plastic surgery might make her pretty again.'

'And will it?'

'Probably. You can get rid of the *external* scars some-times. But once you've been invisible you must always be afraid you'll fade away again.'

He looked thoughtfully at her, reached across and laid his hand over hers in a warm, human touch that could not translate into actual words. Ami stared at him. She didn't want sympathy, either. Ami wasn't sure just what she did want, but incredible as it seemed, at this moment, North Kendrick came close to filling the bill. *Tell me.* No spurious sentiment from North, no clichéd comfort, or slick phrase to sum up the tragedy of an eighteen-year-old girl. At least he recognised the depth of his ig-norance on the subject and gave it the respect of keeping quiet, unlike many people. Or maybe it was a lack of feeling that kept him quiet. The only time he'd shown strong feelings was when his own life was touched. Maybe he didn't feel for others. But Ami looked down at his hand over hers and experienced a sense of comradeship that she surely could never have with someone so disabled. Intuitively she felt they were on the same wavelength. Startled, she met his eyes. He was serious, silently enquiring. As the moment went on, though, his eyes subtly warmed, his nostrils flared and his head raised a fraction, like a hunter sniffing the wind. Flushed, she pulled her hand from beneath his. This was the man who loved a challenge, she reminded herself. There was more than one way to a conquest for a clever man like North.

She put away the damp handkerchief. 'How's Harry?' she asked.

North took some time putting down his coffee cup.

'I thought you might tell me,' he said levelly. 'He's gone again.'

She didn't quite hide a laugh. At seventy-one, Harry had become the worrisome runaway teenager and North his anxious keeper.

He glowered at her. 'You think this is funny?'

'I think you take your responsibilities seriously. Maybe Harry is trying to tell you that he's not ready to be your responsibility.'

'He's not my *responsibility*—he's my father.'

Ami looked more carefully at him. 'When he's ready, I'm sure he'll turn up again, like he did last time,' she said.

North toyed with a teaspoon, digging it into the sugar to load it, holding it up a little to let the sugar trickle out. He had a worried look of concentration that reminded her of the photo of him as a child, in the sand with his bucket and spade.

'He's been trying to trace old pals of his, writing to relatives he hasn't been in touch with for decades.' He shovelled sugar with dedication. 'Amost as if he's—tying up loose ends.'

A man of seventy-one, tying up loose ends? Ami felt a pang of anxiety, closely followed by denial. Not Harry—she couldn't lose Harry, not when she'd only just met him. 'He's just been in hospital, probably had time to think about all the things he's been too busy to do and decided to catch up on old friends and family. A crisis can make you value those things.'

'Yes, you're probably right,' he said, visibly relaxing.

'He said you were trying to talk him into selling his house,' she said, striving to keep any hint of criticism from her voice.

He gave a rueful laugh. 'Talking Harry into anything is more difficult than I imagined. I haven't seen a lot of him over the past ten years. I'd forgotten how determined he can be. He sets his mind on something and doesn't let go until he has his way.'

'Like father, like son?' she said dryly.

His eyes glittered. 'I usually get what I want.'

'Even if you have to deprive someone else,' she mocked, thinking of the business opponents who had cause to regret his determination.

His smile uncurled, slow and languid as smoke. 'I don't think someone else would necessarily feel *deprived*,' he said, obviously not thinking of his business opponents.

Ami lifted her cup a little too quickly and froth slipped down the side. 'How would you ever know? Do you ask the people you've taken over if they feel deprived? Do you ask your *conquests* if they mind being conquered?'

His irritating complacency grew. 'I've had no complaints.'

'Maybe they fake it.'

And the reminder of her own successful faking took the complacent tilt off his handsome mouth. Ami regarded him over her coffee cup, pleased that she still had an edge. She felt a sudden, urgent need for it because she was treading dangerous paths, imagining him as a lover and herself as his. Stupid, when she knew his pursuit was more to do with payback than love or desire. Maybe nothing short of possessing her would restore him, that age-old symbol of triumph and male superiority. She set her cup down hard. Coffee slopped onto the table.

'It must be difficult for Harry, being immobilized,' she said to correct this dangerous detour. 'I get the impression he's always been very active.'

North acknowledged the retreat with a quizzical smile.

'Active is an understatement. He used to take the back steps three at a time, he had so much energy. I remember him climbing up to lop the poinciana tree, hefting an axe—he used that axe to cut down a Christmas tree every year, too—' North picked up a teaspoon, turned it over and over, looking into the distorted reflections as if it was showing him pictures of the past.

'You had them growing—Christmas trees?'

'We used to drive out towards the Blue Mountains to a farm every Christmas Eve. The best part of Christmas—walking around the paddock of pines, deciding which tree.'

'And Harry cut it down?'

'A couple of strikes with the axe and—' North used the side of his hand to recreate Harry's decisive strikes and the toppling of the tree, with the male appreciation for technique. 'Harry was very good at things like that. A natural athlete. He rode in bike hill scrambles and that's as rough as it comes.'

'You *do* remember his racing days, then?'

He gave a snort. 'Does a kid forget a thing like that? I used to go and watch him race, work on the bikes with him, when he'd let me, until we just seemed to...for competitions he wore long, black bike boots with straps and silver buckles.' A faraway smile transfigured his face. 'God, how I wanted those boots—you know the way a kid covets adult things. They were huge, but Harry used to tell me one day I might be big enough to fit into them.' He gave an odd self-deprecatory smile. 'When I saw him in hospital, then in the wheelchair, I couldn't believe it. He'd changed—I don't know, grown smaller or something, and I hadn't noticed. The only thing that hasn't changed is that he's just as hard to get along with,' he said, his mouth set. Ami studied him, thinking of his irritation so hard on the heels of barely disguised hero-worship.

'Are you annoyed with Harry for getting old?' she asked.

North looked at her in dislike. 'No, I am not *annoyed* with Harry for getting old,' he mimicked. He tossed the teaspoon onto the table and studied her for a few un-nerving seconds. 'Your mother told me your father is a doctor.'

'A surgeon. Didn't your credit card investigation tell you that?' she mocked.

'She also told me about her agency and her writer client. Your mother said you often take on unusual jobs.'

'My mother seems to have said a great deal.'

The merest flicker of his eyelids gave him away. Ami grinned. 'She's hard to stop once she gets started, isn't she? Serves you right. Did she persuade you to part with a nymph for the raffle?'

'I've agreed to a painting. We're...negotiating on the nymph,' he said straight-faced. 'Shall we go?'

Negotiating. Ami didn't like the ongoing sound of it.

Outside on the pavement, he turned to her and said, 'If Harry contacts you I would appreciate a call. I'd—just like to know that he's okay.'

I would appreciate. Not *I want*. North must be more worried than she thought. 'Is there something you're not telling me about Harry's departure this time?'

He studied the passing traffic for a moment. 'He didn't take any clothes and he left his wheelchair behind,' he said, his brow creasing. North shuffled his feet and bent an intense gaze on a boutique window display. 'I wouldn't be so concerned about that except that he had his solicitor call around the other day. To finalise a few things, he said.' North hesitated then went on. 'It sounds stupid, I know, but sometimes I'm afraid he might—' North took a deep breath and sidestepped the obvious phrase as if to name it would be to make it more possible. 'He seems rather...depressed,' he said lamely. 'I thought he might be hiding some condition from me, something incurable, but I talked to his doctor and she said there is nothing like that.'

'Harry wouldn't do anything silly,' she said but she remembered something Harry had said. *There'll be no more birthdays after this one.* And, *It's too late for that, now.* Something must have shown in her face for North took her arm and said, 'What's the matter?'

'It's nothing. Where did you see him last? What was he doing?'

'On the terrace, looking through those binoculars.'

Something stirred in Ami's memory. Harry and the binoculars and something he'd said. 'He showed me a hotel he'd worked on as a young man,' she offered slowly. 'Said it still operated as a hotel and he would like to see it again. I wonder...'

They drove to the Avalon in North's magnolia Jaguar. Ami stood on North's terrace and searched with binoculars for the old hotel building Harry had shown her. It took her nearly ten minutes to locate it. 'There,' she said. 'I can just make out the name—the Century.'

* * *

Harry was seated at the bar of the Century Hotel, walking sticks leaning against his stool. He had a schooner of beer in one hand, a forbidden cigarette in the other, and looked far from suicidal. He broke off from a conversation with the barman when he saw North and Ami and made an involuntary effort to hide the cigarette before he defiantly changed his mind and flaunted it. 'What are you two doing here?'

'Harry—are you okay? Why didn't you tell me where you were going? You left your wheelchair, you'll end up in hospital again,' North said in a tight, scolding tone that failed to convey the concern Ami had so clearly seen.

Irritation flitted over the old man's face. 'I don't have to tell you what I'm doing every minute,' he said mulishly. 'I just came down here for a drink and to look at the work I did on that cedar panelling, see? I'll be back for dinner, all right? You're a sight for sore eyes, Amelia,' he added, his faded blue eyes sharply speculative about her arrival with North. The following communication between the two men was terse. All North's stiff persuasion failed to move the old man, who said he would call a cab and come home when he was good and ready.

North was silent as he drove her back to pick up her car. Ami glanced several times at his profile, which relief had rendered no less severe. 'Those boots Harry used to wear for bike racing,' she said lightly, for something to say. 'Did they live up to your expectations when you eventually grew into them?'

North concentrated on swinging the Jaguar in next to her car. 'I never got to try them. Harry gave them away when I was sixteen,' he said, glancing at her.

'Oh.'

North opened the door for her, walked to her car with her.

'Thank you for your help,' he said. 'I wouldn't have believed Ami Winterburn could contribute to my peace of mind, but today, you have.'

'Ah, well, you don't know me very well,' she said lightly.

'No. That might take more time than I thought.' He eyed her with a certain calculation that made her think of takeovers and financial coups.

'More time than you're prepared to spend,' she told him. 'I am very complex.'

'I'm a quick study. I was a boy genius, remember?'

Smug devil. She resented the way he made her feel frail and hunted. Let him hunt. She wasn't going to fall for his strategies. Getting to know her wasn't his aim, except in the biblical sense. 'You can forget it, North,' she snapped. 'You aren't going to rumple my sheets!'

He burst out laughing and for the first time it was audible, a pleasant, tenor sound that was warm and uncomplicated. How very amusing he found her, she thought wrathfully.

'I mean it, North,' she said. 'It was the purest accident that we met. You are definitely not my type.'

His expansive good humour disappeared in a hurry, she was delighted to see. Mr. North Kendrick, handsome, rich, eligible, was used to judging women but not, perhaps, used to being judged unsuitable himself. 'I wonder how you kiss men who *are* your type,' he said sardonically. 'The poor devils must melt down in the heat.' When she didn't respond, he said, 'Well—if I'm not your type, I have to accept it. I don't make a habit of pursuing women who don't want to be pursued.'

Ami regarded him with suspicion. 'Very civilized of you.'

'But why don't we agree to a truce relationship, for Harry's sake?' He held a hand out to her and she looked at it, her back against her car and an odd feeling that she might as well have been against a brick wall. 'He's fond of you. It would be silly if you felt you couldn't visit him because of any, er, tension between us.'

'I'm surprised you'd encourage my friendship with Harry, considering the way I met him. Doesn't it have unpleasant associations for you?'

'And some extremely pleasant,' he said with a nostalgic air.

'This doesn't sound like a truce relationship to me.'

'Will it help if I don't mention the pleasure you've brought me?' he enquired. 'What else should I not mention? Your eyes—your mouth...' He leaned an arm on her car so that his face was tilted quite close to hers. 'Better not mention your hair, your legs, those arm movements...'

'If you think I'm flattered by this, I'm not,' she said, fighting the candlelight mood he was generating in a parking lot in brilliant sunshine. 'I'm a great deal more than superficial things like legs and—and green eyes. I'm a lot of other things, too, an entire person, not just a collection of curvy bits like your sculptures. So don't imagine you're going to add me to your collection.'

'That's not what I imagine,' he told her, his grey eyes warm. It would be so easy to have a physical affair with North Kendrick. She would hate herself for it afterwards. But oh, she would love it for a little while.

Colouring, she said tartly, 'What did you mean—arm movements?'

He straightened, threw his arms wide in mimicry of her habitual gesture. His teeth showed in a smile that took her breath away. 'I get this mad urge to run into them.'

He had always stared at her when she did that, she remembered, right from the start. North Kendrick, running into her arms. It should be ludicrous but it wasn't, it was appealing. Her heart beat heavily, faster. A mad urge. She hadn't thought of him as a man who had mad urges... She caught herself in time.

He was very, very good. Her face flamed as she turned away to set the key in the lock. North had simply changed tactics. She was being shown an example of the long-term planning for which he was famous. If he had any mad urge associated with her, it was a very basic one.

So when he held out his hand again, she took it for Harry's sake, understanding that North's idea of a truce was simply another move in the game. And as long as she knew that, she was in no danger, was she? His hand closed strongly around hers and he looked into her eyes with some indefinable expression that made her assurance seem foolhardly.

'Come to dinner tomorrow. With Harry, of course,' he said.

'Sorry, I can't. I have an appointment with the dressmaker. My bridesmaid's dress. It's urgent because the wedding's only a couple of weeks away, and it's out west so I have to be ready to leave days before,' she said, babbling out unnecessary excuses. 'Some other time?'

She drove away thinking that almost every female she knew would think she was crazy to turn down Kendrick. One part of her said, well—why not let it take its course? However base North's motivation, he would be a great lover. He treated his collector's items very well, while he treasured them. She screeched to a halt at traffic lights, wishing she could relegate him to the ranks of the purely superficial. But she thought instead of North, the cool, level-headed man of business, worried about losing his father. And she thought of the father who'd been such a forgetful hero that he'd given away to someone else something he'd promised his son.

She was moved, as she always was by North's vulnerable side. 'Oh, grow *up*!' she said out loud. The man had had too much power too soon and was unbearable. He was a collector, remember that. And anyway, he was probably a lousy lover.

CHAPTER SEVEN

AMI slid under her car. It had been quite cool that morning when she and Harry had set out after their overnight stop, quite tolerably warm by the time she had dropped him off at Swagman's Creek, to which tiny country town he had traced yet another of his old cronies. But when she'd travelled on alone, the day had heated up as midday approached and passed. Ami had developed a parched, painful throat and a nagging headache from the dust and hot air. At least, she thought, it was marginally cooler *under* the car.

She unrolled the canvas tool kit, more to counter the dismal feeling of helplessness than anything. Somehow she felt the exact nature of the damage was more likely to reveal itself to someone with a spanner or a hammer in their hand.

'Ugh,' she muttered, wiggling around a spill of some oily black substance. She had only pulled over for a few minutes to drink some water and take an aspirin, and when she had headed back to the road the wheels had dipped into a rut and the car had hit something. In vain, she tried to see signs of damage but realized she would need the torch.

As she slid out again, she heard the scrape of leather on stones. In the aperture between the ground and the underside of the car, she saw clumps of grass crushed beneath two shoes. Help, at last. Hastily, she wriggled out, almost blinded in the sunlight after minutes in comparative darkness. The shoes were attached to widely planted legs clad in denim. A buckle glinted between two large hands clasped around the leather of a belt.

Glare hazed the man's face but she recognized those hands. She lay flat on the stony ground, heart hammering, wondering if this was one of those famous outback mirages. Because North couldn't be here. He was on a business trip in Malaysia, according to Harry. Expected to be away five days.

'Very appetizing,' he said, looking over her bare legs, the crumpled shorts, the thin cotton shirt, soaked with perspiration and clinging to her breasts. 'But asking for trouble on a lonely road.'

She scrabbled to leap up and her head didn't quite clear the car underside. A hollow clang echoed inside her head as she hit herself, but she yanked the black denim cap down on her head and shook off North's helping hand to stagger up fighting, a spanner in her hand.

'Asking for trouble? *Appetizing*?' she rasped. 'I've been stranded here for over an hour, waiting for help! My hands are a mess—' She thrust out her greasy hands that were cut and grazed. 'Half a million flies have discovered I'm the only moving thing for miles around and I haven't got anything left to drink!' She threw the spanner down in a fine temper and put her hands on her hips. 'And all you can do is leer and tell me I'm asking for trouble by being provocative enough to wear *shorts* in one-hundred degree heat! *Trouble*?' she yelled in his face. 'I've already got trouble, so you can take your leer and your damned male superiority and shove off!'

Her voice screamed on the still, hot air. Ami heard the note of hysteria in it and hoped she wasn't going to cry. North slowly removed his sunglasses and blinked at her, a slight frown cutting above his handsome nose. And even as she noticed the beguiling look of concern in his grey eyes, half his face disappeared. In panic, she reached out to him, grasping his solid shoulder. 'I can't see you properly. North, what's happening? I can't *see* you!'

He made some exclamation, took her by the arm. 'Sit down.'

'North?' she said, on a rising note. She screwed up her eyes, rubbed at them and one of her hands came away sticky and warm with blood. Her knees went weak and she sat down under the pressure of North's hands on her shoulders. She heard him walk away, open a car door, and she called in sudden panic, swivelling her head for a partial view of him. 'Where are you going? Don't leave me. Oh, you rotten, chauvinistic swine. I suppose you'll take me at my word now and shove off just when I *need* you!' She stood and wiped ineffectually at her clouded eye, thrust her arms out wide in entreaty and yelled, 'North!'

A dark shape loomed up and he said, 'I'm here,' and stepped inside her outstretched arms to pull her close. Her arms went around him and she held on to him and snuffled into his shoulder. After the privations of the day, the frustrations and the pain, it was heaven to let herself go and cry. Home to heaven, she thought irrelevantly, sliding her arms around his back, turning her cheek against his neck so that her lips brushed his warm skin and she smelled the fresh tang of him.

Self-consciously she withdrew her arms from around him and found herself guided onto the ground, nudged against a tree. He removed her cap, used a cloth to wipe her eye and when she blinked again, her sight was blurry but almost back to normal. He showed her a vacuum flask and poured orange juice into the lid. The jangle of ice cubes was a sound so sweet that she felt an overwhelming affection for the man who provided it.

'North Kendrick, I take back all the disagreeable thoughts I've ever had about you,' she said fervently, swamping down half the juice with such enthusiasm that it dribbled down her chin.

'All of them—just for orange juice?' he murmured. 'What would I get for French champagne?'

'There speaks the man of business—looking for a return on everything. Profit from money invested, favours in exchange for gifts. Any advance on French champagne?'

'The world does tend to work that way, doesn't it? But please consider the orange juice a gift. No strings,' he said dryly and, kneeling beside her, opened a first-aid kit. He leaned over to part her hair, walked his fingertips through it until he found the source of the bleeding. He removed a hairpin and took her face in both hands, tipping her head so that he could see. Ami closed her eyes, listened to the buzz of flies and the warble of magpies and the deep silence of the countryside. She felt the heat of the sun, dappled on her skin, and the pleasurable, dry warmth of North's large hands across her temples and ears. Nice, she thought hazily, wondering if she might be concussed.

'That blow pressed the hairpin into your scalp and cut the skin. The blood soaked into your cap then trickled down into your eye, blinding you for the moment,' he said, shaking some antiseptic onto cotton wool. The sting of the cut had dulled to a throb and Ami found the tiny tugs on her scalp, the tender progress of his fingers through her hair unexpectedly soothing.

He shifted so that he sat cross-legged beside her, lifting her leg over his knees so that he could clean the grease from a long scratch on her thigh. Ami jumped at the intimate touch. Orange juice slopped over her shorts.

'I can do that myself,' she said.

'Sit still.' He wiped the scratch clean and pressed an adhesive strip over it. Every tiny prod of his fingers produced a flow-on effect, like pebbles tossed into a pool that made ripples and still more ripples. He curved his hands to her thigh and lifted her leg from his knees, then sat, looking her over.

'Better?' he asked.

Better and worse. She nodded. North got up and bent to haul her onto her feet, and the sudden change made her dizzy enough to grab him for support. 'Sorry. I saw stars,' she muttered into the junction of his neck and shoulder, which was hunched into a protective curve for her benefit. She wished she didn't have this absurd wish to touch him there, wished she hadn't clutched at his muscular arms so needily.

North held her with one arm, letting her get her balance, not suspecting, she hoped, that it was achieving the opposite. 'Are you okay?' he said, so close to her ear that she felt the ebb and flow of his breath. He tilted his head downward and his mouth brushed across her temple, her cheek, touched the corner of her mouth. A breeze rippled the tree above and golden flecks of sunlight shimmered on his face as he looked down at her, his eyes gleaming silver, his mouth parted and sensual. She meant to say something prosaic like, 'I'm okay,' or, 'Can you send a breakdown truck,' but she left it too late and North's mouth came down on hers. He kissed her lightly and withdrew, rimmed her lips with the tip of his tongue, leaving them moist and temporarily cooling in the warm breeze, while he pressed his mouth time and again to her neck, her ear. And his hands were in her hair, lightly on her shoulders, sliding beneath the shirt collar. He inched her shirt aside and bent to kiss her exposed shoulder, stroked his mouth along her collarbone and, as she swayed back against the tree, unfastened her shirt buttons and lowered his mouth to the upper curves of her breasts. Ami's head dropped back against the rough bark of the tree. Bright specks of sun dazzled her and giddily she closed her eyes, murmuring her pleasure at North's touch. She stroked the contours of his shoulders and arms, recreating the image of him behind her closed eyelids from touch and smell and the messages jamming the lines of her nervous system. Her fingers trailed along that intriguing line of his shoulder and neck and she smiled dreamily as he shuddered in response. The short hair on the back of his neck bristled beneath her exploring fingers and still she kept her eyes closed, lost in a world of texture and sensation, scarcely able to tell whether it was North, or the breeze, or the sun that touched her skin with exquisite tenderness.

But his hands circled her hips, tipped her towards him in an earthy little movement that penetrated her dreamy self-indulgence. He wanted her, of course he did. Her hands flexed on his fabulous arms, she gave an audible gasp and her eyes flew open to see the gleam of triumph in his. A delicious panic assailed her, a sense of having come to a point of no return. Excitement welled up in her and a desire that rocked her to the soles of her feet.

North unclipped the front of her bra, brushed aside the lace and cradled her breasts in his big hands, bending to draw a nipple into his mouth. Ami's broken sigh of pleasure hung on the hot, still air, was drawn again from her as North repeated the magic. A curious humming sound was in her head, growing ever louder towards crescendo. In mounting passion, she spread her hands on North's backside, traced the hollowed sides and the hard muscularity of his flanks. A growl came from him and Ami exulted in the sound, in the clench of his body against hers. And the humming sound suddenly was a roar with an accompanying rush of airborne dust. A car horn honked and men's voices shouted.

Ami pushed herself away from the tree, clutching at her unfastened bra and shirt. Horn still honking, a truck crawled away down the road with a man leaning from the passenger window and another, in the back of the truck, waving his hat and grinning. North put his hands on his hips and gave a rueful smile. 'No traffic for the past hour and they had to turn up now. Their timing is as immaculate as your mother's.'

Their timing, Ami thought, turning away to fasten her clothes, was about ten minutes too late. Ten minutes?

Was that how long they'd been here, making love under an ironbark tree on the side of the road? Her face turned scarlet. Ten minutes, fifteen. Thirty. She had had no awareness of time passing. She had been in a dream world, all sense and delicacy suspended.

North came close behind her, slid an arm around her waist.

'Okay?' he said softly, dropping a light kiss on her neck. Ami pulled away with such fervour that dizziness overtook her. She put a hand to her head, which was aching badly. Now she was sharply reminded of the sting of cuts and bruises. Her knuckles ached. Her knees and elbows. Everything.

North's eyes narrowed. 'Suddenly you object to me touching you? I thought we'd passed that point.'

She clamped a hand to her head. Concussion. It was the only reason she could have been so daft. '*We* haven't passed any point.'

'We were making love, Ami,' he said. 'In broad daylight, in public and neither of us gave a damn. If the truck hadn't come, we'd still be making love.' His nostrils flared. 'I wish we were. I want you. And you want me.'

She took a step back but he didn't move, just stood there staring at her with that need to possess written on his face, the desire of the collector for another acquisition. And it wasn't just that, she thought, appalled to realize how close she'd come to being collected.

'I'm half concussed,' she snapped. 'And you took full advantage of it, didn't you? Nothing for nothing, that's your motto, North.'

'What the hell are you talking about?'

'You're an opportunist, always looking for a weakness, always working a strategy to get what you want.' She picked up the spanner, the canvas tool kit, and her head swam, but she strode to her car, opening the boot. The tools clanked when she tossed them inside. North came up alongside her.

'Opportunist?' he said between gritted teeth. 'Explain.'

'When I turned up as Amelia, you soon used her to turn a potential disaster into a PR triumph. *Then* you decided to use her as an elderly sounding board for your problems with Harry. Oh, yes. You were quick to find a use for Amelia to compensate for any trouble she cost you. And when I turned up again as myself—you had a use for *me*, too, didn't you? You never waste anything. I should have known when you were playing doctors, tending my wounds, that there would be a price for all that lulling tenderness. You invested precious time anointing my scratches, so why not expect a little return on your investment? After all, that's the way the world works, isn't that what you said?'

North's face was a cold mask, flushed on the cheek-bones, white at the corners of his mouth. He reached past her and slammed the boot closed.

'I'm looking for Harry,' he said between his teeth.

'You're always looking for Harry,' she said, hearing the words thicken on her tongue. 'Why did you come all this way?'

'I flew back early. I have a few days unexpectedly spare and I want to spend them with my father,' he snapped. 'At least this time he left me a note to say he was headed in this direction with you. I suppose that's progress. Where is he?'

'He wanted to look up an old mate of his who had moved out west. You were overseas on business, and I was passing through the town on my way to Emma's wedding, so I offered to drop him off. He's with Ken Drummond in Swagman's Creek now. You passed the turn-off a way back.' She waved her hand in the general direction. 'I left him and Spritz there this morning and I'll pick them up on my way back from Catastrophe in three days. That's where my friend is getting married.

I'm supposed to be there tonight,' she said, with a disconsolate look at her stranded car.

He walked to his own vehicle. 'If you want a lift back to Swagman's Creek, get in.'

'I'll wait with my car, thanks,' she said stiffly, then, crushing her pride, said, 'could I ask you to send a tow truck out, please?'

He smiled nastily. 'Aren't you afraid of what it might cost you?'

She watched the frosted magnolia Jaguar go, its image dissolving in the heat waves on the crest of the road. A short time later another image appeared, coming towards her. It was the truck that had passed earlier. The men's grins were detectable from a distance and she was painfully aware of how she must have looked last time they saw her. Half undressed, writhing in a man's arms. And now that man was gone and she was still here. She opened her car door, undecided as to whether this was rescue or trouble, when a horn blasted in the distance and the Jaguar appeared. North had come back.

The truck had slowed, but when the men saw the Jag, they speeded up and passed her, shouting something vulgar about what treats she had missed. If they had been offering rescue, they had been offering trouble first. North's car screeched alongside her, raising a cloud of dust. The passenger door sprang open and Ami got in. She held a hand to her head. It felt fuzzy and ached abominably. The big car turned around and raced towards Swagman's Creek. It was air-conditioned and deliciously cool. No dirt and sweat for North. The seats were softest leather, cushioning her hurts. Home to heaven, she thought yet again. After a while, she glanced at North's granite profile and said, 'Thank you.'

'They were parked on the roadside farther up, eating, and when they saw me pass by alone, they turned back,' he said grimly. 'There are times when I'm ashamed to be male.'

'Maybe they thought I was just a nice girl selling magazine subscriptions,' she said, unable to resist the barb.

North's mouth contracted to the count of ten. 'When we get to the town, you can show me the way to this place where Harry is staying, then I'll drop you at the local garage.'

Ami swallowed hard. Her throat was raw, her head pounded and she thought miserably of having to make arrangements for a tow truck, having to wait around in the heat while repairs were done, when what she really would like was to lie down somewhere cool on a soft mattress. 'Fine. Thanks,' she said hoarsely and felt North glance at her. Her eyes closed and she drifted off into a curious space dotted with bright, sparkly things. After a while, she heard her own voice, counting. '... Fifty-one, fifty-two...'

'Fifty-two what?' North said.

'Stars,' she said, opening her eyes. 'I have to count the stars. Oh!' she said in annoyance. 'I shouldn't have opened my eyes. I've lost count—have to start again.' She lay back, closed her eyes. 'One, two...'

The car came to a halt. She felt a hand on her forehead, a delightfully cool hand. Ami took hold of it with both her own and held it to her hot cheek, rubbing against it.

'You're burning up,' North said in a curious voice. 'I'll get some aspirin from the first-aid kit.'

'Burning up,' Ami repeated. 'Never play with fire,' she said solemnly. She swallowed the aspirins he gave her, washed them down with a mouthful of orange juice and closed her eyes. 'Eight, nine, ten—oh!' She gave a groan.

'What is it, Ami?'

'I've lost my place again.'

*   *   *

The aspirins brought her fever down and she was lucid when North ushered her into a hotel room in the tiny country town where Harry was staying with his friend.

'The doctor will be here soon,' he told her, pushing her down onto the bed. Ami caught sight of herself in the tilted dressing-table mirror. Her hair was matted, flecked with bits of leaf and twig, strands stuck together where North had tried to wash off the blood. Tear stains made a clean track through grease and dirt on her cheeks. Ami bit her lip, made a few half-hearted stabs at tidying her hair and gave up, exhausted. Tears welled in her eyes.

'Lie down,' North said. He pushed her down, lifted her legs onto the bed and leaned over her. 'The fever's rising again.'

There were rust-coloured patches and grease on the shoulder of his lovely, fine cotton shirt, Ami saw. She must have transferred blood and dirt to him when he held her. Staring up at him, she thought vaguely that it was funny for North to kiss such a scarecrow. He liked his women beautiful. 'I look terrible. Nothing like a nice piece of sculpture, not even a chipped one,' she said pugnaciously, in case he thought she didn't know how awful she looked.

'A work of art you are not,' he said dryly.

Ami smiled. 'Good,' she said.

So why on earth did that please her so much? North showed the doctor in and waited outside. Most beautiful women would be riled at such a comment, and even though she was sick, he had meant to rile her. Ami Winterburn. A most contrary woman. And even in a mess, still appealing. In the beginning, he had wanted her for that face, the creamy perfection of her skin, the full, fabulous mouth, the stunning aquamarine eyes. That streaky hair that almost crackled with energy. And he'd wanted her for her dancer's body—tall and slim and athletic. Long legs and those breasts. He closed his eyes briefly and did homage to her breasts. A beautiful woman, Ami Winterburn. A desirable woman. He wanted her. But.

But it wasn't going to be enough, he thought suddenly, in astonishment. To pleasure her and take pleasure from her. It would be extraordinary, exhilarating. His pulses quickened at the mental picture of Ami in his arms, in his bed. Whereas once the picture had been a goal, an end in itself, now he felt a curious incompleteness about it. Not enough? Why not? Now that he knew she wanted him, now that he had come close to having what he wanted from her, there was something else eluding him. Her mind, he thought, trying to get a laugh out of it. How many men thought about Ami Winterburn's mind when that lovely exterior was so distracting? But the truth was, he didn't quite know what or who he was dealing with. Hell, he hadn't even sent her flowers yet. North considered the omission in surprise. It was what he usually did when he was interested in a woman. Flowers. Fly to Melbourne for dinner. Perfume. Eventually jewellery. It all seemed so shallow now, faced with Ami Winterburn. He was a rich man but he had a feeling there was nothing he could buy for her that would impress her. It engendered a reluctant admiration in him, but irritation too because buying things was easy—he had a very efficient gift-buying service for busy executives. All he had to do was phone them, give a description and vital statistics and a perfectly wrapped gift was delivered within hours, with a discreet description of the contents sent to him. He was used to women who responded with approval and pleasure to his merest efforts. Of course the nature of his relationship with Ami was such that it had precluded gifts. She would have tossed them back at him. Perhaps now... He imagined giving her description over the phone to Monica, the gift buyer extraordinaire—how the hell did you describe Ami? Blonde, aquamarine eyes, five foot ten, long neck, long legs, hands that had a language all their own—the obvious features only told half the story, anyway. He imagined those eyes quizzing him steadily over a lavish bouquet of flowers or a flagon of expensive perfume and said out loud, 'Oh, yeah,' unsettling two passing guests. Grinning weakly at them, he thought in dismay that the damned woman had virtually brought on an identity crisis for him. She had made him doubt the worth of his own career, now she was making him feel that even his wealth gave him no advantages. 'Ridiculous,' he said. A passing housemaid threw him a cautious look. North scowled. He was muttering to himself like some old hobo, all because of a make-up girl.

She'd fooled him once and the memory of it still burned. And beneath that wrinkled disguise she'd worn had been the face he'd first seen. The thing was, what was underneath *that* face? Ami refused to fall into any category he'd ever encountered. She was so adept at illusion that she'd made him believe her an old woman, so how would he ever be sure that her current face was the real one? Never one to abandon a line of action once he'd decided upon it, North nevertheless thought it might be wise to back off from Ami Winterburn. There were less complicated ways, more comfortable ways to have a woman in his life, surely. But as he waited, hearing the murmur of her voice through the door, he could only think of Ami, holding out her arms to him in one of those big, embracing gestures she was always making. He'd joked about it with her, using it deliberately to try to seduce her with some small talk. Uncomfortably, he realized that, as usual with a joke, there was truth behind it. He did want to run into her arms. Today, when she'd held them out to him and said she needed him, when she'd rubbed her cheek on his hand like a kitten, he'd felt almost as if... The door opened and the doctor emerged. North was singularly pleased to have his thoughts interrupted.

In her dreams, Ami cried that she would be late for Emma's wedding. North appeared and she grabbed his hand and babbled out her fears that someone would steal her bridesmaid's dress from her abandoned car. Then, in the dream, her dress appeared, covered in plastic. 'Here it is,' North Kendrick said, hanging it on the wardrobe door handle where she could see it. 'Everything is fine.' In her dreams, too, she burned in desert wastelands and stood under cool showers until she shivered. And she argued with North, who wore a cheap checkered shirt and who sometimes stripped her clothes from her, and sometimes dressed her in them again.

But when she eventually woke, the dress for Emma's wedding was hanging on the door handle, just where it had been in the dream, and she wondered if maybe the rest of it had really happened, too. A moment of anxiety passed. But of course, it was all a dream. North Kendrick wouldn't be seen dead in a cheap checkered shirt.

She sat up, feeling seedy but minus the pain that had pounded in her head and body. Anxiously, she went to the bridesmaid's dress, fingering it through the plastic to reassure herself that it was okay. As the door opened, she turned too fast and staggered. 'North,' she said. He caught her around the waist, bent and lifted her. Her hands grabbed at his shoulders, took hold of cotton material coloured blue, red and grey.

'You're wearing a cheap checkered shirt!' she accused.

'Snob,' North said, walking to the bed with her. 'I ran out of clothes and the manager's wife bought it for me at a chain store across the road.' He stood a moment, holding her aloft, looking closely at her. 'No fever. You look better.'

Ami released his shirt, self-consciously felt her hands slide a little over his shoulders. He looked as if he could use a shave. His hair, instead of being neatly brushed back, had fallen in a dark, wavy mass onto his forehead. The checkered shirt fitted closely, she could see the strain on the stiching around his well-muscled shoulders. Ami lifted her fingers from further temptation, tried to find an uncontroversial place to put them, but couldn't. She tried to hunt down the details of those dreams featuring the blue, red and grey shirt but all she could recall was a kaleidoscope of fractured images, most of them involving her naked body. Her colour rose.

'Memory troubling you?' he said, perceptively.

She bit her lip. 'I thought I dreamed the checked shirt, along with all the rest—'

North set her down in a businesslike manner on the tangled sheets of her bed.

'Don't trouble yourself. You were sick. I did what needed to be done, no more, in spite of my opportunistic streak.'

Ami stared at him, surprised to see that it still rankled. He *had* undressed her, looked at her naked, touched her. Ami felt she'd been stripped of more than clothes. She was bereft of defences. This man had started off by watching her while she was in blithe ignorance of him and now he knew things about her that she would never willingly have let him see. Her fists bunched in frustration. North Kendrick already had so much power. Why did fate have to hand him still more?

'Well,' she said stiffly. 'I suppose I should thank you.'

'Don't choke on it,' he said, moving to the door. 'I'll see if the kitchen can rustle you up something to eat. Now that you're better, I'll go visit Harry.'

She nodded, suddenly ravenous. '*Wait!*' she said, as he opened the door. 'What do you mean—you ran out of clothes? How long have I—' she looked over at the other single bed '—we been here?'

'Two nights.'

With a small scream, she slid out of bed. 'Two *nights*! Then today is Friday—Emma's getting married *tomorrow*! And my car—'

'Your car is with the mechanic. It needs parts freighted in from Sydney and will be ready after the weekend.'

'But then—I have to—Emma will be wondering—where are my clothes?' Distractedly, she plucked at her pyjamas, looked around in vain for some street clothes. North put a hand on her shoulder and steered her back to bed.

'I've been giving regular bulletins to Emma. You had her phone number in your diary. She and Matt are expecting you there tonight, so be a good girl and go back to bed.'

She glared at him. 'Don't patronise me. I have to make arrangements to get there. Hire a car—'

'No hire cars available, I asked,' he said smoothly. 'I'm driving you.'

'But it's a hundred miles away,' she objected, thinking of a hundred miles in the magnolia Jaguar with North, a prospect both intriguing and offputting. 'And how will I get back here?'

'The same way. I've talked so often to Emma and Matt, we're practically old friends. They've invited me to their wedding. Isn't that nice?'

'Emma—how could you invite him to the wedding?' Ami said in an undertone to her friend that night.

'How could I not?' said Emma. 'He was nursing you on your sickbed, offering to bring you here because your car was defunct. Besides, he sounded nice.' Emma's eyes strayed to North, who appeared to have struck up an instant rapport with the groom. And why not, Ami thought darkly. Matt Mackenzie was another arrogant male used to getting his own way, even if falling for Emma had brought out his better side. She deliberately recalled Mackenzie as he'd been two years back, raging into her shop looking for Ami, rather than the sensitive man who'd had to come to terms with the loss of a close friend just months ago.

'Nice?' Ami hissed. 'People who are used to having anything they want when they want it are rarely nice. He's a very successful manipulator and his strategies don't end at his office desk. North Kendrick never stops doing deals.'

'What deal was he doing when he was sponging your fevered brow?'

Ami flushed. 'I know I sound ungrateful, but you don't know him. There are no free lunches as far as North is concerned. Both he and his father do it—manipulate people.'

'That's not what's troubling you,' Emma said, eyeing Ami shrewdly. 'You've already half fallen for him, haven't you?'

'Half fallen is a retrievable position,' Ami said stoutly, not bothering with denials to this friend who knew her very well. 'I could never really fall for a man unless I knew he could see more about me than my face and figure.'

Her friend pulled a face. 'You mean you could believe in his sincerity if you were plain and dumpy?'

'That's just the point. I wouldn't have any problem with North if I was plain and dumpy. I'd be invisible to him.'

'You have the same problem as the original poor little rich girl. The only way she can ever be sure a man wants her for herself and not her money, is to get rid of the money,' Emma said, her gaze settling fondly on her husband-to-be. 'Men are such complicated creatures— they often hide the best about themselves and flaunt the worst. If you think he's so superficial and you've half fallen for him anyway, maybe your intuition is trying to tell you something.'

'My intuition, ha! If women's intuition is so good, why aren't we running the world?'

The four of them had drinks on the veranda and watched the stars come out.

'Do you think it will rain tomorrow?' Emma said wistfully, as many a bride must have said on the eve of her wedding.

Matt Mackenzie studied the sky with an experienced eye.

'Not a chance,' he said.

'Oh, darn,' Emma said with a sigh. Ami laughed softly. At North's look of surprise, Emma said by way of explanation, 'Mackenzie grew up in a drought. We're both rather partial to rain.' She and Mackenzie exchanged a slow, smouldering smile. 'But we'll just have to make do with sunshine.'

Emma Spencer and Matt Mackenzie were married in the sunshine, in the courtyard of his homestead, Falkner's Place. Matt looked magnificent in formal clothes, Emma glowed in ivory silk, flowers in her plaited hair. A lump in her throat, Ami stood alongside Steve Mackenzie, the best man. Emma had planned never to marry again after a disastrous attempt years earlier, but blunt, bearlike Matt Mackenzie had changed her mind. If ever there was a moment that confirmed the existence of real love, this was it. It had grown from many things—instant attraction, friendship, hardship and passion, and in the end, patient compromise on the part of both of them to overcome a host of difficulties and delays. They had literally run through fire together. Matt and Emma looked in each other's eyes and made their promises from the heart. They were lovers and friends. There was mutual respect and liking as well as love between them. Their marriage would be built on bedrock, Ami thought, feeling a twinge of envy. That's what I want. She glanced around until she saw North's black hair and hawkish profile. That, or nothing.

It was some time after the formalities before she came across North in the crowd. 'Your scars have vanished,' he said. 'Is that a quick healing process, or a demonstration of your gift for illusion?'

He had borrowed a tuxedo from one of Matt's many friends and it was a little old-fashioned and, she noticed crossly, very fitting around the shoulders. Ami drank a large mouthful of punch, her intuition twanging like a bow that had just released an arrow. Half fallen was a retrievable position, she'd told Emma. Oh, lord, what a fool she was. If she was anywhere else, she would cut and run right now. But it was her best friend's wedding and she couldn't walk out. If North asked her to dance, she would be ready with a refusal.

'Oh, it's pure illusion,' she said, rallying with a light tone and holding out her hand to display the touched-up scars. 'The scars are still there. You can see them if you look closely.'

'You carry that theatrical bag of tricks the way a doctor carries his medical bag,' he said, and, looking at a very brown, very lined woman in her sixties, said dryly, 'I'm tempted to think that's more of your work and that she's really only twenty-six.'

Emma laughed. 'No. Joyce is Matt's aunt, the genuine article.'

'The genuine article,' he repeated, giving Ami an odd look that skimmed over her classically knotted hair with the spray of delicate flowers, her pale green silk tabard and skirt. For a moment she was certain he was about to ask her to dance and her heartbeat quickened. Instead, he said, 'I must make the acquaintance of this rare creature.'

With that he excused himself and a few moments later, Ami saw him dancing with Joyce. After that, he danced with any number of appreciative women, some young, some old. He never did ask Ami to dance although she remained ready with a refusal all evening. It nettled her that she didn't have a chance to say no to him. And that, by staying away from her, he had managed to dominate her thoughts just as much as he would had he pursued her.

The bride threw her bouquet and it was caught by Sara Hardy, a local woman and writer who had found unexpected success with Emma's production of her first play. She plucked a single rose from the bouquet and tossed it back to the bride in thanks.

Emma and Matt flew away in his helicopter and the guests partied on for a while then gradually drifted home until only those guests staying overnight at Matt's homestead were left. After coffee, Ami went to bed, leaving the others drinking brandy and playing poker. North didn't even look up when she said good-night, just muttered a preoccupied, ''Night.' Which was fine by her. Just *fine*. Ami showered and slipped into a silk night shift, reflecting that she'd got accustomed to being pursued and this sudden change for the better took some adjusting to. The viral illness had left her more tired than usual and she drifted into a restless sleep dominated by dreams of scars and tight tuxedos.

CHAPTER EIGHT

SHE woke with a sudden thirst hours later and found the tumbler on her bedside table empty. Half asleep, she went into the adjacent bathroom to fill the glass, navigating her way by the moonlight flooding in from the uncurtained windows. When she came back, North was by her open bedroom door.

He was shouldered in against the doorframe, the picture of disreputable glamour—in need of a shave, his ruffled shirt open halfway down his chest, his bow tie hanging unknotted under his collar, traditional braces holding his borrowed pants a fraction too high. 'Beautiful Ami,' he said, crinkling his eyes. 'Can I have this dance?'

Her heart thudded. 'Are you drunk?' she said.

'Just a few brandies.' He looked appreciatively at the thin-strapped night shift, which only just covered her thighs. Ami went into her room, set down the water and snatched up her robe and when she looked back, North had stepped inside and closed the door.

'Everyone's gone to bed,' he said. 'Don't want to disturb them.' He put a finger ot his lips in the classic manner and she might have laughed except that his efforts not to disturb others so disturbed her. Pulling her wrap around herself she belted it tightly, as if she might suppress any response to this boyish, captivating Kendrick.

He eyed her bed, which was in the usual riotous tangle. By now he was well and truly aware that her rumpled sheets were routine, not the result of 'heavy nights.'

'It's nearly three in the morning. Why are you here?'

'To tell you we're driving back at nine tomorrow. Okay?'

She nodded.

North held out his hands. 'And to ask you to dance.'

She gave him a snort of impatience. 'It's a bit late for that. You should have asked me earlier, when the band was playing, but you were too busy being Mr Popularity.'

'I wanted to ask you to dance but—thought it best not to. Can't keep my distance if I'm holding you in my arms, can I?'

Her pulses thundered in her ears. 'Why, suddenly, do you want to keep your distance?'

'You're too much for me,' he said seriously. 'Better to stick to someone like Fran. I know Fran, understand her, understand what motivates her. Can't figure you out. Might never know what's underneath.' He reached out and drew a finger over her cheekbone, down to her chin, almost as if he expected the skin to peel off like a mask. 'Is this the real Ami Winterburn tonight? Looks like a temptress, acts like a severe nurse?'

'A temptress?' she snapped. Well, then, let him stick to Fran and that barren relationship, she thought in sudden rage. They could form a corporation. Poor Francesca, she thought in sudden sympathy.

He put a hand to her waist. 'Shall we waltz?' he said ironically. 'We waltz well together.'

His handprint was surely etched on to her skin. He's going to stick to Fran, she reminded herself. He still wants you but he's not going to chase you anymore. What, she wondered, had made North abandon the chase? But it was the conviction that he had that stopped her pulling away. It might be the last time he touched her. 'If I'm too much for you and you want to keep your distance, why ask me to dance now?'

North pulled her close, looked down at her affectionately. 'I'm drunk,' he explained, grinning.

She gave a shaky laugh but the laughter quickly died as he clasped her hand and hunched down, cheek to cheek, shuffling his feet in a parody of dancing. 'Mm,' he murmured, nuzzling her neck. 'Ami Winterburn,' he said, rolling her name out like the first line of a poem. He often said her full name like that, as if there was something else to come after it if he could just think of the next line.

Ami attempted to free herself, but she was half-hearted and in the process her arms slipped around his broad back and her mouth touched his neck and the scent of his skin assailed her. Ami closed her eyes. Just one cuddle while he was in this odd, boyish mood. Lucky Francesca, she thought, knifed by jealousy. They shuffled a few steps this way, then that, and suddenly North stopped. He looked at her, his hair falling over his forehead, and she saw the glitter of desire in his eyes.

'Ami Winterburn,' he whispered, laying a hand along the side of her face, and her name hung there, oddly unfinished, as he stroked downward, plucked the end of the silky belt and unravelled it. At his feather-light touch, the robe slithered from her shoulders. North held her close, bent his head to nuzzle in close, gathered up a handful of hair to expose her neck for his kiss. It was too much—the silken caress of his palm through her shift, the play of his fingers through her hair, the moist warmth of his mouth on her skin. He slipped the shift over her head, tossed it into the air and it fluttered in filmy slow motion to the floor. He drew back to look at her, naked now except for briefs. 'Beautiful Ami,' he said. In a new dance, they circled, locked in each other's gaze. Ami felt the edge of the bed behind her and sat down. North knelt and ran his hands over her in a delicate, tormenting exploration. 'Superb,' he said as he kissed her thigh. 'Magnificent—' he breathed, his head at her breasts. And Ami arched back, barely supporting herself as he suckled and fondled and pleasure rippled through her body. A sigh broke from her. North laughed softly and stood up to pull his shirt free of his waistband. Moonlight threw shadows down one side of his body, accentuating the hollow beneath his collarbone, the sculptured curve of his chest and the small, neat nipples. Her fingers tingled. Ami reached up and stroked the junction of his neck and shoulder. North's eyes closed. 'Do that again when I have my hands free,' he said huskily and hurried to get the cuff links from his shirt sleeves. She stood and put her mouth to the same place and he groaned and gave a delicate shiver, lifting his shoulder into a defensive curve.

'How to make an angle into a curve,' she whispered against his neck.

'Physics at a time like this?' he said huskily, doubling his efforts. 'Damn all cuff links!'

Smiling, she let her fingers trail lower, to his waist. North's chest heaved. Looking at him, seeing the expression of delicious strain on his face, she felt a heady rush of power. She dipped lower still until she held him in the palms of her hands.

He muttered something under his breath, ferociously shook his shirt sleeves free. Laughing softly, she stretched out on the bed and watched him in the moonlight, admiring the aesthetic lines of his shoulders and arms, anticipating his strength, a lazy sensuality circulating in her body. She heard the soft burr of a zip, the rustle of his trousers, a clatter as a metal braces clip caught the frame of the bed. Then the bed bounced under his weight and she was in his arms, kissing him wildly, lost in a starry space. He grasped her hips and tilted her evocatively against him, an unnecessary action for she was already breathless with the columned promise of the beautiful, powerful body beneath her. North took some deep breaths, which she rode in delicious anticipation.

'Ami,' he murmured. His strong hands were in her hair, gathering it up with tenderness, forcing her eyelids closed with the sheer hypnotic pleasure of the small caresses on her scalp. 'Is it safe?'

Safe. She rubbed her cheek against his hand, as mindless and sensual as a cat. 'Safe for what?'

'For us to make love.'

She smiled. Sexy North Kendrick was also thoughtful and responsible. She felt a surge of love for him. 'Yes. Thank you for asking.' She kissed him passionately then slid off the bed to step from her briefs, deliberately slowing the moment, letting the anticipation build.

'Mm,' North groaned, watching her. He rolled on his side and reached out to curve a hand to her thigh. 'Exquisite,' he said.

It was as if something switched in her head. She looked down at him, saw the heavy-lidded look of the lover and her body throbbed in response. But when he raised his eyes to her face, she saw the glitter of triumph there. And here she was, as frozen as one of the bronze torchbearers outside his hotel, with his hand on her in ownership. His fingertips moved gently on her skin as if he was appreciating her flesh-and-blood smoothness the way he'd appreciated the smoothness of the bronze. *Beautiful. Magnificent. Exquisite.* She was almost part of his collection. She reversed the direction of her briefs. 'Maybe I should be holding a torch,' she said, raising her arm, striking a pose.

North stared at her, his spurned hand poised in a frozen caress. 'A *torch*?'

'Or a sheaf of wheat or something,' she muttered. Ignoring the silk shift on the floor, she snatched up her robe and turned her back to put it on. Was there anything more embarrassing than reclaiming in cold soberness the clothes discarded in mindless passion? She winced, switched on the bed lamp and gave herself a few moments before she looked at North. He was hitched up on one arm, his hair black as night, his long, muscular body golden in the lamplight. Ami closed her eyes as her resolve weakened.

'Wheat?' he repeated carefully. 'You did say— *wheat*?'

'You're very good,' she said coolly.

His eyes narrowed. 'You stopped before you found out just how good.'

She flushed. 'You should be on the stage, North. You had me really believing in that boyish, affectionate persona.'

'Did I?' he said harshly.

'You aren't drunk. I daresay you've had a brandy or two but you're cold sober and as calculating as ever.'

North got up and put his hands on his hips. A formidable sight, almost naked as he was. His hands slanted down and inward like arrows and she turned away as her body mourned the pleasures she was rejecting.

'You do intend to enlighten me, I hope? I don't know what the hell you're talking about.'

'Oh, yes,' she said whirling around, picking up his clothes, her face burning as she remembered helping him off with his shirt, aiding and abetting him in her own acquisition. 'It was a good idea—a *great* idea. This is what you've been aiming for since the moment you decided you had to pay me back for humiliating you. You had to have me! Kendrick the Conqueror! All that rubbish about truces! Just Kendrick tactics like the charming little-boy-lost act—so appealing and frank because you've had too much brandy. Well, it didn't work!' she said, throwing his clothes at him.

North's head went back as he caught the bundle and the braces flicked at his face. His eyes looked cold as ice. 'It almost worked,' he said. To emphasize his point, he leaned down and picked up the silk shift, tossed it in the air, and its slow-motion descent created a time warp. Ami watched it, her mouth dry as the sight triggered a rush of desire.

'Like I said, you are very good at using your opportunities,' she snapped.

He shoved his arms into the sleeves of the frilled shirt and she thought she heard the sound of tearing stitches. 'I really must insist that I was—am—the worse for wear from too much brandy. Why would I be so stupid as to get mixed up with you again, otherwise?'

'So worse for wear that you could coolly check on— on—whether or not I—'

'On birth control arrangements?'

'I suppose you came with a prophylactic tucked away in your pocket!' she said contemptuously. 'Because you came here tonight with one purpose in mind.'

North pulled on his pants and snapped the zip. He looked at her with dislike. 'You don't know that. Even if it was true, you can't have it both ways. A man who doesn't give a damn is insensitive and irresponsible. A man who comes prepared is calculating.'

She blinked at the truth of that, knew she was being unfair but she had to persist because he was still here and in spite of everything she knew about him and the way he thought, she could so easily go to him and make love with him until morning, then wake up to find herself another exhibit in North's life. There was the staccato sound of a zip. The braces twanged.

At the door North looked again at the bed, which was now practically denuded of linen, the coverlet and top sheet flung in folds on the floor, the mattress cover showing. 'I'm afraid I've rumpled your sheets,' he drawled before he left.

Ami shut the door with a slam that brought muffled queries from other rooms and set Matt's cattle dogs barking. 'How could I?' Ami muttered as she remade the bed. 'Because I am an idiot!' Burning with self-censure, she got into bed to reflect upon her foolishness. But as the dogs quietened and the house fell silent once more, she reflected instead on what she would be doing had North stayed. She would even now be in those strong arms had she not come to her senses. She would be stretched over his beautiful, hard body now if she had not seen how degrading it all was. She would be holding him inside her now, feeling the intimate flex of his muscles, deliciously aware of the latent power in him as he moved, just a little at first... If she had not seen through North's games-playing in time. As the silent morning hours passed she told herself it was a lucky thing that she wasn't some young, foolish girl to fall for his charm and expertise. Eventually she slept and dreamed she was a young, foolish girl.

It was late morning by the time they arrived at Ken Drummond's place in Swagman's Creek the following day. After knocking fruitlessly at the front door, they walked around the back of the small, timber house and found Harry propped on his walking stick beside a motorbike, the best-preserved of several dilapidated vehicles that were scattered around the large, untidy allotment on the edge of the tiny town. His old friend was hunkered down beside him, pointing out something with the zeal of the enthusiast. Spritz came bounding towards them, as pleased to see North, Ami thought resentfully, as the owner who lovingly fed and groomed her.

North came to a halt, watching his father. He wore sunglasses as he had during the journey and Ami could only guess that the degree of frost in his eyes paralleled that in his voice. North was either genuinely offended by her accusations last night, or just a bad loser. She opted for the latter. His mood improved with Spritz's unqualified adoration, but dissipated quickly when Harry greeted them.

'Driving back with us?' Harry said eagerly to Ami. She shook her head.

'My car is ready. I'm driving back just as soon as I pick it up.'

Harry was clearly disappointed. 'In that case, maybe it would be better if I waited and drove back with Ami,' he said undiplomatically to his son. Harry couldn't make it clearer that he preferred her company to that of his son on the long drive back to Sydney.

North's jaw tightened and Ami would have left then except that Harry's bachelor friend pointed with sheepish pride to a ramshackle outdoor table set with four mismatched teacups, a pint jug of milk, a plate of thick fruitcake slices and a tin of biscuits. 'Don't often have company,' he said, pink-faced, to explain such an elaborate table. 'I'll bring the teapot.'

He duly brought it and went back to contemplate the bike with the other two men. Ami sighed, realizing that she had been assigned to pour the tea as a natural consequence of being the only female present. As she did so, the motorbike started up with an ancient shriek. To her surprise, she saw North was riding it, skillfully dodging the various back yard obstacles, including a sheep that placidly cropped grass in the midday shade of a row of camphor laurel trees that stretched to the back boundary. Harry and Ken absently took the tea she handed them, watching North's progress with the kind of attention and approval only males can give such an activity. On Harry's face was also a look of deep envy. He grimaced at Ami. 'I'd give a lot to get on a bike again, but my legs—' he said wistfully.

North, his black mood considerably reduced by the ride, throttled down and parked and the three men had an earnest exchange based on the sound of the revs. Ami stared at North, the usually immaculate company director and art collector who was now crouched down, sunglasses off, pointing out something in a rusting old heap of machinery that emitted an unearthly sound. The noise would be horrendous to a man who really had imbibed too much brandy the night before, she thought, unable to detect the slightest flicker of his eyelids. Harry ran a fond hand over the bike handles and the fairing and, following the movement, North said, 'Whatever happened to your bikes, Harry?'

'I've still got one. It's in my shed. Was always going to fix it but it'll never run again,' he said flatly. 'I gave the others away.'

Harry, Ami thought, had given a lot of things away. North looked thoughtful and the three men stood in a circle, arms folded, united in the mysterious masculine passion for machinery. Ami took advantage of their pre-occupation to leave before she was dragged into a fight between North and his father about the journey back. She left a note on the table to say that she was walking to the garage to pick up her car, took her suitcase from the Jaguar and set off up the road with Spritz beside her. The drone of the motorbike made her look back. Beyond the stripe of the camphor laurels' dense blue shade, the rough ground of Ken's paddock was a hazy yellow in the sun. She caught a glimpse of the bike in the bright spaces between the trees until it emerged into the open. Ami laughed.

'Oh, Spritz, look at that,' she said, shading her eyes. She thought of that photograph of a young North, his face showing anxiety and pleasure and pride, riding pillion behind Harry all those years ago. Now it was North with Harry behind him, holding on, making good his wish to get on a bike again. Unseen, she stood and watched until the bike turned and flickered from view behind the line of trees.

Ami walked on down the lane, her eyes watering. Why did it matter to her whether North made peace with his father? Why on earth should she feel this flutter of anxiety lest he make a mess of what might be a tentative reconciliation? Because she cared. 'Oh, you *stupid*!' she said out loud, kicking a twig off the road as if she was kicking North out of her mind. Spritz pounced on it and brought it back to her. Ami tossed it into the scrub at the side of the lane. Half fallen was a retrievable position. It had to be true. She couldn't face the prospect of falling in love with a man who liked his champagne cold and his women beautiful. The dusty lane stretched out ahead. The sunlight limned tall seed heads in the waist-high grass along the road. The sound of the motorbike followed her in fits and starts like the sound of an exuberant insect on the still, country air.

Spritz brought the stick back again and again and insisted on taking it into the car. It was still in the car when they reached Sydney where she tossed it out. Out of sight, out of mind. Unfortunately the same could not be said for North.

North himself phoned her on the Friday following Emma's wedding.

'Ami,' he said briskly. 'I haven't got much time. Can you come over to the hotel?'

She felt the usual dual irritation and excitement at his voice and the prospect of seeing him again. 'I haven't got much time, either,' she said coolly. 'What is it about? Is Harry all right?'

'He's fine,' he said impatiently. 'I can't go into it on the phone. How long will it take you to get here? Half an hour—forty-five minutes?'

'Just a minute! I'm not going to drop everything—'

'And don't make any plans for this weekend,' he said.

She took a deep, deep breath. Adrenalin pumped into her system. 'The weekend?' The ragged nature of her heartbeat aggravated her. 'Look,' she said, opting for anger rather than this weak-kneed speculation. 'My weekends are none of your business.'

'This one will be,' he said smoothly. 'I'm calling in a favour, Ami Winterburn. And if you don't like it, too bad. You shouldn't start things you don't intend to finish.' He gave her a moment to digest that and added, 'If you set out now, you can be here in forty minutes.'

She bridled at the gall of it. 'And I suppose if I don't I can expect a letter from your lawyers?'

She thought she heard him swear under his breath but when he spoke, his voice was silkily earnest. 'I would hate to implicate your partner in the irresponsible hoax that was, after all, exclusively *your* idea, but—'

'All *right*,' she snapped. 'You really are the lowest—'

But North had rung off.

The threat was possibly a bluff but she wasn't sure enough of him to call it. Even if things had improved with his father, his mood would be anything but benign where she was concerned. It would not be often that North was rejected in the middle of lovemaking. In the middle of his best-laid plans.

Almost-laid plans.

Her face flamed as precise images from that night presented themselves yet again to her. She had let him take her in his arms against her better judgment. She had danced with him in her bedroom when she'd planned all along to refuse, when she *should* have refused. She'd sprawled on the bed, ogled him. She'd caressed him, held him in the most intimate way... her fingers tingled. She drifted off for a few hectic moments.

How unfortunate the timing had been. Every year when Emma and Matt celebrated their wedding anniversary, she would be forced to remember her folly with North in the west. She gave a wry laugh.

The memory triggers were mounting up. The waltz from *Rosenkavalier* could set her thinking about North. The fragrance of a gardenia. Her best friend's wedding date. The dog. Motorbikes. Santa Claus suits. Viruses. Cheap checkered shirts. The kitchen sink...

As she drove to the hotel, she dissected his words, read between the lines. *You shouldn't start things you don't intend to finish.* A deep foreboding filled her. What if he wanted to finish what she had started that night? No, surely not. Manipulation and blackmail might be in the Kendrick genes, but she couldn't see North demanding sexual favours in exchange for amnesty over her masquerade as Amelia.

Still, she sailed past the torchbearers with a distracted air. She nearly missed seeing the tall woman in the tight, black leggings and the blue sweater with alphabet letters printed on the front. But she turned at the Avalon doors and saw the blonde approach a man, with an unlit cigarette between her extended fingers. Ami saw her lips move in the classic words, 'Got a light?'

So that was her doppelgänger, she thought. It did nothing to endear her to North, knowing that she did loosely fit the description on his security records. Even if she *had* turned out to be the woman on the street, he had no business being so patronising, so downright arrogant on the day of the gardenia. Ami felt like warning the woman that she was probably even now under surveillance, but when she looked again, she had disappeared. The hawk-eyed Morgan, she saw, as she passed through the doors, had not noticed the woman, which gave her spirits a curious little lift.

The concierge sent her to the floor below North's penthouse. 'You'll find Mr. Kendrick in the Celestial Suite.'

The door was ajar and Ami went in. North was standing by a glass wall that overlooked a breathtaking view of Sydney seen through swathes of sheer fabric. He was on the phone and turned around when she entered. He waved her towards the lushly upholstered armchairs. Ami was forced to cool her heels while he continued his call and she thought bitterly how very well he used the tools of technology to give himself an advantage. She paced the length of the room, which was furnished rather floridly with divans and chairs covered in mauve and

turquoise brocade with tasselled cushions. On low tables
stood huge oriental jars filled with tiger lilies, strelitzia
and jasmine, the origin of the perfume in the air. The
lavish interior hinted more of earthly than celestial
matters. All it needed was a sheikh and a dancing girl
with a diamond in her navel. Her eyes flicked from the
lush fabrics to the frankly sexual tiger lilies to North
himself. His eyes followed her every move. What did he
want? What did he mean—*you shouldn't start things
you don't mean to finish*?

He put the phone down and her muscles tensed as he
studied each small detail of her appearance. If he took
as much interest in the inner woman as he did in the
outer, she thought prudishly, he would be a prince among
men. He wore one of his superb three-piece suits with a
blue shirt that tinged his grey eyes with its colour.

'You took off rather suddenly from Ken's place,' he
said. 'I would have driven you to the garage eventually.'

'What's this about, North? What is this *favour* I owe
you? If it's payment you want for nursing me through
a viral illness, then I'd prefer to write you a cheque for
your time.'

There was a pause, during which Ami realized just
how insulting that sounded, even to someone like North,
who thought the world operated on those terms. His eyes
glittered. 'No, no,' he said in that silky voice that filled
her with misgivings. 'I feel you repaid that debt the night
of the wedding. Perhaps not quite in *full*—' He gave a
wolfish smile, as if remembering how close to full
payment she had been. 'I'm still puzzling over your reference to a sheaf of wheat. It was wheat? Do you have
a cereal fetish, or something?'

Flushed, Ami looked at him with dislike and suspicion. 'I'm very busy. What do you want?'

'Like I said, I'm calling in a favour—you owe me,
Ami Winterburn...' As usual, her name did not quite

finish the sentence. But there was no more to come save a very explicit scrutiny that made her wonder if the room was unseasonably heated.

'How do you like your suite?' he said at last.

Ami stared around at the opulent interior. '*My* suite?'

'Yours,' he confirmed, watching her the way a cat watches a mouse.

'What are you talking about?'

'I—feel I want you near,' he said, walking around her, looking her over. 'So that we can finish this business once and for all. I'll be here in Sydney over the weekend and it would be—*convenient* if you were handy.'

'*Convenient*!' A pulse hammered in her temple.

'I'm a generous man. I've even provided a new wardrobe for you to use while you're, er, staying with me.'

'You *can't* think what I think you mean!'

'You once asked what would satisfy me,' he murmured. 'You can't be so naive not to know the answer.'

She felt a shaming little thrill that made her cut the air contemptuously with the edge of her hand. 'Forget it. I'd dive into a tankful of sharks before I'd go to bed with you.'

His brows went up in mock surprise at such plain speaking. 'I suppose that explains that little interlude we shared after Emma's wedding,' he said blandly. 'You couldn't find a tankful of sharks? Scarce in the outback.'

'Very amusing,' she snapped, feeling a furnace heat in her cheeks.

'You made a fool of me, Ami Winterburn. I didn't like that.'

Ami tried to read the conflicting messages in his eyes but was defeated by a recollection of him in his underwear, by lamplight—the frustrated, baffled lover. She felt some vague pangs of guilt in spite of her knowledge of his devious behaviour.

'I have to—how did you put it? Restore my self-esteem. All I want is your—company, for a short time. To, um, finish the affair properly,' he said with a look so wolfish it just had to be fake. She frowned at him, suddenly realizing that her intuition was telling her there was something wrong here. But his expression grew so smug that her normal thought processes were blocked by anger.

'Come, take a look at the clothes I've bought for you,' he said, showing his teeth, and she abandoned her battling intuition. She was still trapped in that dangerous habit women had, she thought in self-disgust—trying hard to believe that no matter how manipulative and selfish a man was, he couldn't be all bad.

North walked through an adjoining door wondering if sheer curiosity would make her follow him. It did. He smiled as he heard the outraged rustle of her clothes behind him. There were massive jardinières here, full of exotic orchids in the fleshy pinks and decadent purples the decorators deemed correct for this most bordello-like suite in the hotel. There was an enormous, cushioned bed on a dais, silk-draped from the ceiling. Tassels everywhere. North mounted the dais and delicately tested the mattress with spread fingertips. Pure corn, he thought, glancing over to see if she had twigged yet.

She was clearly torn between fury and a hysterical desire to laugh. But her normal very reliable sense of the ridiculous was being suppressed by some other strong feeling and she fell for it. North was elated. He still had some old scores to settle with Ami Winterburn.

'You *can't* be serious?' she said scathingly.

'Being serious is a failing of mine,' he said. 'I'm sure you recall Harry pointing that out. Here's the wardrobe.'

At his touch, large carved doors opened to reveal some clothes still wearing the maker's tags.

'I can't believe even *you* would be so crass as to—to proposition one woman while you're on the brink of marriage to another.'

He blinked a bit at that, not aware that he was on the brink of marriage but quite prepared to play along with it. 'But as you've remarked in the past, I never waste an opportunity,' he said dryly, thinking of that night that was so frustratingly hazy when he tried to remember just how it had felt to have her naked in his arms, yet so painfully clear when it came to her denouncement afterwards. He took out a garment and arranged it over his forearm, as if he was an old-fashioned draper, inviting her approval.

She did hesitate for a moment then, as if she was picking up the clues but something was interfering with her judgment. The confident, articulate Miss Winterburn was red-faced, her magnificent breasts were heaving as she grabbed the dress and flung it on the floor. 'Keep your harem clothes for some other—' The fallen garment caught her eye at last. Powder blue linen. Long sleeves, buttoned at the wrist. Tiny pearl buttons up to the neck. Neat collar with guipure lace.

She spun around to the wardrobe, riffled through the clothes. North grinned when her straight back stiffened as she got a closer look at the harem clothes. A dove-grey dress and jacket. A pleated skirt, a matronly blouse and cashmere cardigan. Refined clothes for the older woman. Monica from the executive gifts service hadn't turned a hair when he'd given a description and estimated vital statistics of the widow Anderson.

Ami seized a pair of shoes from a shelf. Her size, but high-cut, lace-ups with sensible heels.

'Built in arch supports,' North said helpfully, pointing over her shoulder. 'So essential for legs that have been through so much.' He smiled fondly at her. 'Amelia.'

She swallowed, put a hand to her forehead as she finally twigged. Miss Winterurn was very slow on the uptake today, which meant that whatever was on her mind was something very weighty indeed. North found it a source of great optimism.

'You mean—stay here as Amelia *Anderson*?'

'My favourite old lady. I invited her to stay, free of charge, remember?'

CHAPTER NINE

SHE had forgotten all about Amelia Anderson, had lost her cool entirely and plunged headlong into assumptions that might be all too revealing. Ami closed her eyes briefly, winced at the echo of her babble about sharks and harems. She had come here with her thoughts firmly stuck in that time warp, the night of Emma's wedding when they'd started something and hadn't finished it. With luck, he would get so much enjoyment out of making an idiot of her that he wouldn't notice.

'I've been pestered by reporters wanting to follow up on the heart-warming story of the elderly gatecrasher having her free holiday in the Avalon. I've managed to put them off with excuses until now. You'll be interested to know that since she gatecrashed my party, Amelia has had a nasty bout of flu and has been to visit her son in New Zealand—or was it Canada?'

She glowered, not trusting herself to speak.

'Somehow I assumed they would lose interest in the widow but it's nearly Christmas and you know how the papers love human interest stories in the season of goodwill.'

'But it's a risk,' she said, aghast. 'What if I'm sprung this time?'

'This isn't like you, Miss Winterburn,' he chided, giving her a hearty slap on the back. 'Where is all that immodest confidence in your skill? Besides, I'm not giving you a choice. How would it look if I can't produce the widow Anderson cosily enjoying the holiday I promised her? Some nosy reporter might run a check on social security and discover there is no Amelia Anderson.

There are only two conclusions that could be reached
from that—one, that I was properly fooled, or, two, that
I knew about the impersonation and knowingly made
idiots of my guests and the press. I,' he told her softly,
'have no intention of being labelled either fool or cheat.
You've been successful in audition at last, Miss
Winterburn,' he said maliciously. 'The part of Amelia
Anderson is yours. Playing this weekend by popular
request.'

She stared. So that's what he meant by finishing what
she'd started. To finish the affair properly, he'd said.
The affair of Amelia Anderson. The affair of the gardenia. There was a certain crazy logic to it, she supposed. She could once and for all allay those feelings of
guilt she had over the impersonation. Make up for wit-
nessing his humiliation, give Harry one last thrill but
this time with his son in on the joke, which would help
to paper over the rough edges between the two men.
Rather than a tedious, unsatisfying fade-out, a definite
event to mark THE END. It appealed to Ami's sense of
drama. Amelia's swan song would be hers, too. She
swallowed.

'Surely not the entire weekend,' she objected. 'It would
only take an hour for a press photographer to take some
shots.'

'Two press photographers,' he corrected. 'One on
Saturday night, one on Sunday sometime. You'll stay
overnight and make yourself seen around the hotel.
Several guests have enquired about dear old Amelia. You
have tugged at so many heartstrings.'

'And what am I supposed to do about Spritz?'

'I'll spring for the cost of a kennel—which is more
than fair in the circumstances,' he said. 'After all, *I* did
not create the widow Anderson.'

'You could have simply *told* me the press were being
a nuisance,' she said, with a sigh. 'I do have some sense

of responsibility, you know. I don't have to be coerced into helping in a situation I helped create.'

'I know that,' he said, amused. 'But you have such a poor opinion of me—I couldn't resist stringing you along when I saw your suspicions written all over you.'

She snorted. 'Childish.'

'Put it down to my atrophied sense of humour,' he said ironically and she saw with surprise that Harry's criticism still stung. He bent to pick the blue linen dress from the floor. Flicking her a wicked glance, he shook it, slipped it on the hanger and put it away. Ami had to press her lips together to hold back a laugh at the recollection of herself, flinging it to the floor as if it was a black lace negligee with strings attached.

'You made quite a few assumptions there,' he commented, touching a long spike of orchids. The flowers trembled and he plucked one, casually raised it to his nose as they walked out to the sitting room. 'Jumped to conclusions that I'd inveigled you here to force you into bed with me.' He paused, looked expectantly at her but she refused to bite. 'Psychologically speaking, we tend to make assumptions based on what we *fear* might happen, or on what we *want* to happen. Which was it in this case—maybe a bit of both?'

'Maybe you should apply that theory to some of your own assumptions, North,' she retorted. 'You've jumped to conclusions almost every time you've met me. And every time they've led you to want to throw me out.' She paused alongside him, looked mockingly at him. 'Psychologically speaking, we tend to want to exclude things that frighten us, or are too complex for us to deal with. What was it in my case, North? Maybe a combination of both?'

'Touché,' he murmured, staring into her eyes.

It irritated her, that polite, sportsmanlike acknowledgment of a point scored—the kind of graciousness extended by champions who knew they would win in the end anyway and could afford to be generous. But the spurt of irritation was not enough to set her feet moving. Her heightened senses picked up a heady drift of jasmine, the faint, rising sounds of the city through the open terrace doors, the tremor of the breeze in the sheer, swathed curtains. She stood there, held in some mysterious communication that was changing nature second by second. Puzzled, she sought to describe it, but it seemed independent of any words they had exchanged. In his grey eyes she saw the same faint surprise, followed by acceptance. A pleasant warmth came to her, and the magnetic pull of attraction. North, she thought, as if it was on a map. A direction. A destination. Magnetic North.

They moved at the same time, heads tilted until their lips met. A scarce, tender touch as if they were teenagers and it was their first kiss. North sighed and she felt the warm rush of his breath in her mouth. Again they kissed, leisurely, equally open one to the other. There was no other point of contact between them, just mouth on mouth, tongue speaking direct to tongue with no distractions. Language seemed obsolete. There was simply this tender, electrifying, intense communication on some level Ami had never before encountered. In perfect synchronisation, they moved apart again, seeing the shaken realization in each other's eyes, that something new had happened, something that transcended anything that went before. Ami's chest felt tight, emotion welled up in her and for a moment she thought she might cry at the puzzling sense of something beautiful and elusive.

North saved her from anything so foolish. He broke the contact, leaned over and tucked the orchid into her hair.

'I won't throw you out this weekend,' he said, giving her face a little pat.

So much for a mysterious, mutual communication, she thought, deriding herself. So much for tran-

scendence and recognition and some elevated level of
transmission between two people. It was all skill and
technique for North and it was all wishful thinking on
her part to imagine it was anything else.

It was only when she got back to the shop that she
realized why so many people had stared at her along the
way. North's orchid was still tucked behind her ear,
marking his place. Once again she removed it too late
and was only prevented from throwing it out by Helen,
who never got orchids and, scandalised by the waste,
snatched it to the safety of a water glass where it mocked
Ami for the remainder of the day.

Ami duly made her appearances in the hotel on
Saturday afternoon, to give credence to the idea that
Amelia Anderson was a guest. Accompanied by North,
she drank coffee in the coffee shop where he had his
revenge by insisting on an in-depth discussion of lamp-
shade making which tested her powers of invention. She
visited the indoor pool and was introduced to several
guests by a solicitous North who watched her performance critically with the satisfaction of one who was
in on the joke at last. On Saturday evening, when her
skin was itching from the long contact with adhesive,
she posed for a number of shots, ending up in the restaurant, where the newspaper photographer took shots
of the pensioner being wined and dined by the benevolent entrepreneur. The entire business had the
hallmark of North's organization upon it. It was he who
decided where she would be photographed, to ensure the
best possible conditions for deception, and for once she
was pleased that his high-handedness invited no argument from the cameraman. A reporter turned up and
Ami had reason to be grateful again, this time for the
semiinvisibility of an old woman, even one supposedly
in the limelight. North hardly let her say a word and the
young male reporter didn't find it odd at all, that a man

was running the show and spoke on behalf of a woman twice his age.

Because of the interest generated amongst other patrons, North insisted that they sit through the remainder of dinner after the press had gone, when Ami was breaking her neck to escape to her room and take off her make-up. He was expansive and complacent and she glared at him.

'Wouldn't you rather we skipped dessert?' she said primly. 'I'm sure you'd prefer to spend time with Francesca on a Saturday night.'

He laughed and took her hand, patting it kindly. 'It's you I want to be with Amelia, honestly.' He took her hand and lightly bestowed a kiss on the made-up surface.

'The warm and human side of big business,' she said sardonically under her breath. 'The very important North Kendrick being nice to an impoverished, elderly nobody.'

There was a gleam of anger in his grey eyes as he paused, her hand still raised in his. He turned her hand over. 'The very irritated, besotted North Kendrick trying to find a chink in the armour of the infuriating, desirable Ami Winterburn...' he murmured. Eyes never leaving hers, he put his mouth to her palm, the only available part of her that was not defended by disguise. The warm caress of his lips sent a frisson down her back. She jumped at the sly touch of his tongue.

Besotted? she thought, staring into those silvery-grey eyes.

'Did you say—' she began, when Franesca showed up, elegant in black with a tiger-skin-patterned silk scarf thrown about her neck, its ends floating to her knees.

Francesca said a polite hello to the widow Anderson, averting her eyes quickly from the threatening vision of age and wrinkles. 'You've been simply ages,' she said to North, an excited light in her lovely eyes. 'I'm dying to talk to you.'

Besotted, Ami thought derisively, as they left the restaurant. Of course he hadn't said besotted. Or if he had, it was an ironic turn of phrase.

Gloomily she tried to achieve some professional satisfaction at carrying out yet another performance without giving the game away. One more performance the following day and the affair would be finished once and for all. But her mind was on North and Francesca, who had disappeared, arms linked, having escorted Ami to her room. By now they were probably on their way to some intimate little place where they could dance cheek to cheek . . . and Francesca could whisper in North's ear whatever it was she was dying to tell him.

Harry phoned her when she had finally cleansed her face and let the skin breathe. 'Come on up and have a drink with me,' he said.

But when she got to the penthouse she found that North and Francesca were not in any cosy little restaurant, they were here with Harry.

Francesca looked at Ami in puzzlement when no-one introduced her to the stranger. 'I thought you said Mrs. Anderson was coming up to stay a while with you, Harry?'

The old man gave a wheezy laugh. 'Oh, this is her, er, goddaughter, Ami,' he said at last.

'The fairy goddaughter,' North murmured, a gleam in his eyes.

They left and Ami stayed for an hour in North's home, vowing never to come here again. As she talked to Harry, her eye was drawn from one work of art to another— paintings, sculptures, the ancient Grecian pots in their lit display dome. How long would North keep these, she wondered, before his enthusiasm waned? Besotted one minute, indifferent the next. Poor Francesca.

Back in her suite she was so restless she knew she wouldn't sleep. It was after eleven when she changed into the leotard and tights she had packed, put on some

battered practice dance shoes and attempted a work-out.
She gave up in frustration, for the suite, though spacious,
was not nearly spacious enough to give vent to her
feelings. She would need a space the size of a ballroom
to do that tonight.

A ballroom.

Ami's heartbeat quickened. She visualised that vast
space. It was probably hired out for a wedding or twenty-
first birthday party, crowded with tables and chairs and
guests. But it would do no harm to look. She pulled on
a long sweater over her tights, cinched her hair into a
ponytail and made her way to the Avalon ballroom. It
was empty save for clustered tables, a lectern and stacked
chairs at one end left over from a conference.

She found a switch, turned on some recessed lighting,
which shed a candle-like glow along the mirrored side
of the huge room. Using one of the chairs as a *barre*,
she warmed up with some exercises. Then she removed
her sweater and progressed to centre practice, slow, fluid
movements, then small jumps. The shiny expanse all
around her went to her head and she moved into quicker
movements, travelling the length of the ballroom in a
series of leaps and turns, her feet making soft, rhythmic
thuds on the floor, her image flickering alongside in the
mirror. She stopped at last for a breather and warm-
down, one leg raised on the back of a chair, her head
thrown back. And she saw the other image in the mirror.

North. Her heartbeat, slowing already after the
workout, bumped into reverse. The sound of her
breathing seemed abnormally loud as she looked at him
in the mirror, wondering if she had gone right off the
rails now and was conjuring up his image like a fey ballet
heroine languishing over her imagined prince. Music
started up, in her head or in reality she wasn't sure.

'It's after midnight,' he said, removing any doubt of
his earthly nature. The sound of his shoes, measured on
the fine parquetry flooring, kept time with the boom of

her heartbeat. 'I thought fairy goddaughters were supposed to turn into pumpkins at midnight.' Closer now, his gaze dripped warmly down over her body.

Supremely aware of him, she continued her warm-down exercises to the music that was, she realized, coming from the hidden speakers. It was the tail end of something by one of the Strausses and it concluded with a rousing blast before silence fell. 'I hope you don't mind me using the ballroom,' she said huskily.

'I saw you dance. You take my breath away.'

He'd taken hers. Ami stared at him, while on the edge of her vision she could make out his image and hers in the mirror, facing each other motionless like two inhabitants of a Degas painting. She with a leg raised and outstretched, one foot still resting on the back of a chair, he with an arm outstretched to the same resting place, his hand beside her foot. The music started again, the first celebratory whoops of orchestra brass followed by strings as the music swelled from the introduction into the waltz from *Der Rosenkavalier*. There were words to this music, she thought. Something about the night being too long...

'They're playing our song, Ami Winterburn...'

Some part of her listened for the unsaid words following her name, but there was only the music.

'Dance with me,' he said.

She'd meant not to dance with him the last time. There were more reasons than ever to refuse now. Reason number one—look what happened last time. Reason number two—if she kept clear of North, she would be finished with this affair in a matter of hours. Reason number three—she was more than half in love with him, but he was still the wrong kind of man for her. Four—Francesca. Five—*look what happened last time*. Six—*Francesca*...

'What about Francesca?' she said abruptly.

'She doesn't want to dance with me.'

'How do you know?'

'She told me tonight. Doesn't want to dance with me, ever,' he said, placing his hand firmly on her ankle. Ami drew in a sharp breath at that imprisoning, pleasant grip. 'She said she thought I was a sexy brute but she couldn't ever fall in love with me.'

'That's what she was dying to tell you?'

'That's it, broadly speaking.'

'But you were going to marry her, always supposing she would have you,' she said dryly.

'I might have considered it, in my ignorance, before—'

Before what? She waited but he didn't finish it. It was a habit with him, she thought, those unfinished sentences. He had been going to stick with Fran. Whether he would have or not was purely academic because Fran was not going to stick with him. This was nothing to celebrate, she told herself as her heartbeat sped up. This made no difference to her. He was still the kind of man who could contemplate such a lukewarm but convenient partnership. The man who liked his women beautiful, his champagne cold and his collector's items new and fresh. He would find another Francesca in time. But he was here now, his touch warm on her body, and her blood pounded in her veins and the tempo of the waltz was inside her. How did the words go? *Something, something, keine nacht ist zu lang.* The night was too long? She struggled with her schoolgirl German to translate. *Something, something, no night is too long.*

Impatiently, he dragged the chair aside, removing the barrier between them with a rasp of chair legs on the polished floor. Then he caught her close to him and they waited there a moment staring into each other's eyes while the music slowed to one of those breathless pauses when every nerve in the body anticipated the resumption of the sound. When it came, they went with it, slowly at first, locked together, intent on each other, hardly admitting the music. But as the rhythm quickened, they spun to the exuberant rhythm. This time Ami wasn't pretending to be anyone else, wasn't pretending anything at all. The ballroom whirled by, a blur of light and shadow, the only constant North himself, smiling, holding her fast in a dizzy world. *With you, with you, no night is too long.* I love you, she thought, feeling the forbidden words bubble to the surface, not quite spoken. The music slowed and released them, breathless and exhilarated.

'I wondered what it would be like to dance like that with you, that night when you waltzed me around cautiously as if I might break.' Ami threw back her head and laughed and North caught in a deep breath, hauling her hard against him.

'I don't think I can be cautious tonight. Will you break?'

His eyes glittered, his nostrils gently flared and she felt a rush of desire, a heightened sense of danger and aliveness. Like teetering on a high, narrow ledge, the risk of losing life making life more intense.

'What would you do if I did?'

North put his mouth to her ear. She could feel his smile on her skin. 'I'd mend you,' he murmured, suturing an imaginary line along her neck with a series of kisses and flicks of the tongue that made her gasp out his name.

She felt the jolt of his response to her ragged cry. He crushed her in his arms, kissed her mouth, hotly forging an entrance, filling her mouth with the taste of him. Stooping, he picked her up bodily and walked from the ballroom, his mouth on hers, her arms wrapped around his shoulders.

'Let me down,' she said indistinctly as they stopped by the lift and he punched a button with his elbow. 'Someone might see.'

'I don't give a damn if they do,' he growled. He jabbed the button. 'What's taking the damned lift so long?'

'Am I getting too heavy?' she said innocently, taking a nibble at his ear lobe.

He gave her a look so warm that she wondered if her hair was singed. 'No. But if the elevator doesn't come soon, I might make love to you here on the floor.'

And so in tune with him was she that the prospect was hardly shocking at all. But the lift came and by the time they were inside Ami's suite, her hair was streaming loose and North's shirt was unbuttoned beneath his jacket and his tie hung over his beautiful bare chest. North set her down and his hands roved the resistant, seamless Lycra dance gear and his urgent, escalating efforts to remove it sent shivers of delight and apprehension through her body. He was so strong, so passionate, so impatient and she suddenly panicked as his will carried her too fast, too soon. Whether or not he sensed something, he paused, his hands stilled, defeated by the impenetrable, skin-tight Lycra.

'Ami Winterburn... still encased in armour,' he said huskily, holding her at arm's length suddenly. He took several deep breaths and curbed his ferocity. Ami saw the gleam in his eyes as he forced himself back from the brink. Her mouth went dry. If there was anything more guaranteed to raise her temperature than North impatient to make love, it was North disciplining himself to match her pace. Making himself wait. She smiled, dazzled by him.

'I could make love to you now, this moment, anywhere, I don't care.' He took her hand, raised it to his mouth. 'But I want to make it last...'

He made it last and so did she, for how long she couldn't say. A tender, mutual exploration that set her senses reeling, made her wonder if she'd ever known what it was like to be really alive outside his arms. North was a lover to cherish, she already knew that. A strong, vigorous lover who kept his power in check, making it all the more exciting. She stood before him as she shed the tights and North took a long, long time to smooth her underwear from her with lingering, seductive strokes down her thighs and calves. He pulled her along with him and sat on a divan, spinning her at the last moment so that she sprawled on his lap, her back against his bare chest, her head dropped back into the mellow curve of his neck in a pose of sheer abandonment. And if she thought she had been aroused before, she found now that there were higher planes of arousal and higher still as North played her body like an instrument, his hard heat behind her, his fingers moving over her skin, fondling, finding all the secret parts of her. 'North,' she cried raggedly, urgently.

'North it is,' he murmured in her ear and moved his hands northwards to her breasts, where he produced sensations that kept her on a plateau of pleasure with the promise of high mountains and an endless sky. And just when she thought she might make the journey alone, he turned her to face him and she wrapped her long legs around him and he spread his hands over her hips and looked deep in her eyes. 'Ami Winterburn,' he said softly, lowering her to him, inch by tormenting inch. Her eyes almost closed with pleasure but she forced them open, watching North's flickering lashes, the glaze in his eyes, the flush high on his cheeks as he entered her. She kissed him, filled with love and a peculiar joy she'd never experienced. Locked together in intimacy, they were still, her head on his shoulder, his arms close around her. Every nerve in her body tingled with anticipation, waiting for the music to resume. And when it started, it ran away with them, faster and faster. Through the window behind North, the glittering city was a mass of shifting light points—stars slipping from their places in the sky. Her mouth was against his forehead, her arms close around the rippling muscles of his back, and she thought she might have called out something about love when she left the glorious plateau for the mountains and then the sky, the great, glittering, immense sky that went on forever...

Later, smiling, they stretched out on the divan with its cushions scattered to the four winds in testimony to their activities. They wore the towelling robes provided by the hotel and sipped at coffee made by Ami. She flushed, gradually growing self-conscious as North's eyes roamed over her, his intimate knowledge of her making them warm and lazy. The heat of passion began to seem just a tiny bit silly as her head cooled. 'That was—' she began, and bit her lip.

'What?' North prompted, lifting a heavy swathe of hair from her face with an index finger. 'Good, bad, indifferent?'

His grin was so complacent that she was peeved. No doubts for North Kendrick. No lingering little worries that he might not have been a satisfactory lover. She'd left him in no doubt with her moans and cries. There were even the marks of her fingernails visible on that juncture of his neck and shoulder exposed by his loosely tied robe. Ami averted her eyes from them, irked that she had left the visible signs of her pleasure for him or anyone else to see. Red-faced, she said rather more sharply than she intended, 'I suppose I should be glad we made it as far as the divan. You did talk about throwing me down in the corridor...' Her colour deepened at the idea that hadn't turned a hair of her head when she'd been in the throes of desire.

North looked at her with great interest. 'Was it a bit too unconventional for you, Ami?'

'Yes. No! I mean—oh!' she said crossly, pulling the edges of the robe primly over her knees, a move that amused North no end. What on earth did she do now? Would he get up and leave? Thanks for the coffee. See you in the morning. It wasn't as if she'd never had a lover, but this was North and she was already dying of embarrassment. It made her acerbic. 'It just seems more—civilised to use a bedroom,' she said, scowling.

'You're embarrassed,' he said softly.

'Not at all.'

'Ami Winterburn...' he said, smoothing her hair again, and she thought for a moment he was going to add something to her name. 'Fearless Ami, embarrassed by her own fervour.'

'Fervour?' she said, attempting nonchalance in vain.

'You are a tigress,' he said, growling in the back of his throat.

'An embarrassed tigress? Isn't that rather unlikely?'

'You are a woman of great contradictions. This coffee is good.'

'Does that surprise you?'

'Not at all. It's hard to go wrong with instant coffee,' he said equably.

She glared at him. 'I meant—that I'm a person of contradictions?'

'Nothing about you could surprise me anymore,' he said, putting down his coffee cup. He rose, took her hand and pulled her to her feet. Ami's heart began a heavy, pounding beat as she found herself in the circle of his arms, his mouth lightly on her temple. Taking her by the hand, he set off across the room.

'What are you doing?' she said.

North smiled wickedly at her. 'I've got this sudden craving to be conventional,' he told her as he tugged her into the bedroom with its silk-draped bed on a dais. She stared at him as her body revved into high gear again. His towelling robe gaped to the waist, showing large tracts of very desirable man. His eyes had the sheen of the hunter and she found that suddenly much more exciting than worrying. She wanted to touch him, to be in his arms again.

'Are you sure?' she said, feeling a rush of euphoria.

He grinned, let his eyes flick downwards once. 'Very sure.'

'But you've just got through being *un*conventional,' she said as he drew her closer to the bed.

'You want proof?' He yanked her down onto his towelling-clad body and irrefutable proof. And this time, it was Ami's caresses that brought inarticulate little sounds to the articulate North Kendrick's lips. It was her hands and her mouth that stroked and fondled and encompassed until he sighed and begged—'Yes, yes—no, no, stop!' And when she laughed in triumph at her power over him, he rolled over and spread her on the soft, quilted bed and covered her body, filled it with his so that she couldn't think at all, only feel as they combined their power to climb the heights.

Eventually they lay together, lazily loving. North nuzzled her ear, said, 'Conventional enough for you?'

Positively primitive, she thought, as small shivers of completion still rippled on her skin. 'Very civilised,' she said demurely.

North was gone in the morning. He'd left a dozen red roses on the pillow next to her, with a note. Smiling lazily, Ami opened the envelope, wondering how many men could lay their hands on a dozen dewy red roses on a Sunday morning. He would probably appear through the doorway in a moment with fresh-baked croissants and brewed coffee.

'Darling,' the note began in large, hasty script. *Darling*. Ami's smile widened and she lay back on the pillows and closed her eyes dreamily for a moment, the note held to her chest. Her first love letter from him. She felt like a schoolgirl.

'The second newspaper has cancelled, so the widow Anderson is no longer required.'

Ami sat up, frowning at this unloverlike tone.

'Something urgent has come up and I have to fly to UK for a few days. Damned awful timing. Keep Wednesday night free for me. North. P.S. Last night was wonderful.'

She turned the note over, hoping for something more. But it was no love letter in spite of the postscript, she thought wryly. Ami picked up the roses and breathed in their perfume, aware of a niggle of disquiet. Words had always been important to her. She could pick up a page of script and an innocuous phrase would leap out at her, seemingly more significant than the rest. But she reread the note and failed to identify the part that was bothering her. It was just, she decided, that she was disappointed not to see North today when she was filled with tenderness for him. Flushed with the pleasures of last night, she wanted to look at him over breakfast, touch his hand, share the look of lovers who knew each other intimately. But North had gone north. She laughed softly. 'I love you, North,' she said to the roses, then phoned Harry to tell him she was going home, as she and her disguise were no longer needed.

'Come on up before you go,' he said. 'I'll send the lift for you.'

There was some delay with the private elevator but eventually Ami was delivered to the penthouse, her eyes averted from the mirrored lift walls. One look at her and she felt certain that Harry would know she had been cavorting all night with his son.

As she stepped into the penthouse foyer, she heard a woman's voice, rising and fading as if she was walking about facing one way, then another. Francesca's voice, full of gaiety and archness and raised as it always was when she spoke to Harry, convinced as she was that all elderly people were deaf. 'I shouldn't be saying anything because we're keeping it quiet just yet, Harry, but North must have already told *you*—' Ami caught the word *divorce* loud and clear, then an indistinct jumble before

the next distinguishable phrases that came so rapidly and
breathlessly Ami thought the brunette must be turning
pirouettes. '—second wedding—so thrilled—for keeps
this time—white wedding, just like...'

'Well, congratulations. That's the best news I've heard
in a long time!' Harry said and Ami flinched at the hearty
approval in his voice.

'Oh, *here* it is! Thank heavens,' said Francesca. 'It's
my favourite scarf, I'd hate to lose it.'

Ami backed into the lift, driven to escape before
Francesca could appear, wafting that filmy, tiger-striped
scarf like a victory pennant. *Second wedding.* She felt
quite calm as the doors silently closed and she glanced
at her reflection. No secrets to be seen in the inscrutable
face that looked back at her. *North must have already
told you.*

From her suite she phoned Harry and said she had to
go, would see him later. Still in a numbed state of calm,
she left, picked up Spritz from the kennels and went
home, did her chores, washed the car, mowed the grass.
The widow Anderson is no longer required. Ami
pushed the mower to cut another straight swathe on the
half-mown lawn. She turned for the return trip and
yanked the heavy mower around with sudden savagery.
It was a hot day and she hadn't bothered with gardening
gloves and her hands were already developing sore spots,
but the hurt inside her was so bad, she only faintly registered the lesser pain. She had been so sure she could
trust North. So sure there was something special between them. There had been moments when she felt a
wordless communication in him. The time in that gaudy
suite, was it only two days ago? She'd looked at him
and he at her and she could have *sworn* that... 'Agh!'
Her guttural rasp of pain and humiliation was masked
by the racket of the motor mower. She gritted her teeth.
What had she thought it was? A moment of cosmic recognition? A meaningful meeting of two souls? '*Ha!*'

She traversed the length of the garden again with escalating speed and scant attention to the task in hand, not caring that her normally straight mowing lines were wandering. Perhaps, she thought, in pathetic hopefulness, there was some explanation? The North she had come to know was not such a louse, surely? Maybe Francesca had misinterpreted something he'd said. Ami pondered the idea as she tore up and down the garden, watching the lush summer growth of grass and flowering weed emerge flat and uniform from beneath the blades. North might be a manipulative, compulsive winner but he surely had more style than that. More integrity. More sincerity.

But he was a man who was used to planning his strategies. One of the reasons he had survived a harsh financial climate when others had gone under was his willingness to wait for his investments to yield fruit. So maybe all that style and integrity and sincerity she thought she had discovered in him were just another Kendrick manouvre. All that charm, all that romantic hand-kissing nonsense had been a mood-setting strategy.

She turned off the mower. There were blisters on her hands. The lawn was chewed up, bare in patches, and she realised she had forgotten to adjust the height of the blades. The overspill of grass from the catcher lay in little, crooked lines, showing where she had departed from the straight and narrow. She should have listened to Emma. She should never have gone and walked on North Kendrick's turf.

CHAPTER TEN

A PARCEL, bearing the stamp of a classy jeweller, arrived at the shop on Monday. In a velvet box was a silver bracelet to match the ones Ami so often wore, but this one was studded with diamonds.

'It's fantastic,' Helen breathed, looking over her shoulder. 'You're not sending it back!' she exclaimed, when Ami repackaged it.

'Absolutely,' she said. 'I only opened it to see—' To see just how wonderful he had judged the other night. Her face flamed as she scrawled North's name and the hotel address on the wrapping. Had his executive gift-buying service organised this little token from him? Was this by way of reimbursement for a willing lover? She felt cheap and degraded.

'You toss his orchids in the bin and send his diamonds back! Most women would give their eyeteeth to be in your position.'

'I'm very attached to my eyeteeth.' If it was only a matter of eyeteeth, she thought wryly. She had given too much of greater importance. Her self-respect. Her love. Besides, many women probably *had* been in her position—ex-lover, ex-ornament in North Kendrick's life. The only offering he could make was material, which was why Francesca really was the perfect partner for him. She felt a certain strength flow back when she realised that nothing had changed. So, she had confirmed that North was a manipulative bastard—she'd always known that. So, she had made love with him. She was a grown woman and everyone was entitled to one big affair, one big mistake. So, it was a fleeting romance, all over. It was best that way. Even if North loved her, he was not for her. He liked his champagne cold and his women beautiful. She had to know that the man in her life appreciated those things about her that would last, not just the outward things that by chance pleased him right now. She refused to be like Francesca, checking in every reflective surface, fearing her looks had diminished and her lovableness with them. Poor Francesca. She worked hard to pity the woman who would have North for a while, at least.

She received a message from North via his secretary on Wednesday. 'Mr. Kendrick regrets he has been delayed in negotiations in London and can't make your appointment this evening,' she told Ami.

'Surprise, surprise!' Ami drawled.

Disconcerted, the woman said, 'He'll, er, be in touch soon.'

To retrieve some shred of self-respect, she spent that night composing a letter to North. She was darned if she would play the part of the starry-eyed lover, the last to know that it was all over.

'Dear North,' she wrote. 'It is with great difficulty that I write this.' That at least was the truth. 'We have had a turbulent relationship since our first meeting and it was inevitable I suppose that we would make love eventually. I was attracted to you from the start and I know it was mutual. The other night was extremely pleasurable. I will remember it fondly,' she wrote, her hand clenched into a claw on the pen as she strove for the tone of the liberated woman who liked her lovers but didn't want them hanging around underfoot. 'However, for me the other night was an isolated incident. I do hope we can remain friends for Harry's sake.'

After some consideration she crossed out 'extremely pleasurable' and substituted 'most enjoyable.' Why give North's ego an unnecessary boost? She copied out the final draft and sent it to his secretary with a request to forward it on, then asked Helen to say she was out in the unlikely circumstance that North phoned the shop. Her phone rang once or twice at home in the evening, but she didn't answer it. Another dozen roses, yellow this time, arrived at the shop with a card that said, 'Missing you. North.' She gave them to Helen. A week later a bouquet of November lilies arrived. 'Thinking of you. Love, North.'

Love, North. The words leapt from the card, almost fluorescent with significance. Ami wanted to believe it. Holding the flowers, she felt the treacherous leap of hope. Maybe he wasn't just playing games. Maybe he really did care, really did miss her and think of her. But there was Francesca. What was she going to do? she thought, unable for the first time in her life to think her problems through clearly. Was he an unprincipled swine or not? *Love, North.* The words echoed in her head, scattering reason. And to stop herself mooning she forced herself to consider an obvious reason for this continued courting. North might have in mind an affair to run concurrently with his engagement and eventual marriage. It helped her work up a nice feeling of outrage and she plunked the exotic flowers in Helen's arms.

Harry moved out of the Avalon, back to his own house. By way of compromise, he had allowed North to arrange a weekly call from a nurse-helper. Ami gathered that Harry had planned on training a nice young woman to his own way of thinking. As North had hired a crew-cut male nurse-helper with muscles, a tattoo and a motorbike, Harry was enlivened by a new challenge. The old man phoned Ami several times, anxious over his Christmas plans. His daughter and her family were coming from Melbourne to stay with him. 'I had one hell of a free-for-all with North over it,' he said with the relish of a winner. 'Had to promise to get The Terminator in to help with the arrangements. He had the family Santa suit dry-cleaned and bought me one of those fold-up Christmas trees—I suppose it'll have to do.'

Ami's parents planned to fly to Tasmania to Lenore's sister for the celebration. 'I wish you'd come with us,' her mother said. 'I hate to think of you stuck in Sydney alone for Christmas.'

'I won't be alone,' Ami assured her. 'I've heaps of invitations.'

One from Harry, to join him and his family on Christmas Eve, and she wasn't likely to accept that. One from Emma and Matt, and only an insensitive clod would intrude on the first Christmas of newlyweds. One from Helen, for drinks in her starry-windowed lounge. Several from friends. Heaps of invitations.

As December heated up, Ami sold dozens of her light-weight tropical Santa beards and eyebrows. Sydney's Christmas lights were switched on, the city's buildings were decked with holly, Santas, reindeer and ropes of flashing lights. A giant Christmas tree went up in Martin Place, and the flower sellers' stalls were stocked with Christmas bells and bronze-red flowering native Christmas bush. Silver and gold stars everywhere. At the Avalon, Ami saw as she passed once, the lollipop trees were tastefully hung with bauble-like red apples and the pots were swathed in Victorian-style garlands. Morgan had a sprig of holly in his lapel. Not a garish Santa, reindeer or flashing light to be seen. No stars. Home to heaven.

Ami assumed North must have received her letter and cancelled any further tributes with Monica's gift-buying service, which was just as well because Helen's husband had flown into a jealous rage when she kept taking flowers home. Ami wondered if North would be putting on the family Santa suit. She imagined him dressed in it, a pillow tied around his middle, heaving a sack of toys for his nieces and nephews. Lousy, manipulative, selfish, chauvinistic Uncle North. His lashes would be impossibly thick and black for a Santa. His teeth impossibly white. Shoulders athletically broad. 'And what do you want for Christmas, Ami Winterburn...'

Peace on Earth.

Goodwill to all.

Amnesia.

Ho, ho, ho.

Sales slackened off at the shop as the schools performed their end-of-year plays and wound down for the summer holidays. She threw herself into a reorganisation of the shop, and fell off a ladder while clearing a top shelf at the shop. Her weaker ankle was badly sprained, and she spent two days resting it. Her mother, who had nursed Ami's weak ankle through years of ballet, insisted on sending someone from the agency to cook, clean the house and answer the phone. Her mother also sent magazines, and in one of them was an article about Francesca entitled, 'The Second Time Around.' She tossed it aside but the photograph of the fashion designer in the arms of her man landed upside down on the carpet and Ami couldn't resist a peek. But even before she turned the picture right way up, she could see the man was not North. Ami frowned, seized the magazine. 'Fashion designer Francesca Parelli, marrying for the second time next month, will have a hard time finding the traditional "something new." She will be married in the church where she was first married, will wear the same dress and be attended by the same bridesmaids. Even the groom will be the same.'

'What?' Ami read it again, attempting to hold back an idiotic pleasure that Francesca's bridegroom was losing his hair and had a moustache.

'Francesca and Antony will celebrate their reunion after a six-month separation by renewing their vows. "This time," Francesca says, snuggling up to her first and second husband, "it is for keeps."'

Ami gave an embarrassed laugh, mortified that she'd so badly interpreted a fragment of conversation yet relieved that North had not lied to her after all. Her intuition had been right. He wasn't the kind of man to propose to one woman and sweep another off her feet all within twenty-four hours. The news Francesca had been dying to tell him that night was not that she and her husband were to be divorced, but remarried. Ami felt a surge of spirits that waned as she remembered the letter she had sent him. Biting her lip, she wished she had waited a little longer before mailing it. But on reflection, she decided it was just as well.

It was a warm, wet night a week before Christmas when she gave her last class for the year at the Shoelace Theatre. To protect her ankle, she made use of some stage crutches to move between the students as they emulated her make-up techniques. Once again, she had demonstrated first on her own face.

'I can't believe you can look so gross,' one of her students said as the lesson drew to a close. 'Ugly as sin— on your left side, anyway.'

'Beauty is only skin deep,' Ami said with a horrible grin.

The subject tonight had been distortion, the ruined Phantom of the Opera face, and she had disfigured one side of her face, closed one eye to a mere slit and drawn the lid downward, puckered her skin, twisted her mouth and slashed a horrible, partly healed scar across one cheekbone.

'Beards and moustaches next week,' she told them as they cleared away their equipment to leave. 'Bring photos and false hair for practice.'

They left and she stacked the chairs, gathered up the waste tissues in a bin, turned off all but the nominal lighting in the auditorium. Before she could remove her make-up, she heard a door shut and footsteps in the auditorium. She went through the wings onto the half-lit stage. 'Is that you, Mr McShane?' she called, looking around the rows of seats for the security guard.

'No.'

Her heart flipped. She followed the voice, saw North over to her left. He looked marvellous and she drank in those details of his presence available to her, like a woman offered drink in the desert. The dark hair, glistening with raindrops, the handsome nose, shadowed and emphasized by the side lighting, the contours of his lean cheeks. He wore dark jeans and a shiny black rain jacket with the collar turned up. His hands were thrust into the pockets as he stared broodingly at the stage from the tiered auditorium.

'You look like a movie bad guy,' she said with a nervous laugh.

'You typecast me long ago,' he said dryly. 'How's your leg? I only found out about your accident last week. Harry told me you were in hospital but were okay now.'

'How did he know?' she said inanely, as if she cared when North was standing out there alongside row M.

'He phoned your place and spoke to a nurse or someone.'

'Oh,' she said. A deep silence ensued. Hospital? she thought. She'd only been in the casualty ward, where Helen had frantically taken her, for a few hours to X-ray for fractures. North stayed where he was, leaning on the seat beside him so that his body took on a sideways slant.

'I have been trying to get in touch with you ever since—'

He stopped short and she wondered just what phrase he would use to describe the occasion. Ever since our one-night stand? Evern since I left a dozen roses in my place and ran out?

'You could have written,' she said stroppily.

'I don't express myself well in writing,' he said.

'You made your meaning very plain in the one note you left for me.'

'Did I?' he said harshly. 'That's more than I can say of that piece of hypocritical, pseudo-feminist garbage you sent me.'

'*Your* note was more in the nature of an interoffice memo—"the widow Anderson is no longer required. Please keep Wednesday night free,"' she mimicked in a deep voice. 'You only managed to remember how *wonderful* our night together had been in the postscript!'

He moved down to row K, the raindrops on his hair and jacket turning red as he passed a neon exit sign.

'I could have said our night together was "most enjoyable,"' he said through gritted teeth. 'I could have said I'd remember it "fondly."'

'Well,' she said, flushing slightly. 'It's true.'

'Don't you bloody *dare* remember it fondly.'

'You're a powerful man but you can't dictate my memories.'

'I will *not* be remembered *fondly*!' he said louder. 'Like a—a discarded teddy bear!'

She laughed but North stared at her with a thwarted expression. He was serious, she thought, swallowing hard. Her heartbeat raced.

'When I got that letter,' he said deliberately, 'I thought, to hell with her. Stop trying to phone her every night and every day. Stop sending flowers. Stop thinking about her. Don't see her again.' He flicked a descending raindrop from his forehead with a small, violent gesture, added with self-contempt, 'But here I am.'

'Um, I was upset when I wrote that letter. I heard that Francesca was getting married again and I thought it was to you, and that you'd lied to me about your involvement with her so that I would, er...'

There was a visible straightening of his spine as if he'd been given an infusion of confidence. His hands came out of his pockets, went to his hips, pushed back the black jacket. Ami hastily reviewed what she'd said to account for this sudden power swing in his favour.

'You thought I made love to you while I was planning to marry Fran?' he said, shaking his head. 'You really do have me cast as the villain, don't you?'

'I'm sorry,' she said, shrugging. 'But you have to admit that basically, what I wrote is true. I mean, you and I—we—well, it's a physical thing, really, and very nice, but—'

'Very nice? Very bloody *nice*?' he roared. 'I don't know what you feel for me, but I love you, Ami Winterburn, I love you.'

It sounded like a declaration of war rather than a declaration of love. But the phrase echoed around beneath the rafters, proving that the expense of acoustic linings had been warranted. Ami Winterburn, I love you. A couplet sweet as any Shakespeare had written.

'Well—*say* something!'

Her heartbeat was deafening. 'I—I—' she croaked and he seemed to find something encouraging in her stuttering response.

He cut down through row E to the centre aisle, moving fast, below her now, a man with a sense of purpose. He was powering towards the stage when he looked up at her again and stopped, horror on his face. 'Ami—oh, my God, Ami darling—the accident— Harry didn't tell me.'

He stood stock-still, his face working. His nostrils flared. '*You* didn't tell me,' he accused, pointing a finger at her. 'Why the hell didn't you tell me?'

Ami gaped at him. She put a hand to the artificially distorted side of her face, visible now to him. North was talking about that, staring at it in—what? Revulsion? Loathing? Panic? She saw the pallor in his face, and the blood drained from her own head. North thought her face had been injured in the accident, too. She watched him absorb this new, hideous image of her and waited in a fatalistic calm. Perhaps he was already discovering that he couldn't love her, after all. North preferred his women beautiful.

'Imagine waking next to a face like this,' she said, making a stab at a light-hearted tone. In a moment she would have to tell him it wasn't genuine. And that would be worse still. She wondered what would hurt him the most—his horror at her ruined face or his relief that it was a fake. 'I'm afraid this face doesn't meet your high aesthetic standards, North,' she said in a high, strained voice.

White patches showed beside his mouth. 'High aesthetic standards! You make me sound like a bloody quality control officer or something.' North's eyes narrowed on her suddenly as a suspicion struck him. 'Hell,' he said, clapping a hand to his forehead. 'I've fallen for it again.' He ground his teeth then strode across the auditorium to a side door. Ami heard the stamp of his footsteps up the steps, across a concrete apron, traversing the control console until they echoed on the stage itself. She turned awkwardly to confront him. North glared at the left side of her face. He ran a fingertip over the texture of it. 'All your own work, of course,' he said tautly.

She nodded.

'So it is just your ankle that you injured—you're not hurt otherwise?'

'I only fell off a ladder,' she said. 'And the reason you only heard about it yesterday was because it only happened yesterday.'

'What? Harry said—I got the impression it was more serious, that you'd been laid up in hospital for a week.' He gave a dry laugh. 'That old meddler, playing cupid, I suppose.' He hauled her close, suddenly angry again. 'I should have realised you wouldn't be walking around with week-old injuries like this, but logic deserts me where you're concerned.' And he kissed her with savage passion, bending her backwards beneath the force of it. His hands swept over her back in a rough caress, spread on her rear, tilting her more intimately against him. Ami gasped, dropped one of the crutches and it clattered unheeded to the floor. It was so long since she'd been in his arms, smelled the mix of fragrances and odours that were distincively his, kissed him. Making up for lost time, she kissed him now, feeling the friction of his teeth on her tongue, tasting the sweetness of oranges in his mouth. He straightened suddenly, looking at her with a glitter of combined desire and anger in his eyes.

'So. I failed the test, I suppose,' he said harshly, under his own breath. 'That's why you didn't tell me you were made-up, isn't it? You thought, let's see if this man of superficial feelings and trivial values will say he loves me with scarred skin and a drooping eye.'

'North, it wasn't like that. I had just finished doing a class. When you walked in I—forgot I was wearing make-up. When you saw it you assumed it was real—'

'And you let me! Because you thought I'd run screaming, didn't you?' He clasped her arms tightly, gave her a small shake. 'All that stuff about wanting the entire you, not just your lovely hide—you had to check it out, didn't you?'

She twisted away from him, angered. 'And the fact is, I still don't know, do I?' she snapped.

His face looked ashen in contrast to his black clothes.

'Well, then, you're going to have to work it out for yourself, aren't you, Ami?' he said quietly. 'I don't understand this obsession of yours.'

He stepped back, let her go, only grabbing her arm once more for a few seconds to support her as she wobbled. He picked up the second crutch and handed it to her. 'I love you,' he said roughly. 'I want you so bad I could make love to you right now, standing up, on this stage, and I wouldn't care too much, frankly, if there was an audience here.' Ami flushed a dark red.

'But then, I would say that, wouldn't I? Because I know you're really beautiful under that stuff and trivial, shallow types like me can't contemplate anything else,' he said in a low, guttural voice. 'I'd better leave before we have another *isolated incident*.'

He left then, retracing his steps until the sound of his leaving faded into the space of his arrival. Ami was shattered, remorseful, angry. Tears in her eyes, she removed the illusory effects from her face, not caring if she tore the flimsy pieces of latex. Was she misjudging him? She wanted to believe it, but years of accumulated fears and the many Mirandas she had known got in the way.

His mood was unsociable and he should have declined Lenore Winterburn's invitation to her harbour home to discuss the donation of a sculpture from his collection. Curiosity and a renewed hopefulness, which he refused to acknowledge, made him go. This was where Ami had lived, he thought, looking around the lovely house that was expensively but unpretentiously furnished for comfort. A cluster of photographs drew his attention, and he stopped, picked up a print of a plain, skinny little girl, all arms and legs, pushing a miniature wheelbarrow. He ran a finger over the face, smiling at that familiar, level expression in the child's eyes. 'Oh, I'm sorry,' he said, putting the photo down as he felt Ami's mother watching. He flushed. If he was not careful, he would find himself wallowing in sentiment, he thought in disgust, singing bursts of 'On the Street Where You Live.'

'Come and meet my husband,' Lenore said cosily. North was not misled. Lenore Winterburn was a shrewd, intelligent woman, sharply observant and stubborn as an ox, he guessed, once she'd made up her mind. His chances of getting away without donating a sculpture to her charity were nil. A formidable woman. Like mother, like daughter.

Steven Winterburn was in his study, a large room lined with bookshelves and hung with startling before-and-after photographs—faces smooth, faces ruined and distorted. After the formalities, North's eyes were drawn to them. He frowned. 'I thought for a moment they were photographs of Ami's work,' he said, taking a closer look.

'Mine, actually,' said her father with a smile. 'But I see what you mean.'

'Steven is a reconstructive surgeon,' Lenore said. 'These are some of his patients before and after surgery.'

North looked more carefully. Not faces ruined, but faces restored. 'I suppose Ami took on the therapeutic cosmetics because of your involvement in reconstruction,' he said, thinking hard.

'Yes. She has always been interested in my work,' her father said. 'From the time she was a little girl she would come in here and ask about the people in the photos. Not the most pleasant side of life for a child to confront,' he said dryly. 'But Ami was never the kind of child who could be fobbed off with pretty answers. She was quite critical of fairy tales, I remember.' He smiled.

'I can imagine. Snow in summer,' North said half to himself, moving from portrait to portrait.

'Quite,' Ami's father said uncertainly. 'Cosmetic therapists are few and far between—the stress of dealing with disfigured people gets to them, you see. When we lost our last one and there was no-one to refer patients to, Ami took it on. She says she copes with it okay.'

'She cries, but not in front of her students,' North said absently.

Ami's parents exchanged a speaking glance. 'You must know our daughter very well,' her father said, looking him over with a more critical eye.

'I think I know her a little better now,' he said, with a last look at the studies of faces ruined and mended. He thought of a little girl, growing up with this acute awareness of the evanescence of beauty or normality and the need to look beneath the surface. In a rush of enlightenment, he remembered something Harry had said. Joking, North had studied a stooped, lined woman passing by and said, 'Thanks to Ami, I can never see an old person anymore without wondering if there's someone young underneath.' And Harry had said, 'Don't wonder, son. There always is.'

With understanding came a feeling of helplessness that made North grind his teeth. How the hell was he going to convince Ami that he loved her, the real her? His track record didn't help him, he admitted ruefully. She loved him, he knew it, *felt* it. But she had grown up with those photographs and the small, tragic stories that went with them and she had him taped as exactly the kind of man she couldn't be with—a man with only some of his senses in working order, blind to her qualities save those that afforded him direct pleasure. Surely, she could see that might have been true once, but not any more? But she was so damned stubborn, so strong, so determined.

Before he left, he donated a nymph to Lenore's charity. Like mother, like daughter, he thought, his head reeling from the experience. He called up a four-letter word he hadn't used since early adolescence. 'Help,' he said out loud as he drove away.

A postcard came from Emma, still travelling in Europe on her honeymoon. The small space was crammed with tourist anecdotes and glowing description as well as some pithy advice. 'Regarding that supercilious swine. Don't be too hasty. Any man who can nurse you through a virus and still fancy you—and be "just good friends" with the gorgeous Francesca—is not an empty vessel. Home on twenty-third. Having a wonderful time. Do *not* wish you were here.'

Her mother phoned. 'Darling, you remember my writer? He's abandoned that book he was working on and wants someone to tap-dance in an elevator so that he can study the reactions of the occupants. Naturally, I thought of you. Your ankle's okay now, isn't it? Have you still got your tap shoes?'

'He's abandoned the *book*?' Ami shouted. 'I went and asked his stupid questions, which changed my entire *life*, and he's abandoned the *book*? No, I will not tap-dance in an elevator!'

'I see,' her mother said. 'By the way, we got our nymph.'

Ami's senses quickened. 'Oh?'

'North came to see us. Are you in love with him as much as he is with you?'

She clutched at the phone. 'What makes you think he's in love with me?'

'It must have been the way he mooned over that picture of you on the hall table. I mean, I love you dearly, Ami darling, but even I have to admit you were the plainest little thing on two legs until you were fifteen. He looked as inspired as if you were Helen of Troy. Poor man, he blushed when he saw that I noticed.'

'*Blushed*—North?'

'So you won't take the tap-dancing job?' Lenore went on aggravatingly, when Ami would have liked to hear more about this mooning, blushing North. 'I can't say I blame you. I'm not keen on elevators myself. Bye— your father and I will phone Christmas Day from Tassie.'

Ami hung up and sat a while. She picked up the phone, took a deep breath and keyed in North's office number at the Avalon. It was only a temporary arrangement and Mr. Kendrick had moved back to his customary office in Crows Nest, a woman told her. But North wasn't there, either.

Christmas Eve. Sydney's weather was sultry, the skies blue. The office parties were over. Last-minute shopping and trading. Christmas decorations were going cheap.

The Salvation Army played Christmas carols for the fortunate and prepared Christmas dinners for those less so. Cars packed high headed in slow lines across the Harbour Bridge, heading north, heading south to beaches, campgrounds, holiday houses, to Christmas reunions with parents, children, family, friends. The city's churches proclaimed the birth of the Christ child. Ami slipped into St. James, near Hyde Park, to reflect on love and hope and peace on earth. They closed the shop at noon and Ami delivered gifts to special customers and friends. She kept Harry's present till last.

Harry's house was a modest brick bungalow in an old inner-west suburb greened by mature oaks and fig trees and woody roses. Ami found a parking spot in a row of visitors' cars parked in the street and walked up a path across a lawn bordered with plumbago hedges. There was no answer to her knock and, after a while, she walked around to the back of the house. The back garden was long and narrow with the parasol canopy of a poinciana tree bearing garlands of red flowers. At the end of the garden, beneath the arching boughs, was a large shed. Its timber doors were flung wide open and, framed in the aperture, lit by bright sunlight against the dark interior, were Harry and a partly dismantled motorbike. And North. Ami felt a rush of pure delight, a sudden piercing happiness. The sight of him, on his knees, obviously doing Harry's bidding made her think of the day he'd been on his knees beside her, daubing her with antiseptic.

'No, no, *no*,' Harry was saying, shaking his head and pointing. 'The *other* one!'

'Aw, Dad—give me a chance!' North protested. He worked something loose and showed it to his father then wiped a hand across his face. 'If you're going to supervise every nut and bolt in this project, I think I'll—' He broke off as he saw Ami.

The sense of buoyancy heightened. She smiled at North, unable to keep the feeling to herself. Somewhere, in her reflections on love and hope, she had made a quantum leap past her doubts. This was right. North was right. *I love you, North.* He stood up slowly, eyes fixed on her face, reading the scattered clues there with all the intense speculation he had once devoted to her alphabet sweater. He wore faded overalls that were too tight over the shoulders. There were smears of dirt and grease on his face, his hair flopped over his forehead, he needed a shave. The man was a mess. He looked wonderful, strong and vibrant, a man in his prime.

'Ami Winterburn,' he said, turning her name over on his tongue as if it was the first time he'd said it. He stuck his hands on his hips but in spite of the muscular assertiveness of the pose he looked uncertain.

She walked down to them. Harry beamed a welcome at her.

'We're renovating one of my old racing bikes,' he told Ami.

'You mean *I'm* renovating your old racing bike—you're supervising,' North said with a snort.

'He's always around here lately, tinkering with stuff on the workbench. More inventing, I shouldn't wonder,' Harry said.

'*Tinkering*?' Ami looked at the bike. Not partly dismantled, after all, but partly rebuilt, which was quite different. Smiling, she looked at North as he stepped out from behind the Ducati. Her gaze came to rest, askance, on the rolled-up trouser legs of his overalls that hung incongruously over boots.

'What do you think of them?' Harry said, seeing her interest. 'The boots. I used to race in them.'

Black bike boots with straps and silver buckles. The ones North had coveted as a kid, the ones Harry had said he might grow into one day.

'I thought you gave them away to someone else, Harry!'

'I told him that, just to punish him,' Harry admitted sheepishly. 'He was thick as thieves suddenly with his science teacher—the one that took out patents for him. He didn't need me anymore, I thought. He'd left me behind, so I hid the boots away and told him I'd given them to someone else.' The old man pulled a face. 'Thought he might have grown into them at last so I gave them to him today. And what do you think—they're a perfect fit.' Harry gave his wheezing laugh and winked at Ami.

North didn't notice. His attention was on Ami, compelling her attention back to him. His grey eyes beamed a warmth her way that had nothing to do with the brilliant sunshine. It was a look she had seen many times. When she'd been dirty and scratched and dishevelled by the roadside, when she'd been sweating and sick with a virus, the last time she'd been disguised as an elderly widow, wrinkled and worn with time. At her best and at her worst he had looked at her just like this.

Harry flicked a look between North and Ami. 'Well, I've got things to do. The rest of the family are arriving about ten tonight and I still don't like that darned Christmas tree . . . too *glittery*, if you ask me.'

'I don't want to interrupt anything,' Ami said.

'North only called in for some advice and I've given him that,' Harry said, scarcely leaning on his stick as he walked towards the house, humming under his breath.

The screen door banged ostentatiously behind Harry. Ami looked at North. He yanked the front of the overalls and popped the studs, then peeled the faded drill down, shook it free from his booted legs. Underneath he wore a burgundy T-shirt and jeans tucked into Harry's old bike boots. He tossed the overalls aside and surveyed her, hands on hips, that hint of uncertainty about him making her heart turn over.

'You, the boy genius, asking for advice?' she said with a nervous laugh, thinking how it had put a spring in Harry's step.

'Where you're concerned I could use a panel of advisers.'

'I heard you'd donated a nymph to Mum's charity. That was generous of you.'

'*Wise*, anyway. I wouldn't want to start off on the wrong foot with my future mother-in-law.' His eyes narrowed as he assessed the effect of this breathtaking assumption.

Her heartbeat quickened. 'North, what are you saying?'

'Just that I've met the only woman I ever want—as my mother-in-law.'

'The *only* woman?'

'It's her or no-one. Do you think she'll—like the idea?'

Ami smiled brilliantly. Any minute now she was likely to pirouette around Harry's back garden. 'She'll *love* the idea.'

'You're sure about that?'

'Absolutely.'

'She'll say yes?'

'Oh, yes.'

'In that case, I'll ask her—when the time is right.'

'You weren't going to risk a no? Coward.'

'Absolutely.'

He smiled at her and she at him and it was happening again. That peculiar communication without words, a thing at once primitive and more sophisticated than any artificial means of communication devised by humanity. If Harry was peeking through his window he would see them standing metres apart but they were as close as two people could be without touching.

'I went into your father's study when I called at your house. I saw the faces of his patients in those photo studies. It made me realize how serious you are about superficiality, how you might guard against it. It seemed obsessive to me, I didn't understand, but I think I do now. I came away a desperate man, wondering if I'd ever be able to convince you that I love you—the whole you, not just the pretty bits.'

'I knew you did. It was buried deep, that's all—under fear and cowardice. I just needed time.'

'That's what Harry said, when I asked his advice. He said you loved me, that I should be patient, and wait.' North studied her carefully, folded his arms and leaned against the shed door, waiting, the picture of patience spoiled only by the growing gleam in his eyes.

'But you have to admit,' she said, reacting to his growing complacence, 'that you seemed to be all the things I always said I would avoid. For a start, you were so arrogant—'

He opened his eyes wide in surprise.

'Talking about women as if they were mere commodities in our life—all the women you met were either "too young, too old, married or feminist academics,"' she quoted.

'Ah. Yes,' he said, conceding the point with a grimace.

'You collected painting and sculptures and when you got tired of them just packed them up and sent them somewhere else. It seemed to me that you might regard women like those nymphs—nice to own for a while but replaceable. I thought I might end up like one of those torchbearers outside the Avalon, or like one of your mooning, pale pre-Raphaelite heroines.'

'Just for the record, I never tired of them. But the collection has grown so large and a southern college has been pestering me for years to turn it over to them as a public exhibition and resource for students and—' He shrugged. 'Up until a few months ago there had been a certain lack of meaning in my life, so I decided public works might be a good—' He stopped, struck by a thought. 'The wheat!' he said. 'Pre-Raphaelite women— that's what you meant.'

'Has that been bothering you?'

'When the woman of your dreams leaps naked from your arms babbling about wheat, it causes some serious problems for the male psyche.'

'Oh, really,' she said sceptically.

'I found myself going over that night trying to think where it might have gone wrong and how the hell wheat came into it. It was all a bit hazy because of the brandy. That was true, you know.'

'If you had a hangover the next day, you were heroically unmoved by the sound of Ken's motorbike,' she said dryly.

'I was so thrown, the headache the next day was the least painful thing about it. But I kept reliving every moment of the night that I could remember.'

'Every moment?'

'Over and over.'

'That must have been very irritating.'

'On the contrary. I found it "most enjoyable".'

She chuckled. 'In my first draft I said "extremely pleasurable".'

His teeth flashed in a cocky grin that made her heart bump. Ami held her arms wide and he took two giant steps and hauled her close, held her there a moment before he kissed her hard on the mouth. 'Woman of a thousand faces,' he muttered into her hair. 'I love all of them—all of you. There never will be just one face to Ami Winterburn, will there?' He framed her face in both hands. 'For someone supposed to be smart I can be very slow.'

'Surely not!' she said, opening her eyes wide.

'But I finally saw it was stupid to resent you fooling me with your Amelia disguise because that was you, too,

just in another form. You'll always be changing—
growing—there'll always be a new face. I love that.'

He gathered her close and kissed her again,
thoroughly. 'Ami Winterburn, I love you,' he murmured. 'And I want you...and while I could easily make
love to you on a roadside or standing up on a stage, I
draw the line at my father's back yard.'

Holding hands, they walked down to the house.

'Come for a drive with me and Harry?' he asked.

'I'd love to.'

'Don't you want to know where to?'

'Nope.'

'It might be a long, long way.'

'I hope it is,' she said.

It was over an hour's drive, west, straight into a blazing
late afternoon sun that was dropping down towards the
craggy Blue Mountains range.

'You mean you're looking for...' Harry said, as he
figured out where they were going and then, 'it won't
still be here. Probably got town houses built on it now.
Or been turned into a mini golf course or something.'

But it hadn't been. A hand-painted sign, propped on
a side road, announced Christmas Trees—Select Your
Own. Down a long, dusty driveway they went, following
hand-painted arrows past a house to an untidy plan-
tation of slash pines in long grass. There were two small
groups of people, one wandering about, another cutting
their tree. Their voices and the ringing cuts of the axe
carried on the air. Music drifted from the house.

Harry sighed. 'Fancy that—some things don't change.
The same people must live here.'

'The daughter of the people we used to see,' North
said.

Harry swallowed hard and said stroppily. 'Bet you
didn't bring the axe.'

'It's in the boot,' North said.

Harry sighed again and got out of the car, headed off between a row of trees, slapping at a slender trunk now and then to test for some obscure quality. North stood a moment watching him, then, smiling, took out the axe and a small handsaw.

'We always cut the tree several feet above the ground. That way it doesn't die but grows again. Once, when I was fifteen, we cut our tree from the same one we'd had when I was five.'

Ami looked around at the clumping, erratic regrowth from the post-high stumps, evidence of past Christmases. She thought of North brought here as a boy by his father, choosing a tree. He watched Harry's progress, smiling slightly. 'I think we'll let Harry pick the tree. He seems to know what he's looking for.'

North hefted the axe over his shoulder, took Ami's hand. As they moved onto the rough ground between the pines he made a muffled sound and hobbled a bit. Ami looked enquiringly at him.

'Those boots—' she began.

'Don't you dare tell him they're too small,' he growled.

Ami remembered Harry's wink and laughed, her heart contracting at North's protectiveness. 'I love you,' she said. 'My mother and my best friend vouched for you, so it isn't surprising.'

'I've always believed in the superior perception of women,' he said brazenly.

'But I think it was the gardenia that did it.'

'The gardenia?'

'If it hadn't been for that I wouldn't have felt so upset about you throwing me out. But you tucked that flower in my hair so gently that it ruined my image of you as an out-and-out rotter. I doubt that I would have turned up as Amelia to gatecrash your party, if it hadn't been for the gardenia. I couldn't forgive you for it because it made you unforgettable.'

'You mean there was only a flower between me and life without Ami Winterburn? Remind me to recommend a raise for Morgan.'

The air was mauve with early dusk and shimmering still with the departed radiance of the sun. She had the strangest feeling of timelessness as she walked, her hand in North's, through the field of trees harvested, growing, regrown. The links of tradition. Parents and children. Children and parents. Christmases past. Today, this Christmas Eve. Christmases to come. 'We'll come here for our Christmas trees,' she said.

'I thought you didn't approve of all this pine-tree stuff in the land of gum trees and palms.'

Ami threw her arms wide. 'Oh, I always say that in September,' she said. 'But by December, I always come around to the idea of pine trees and summer snow.'

Harry's voice carried on the still air. 'Now that,' he said, 'is what I call a Christmas tree!'

There was some bickering between father and son as North shaped up to cut Harry's tree. Happiness, Ami thought, was something you either remembered or yearned for. Hardly ever did you recognise it at the precise moment. But this, right now—this was pure happiness, watching North heft the axe in both hands. His shoulders and back rippled as he brought the small tree down with a couple of strokes. Harry seized it and dragged it off towards the car, refusing all offers of help.

North used the saw to neaten the cut. The dusk deepened and the first star appeared in the sky. He threw down the saw and looked at it a while with Ami. Then he held his arms wide, and where else would she go except into them? 'I love you, North,' she said, wrapping her arms around his neck as she kissed him. It was too far away to be possible but Ami thought she heard a wheezy kind of laughter. Her eyes closed. 'Fifteen,' she said, after a while.

'Fifteen what?'

'Stars. Or was it sixteen? I lost count.'

He smiled, looking deep in her eyes. 'Just have to start again.'

Ami sighed. 'Darling North. That sounds most enjoyable.'

This month's
irresistible novels from

Temptation ®

SANTA IN A STETSON Vicki Lewis Thompson

It Happened One Night

Jo Cassidy had always had a weakness for strapping, sexy devils like Russ Gibson. Now in one short night, he'd loved every inch of her...and then walked out. That was it for Jo! She slipped a ring on her finger and invented a husband. The next time she saw Russ, she was going to appear *unavailable*!

CAUGHT UNDER THE MISTLETOE! Kate Hoffmann

The Men of Bachelor Creek

Julia Logan couldn't believe it. Her son had gone to the North Pole to find Santa! But instead he'd come across a sexy-as-sin hunk. If only Tanner didn't live in Alaska... But after an incredible night in Tanner's arms, geography was the last thing on her mind!

MY JINGLE BELL BABY Leandra Logan

All Alec had asked for this Christmas was a rest. Pulling Sara Jameson's car out of a ditch was not part of the plan! Neither was helping her and her baby hide from whatever they were running from. Still, sharing a B & B with beautiful, passionate Sara had its compensations...

THE GRINCH MAKES GOOD Alison Kent

Christmas was Dr Duncan Cox's *least* favourite time of the year. But Brooke Bailey was determined to spread Christmas spirit among all her neighbours—of which he was one! Could this mismatched couple be heading for a passionate affair? Only in the season of miracles...

He's a cop, she's his prime suspect

MARY LYNN BAXTER

HARD CANDY

He's crossed the line no cop ever should.
He's involved with a suspect—his
prime suspect.

Falling for the wrong man is far down her
list of troubles.

Until he arrests her for murder.

Available from 18th December 1998

ELIZABETH GAGE

When Dusty brings home her young fiancé, he is everything her mother Rebecca Lowell could wish for her daughter, *and for herself...*

The Lowell family's descent into darkness begins with one bold act, one sin committed in an otherwise blameless life. This time there's no absolution in...

Confession

MIRA®

AVAILABLE FROM JANUARY 1999

LINDA HOWARD

DIAMOND BAY

———✦———

Someone wanted this man dead. He was barely alive as
he floated up to the shore. Shot twice and unconscious.
Rachel's sixth sense told her she was his only hope.
The moment she decided not to call the police
she decided his future. As well as her own.

"Howard's writing is compelling."

—Publishers Weekly

MIRA®

1-55166-307-4
**AVAILABLE IN PAPERBACK
FROM DECEMBER, 1998**

SHARON SALA

Tory Lancaster is a woman trying to
leave behind a legacy of abandonment and sorrow.
She is about to come face to face with her past. A past
she must confront if she is to have any
hope of possessing a future.

SWEET BABY

MIRA

1-55166-416-X
**AVAILABLE IN PAPERBACK
FROM DECEMBER, 1998**

LYNN ERICKSON

The Eleventh Hour

Jack Devlin is on Death Row, convicted of murdering his
beautiful socialite wife. But the evidence is too cut and dry
for lawyer Eve Marchand. When Jack escapes and
contacts Eve, she is forced to make a decision that
changes her life.

*"Lynn Erickson joins the ranks of Sandra Brown
and Nora Roberts"*

—The Paperback Forum

1-55166-426-7
**AVAILABLE IN PAPERBACK
FROM DECEMBER, 1998**

MIRA®

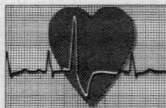

MILLS & BOON®

Next Month's Romance Titles

♡

Each month you can choose from a wide variety of romance novels from Mills & Boon®. Below are the new titles to look out for next month from the Presents™ and Enchanted™ series.

Presents™

TO WOO A WIFE	Carole Mortimer
CONTRACT BABY	Lynne Graham
IN BED WITH THE BOSS	Susan Napier
SURRENDER TO SEDUCTION	Robyn Donald
OUTBACK MISTRESS	Lindsay Armstrong
THE SECRET DAUGHTER	Catherine Spencer
THE MARRIAGE ASSIGNMENT	Alison Kelly
WIFE BY AGREEMENT	Kim Lawrence

Enchanted™

BE MY GIRL!	Lucy Gordon
LONESOME COWBOY	Debbie Macomber
A SUITABLE GROOM	Liz Fielding
NEW YEAR...NEW FAMILY	Grace Green
OUTBACK HUSBAND	Jessica Hart
MAKE-BELIEVE MOTHER	Pamela Bauer & Judy Kaye
OH, BABY!	Lauryn Chandler
FOLLOW THAT GROOM!	Christie Ridgway

On sale from 8th January 1999

H1 9812

Available at most branches of WH Smith, Tesco, Asda, Martins, Borders and all good paperback bookshops